THE NEW
DARK LORD

THE NEW DARK LORD

BOOK ONE

Ian B. Urns & A. C. Erinle

Podium

To Vanessa and Kemi

Cover design by Jason Nathaniel Artuz

ISBN: 979-8-89539-360-4

Published in 2025 by Podium Publishing
www.podiumentertainment.com

THE NEW
DARK LORD

Prologue

The chamber had been constructed to Silenos's exact specifications, demanding every scrap of House Shaiagrazni's not-inconsiderable technologies to ensure that it conformed to every minutia of his designs. The work had been long, tedious, slow. But now it was finished, and he gazed upon the result with a scrutiny born from self-preservation.

A dull, silvery surface extended outward, elliptical in shape and rounded on each of its faces. At its broadest point, the room was just over nine meters across. At its tallest, it measured five and a half from floor to ceiling. Silenos strode through the interior and noted the absence of any strong reverberations or yield within the ground.

Tungsten was its composition, a third of a meter thick and worked with the most powerful magics available. It would have turned aside cannon fire at point-blank range without so much as a scratch, withstood engulfment in temperatures able to burn iron into vapor without losing its solidity, and weathered forces able to collapse mountains with its mass barely shifted at all.

Silenos estimated that it might be enough, should the worst occur, to slow the Entity down long enough for his ritual to be halted from the outside. If not, disaster would reign.

But there could be no progress without risk; he'd learned that during his earliest days in House Shaiagrazni.

"Are the sigils prepared?" Silenos asked, glancing at his idiot apprentice. Adonis was short, squat, and black haired, with a pudgy face that betrayed poor control over his gut's impulses and sweaty, clammy skin born from a life of living close to the limits of his stress threshold. It was not an uncommon appearance for Shaiagrazni apprentices.

House Shaiagrazni was the greatest and oldest institute of magic the world had ever known, and it achieved this position through its unending demand of excellence.

To gain the name Shaiagrazni, and be adopted into the household, an individual would have to prove themselves a prodigy beyond prodigiousness and amass knowledge and power that most experienced magicians could only fantasize about.

The process of achieving such things was not easy, even for those with the inherent gifts that made it possible. Silenos's own studies had lasted him forty years, then another sixty to advance once he earned the name Shaiagrazni and became a house elder.

In the half century since, he had taken on more than a dozen apprentices. Only Adonis had remained with him for more than a year. Talent and resilience keeping him in place.

"The preparations are complete, master," Adonis replied hastily, as he always did. The boy didn't meet his eyes, which was good. Silenos had already punished an act of just such defiance one month prior, and twisting the boy's spine had been tedious enough that he was in no mood to find another, more creative punishment.

Moved by instinct, he took another glance at the room around him. It remained as blemishless and resilient as his first study had betrayed, but something still gnawed at Silenos. He crushed the sensation. Now was no time for abstract worries and insubstantial fears; there was work to be done. Work that would shape the next century of human history.

The chamber was assembled, the bindings complete. All that remained was for Silenos to draw the Entity out into his world and strike his bargain. He stepped forward, readying his magic and calling out to all present.

"Leave," he ordered. "Save for Adonis, I want none here to disturb me."

At best, the attendants and servitors would distract him, and at worst, their fragile, inferior minds would provide the Entity with handholds on the world. The magics it could unleash through a human vessel were limited, but an Entity of the magnitude he was calling on might well overpower him regardless, or shatter its bindings from the outside to bring forth the full volume of its power.

The former would kill him; the latter would kill millions.

Silenos inhaled, focused, then let his magic ooze out to infuse the sigils carved around him. They drank it hungrily, feeding on the nourishing flow of his power, refracting arcane energies into light, heat, and every other facet of electromagnetism Shaiagrazni had yet discovered. The chamber was sealed behind them, cutting off the flood of light from its open door, but by then the interior was already illuminated by raw power.

Adonis kept silent, and Silenos used the quietude well. Continuing to supply the lattice of runes with power, patiently waiting as he measured volume and frequency, allowing the chamber's sigils to swell and glut themselves upon it. Moment by moment, the preparation all came to fruition. Ritual nearing completion, he felt a bead of sweat upon his brow.

It had been years since true worry had racked Silenos; he'd almost forgotten how it felt.

The Entity manifested with a crack of air, the atmosphere crystallizing solid, then snapping in half. A choir sang out from nowhere, their voices straining to sing a note of purple coloration, their vocal cords tightening amid muscles made of snakes. Something slithered up from the universe's ceiling, yet somehow descended in doing so, and its form grew corporeal and substantial before Silenos's very eyes.

It was not a thing of matter, or at least not any matter that could take sustainable shape under the harsh governance of physical law. More akin to some interaction of forces and principals, though even that implied a degree of consistency not native to the Entity's nature.

Silenos watched and waited as the shifting volume of nothingness found itself, congealing and writhing, spending its earliest moments in his world becoming master of its laws. Then it spoke.

The creature's voice ran through him, bypassing the air entirely and carrying itself on waves of magic rather than sound. It was a million things, the sound of steel grating on flint, acid eating lime, a wife being beaten, and an old man's life ending at last. Silenos spent his own time accustoming himself to it, adjusting and interpreting the alien tones, picking out the sentiments and words they conveyed.

I have been summoned. What for.

The Entity's voice did not contain any semblance of emotion or impression, yet it was far from stoic. An inconsistent, shaking tone that seemed to begin each syllable at a different volume and pitch from the last, entering Silenos's mind like nails scraping across a chalkboard. He was well used to such effects from Entities, however, and moved past them to recite his introduction.

"I am Silenos, senior of House Shaiagrazni, and I wish to make a bargain with you. Ask of me what you will and I will grant it, provided you meet my terms."

It was not necessary to speak with vocalized words; the Entity would hear any thoughts Silenos directed its way. Still, habit held strong. He waited for the Entity to respond. Sometimes they took as long as a human, sometimes no time at all. And sometimes they could take years to answer. Silenos had no intention of giving it that long, but he was well prepared to tolerate the idiosyncrasies of such things. The rewards were well worth it.

What is your request.

He told the Entity. Silenos had dealt with two of its kind already, and walked away stronger from each encounter. One had allowed him to see magic itself—an ability so vanishingly rare that most among his own household still did not believe he had it. The other had lengthened his lifespan, and thus allowed for centuries more knowledge to be accrued before death began its approach.

This time, however, he wanted something more. Raw power, that rarest innate gift that segregated the strongest of magicians from the rabble at birth. Among the thousand named of House Shaiagrazni, close to a hundred exceeded him in magical strength. He aimed to fix that.

I can grant this.

Silenos waited for more, and sure enough the Entity continued.

I demand five thousand beating hearts be cut from their owners while they still live, and for you to pledge yourself to me. In exchange, I shall grant you the power you seek.

He almost laughed. Entities asked for pledges of servitude constantly; it was always the gold standard of dealmaking for them. To earn a permanent mortal puppet was to gain some long-standing means of influencing the world. Even House Shaiagrazni's tolerance of forbidden magic and dark knowledge did not extend so far as to permit that.

"I will not be making such a deal," Silenos said, forcing himself to look straight on as the conjured Entity spasmed against the corners of reality. He could see the world liquefying somewhat where its body intersected and forced himself to ignore it.

As a senior, it would be well within your powers, and your mentor would be no issue.

He froze, thinking for one long moment at the Entity's words, as the truth slowly dawned on him. Lethargically, Silenos turned to look at Adonis and found the boy staring with wide eyes at the conjured presence before them.

Decades in House Shaiagrazni had taught Silenos many things, and the tell-tale sight of terror was chief among them. He saw it in the boy's face, and he saw an undeniable direction to it. The look of one who had been caught and knew they were guilty. He took a step toward him, preparing his own powers.

The Entity didn't need a person to speak vocally; it could communicate by simply hearing the words in their mind. Adonis had been speaking with it from the start, not Silenos, and a deal was about to be struck.

His power reached the air, thickening, drawing close to wrap around Adonis and burst him like an overripe grape. The Entity's was quicker still.

Silenos felt the world itself split like a jagged wound torn across taut skin, the air churning and boiling as it was snatched into a roaring gale and dragged into the schism. He felt it tugging at his body almost instantly, pulling like great invisible fingers hooking their way into the robes about his frame and the hair atop his scalp.

Adonis smiled. Damn him, he smiled! A sneering, smug rat in human skin, actually daring to feel pride for overturning a ritual painstakingly designed by his superior. Silenos could feel the weight of power at play. It was an amount he had no hope of matching.

Through making its contract with his apprentice, the Entity had managed to exert more of its strength upon the world. Such was the basic function of summoning it at all—and yet finding it turned against him, Silenos could only curse the fates for letting such an irony strike him down.

His feet didn't leave the ground. Rather, the ground left his feet, and then the world left his skin. Silenos observed it all with a distant, sick fascination. He felt himself drawn high, long, low, and inward. Felt himself unmade, then remade, then shuffled back to how he'd started. He felt an uncountable volume of events and nonevents pass him by, and through it all a blinding light grew ever more intense as it coalesced around him.

The last sight he caught of his reality was the triumphant, arrogant grin of an upstart apprentice.

CHAPTER ONE

Silenos was in a chamber once more, but one far more primitive than the containment he'd constructed for the Entity. Its surfaces were of stone, not tungsten, and were bare of any runic workings that might have functioned to conduct magical energies. The place was cold, made colder by his being naked. Evidently, whatever magics had been called on to displace him, they had failed to permit his clothing passage too. An inconvenience. He'd had a great many useful tools and relics upon his person. Being without them would impede him.

But he had more immediate concerns. Around him, Silenos saw a gathered crowd of people, circling him entirely and standing some half dozen strides back. Eyes wide, faces slack with awe, postures cautious and tentative. They were headed by a woman of golden eyes and hair, taller than most, slenderer than many, and stupider than practically all. Surely stupider, to be eying him with such open ferocity and conviction.

"It worked," the woman whispered, as if disbelieving what her eyes told her. Silenos found that more irritating than anything else. Incomprehension had always needled him, as it might any other of House Shaiagrazni. He felt the draft, suddenly, and considered making the people around him into clothes. As a fleshcrafter, he could work living tissue well enough that even a single one could have covered most of him.

That train of thought was interrupted, however, as the woman spoke again.

"Forgive me, Savior." She lowered her head at the words, reverent. Silenos watched as all present mimicked her. "I welcome you to our world and thank you for coming to save it."

Silenos paused and reconsidered. He wasn't certain what these people thought to be calling him Savior, but if nothing else they clearly acknowledged the respect he was due. That much was reason enough to leave them alive, for the time being at least.

"Who are you, and where am I?" he asked, aiming his question at the woman. With luck, the savages now surrounding him had reason to have selected her as the speaker among their number, perhaps even good enough reasons for Silenos to receive some straight answers.

"Forgive me for not explaining already," she replied, bowing her head so ludicrously low, Silenos suspected it might have injured her neck. "You are in the nation of Elkatin, and my name is Ensharia. We . . . are in need of your help."

Silenos could have guessed they needed help from their calling him Savior, but he decided to forgive the tautology. Plenty more information had been passed his way, in any case. Most important among it the fact that neither name Ensharia had spoken correlated with any he was familiar with.

"Help dealing with what?" he asked. "I take it you are being . . . attacked?"

"Oppressed," she replied, spite dripping from her lips. "The Dark Lord, he calls himself, a magician of unrivaled power and evil. He uses his foul magics to ravage our lands with necromantic armies, twisting the very elements against us."

He observed several things in rapid succession, the most important being Ensharia's description of necromancy as foul. It would appear that the magics forbidden to most of Silenos's world were just as taboo in this new land, at least within the nation of Elkatin. That might cause issues. As a necromancer himself, Silenos was well familiar with idiots attempting to kill him in some misguided zeal, but that didn't mean he wasn't well aware of the danger they posed. Taken off guard and unawares, even a magician of his prowess could be slain. All it would take was a single stroke of luck at the right time.

But there were other things to be considered too.

"How large are these armies?" Silenos asked.

He had no intention of actually helping, not in the slightest. Whatever these idiots thought they'd done to call on a savior, he could only conclude it had failed. House Shaiagrazni did not protect those too inept to defend themselves, nor did it risk its members in useless endeavors. But if Silenos was to navigate his new surroundings, he'd benefit from learning the scope and scale of its apparently largest threat.

Ensharia paused though, mouthing out in silence for a few moments before she finally answered him.

"It may be best if you follow me, Savior. My king and queen can give you more in-depth information than any here."

Resisting the urge to ask why *they* had not greeted them, Silenos merely nodded and stepped forward.

"Take me to them," he instructed her.

The woman hesitated.

"You . . . would like some clothes first, yes?"

Silenos glanced down, then sighed.

"If you insist, yes." He did loathe wasting time, and it was far slower to don new apparel than simply craft it around him from raw material, but he suspected that using his fleshcrafting upon those now watching him would lead to tenuous diplomatic relations.

Fortunately, the idiots had some clothing prepared for him. It seemed well-made enough, largely silks and linens, fabrics Silenos didn't see in the apparel of those around him, and with far greater craftsmanship. He supposed it was considered good work by the standards of the savages around him now.

Ensharia led him alone, which left Silenos to wonder about the purpose of her company. He eyed them as they made their way out of the chamber, considering the zeal and trembling hands so common across them. It was hard to imagine any people of substance would conduct themselves like that, but harder still to think ordinary rabble might have been given audience to the arrival of their land's savior. An irksome conundrum, and one Silenos was not given long to consider.

Winding corridors awaited him ahead, and he navigated them with Ensharia's guide. Carefully committing the turns and twists to memory, employing the mnemonic techniques he'd spent a century accruing. Their walk lasted them more than a few minutes, betraying the scale of the surrounding building itself, and Silenos was able to glimpse it more directly as they passed by a long window betraying the sight of sprawling courtyards and towering spires outside.

"Admiring the view, Savior?" Ensharia asked, looking rather pleased to see him studying it. "Castle Vardrire is one of the largest in the world, dwarfing any other structure in Elkatin."

In fact, he'd been trying to hold back a sneer. The architecture was primitive, betraying a lack of any complex working of glass or large-scale production of steel. He could only imagine it was wrought by a people too simple to manage such technologies.

"It must have taken considerable time," Silenos replied. Typically, the woman interpreted his words as a compliment.

"Almost sixty years," she replied happily. "With some of the finest architects in Elkatin dedicating decades of their lives to its various stages."

Silenos knew some, a very fair few, who might have made a similar structure themselves in mere weeks, using nothing but their magic and the necessary raw materials. It seemed strongly evident to him that the nation around him had few magicians of power comparable to his own.

His pondering was interrupted as Ensharia took him to a large set of double doors guarded by a pair of tall men in glinting plate. Curious armor, Silenos could tell it was not steel by its coloration, and a glance with his arcane sight showed flickers of magical energy infusing the metal. That it had been worked into such large planes and articulated joints betrayed a level of craftsmanship he'd not have expected from the architecture, and both moved without the need for verbal communication or order.

The door swung open upon near-frictionless hinges, revealing an expansive hall on the other side.

At one end of it, a pair of thrones were seated, carved of smooth stone and occupied by an aged male and female. The space between Silenos and them was carpeted in a long crimson streak, with great stone pillars connecting floor to ceiling on either side like the bars of a cage. Ensharia was immediate in making her way forward, taking a dozen steps, then dropping to her knees before them. Silenos followed after but did not prostrate.

Whatever world he had found himself in—and he was growing increasingly certain that this land did not share a planet with his own— he remained a senior of House Shaiagrazni. Some could kill him; none could make him kneel.

"My king," Ensharia declared with her face aimed toward the ground. "The ritual was a success. I present to you the Savior."

Silenos moved his eyes to the male, meeting the old man's gaze. He looked to be between sixty and seventy, physically speaking, but by the creases of stress and worry upon his brow, the man may well have been younger than his flesh would claim. Wispy silver hair clung lightly to his scalp, drifting as his head was animated by speech.

"It is an honor," he said, surprising Silenos by nodding deeply enough to almost approximate a bow himself.

Resisting the urge to let himself soften at the show of deference, Silenos spoke.

"I have been told your people are being assailed by forces external to your nation and that you expect me to aid in your plight. How, might I ask, was I brought here?"

The king did not seem surprised by the question, while the queen did not seem to consider it at all. Silenos could only assume the males of this new land held rulership over the females. It was a common enough system. Many civilizations— or things that thought themselves civilized—fell into it. A simple evolutionary flaw, he suspected, of one sex being larger and stronger than the other among a species that fought and hunted for survival long before accumulating the resources to build cities.

"There are stories in our nation," the king replied, at last. "And there are truths in those stories, secrets . . . Rituals among them. One such ritual was known to have possessed the means to bring forth a being of great power and greater danger. We used it during our time of greatest need, and it promised us a Savior. You."

House Shaiagrazni respected the value of knowledge above all other things, and so Silenos never quite escaped a state of awe upon seeing it handed out so freely by those in other orders. He'd just found himself saved asking another half dozen questions.

"I see," he replied. "And what, exactly, do you require me to save you from at the moment? I am aware of your general predicament, but what imminent threats are there?"

Another pause followed, forcing onto Silenos the choice of either allowing his displeasure to show or making the effort of keeping it contained. He did the latter. It was to be suspected, he knew, that mental sluggishness was commonplace in this land, for it was rare that any human civilization evolved a culture as meritocratic as House Shaiagrazni.

"As we speak, the Dark Lord's forces are marching on our city, the capital of our nation. Scouts have reported that they number in the hundreds of thousands, undead in almost their entirety, rotting, vicious abominations sustained only by magic. Our defenders number a mere ninety thousand, with a further forty thousand conscripted from the general populace. Historically . . . this has not been a ratio that serves to our advantage."

Silenos considered that.

"How many magicians are counted among your defenders?"

"One hundred and six magicians of war," the king replied. "Bolstered by a further hundred and nine conscripted from the city's general populace."

It was a meager number. House Shaiagrazni's surrounding nations had magicians numbering at one among every four hundred ordinary humans and would have mustered several times as many in such a population. And as a rule, scarcity of magicians correlated with the talent of those magicians in a given population. Silenos worked through the relevant calculations in his head.

"When will this army be arriving?" he asked distractedly. The king surprised him at that.

"It arrived before you did and encircles our city as we speak."

Silenos was led by Ensharia to see the army outside, rather quickly demanding that he be allowed to study it himself, and thinking as they went. There were few reasons for him to stay, as he saw it. A magician powerful enough to conjure armies was likely more than worthy to dominate the primitives around him now, and far be it from Silenos to interrupt the natural order of things. Still, knowledge was useful. He needed to see the forces in question.

They were, as it happened, rather numerous. Covering the landscape as a writhing black carpet of rotting meat and rusting metal, stretching out almost to the horizon. As far as armies went, he'd seen bigger. But rarely conjured by one individual.

Silenos studied it with eyes of magic rather than light to see what he might glean of the work. And he felt a stab of disgust.

Different densities of arcane power made themselves apparent to his sight with shifts in shade and tone, and he'd expected a respectable darkness. Instead he saw pale, fragile whiteness only barely discolored at the edges. It was a frail magic that produced such color, and a frail magic meant a frail magician.

This is who these idiots are being dominated by? This . . . incompetent?

It was revolting, disgusting, and unacceptable. Silenos would not stand by and watch people subdued by such a blithering idiot.

They needed some proper leadership.

CHAPTER TWO

I must meet with the general of this army," Silenos declared as he looked up from his maps. It hadn't taken long to have them assembled, to the savages' credit, and they appeared relatively recent. He'd spent the better part of a half hour studying them, committing the etched lines detailing fortifications, streets, and bridges to memory.

"What for?" Ensharia asked, face a canvas upon which her confusion was scrawled with excruciating clarity. "They're undead!"

Silenos did not roll his eyes, but it was a near thing.

"Undead are limited," he explained. "Particularly the varieties congealing outside. I would wager they are being controlled by officers or generals of more . . . sapience."

It was an understatement. Necromancy capable of leaving the subject's mind even mostly intact was of the highest order. Silenos himself could barely manage it, and he had no doubt that anyone inept enough to create the army now threatening him would find it beyond their scope entirely.

He turned back to the maps. The major weakness of Equiscia, the city in which he now found himself, was its river entrances. The waters that fed them had long since diminished in the centuries since their construction, and though they still boasted strong currents, he suspected an undead could easily crawl through. The lack of need for air meant being swept under would be no threat to them, and if they were damaged somewhat by the bludgeoning effects of being carried along, their combat effectiveness would remain at a large fraction of its norm.

Yes, the riverways. Send larger reanimates in first to break apart the aged iron bars keeping them blocked off, then allow the masses to swarm in along with the waters. That's what Silenos would do, if he were attacking. That's what any competent general would do. Anything else would be a mere distraction from the infiltration force.

"Are you listening?" Ensharia demanded, glaring at him. Silenos raised his head, frowning.

"Of course not," he replied. "I was busy thinking. My genius is far more demanding of attention than your babbling."

She glared at him. The woman's veneration remained but had been quickly cut by irritable impatience as she'd gotten to know Silenos. Apparently she was a paladin, a holy knight of her kingdom. Such things had not existed in House Shaiagrazni, but he was familiar with the concept. An odious one, in his opinion.

"I was saying that the Dark Lord's generals might simply take the chance to kill you if you go out to meet them."

Silenos sighed.

"They might try, but I am not unaccustomed to assassination attempts. I suspect I will withstand any they might employ and will gain far more from this than we stand to lose."

A closer look at whatever elites would doubtless be present, for one.

"You're . . . our only hope," Ensharia said after a moment, not meeting his eye, face aimed pointedly at her own feet and pale skin flushed pinkish. "Please, don't do this. If we lose you, we're doomed. I'm . . . not even sure we aren't doomed already."

Silenos studied the woman, seeing the emotion clear as day across her features and feeling an undeniable wave of . . . utter revulsion. What petty mental conditioning had this warrior experienced, to be left so volatile? It was like conversing with an open wound. Pathetic.

He set off soon after, though the woman insisted on accompanying him. Silenos found himself half tempted to kill the idiot as punishment for insulting his powers when she claimed to be capable of defending him with her divine magic, but more pragmatic heads prevailed.

The two of them exited the city shortly, traveling by horse—Silenos decided it was worth accepting the subpar mechanisms of natural selection rather than tip his hand by biomantically crafting a superior vehicle—and headed for the head of the enemy's forces. He weathered the slow, drawn-out travel with eyes kept ahead and open.

A large mass of infantry seemed to be the major core of the enemy army, though Silenos caught other facets to it as well. Dullahan had been gathered in the thousands, their black horses standing twenty hands high, putrefying flesh bloated and writhing with dense musculature almost as much as the maggots lying within. Their armor was dark but, he knew from experience, strong. Headless riders were a higher order of undead than the zombies making up most of the enemy, but they would not be of the most use in a siege. Sieges were the order of footmen, not cavaliers.

Which meant he couldn't be certain that the enemy's forces hadn't been tailor-made for just such an attack. He made a mental note to study them further before an open battle when he got the chance. It would be a useful point of comparison.

"Black riders," he heard Ensharia whisper and turned to see the woman glaring at them. "Fallen knights. I've seen those creatures walk through hails of arrows, split men fully in half from crown to groin. Even withstand a ballista bolt once."

Silenos had seen much the same sort of prowess demonstrated from the creatures, though it had never inspired the awe he now heard in the paladin's voice. He supposed that was consequential of his own world's technology. Dullahan were rather less impressive seen through the sights of a musket than they were from those of a bow.

"Let us continue," he said instead.

The dullahan had been placed around the army's head, Silenos soon found, and he knew which of the numerous undead shielded by their ranks was in charge at but a single glance. The belladonnan puppeteer was a thing of magic powerful enough to register in his vision even without his actively looking for it.

It was not a large thing, which made it uncharacteristic for the stronger undead. The belladonnan puppeteer was perhaps the same height as most men, with any of the surrounding dullahan towering over it by easily two feet or more. Its frame was slender, its body near a state of total desiccation, preserved from rot, yet dehydrated into a withered husk by the very processes that left it free of the decay plaguing its lesser kin. Silenos caught Ensharia covering her nose in disgust from the corner of his eye.

"This is the first time an emissary has been sent by the people of Elkatin," the belladonnan puppeteer observed, speaking with the same emotionally vacant tone that most sapient undead did. "Are you here to surrender?"

An idiotic guess. From what Silenos had seen, this new world's residents were as superstitious of necromancy as his own. They would sooner kill themselves than be at the mercy of such beings. A lot was common between Elkatin and his world, in fact, including the undead. Dullahan and belladonnan puppeteers, two higher-grade constructs he recognized on sight. That was interesting.

"I am here to see if I might deter you from this trivial conflict," Silenos replied.

"Your accent is different from any I have heard," the puppeteer noted, without even acknowledging his words. "And I have heard thousands. Am I to take it you are the savior spoken of in Elkatinian prophecy?"

The paladin stepped forward behind Silenos at that, her voice cutting out.

"How could you possibly know about that?"

Silenos spoke over her before the idiot could have the chance to realize the obvious, that the enemy had informants within their walls, and vocalize the fact of her stupidity.

"I am," he replied. "And I am familiar with your reason for being here. Leave now and there is no need for conflict."

Puppeteers were sapient. Like all undead, they were compelled to obey their creators, but that was nothing more than an impulse. The eternal danger of creating cognitive beings was that their intellects might prove stronger than their instincts. It would not be impossible to reason such a thing out of following its orders.

"That is not an option," the puppeteer replied, and Silenos cut in quickly.

"Yes it is. You know it is. You have doubtless been considering the very fact that it is. You are not forced to obey; you choose to. You can choose not to obey just as easily as you can choose to fart or hold your breath."

A moment passed, but no gesticulation came from the puppeteer. It was to be expected. Though not actively rotting, the being's dead nerves were no more capable of transmitting the spasms of unconscious thought and body language. Silenos watched it more from habit than anything.

"You have two hours to surrender," the undead said at last. He knew then that there would be no reaching it. Though unemotional as any, belladonnan puppeteers had cognition enough that tone could inflect their voices, at least in some small part. He could hear clear as day that its mind had been made up. Silenos nodded.

"Very well then. Ensharia, let us leave." He began walking and spent the first few moments anticipating an attack. None came. The two of them were allowed to take their leave, breathing in air that grew less clotted with the scent of decay with each step away from the army they took. Soon enough they were back at the walls.

"I warned you." The paladin sighed. Silenos glanced at her. She was becoming too comfortable by far around him, but this wasn't the time to correct her. He had more pressing concerns.

"Guard the waterways," he instructed. "The enemy will attempt to enter through there. Where are the city's graveyards?"

She stared at him. "Graveyards? You're worried about them . . . reanimating our dead?"

"That," Silenos confirmed. "And I wish to pay my respects to our fallen."

The woman's face lit up at that, like some simpering dog, and she was quick in directing him. Silenos wasted no time following the path.

Ensharia had watched the Savior leave close to an hour ago, and she was eagerly aware that their time was running short. It had been noon when they'd first summoned him and, not coincidentally, merely two hours from sunset when they'd met the enemy's army. Undead were weakened by the light, the weakest of them at least. When it was fully dark, the attack would come.

She trembled, feeling the familiar convulsions of adrenaline racking her muscles, fighting to remain still where she stood vigil. Her body was encased in moonplate, paler and harder than steel, her fists closed tight about the handle of her shield and mace, her body coiled and ready to loose the strength of fifty men. Still, her mouth was dry, her nostrils stinging with the unmistakable scent of rotted meat as it grew ever stronger on the wind.

Where is he?

The enemy was closing in, she could see now, heading for the city's walls like a giant swarm of cockroaches, crawling over one another, blotting out the ground, moving on inexorably as a wave of pitch. They were on the walls before long.

Arrows flitted down to strike, broadheads and bluntheads to split wide gashes in enemy bodies and break bone. Stones were cast from walls, burning oils poured over, and the waterways turned to a massacre as men stood behind the reinforcements hastily added to their barricades and stopped necrotic flesh from getting through. It was all professional, experienced, well-done. All carried out with the hard-earned skill of men who had fought undead many times. And all pointless.

The enemy were too numerous, and their advantage grew by the moment. Even as Ensharia fought, rupturing heads and tearing off limbs with each swing of her mace, she could feel the battle's inevitable end drawing near. A dullahan beheaded a man with one swing, coming for her wordlessly. Its black blade missed her head by an inch, and her mace missed its chest by a hand. They encircled, trading swings and swipes, thrusts and would-be death blows, then Ensharia broke the deadlock with a flash of holy light. Smoke wisped from the enemy, its flesh burned but not charred by her eviscerating magic, and Ensharia struck while it was distracted. An unguarded blow to the neck, snapping the spine and leaving the horseman to fall.

But there were more. Unmounted, not as deadly on foot as on horseback, but each the equal of a hundred men on their own. Even with the defensive advantage of a fortress, there would be no victory.

The ground trembled, and Ensharia turned to see a horror. It was enormous, towering easily sixty feet high, taller than the walls themselves. Its body was a bloated, bulbous thing, and it reeked of necromantic magic. Its flesh was black, coated in some form of scales, and its strength was palpable in every move, body driven by musculature sufficient to send its hundred-foot limbs darting around with the speed of sling bullets. It crossed the city within a minute, falling upon the defenders at the wall, and Ensharia awaited her death. There would be no fighting such a thing, not even any trying. One swipe of one limb and they would die. She doubted her body would even register as more difficult to crush than any other.

Savior, where are you?

But its swipe didn't come. Not for the humans, at least. Instead the creature stepped cleanly over the walls, its krakenous tendrils swinging along the enemy's army. Hundreds were obliterated. Zombies popped like grapes, dullahan tossed skyward and sent spinning a dozen times before they landed, broken like dolls in spite of their dark plate. Arrows and sling bullets hit it, even artillery, wherever the monsters had salvaged such things. It simply powered on, cutting a path through the enemy's forces and crippling their advance. Ensharia could only watch in awe.

The ruin did not take long to finish. A few minutes, perhaps, then the enemy was retreating. Undead felt no fear, but their leaders were rational. If they fled, it was because they knew there would be no realistic chance of winning. The creature turned its focus onto the city as the horizon grew black with flesh, moving swiftly back to the wall.

Ensharia saw him then, standing atop the stony fortification. Tall, bronze-skinned, and with hair as black as any dullahan's armor. He awaited the monster, watching fearlessly as it came before him and lowered itself into a bow, inky tendrils bent beneath it, stone-hard body glinting in the moonlight. Silenos the Savior watched the thing impassively, merely nodding once at its bow.

CHAPTER THREE

The world was still, save for the beating of Ensharia's heart and the convulsing of blood vessels as they surged with oxygenated power. The Savior was standing still, gazing down at the abomination as it knelt before him. Show of deference seeming somehow out of place, wrong, at odds with everything. Unnatural.

Seen closer, she could gauge more detail in the undead. See the curious, hardened substance that clung to so much of its body, recognize how it thickened and sharpened around the ends of its limbs. Observe how every fractional movement left its limbs practically inflating with muscular strength as the fibers below tensed and expanded.

There was an uncanniness to the way it was shaped, something Ensharia couldn't quite put her finger on at first. Nature created things in particular patterns, allowing natural laws to govern how and why they fit together, limited by chance and single-generational survivability. This thing broke all those laws, less a reanimated animal and more . . . a machine made of meat and bone.

Before she even knew it, Ensharia was heading for the Savior, her feet trudging hard and clumsy along the blood-slick battlements. The air reeked of death and dying, but even that horror barely registered to her compared to the growing terror that took root as she drew nearer to the man and his pet monster.

"You created this?" she asked, glaring at him, past caring at his status, destiny, or the respect it left him due. The Savior turned his head, slowly, to glance at her, as if she were some buzzing fly in the periphery of his vision. Then nodded.

"It is how the greatest undead are made," he explained. "One can undo the putrefaction of mere corpses and use them as material, merge them into something greater."

The way he spoke of it, the way he explained it, the Savior almost seemed proud to have wrought such an abomination. It made her sick, and Ensharia felt her guts squirm as the thing moved again, limbs jostling like the crushing tendrils of a kraken. There was a sharpness to the movements that made a new thought occur to Ensharia.

"It looks like it's in agony." She gasped, staring at the writing thing. "Like every moment is . . . torment."

The Savior's eyes widened, and he stared at her.

"Thank you," he replied, sounding genuinely, sincerely flattered. Without another word, the man turned, heading down from the battlements, leaving Ensharia alone.

She was left there, standing in a field still wet with congealing blood, nostrils assailed by the reek of necromancy. Ensharia took a few moments to fully process what had happened, what she'd seen, what it meant. And then she made her decision. She'd never been one to delay or agonize over a problem. Rapid action was among the tenets of her order; it was needed when one fought against the world's foulest horrors. She would not stand for a false savior, and so Ensharia headed out to make the matter right. Moving toward her king and queen.

More quickly than she deserved, she was granted her audience.

Ensharia's monarchs looked restored by victory, the lines upon their faces thinned, the slumping fatigue about their shoulders reduced. King Arodan's face cracked with a smile as he saw her, eyes bright and glinting.

"I heard of your victory, paladin." He grinned. "It was a remarkable thing. Our savior has certainly not failed to impress, eh?"

The look upon his face was one of such distilled happiness and relief that Ensharia hated herself for the truth she was about to unveil, feeling as though it were the desecration of something sacred.

What isn't desecrated these days? How much more of this world is there left to be fouled?

"My king, I apologize for bringing you such grim news at a time like this, but I fear I would be neglecting my duty if I did not share it with you. It is simply too important to be ignored or delayed."

Instantly, Arodan's features hardened.

"What is it?" he asked, joviality melted away, replaced by a kingly seriousness. Ensharia took a moment to steel herself before telling him, and then she shared all that had happened on the wall, what she'd seen, and whom she'd seen responsible. By the time she finished, her king looked far grimmer and more severe than before. But not, she realized, surprised.

"I had heard of the Savior's use of the dark arts," he confessed after a moment. The words sent a stab of shock through her, like a spear to the guts.

"You know?!" she croaked, mind moving slow, suddenly, uncomprehending as her king nodded.

"I did, Ensharia. I did not tell you because I imagined you would be . . . distracted by the knowledge. We now have some breathing room, thanks to him, however. Which is why I would have shared it with you had you not already known."

"But . . ." Ensharia blinked, fighting her own mind for clarity, trying to carve through the madness of her conversation. "But you were fine with him fighting for you? Turning the powers of evil to your ends?"

She was so wrapped up by the weight of what was being said that it barely occurred to her how dangerously close her tone was to insubordination. How precipitously near the edge of accusation her assessments were growing.

"He is our savior," the king echoed, more forcefully now. "Whatever means he utilizes to beat back the forces of darkness, I think we can agree, is tertiary to the fact that he is using them to do just that. This is not a time to be picky, paladin. A lot of men—a lot of children—now draw breath because we weren't."

Ensharia's disgust was more than she could bear, and she rose, forcing herself to make a respectful nod before taking her leave, trembling with rage. It wasn't right, it wasn't *moral*. The undead were not tools to be wielded at one's convenience; nature could not just be disregarded as became necessary. What she'd seen last night had been a behemoth made from human corpses, corpses that never consented in life to be twisted and mangled with magic. It was an act of perversion to do so.

Outside, in the main hall, Ensharia came past a group of soldiers, four in all. They were twitching with the familiar throes of residual adrenaline, bodies using tiny, jerky little motions to burn off as much of the excess energy as they could manage after mustering everything they had for the fight. None were wounded, she could see.

"You there," Ensharia called. "Soldier, a word." The first among them paused, turning his gaze to her, then froze in realization.

Paladins were not generally feared, and for good reason. They were servants of God, defenders of the innocent, and now above all times, destroyers of undead. Ensharia liked to think that they inspired hope and happiness rather than horror and fear. Despite that, it was difficult *not* to intimidate a man who had seen her fight. There was simply something to the world's Talents that left them unnerving for most to behold.

She saw it now as the man tripped over his words. He probably wasn't a fool, or even a coward. It was just difficult to string a coherent sentence together when it was aimed at a person strong enough to lift a barded warhorse over her head.

"Sir!" he managed at last, back going lance straight, eyes going plate wide. "An honor, sir. We—me and my boys—we saw you fight last night. The way you destroyed that dullahan . . ."

Ensharia wasn't proud of it, for the simple reason that she'd seen the Savior's undead servitor crush half a dozen dullahan with one swipe of its tendril. If she'd had to fight a creature like that, could she have won? She doubted it. And a paladin who doubted her victory against an undead was no paladin at all.

"What did you think of the undead?" she asked the group abruptly. "If you don't mind my inquiring. You know the one. It came from our side of the walls and cleared the battlements out when they were overrun. Walking through volleys of arrows, crushing bodies to pulp."

She resisted the urge to shiver at the memory.

To her surprise, and disgust, a bunch of grins lit up on the men's faces.

"It was remarkable," one replied instantly. "I've never seen anything like it. Didn't even know things could get that big."

"The Savior did it, didn't he?" another asked. "I saw it bowing to him. He controlled it, right? He took the Dark Lord's power and turned it against him, protected us with it."

The others continued in much the same fashion, and Ensharia realized that it had been, perhaps, just a shade foolish of her to expect any different. When given the choice between spiritual fulfillment and their lives, people would invariably settle on the latter. Not everyone could be a paladin, not even everyone with the Talent.

She moved on from them shortly, encountering yet more people, testing them with that same question. All seemed to cling to the same tragic misconception, that their savior had simply seized control over the Dark Lord's magics to fight with. She found that, no matter how many shared the misunderstanding, she could not bring herself to tell them that he was a necromancer in truth. Couldn't bear to shatter that joyous delusion with a cruel reality.

And why should she want to, in any case? The more Ensharia thought about it, the more trivial and fleeting the call of honor and righteousness felt. Such things might motivate a man, might motivate a paladin, but they did not save lives, not as directly as the Savior had. Who was she to put something that had stopped so much death and ruination beneath her own order's tenets?

Pride was the deadliest sin, and it came in many forms. Ensharia's was a pride of purity, she saw that now, and she would not allow her own shortcomings to hurt others. With no small measure of reluctance, she moved to find the Savior, her limbs suddenly heavy beneath her, her chest suddenly tight.

He was not difficult to find, occupying the outskirts of the city, rebuilding and clearing debris with his expression no different to when he'd watched the undead hordes torn apart by his own power. Ensharia came to stop in front of the man, waiting for him to look up and notice her. He did not. She cleared her throat, and still he kept his gaze on the books. Ensharia felt a stab of unpaladinlike irritation at that, finally speaking.

"Savior, might I have a word, please?" she asked. At last he lifted his gaze to affix it onto her.

"Speak," he instructed, and Ensharia noticed for the first time how thick the man's aura of command was. He had surely been a king in his own land, or an emperor, because conveying orders to a paladin seemed as natural to him as breath.

She took a breath of her own, then obeyed.

"I have been having difficulties in coming to terms with your . . ." She looked around, confirmed they were alone, then continued. "Powers. The dark arts, as it were. Necromancy chief among them. For most of today, I've been trying to wrap my head around your usage of such magic or even galvanize others to reject you as Savior and find salvation through less morally compromising means."

Ensharia had expected such an admission to wound, or at least enrage the Savior. For his granite features to finally shift with betrayal, anger, disgust. She did see an emotion flit across them and found herself shocked to realize it was *irritation.* A rat might have chewed through one of his boots and earned the same response.

"However," Ensharia continued, "I took some time to process what you did, as I said. And I spoke with others. I saw the hope you've already inspired with our—your—victory, the fear melting away from people. I heard the whispers of supply lines opening up once more now that your abomination can guard them, and I realized . . . This is bigger than me. Bigger than my emotions and uncertainties, bigger even than the paladin order's tenets. People's lives are at stake, and if you, our savior, are confident you can control such powers, then . . . I will trust you."

The Savior blinked, once, after perhaps minutes of leaving his eyes unmoved as the rest of him.

"Okay," he replied. "If you're finished, then start helping with this debris. I estimate that you ought to be capable of hauling over a tonne from the ground based on the density of muscle fiber and magic in your body."

CHAPTER FOUR

Silenos's position had changed, for the better in some ways, for the worse in others. He was not ignorant as to the tenuous position in which he, and the city, now resided.

Among his advantages was the fact that he had apparently earned some measure of respect and trust through his stratagem and magical aid during the last attack. To his disadvantage was the fact that their enemy would be moving to consolidate with other armies in the region, that the city's defenders had been either killed or wounded in multitudes, that much of their defenses had been weakened by bombardment, and that he had now caught the direct focus of this Dark Lord onto the city itself. There were limits, Silenos knew, even to what a senior of House Shaiagrazni could achieve, and he could sense himself approaching them.

His options, however, were numerous.

Numerous insofar as a pair was numerous, at least. He could flee or stay. Fleeing would guarantee Silenos's safety but doom the city. In doing so it would cost him a powerful potential ally in claiming this world for House Shaiagrazni and would have few benefits save, he supposed, free time. Silenos was confident he could flee from a city falling just as easy as a city awaiting attack.

Which made the decision clear. He would stand with the defense and do whatever he could to make it successful, abandoning it only if his options seemed limited.

Silenos spent the better part of a week acting to add whatever strength he could to the city's martial prowess. He used fleshcrafting to heal those whom he could without exhausting himself, subtly improving their bodies as he restored them for greater strength and speed. The city's waterways, he decided, had held before, and so he did not do anything drastic that might have cut off its supply of drink. The walls were by far his greatest concern.

Trebuchets, the most advanced weapon utilized by this savage world, were pitiful by comparison to the cannons used in Silenos's own land. Nonetheless, so too were these people's fortifications. The walls had been damaged by artillery fire and scaled quickly by siege engines even before that. So Silenos turned his focus to rectifying that vulnerability above all others.

It was not long before the horizon grew dark once more with approaching enemy forces, and the city's triumph melted back into fear. Even Silenos felt a stab of apprehension, for they saw instantly how much larger the new mass was than the last.

There had been three armies within the general region around the city. Silenos had crippled much of one. The remaining two, he now saw, had merged with its remnants. Clearly this Dark Lord had at least enough intelligence to recognize the threat he posed, for the marching bodies drawing toward him numbered in excess of the hundreds of thousands his last had.

He could feel the worry running through his own forces, an uncharacteristically logical response from them. His bag of tricks was running empty.

Many of the corpses in the city had been excavated and destroyed before his arrival, in some attempt by the people to prevent the Dark Lord from reanimating them and adding to his armies should he have taken it. Perhaps it was not such an unwise decision, but given the circumstances, it foiled much of what he might have done to protect them.

His grotesquerie was intact, at least. Silenos tweaked it as the army neared, rethreading its body, maintaining its flesh. Most undead could not regenerate by themselves, though the ability to create such advanced reanimates was hardly uncommon in House Shaiagrazni. Even still, Silenos opted to add a personal touch. The construct alone made up a considerable fraction of their martial power. Had he been able to craft three or four more, there would have been no fear of defeat.

Men took to the walls, and siege engines began their bombardments as the enemy armies closed in. Formations of rotting zombies and withered skeletons flew apart upon the impact of trebuchets, each one obliterating one body in its entirety, then scattering several more around it. The undead were unimpeded, simply marching on past their own devastation, acknowledging it as the triviality it was.

Nearer, nearer, nearer still they came. Returning fire with their own engines and pushing forth others. Siege towers, Silenos recognized them as, great constructs of wood and iron made to allow for easy, covered climbing onto the walls. A single cannon would have reduced one to so much kindling, and yet the shoddy hulls of lumber proved stubborn against mere trebuchet fire.

The enemy was soon close enough for bowmen and crossbowmen to begin peppering them with arrows, utilizing curious blunt-tipped projectiles fired by overdrawn bows. It was a logical innovation. Undead did not care much for skewered organs or ruptured arteries. By far the most reliable way to stop them was breaking their bones. And yet they came on regardless, inexorable march simply absorbing those casualties lost to cracked skulls and mangled limbs. Those undead with broken legs dragged them behind, those with destroyed craniums fell and moved no more, but not one lost its animation.

Silenos found a flicker of something at his heart then. Something that might, before his years of conditioning and ascension, have been accurately described as fear. He crushed it like a maggot underfoot, surveying the destruction.

He had no doubt that less than a twentieth of the enemy would actually fall or be injured before leaving the walls, which meant the battle would be decided on how well those walls held. The siege engines were priority one.

His magic built, a snarling, flowing river of power in his fingers, hotter than magma, thicker than steel, deadlier than any force the primitives around him could muster with their technologies.

Never one to specialize himself for battle, Silenos nevertheless had more than a few tricks up his sleeve to prepare for such things. He called on his necromantic might, breaching that veil between life and death, running mental fingers through it and feeling the slide of souls against them. Silenos ignored them. He wasn't looking for wisps of deceased humanity now. He had no flesh with which to use them; instead he wanted the substance they lived in.

The abyss, made of shadestuff. Unimaginative though the names were, they referred to magics older and more powerful than any individual within House Shaiagrazni. Silenos drew on them, readying a globule of the viscous, fluidlike magic as he pulled it into reality.

Shadestuff was blacker than black and deadlier than death, held carefully from his skin by a lifetime of practiced caution. Taking a moment to get his aim, Silenos propelled it at one of the siege towers.

He had experimented with acid once to see the strongest varieties and their effects on living matter. The most corrosive solution had been able to strip a finger down to bone in mere moments. The shadestuff would have left that bone a swirling mist of carbon within the same time frame.

It crashed against the tower, melting and obliterating wood so quickly there was no time for the effects of inertia and surface tension to be seen. Whatever it hit simply stopped existing before it could even be sapped of speed, projectile tunneling clean through the structure, then falling to snatch away the bodies of a marching undead rank behind it.

Silenos had already prepared another globule of shadestuff, following the first up and obliterating a second hole out of the siege tower. Two, it appeared, was more than the structure could withstand, and its lessened integrity finally surrendered to the assaults of gravity. It collapsed, raining tonnes of wood down upon the undead that continued mindlessly pushing it, even as their work was made pointless.

He barely acknowledged the sight, instead hurling yet more shadestuff. Another tower fell, then another, and soon the enemy had no siege engines left at all. Silenos turned his focus on their ranks instead, feeding undead to the abyss by the dozen. He hurled down pools of the inky void to swallow them as they marched through, concentrated it into a slick, oil-thin stream, and hosed entire formations out of existence. Destroyed hundreds, thousands. It was a droplet in the enemy's ocean of bodies.

The concept of morale did not truly apply to an army of the dead. Their psychologies, if the primitive magics that directed their locomotive forces could even be described as such, simply failed to register the necessary sensations. Fear, self-preservation, panic, confusion. All were irrelevancies. It was why petty necromancers had ever been such a thorn in the world's side. Even a near-total absence of skill could conjure a force that was unrelenting in the truest form. And if an army did not relent, then half the principles and stratagems of war humanity had ever devised were rendered useless.

Siege engines ripped jagged holes in their ranks, bow fire left them twitching and spasming in the dirt, pikes skewered limbs and severed tendons as they shambled up ladders. Some undead even climbed the walls simply by gripping the stone, most falling, but those who made it managing to attack the enemy in the least expected places and further disrupt their defense.

When victory came, it would be upon a mound of ruined reanimates meters deep. But there was no doubting which side would win. Twenty minutes had passed, and Silenos's enhanced cognition counted more than nine-tenths of the enemy still active. A decimation but not a devastation.

The enemy did not experience anything that could be called morale, but undead still required direction. Without a guiding force of higher intelligence they would, at best, continue mindlessly attacking without use of the siege engines allowing them a foothold. Silenos peered through the army to locate his target.

Years ago he'd made his deal to gain the eyes that let him perceive magic as lesser men did light, and he put them to good use in finding his enemy for a beheading strike. It was the familiar glow of power he'd seen surrounding the belladonnan puppeteer, which told him he'd be contesting either the same individual or the same order of being.

Silenos gathered himself and took flight from the castle walls. His back exploded into leather wings of twisted muscle fiber, beating at the air as exothermic chemistry vented pressurized burning gas from vents crafted into his flanks. The propulsion was as great as Silenos had yet managed to engineer, carrying him across the world in moments. He flew over the heads of shambling hordes beneath, arcing straight for the undead's general.

And he changed his body as he did.

Limpet teeth were formed of a keratin-based compound boasting strength an order of magnitude beyond that of steel and retaining it regardless of size. Silenos had studied the creatures to mimic the atomic structure that permitted them such properties, and he now wove it into thick armored plates across his body. Beneath that his skin and flesh changed too, made to a composition similar to that of hair, its shear and tensile yields growing to almost rival cast bronze.

His muscles swelled and rethreaded themselves into tightly woven bundles, ready to elongate or compress by many times their original dimensions; his nerves were reforged as dendrites thickened and myosin sheaths extended across their faces. Skeletal matter was broken down into constituent particles and recombined to be replaced with a boron carbide frame, and a hundred other parts of him were changed, improved, ascended.

When Silenos landed, he was a thing of terror and genius. The dirt compressed underfoot as his taloned feet came down, body bloated and expanded to a height of nine feet and a breadth of three men by his work. Jagged edges of nacre glinted prismatically upon the end of Silenos's arm, forming a great lance, and the world seemed to move at a fraction of its usual haste as sensory information ran along nervous tissue with speed to leave even sound behind.

The belladonnan puppeteer, of course, was the slower of them. Not moving in time to keep his thrust from striking entirely, only turning what would have run its cranium through into a mere shoulder stab. The thing's body was sent spiraling backward, head over heels, and Silenos gave chase. His left arm was equipped with a keratinous mass shaped to a shield able to withstand cannon fire, and he raised it in time to block the jet of shadestuff thrown at him by his tumbling enemy. Still, he felt the organic barrier begin to wither and erode at contact. Few things could withstand such necromantic power even for that long; blocking would not be a sustainable strategy.

Undead congealed out of the ground, surging high like overpressure from a land mine, and Silenos turned his shield to warding off their own strikes next. They were higher grade than the majority attacking, higher even than the dullahan, he knew. Lesser reapers and dreamsnatchers, things of compact frame, dense magic, and deadly glinting-black blades. Shadestuff trailed from their attacks, scratching at his form, and he found himself backing away.

Flames lit the area like a bonfire just moments before the belladonnan puppeteer's fireball impacted him. Silenos felt keratin expand and crack, compacted hydrogen absorbing the heat and dispersing it from his body, yet still leaving enough to sear the flesh. An attack like that would have left steel a semisolid sludge, and there were limits to biological resilience.

Limits to his power in combat too. Had Silenos the time and resource to construct even a single new grotesquerie of considerable size, he would have seen these petty casters crushed between its strength and his own. By himself, against so many, he found himself failing.

Silenos drove his lance through an undead, tearing it apart with a wrench, then felt his war body's tail whip around to break apart the jaw and neck of another. Blades dug into him from all sides, pinpricks and beestings, but the weight that followed them was more concerning by far. It resisted his movement, threatened to hold his body, allowed the puppeteer to ready another fireball. He braced for it.

But the impact never came.

There was a light, harsh and glaring, that left wisps of smoke hissing from the bodies of every undead present, like logs a mere instant before conflagrating. It had an intensity to it that almost masked the newcomer's approach, but Silenos's retinas were polarized against such damaging overload, and he could pick out the form of Ensharia as she charged in.

He had no idea how the woman had gotten to him, so far from the front, nor why she'd chosen to, but she moved with that sluggish, suicidal lethargy that came only from the combination of remarkable courage and weakness. An idiot, to be joining a fight of this caliber, but a useful idiot. He watched as her mace took a creature in its head and cast it down, bone cracking, snapping more heads to her. Then he moved in an instant.

Silenos let his tail whip high as his lance went forth, driving the enemy back just beyond the range of his skewering weapon, and into the wide, sweeping strike of the longer-ranged one. At the last moment, he had the coiled musculature draw back from his limb, cracking its edged tip like a whip and hearing as the half kilogram of nacre left sound itself behind.

The snapping of atmospheric rupturing was so loud, even his supernatural ears barely picked up the sound of bone breaking beneath. The undead stumbled, kept from flying back by the simple physics of such a low-mass collision, and Silenos was upon it in an instant. His lance was blocked, whip too close for use, shield serving only to pin the enemy down. So he closed the jaws of his war body across the undead's neck and bit down.

CHAPTER FIVE

I t had not taken long for the battle to end after Silenos succeeded in killing the puppeteer. As a rule, Silenos had seen enough combat to say that battles rarely lasted long at all when one side was controlled by sapient thought and the other an overwhelming urge to put those sapient thinkers in their stomachs. Without the direction of siege engines and scaling ladders, the undead, remarkably stupid, he thought, even for amateurs, simply couldn't defend themselves against human engineering. Clustering for trebuchet fire to rend them apart, impotently clawing at wooden gates and stone walls while thrown boulders crushed skulls and spines. It took close to a day in all, due to the sheer weight of numbers, but the following butchery had stopped being a true battle hours before it finally ended.

Ensharia and Silenos's deed in slaying the puppeteer had not gone unnoticed, and both of them had been called forth by the king to be rewarded. Silenos suspected he would not really be rewarded, at least not in any meaningful way. These idiots seemed to have mistaken him for an altruist and doubtless wanted to take advantage of that misidentified trait by honoring him through some position or other. General, champion, whichever was most suitable. Highly venerated roles in a society were perhaps the oldest way in all the world that the intelligent had of manipulating the stupid.

If he was given a medal, Silenos might well kill the offending monarch on sheer principle.

"Do you think we'll get a medal?" Ensharia asked from his side, eyes wide as dinner plates, face glowing with naive expectation. Silenos had told her, after the fight, that she had done well to sacrifice her life in order to buy him the chance to strike and had been a useful tool for leveraging his magnificent strength. She seemed to have thought he was joking. The woman's pale skin flushed red whenever a compliment was paid to her heroism, and her eyes glinted with pride at every awed stare Silenos received.

For his part, Silenos could not claim to find the state disagreeable. Word had spread of his power, first from the destroyed siege engines, then the slain puppeteer. People now gazed upon him with just a tinge of fear to supplement their respect. It was, finally, as things ought to be.

The two of them made their way briskly through the castle, which Silenos noted had remained almost untouched despite the carnage outside. A trebuchet had clipped one of the outer walls at some point, but beyond such superficial degradation, it had weathered the siege well. Likely because all its defenders had been dying on the walls at the city's edge, a mile away from it.

Farther still from the conflict lay the king and queen, both of whom greeted Silenos with smiles as he entered, neither of whom had so much as a single scratch upon them. It was very much to be expected. As was the weariness. Silenos saw it, however much they tried to keep it from their gazes. A silent, abstract fear of him, of his power. Good. It was the inevitable reaction of any who witnessed his abilities, and it was as things should be. Those with power needed respect from those without.

"Savior," the king called out, voice carrying across the hall as a booming wave. There were others present, finely dressed and nourished enough that Silenos imagined they were a part of some aristocratic class. By their expressions, they seemed to have heard at least secondhand stories about him. More awe, more fear.

"For your services in the defense of our city, your heroic defeat of the enemy general, and your preservation of the human race, you have my and the nation of Elkatin's thanks. We owe you a debt of gratitude and will repay it however is within our power."

Silenos considered demanding some financial recompense, perhaps a slice of his own territory. Such things would give a useful grounding to eventually establish himself, once he'd spent enough time learning of the new world.

But such a demand would also run the risk of irking his new allies. Better to bite his tongue and accept whatever nonentity of a reward was handed over instead. He could always take a nation himself later.

"I thank you." He nodded, not bowed, doing the king a near-unprecedented honor by treating him almost like an equal of his own. The man did not appear to notice what ridiculous consideration he'd been shown.

"Alas," he continued. "Elkatin is only one kingdom, and you are savior of the world itself. We cannot defeat the Dark Lord with just our own power, however great yours might be."

Silenos resisted the urge to laugh. They'd barely even *seen* his power and couldn't fathom it if they did, but he knew better than to treat himself as untouchable. He'd nearly died in the battle, albeit due to circumstance, and was not capable enough that he could be certain nothing would match him. The Great Ancestor, leader of House Shaiagrazni, they could have let their guard down. But not their lessers.

"What would you suggest we do as an alternative?" he asked the king. Whispers ran out through the court, muttered, scandalized disbelief. Silenos did not dignify them with a glance. He was well familiar with the response inferior minds tended to have to Shaiagrazni's named speaking without undue reverence to their randomly selected leaders. Whispering about it was simply the inanest thing they might have done.

Clearly, though, his question was enough to entice them. Silenos felt the room cramp in as faces studied the conversation ever more intensely, awaiting an answer.

". . . There are others," the king said at last. "People of great power, of magic, knowledge, strength, and swiftness. People who might be turned to pit their abilities against the Dark Lord and remove his scourge from the world."

Silenos glanced at the paladin, Ensharia, keeping his face carefully neutral.

"Would you describe her as such an individual?" he asked.

The woman's eyes fell to her feet. Clearly she was clever enough to realize what he was trying to do, but the king simply thought. Then slowly shook his head.

"Ensharia is remarkable, one of the strongest paladins now active, but there are others in her order of greater power. She is, however, not countable among the foremost warriors of this world. None in the city can match her, but in the kingdom there may be some who could, and in the surrounding lands it is all but guaranteed. We would need a hundred of her to win this war, not a dozen."

It was actually quite reassuring, and simultaneously was not. If Silenos had been sent to gather yet more individuals of the paladin's power, then he'd have been wasting his time. With sufficient preparation, he might have slaughtered fifty of her.

"Where are the first of these luminaries?" Silenos asked. The king waved his question aside so contemptuously he almost killed the monarch on sheer reflex.

"You will be provided with a list, but first we need your assurance that you can find these figures and secure their aid."

He considered the matter.

"I would like Ensharia to accompany me," Silenos said instantly. The woman was at least *almost* passable as a bodyguard, and with his grotesquerie destroyed, he would have to make do. Silenos had not yet coined a way to reanimate an already destroyed undead, and too few defenders had perished to supply him with the many thousands of bodies needed to create such a behemoth.

Silenos winced, his skin experiencing a sudden, phantom spasm of pain. The biomantically grown plates of keratin and hide that had largely been burned in his fight were gone now, but some whisper of the agony they'd been subjected to still remained. He made a note to dampen his pain receptors when next he transformed. Such a reaction might be inconvenient in the heat of battle.

"Done." The king nodded triumphantly. "And the two of you shall have the fleetest horses in Elkatin too!"

They left shortly after, their business done, and headed to prepare. Silenos was surprised by the paladin slowly raising her voice, hesitantly directing a question at him.

"Why me, Savior?" she asked, thoughtful, hopeful.

Silenos threw another glance along her form. Perfectly sized, he thought, to both cover much of his body and be quickly pulled in front of it should he suddenly need a shield.

"Because I see great potential in you," he replied. She beamed as they made their way off.

CHAPTER SIX

House Shaiagrazni had vastly superior means of transportation to horses and carriages, but Silenos had been informed that such things would tend to draw unnecessary attention from the world at large were they to use them. It was unfortunate, infuriating, and inconvenient, but there was nothing to be done about it just yet, and so he simply compromised with reality and allowed himself to be transported by the slow, plodding musculature of natural selection and primitive engineering.

Ensharia, apparently an optimist, had seemed pleased enough with the vehicle. Awed, even, by its construction. From what Silenos could recall, there had been times in his own people's history where such things were a rare commodity, the metal and craftsmanship involved yet to be made common by mass production, and so he perhaps should not have been surprised.

He was, though not enough that he didn't get a lot of work done.

Silenos read during his journey, and read well, having piled the carriage's storage with books covering as many subjects as he could and begun devouring them at a rate of two or three each day. Boredom was not such a crippling barrier for him, not with hours of mere waiting on the road passing them by, and not with the regions of his brain that registered such sensations having long since been flesh-crafted to remove the inconvenient flaws.

Book learning was not a flawless fountain of knowledge, but it was a start. A theoretical backbone that Silenos was careful to strengthen through questioning and inquiry with his new companion. He read of the world's Vigor, a curious form of magic that seemed to dwell within muscle and flesh to leave them hardened past physical limits. Somehow without even being identified by the new world's natives as magic at all.

He learned of the Dark Lord's historic rise several decades prior, the fractured nations that had been so tragically slow in heeding the call of paladins to unite against him. The resulting defensive war that was prepared too poorly and fought too hastily, allowing great swaths of territory to be claimed by the enemy before any serious defense could be galvanized against him by the previously warring or rivaling states.

It was not lost on Silenos that his sources of such information were far from unbiased. Without an invented printing press, this new world's book creation was monopolized and hoarded by those few possessing the greatest wealth, history was recorded only as the people in power wished it to be, and having a paladin to explain their error in disregarding the paladins hardly left him more confident that he'd gained a complete picture. Still, as the days progressed, he learned more than nothing.

Of course, a large portion of Silenos's studies and conversations were directed toward the subject of those phenoms he now rode in pursuit of, and Ensharia was as eager to assist with his learning of them as she was all other things. The nearest, she explained, would be found in the arcane city of Magira, the Great Magus Walriq. As he understood it, the magi were an order of caster native to the new world whose powers seemed most similar to Silenos's own, though still prohibiting necromancy and fleshcrafting as so many of the savages did. He'd yet to see any considerable magic from any of the new world's residents, but apparently Elkatin was not famous for its arcane power, only its holiness. That explained the near extinction he'd arrived in the midst of.

A magus, found in Magira.

Silenos did not comment on the repulsive naming scheme at play coinciding title to city designation, only waited for them to draw nearer their destination. On the seventh day, they came to it. Or rather they came to a small, pristine fountain in the center of a field, circulating water with a fluidity and smoothness that seemed anachronistic of what Silenos had yet seen of the world's primitive technologies.

"We're here," Ensharia breathed, her words distorted by a face twisted toward frowning rather than smiling. Silenos didn't need to ask why.

Around the fountain was a field, grassy and flat. It stretched back for miles, occasionally yielding to hills and slopes, dips and dives in the earthy terrain, before finally fading to woodlands at its farthest perimeters. But there was no sign of any city, magical or otherwise.

"Have we got the wrong place?" Ensharia pressed. "We . . . Surely we can't have. I don't understand."

Silenos did though. He was not what this world would call a magus—his own world had never used that name to his knowledge—but House Shaiagrazni was an order of arcanists more than anything else. One world or another, one name or another, the magics they bound and the ways they did so were similar in nature. Magic was power.

Magi, sorcerers, wizards, casters. Power brought arrogance, and there were few things the arrogant enjoyed more than inconveniencing their lessers with tedious testing.

He tightened his eyes, took in the sight of the fountain, then sighed. It was practically screaming with magical power.

"I can see through your idiot illusion," Silenos called out, letting his displeasure show. "I am Silenos Shaiagrazni, senior of House Shaiagrazni, master of the arcane arts. Arcane arts more complex and potent than your civilization has yet to discover, that is. Reveal yourselves this instant before I grow bored and start destroying things to motivate you."

Fortunately, it did not take long for his calls to be heeded.

The illusion went watery first, physical world distorted. Losing form, as if it were molded wax suddenly left melting under the sun. Within moments it fell away, revealing a hard stone ground leading to a tall metal gate, two men looking down from atop it. Both held crossbows, cocked and readied. Built with gears and pulleys, each one had clearly been engineered to multiply the strength of its wielder, storing tension built by drawing it with the turning of a wheel rather than brute force. Mathematics turned into death.

Silenos resisted his urge to mock the savages for their weaponry.

"Identify," one called, and Silenos affixed him with a look that he could only hope conveyed the true, transcendent stupidity of leveling such a demand at him mere moments after his declarations of name, rank, and loyalties. Ensharia spoke before he could decide on how best to articulate the man's mental deficiencies.

"We are here on the business of King—"

"A woman?!" another one snapped. "There are no women allowed in Magira, girl. Begone with you."

"Or are you one of the new whores traveling with your master?" the first added, thoughtful. Silenos suddenly got the impression that, despite the plate armor encasing her, Ensharia's body was being examined and weighed. Apparently she shared his impression because her disgust was palpable.

"I have a letter of introduction," Ensharia replied quickly, fishing inside her person and producing it with a demonstrable haste. It was the genuine article, signed by the king's own hand to both explain their presence and request entry on his behalf. With their altitude atop the gate, both men took a moment to shuffle down and reach through an opening in the metal to seize it, reading it quickly once they had. Apparently they'd been selected for literacy, or else Magira simply allowed more of its populace to read than Elkatin, because they soon understood the contents and acted accordingly.

"Alright," a voice came at last. "Fine, you can enter, but stick with the man."

A rumble, a rattle, and the gate's mechanisms began to turn as the letter was handed back. Silenos and Ensharia both stepped past the threshold and into the city together, moving fully past the illusion at last.

Everything shifted, photonic trickery breaking down as Silenos bypassed the angles at which it had been woven to work. Illusory magic was a difficult thing to do right. Few even among House Shaiagrazni could cast it precisely enough to be truly indistinguishable by close scrutiny, and so Silenos was not surprised as the city unfurled before him. Buildings reaching high, streets wide and scarcely occupied, everything presenting itself clean, smooth, glinting under the sun and wafting currents of magically sterilized air in all directions.

To his side, Ensharia gasped. He turned to see her eyes wide, face a mask of awe and amazement.

"Incredible," she breathed, staring out at the sights. "I'd heard stories, ridiculous stories, but . . . God, it's like a city of angels."

Magira was a city of magic casters, not an uncommon sight in the lands of House Shaiagrazni. But Silenos could understand the sheer incredulity with which it might be beheld, seen from eyes that were as unused to the arcane as hers. Magic almost invariably found use in architecture first within nations that had access to it. Clearly Magira was no exception. One could build higher with magic by shaping materials more accurately, or else just working harder ones.

Which begged the question of what exactly had been used for this city's construction.

"Diabase," he noted, identifying the stone with a glance. It was one of the preferred materials of a puerile magical society, harder than other stones, not wholly uncommon, and quite workable with the sorts of energy and force that might be mustered by modest power. Ideal for those who wanted to feel as though they'd somehow transcended ordinary rock.

Evidently, his lack of respect for the choice was clear to Ensharia.

"You don't approve?" she prodded. Silenos shrugged as they made their way into the city, still examining it while he spoke.

"Magira is three centuries old, yes?" he asked. She nodded. "Double my own age then, and easily six or seven of your generations. Diabase is acceptable for beginners in the art of magically aided architecture, but I fear its continued use here after so long, even in the outskirts of the city, which must surely have been made most recently, betrays a lack of . . . innovation."

She eyed him, seeming more concerned with Silenos than the city now.

"What are your people like?" Ensharia asked after a moment. "The entire time I've known you, even when bringing you to the greatest wonders I know, you've never so much as arched an eyebrow. Are your people really so unrivaled by this world? Are . . . Are you . . . unrivaled, among your people?"

He cracked a smile, and for once the display was sincere.

"I am not. In House Shaiagrazni, my order, there are perhaps a dozen who exceed me in magical mastery and knowledge, and many more who are my betters in raw power. I am not the oldest, most studied, not the wisest, nor even am I the cleverest or most cunning. I will never rule my people."

She seemed surprised.

"That . . . You always seemed so . . . certain, so demanding of others."

"I am." He nodded. "Of my inferiors, just as my superiors are demanding of me. My people achieved wonders to dwarf those of this world specifically because we believe in elevating the greatest minds and powers to the greatest positions. This world, it would seem, has . . . other criteria."

Ensharia looked at her feet.

"Many magi believe women to be inferior, ill-suited for magic. Too emotional, lacking the discipline needed to control it."

"Hmm," Silenos noted. "Imbeciles."

Misogyny, the word was, if he recalled. An archaic thing long since dispelled from his own people. What mattered was not that flesh found between a person's legs, he knew. It was the firing of synapses between their neurons. How he loathed the idiocy of a civilization that would halve its own potential so arbitrarily. No wonder they were still crawling around with mud bricks.

"Let us continue. We have searching to do," he declared.

Their search was a tedious thing, not least because, despite her clear disapproval of the city's view regarding her sex, Ensharia simply refused to demonstrate any real perspective in seeing the displays around them. Every moment, it felt, he had to remind her to keep focus and not allow herself the distraction of gawking at one thing or another.

Silenos himself hardly saw the appeal. Magic was being used brazenly, indulgently, as it might by the hands of some infant community who had yet to even realize the potential of their own powers. Toys being sold, petty conveniences for warming beds or blocking unwanted noise, massaging devices or servitor golems. It was all so dull.

"Is this not a city of research?" Silenos asked his companion, who looked distractedly back to him and considered.

"They say so, but the magi say lots of things. It's a city of secrets, certainly, the Arcane Council has seen to that."

The Arcane Council, dictatorship split between a dozen. House Shaiagrazni actually used rather similar means in many cases, though was ultimately ruled by a single autocrat. Silenos had heard little of the magus rulers of Magira thus far, and everything he'd seen of their work left him certain they needed oversight just as much as the Dark Lord.

Something bothered Silenos, and it bothered him more the farther they moved into the city. He realized it before long. There were no corpses, at all.

He could smell corpses, or feel them rather, and that sensation was entirely absent.

Cremation, he imagined. Not an uncommon practice in his world—the enemies of House Shaiagrazni had long since learned not to leave their cities filled with potential soldiers should they war with the necromancers—but an inconvenience, nonetheless. He stifled his irritation and pressed on.

As they drew closer to the city's center, Silenos expected to see an increase in guards, soldiers, defenses. He expected, perhaps, to find refugees, given that he had seen none anywhere else. When he did not, he consulted Ensharia once more.

"Magira tends to remain neutral and apolitical," she explained. "Unconcerned with the outside world."

"Including matters of someone attempting to rule and conquer everything in the world?" he asked, not entirely shocked, just finding himself in need of certainty. She nodded.

Imbeciles, as he'd thought. Silenos almost wished he could watch them all invaded and crushed by their own mistakes.

By far the largest of Magira's buildings was its university. That, Silenos had to admit, was a mark to the credit of its savage governors. It was guarded, though not in any way that might have impeded the movements of those frequenting it, and Silenos found himself stopped near the door by yet more gatekeepers. The letter appeared just as effective at granting passage as it had been to the city itself.

Inside, the place was a monument constructed to spellcaster egotism. Everything was either large or absurd. Its ceilings dozens of meters high, its walls littered with relics no doubt pilfered from the past conquests of its owners. The people were similarly . . . absurd.

Robed men, no women. Most elderly, some ancient, all bearing the sharp, straight postures of individuals who were confident in their own power, all bearing the flitting eyes of those surrounded by others they considered just as rightful in being likewise. Silenos recognized the demeanors instantaneously. They really were similar to those of his own people.

Ensharia seemed cowed as they passed magi, despite the limited numbers. Silenos was merely curious. He found a few glances turned his way as they made a path through the university, eyes scrutinous and considering. His features, he had learned, were foreign to Ensharia's people, but here there was a blend of ethnicities almost as varied as House Shaiagrazni. Pale, olive, copper, and ebon skin, curly, straight, and wavy hair. Eyes of brown, of blue, of green, or even of red and black. It was a population clearly extracted from a continental mass, and perhaps even beyond.

That was a good sign. It, at the very least, implied a sample size large enough that, through sheer weight of statistics, there ought to be at least one or two semi-talented individuals among them.

Finally their trek through the ridiculous university reached its culmination, and he and Ensharia stepped into a voluminous chamber with walls of carved obsidian, lit from the center by a great, towering pillar of light. A ley line, he knew.

A crease in the world, where reality's skin was thinner and less separated from the hot magical blood pumping under the surface. Of course the magi had built their university around it; such things were powerful.

But more dangerous. The Entities swam as bacteria in the veins of the world, and it was ever so easy to bring one forth when extracting the fluid in which they bred.

There stood a group of men beside the ley line, whom Silenos recognized instantly as among the most important around. Their magic betrayed that much, considerable in its volume as he studied it with his arcane gaze. Bonfires of power, perhaps small things compared to the scale he might have expected from his peers in House Shaiagrazni, but certainly greater than the spitting hearths that fueled spellwork in most he'd passed.

He hadn't taken so much as a step toward them before another came into step ahead, barring Silenos's way with his body and eying him coolly.

"Do you have an appointment to meet the councillors?" he asked, gruff.

"Your tiny bureaucracy is but a writhing insect compared to the unfathomable might and import of my powers," Silenos replied diplomatically. "Step aside now or I shall obliterate you like the semisapient bacterium you are."

Ensharia was hasty in adding her own voice to the mix, presenting their letter of introduction for the third time.

"Elkatin," the guard read, lip curling with distaste. "You're not pilgrims, are you?"

Silenos had yet to teach himself the new world's languages, not even that of Elkatin itself. It hadn't been necessary as whatever process had brought him here seemed to be translating the natives' speech for Silenos without his input, but he'd been practicing with the letter. Aside from merely memorizing their alphabet and phonetics, he had come to intimately know that their purpose had been made very clear in its wording.

Which told him that this man was merely antagonizing them.

"Step aside," he repeated. "Or I shall move you."

A sneering grin plucked at the man's lips, and he'd just barely opened his mouth when Silenos's thoughts touched his nerves.

It would be politically inconvenient to destroy him entirely, and Silenos's magics were ill-suited for physical displays even in a world where their practice was not illegal. He was ever creative, however.

Fleshcrafting sorceries seeped into the guard's muscles, forcibly convulsing them in the exact sequence needed to send him flying one way under his own strength. Silenos was careful to exert the full range of power available to the targeted tissues, ensuring that the obstacle was displaced a full ten feet by the time he finally stopped sliding on the smooth stone.

All eyes were upon him and Ensharia now, which suited him perfectly well. He stepped past the crumpled, groaning man and closed in on the magi. All were on edge, preparing magic, suspicious, ready for battle. Politely, he refrained from laughing at them.

"I am here to speak with the magus Walriq," he told the group. "Show me to him and I shall be on my way."

The catching of breath told Silenos that these men, at least, possessed the magical prowess needed to observe his own power. That was good. A dash of fear often helped to move conversation along in his experience.

"Walriq is dead," one of the magi replied gruffly. "You're here a week late."

CHAPTER SEVEN

Ensharia gasped, and Silenos felt the convulsive tightening of irritation in his throat.

"How did he let himself die?" he asked, keeping his temper cool. Cellular regeneration, genetic immortality, redundant organs, soul tethering, safeguard bodies. There were a hundred ways he'd found to keep his own existence preserved, albeit most had been left untenable by his sudden transfer. It took a very young and very stupid caster to be *killed*.

"He was murdered." One magus spat, literally spat, a globule passing his lips and hitting the ground in contempt. "His own apprentice, Arion Falls. Walriq is no more."

Silenos and Ensharia took their time gathering yet more information before finally moving once again. Falls was, indeed, the magus Walriq's apprentice, and a point of pride for even him. A wind mage, he was apparently the kind of prodigy who emerged only once every few centuries and had been expected by most to surpass even his mentor despite being only twenty years of age.

It was believed, likewise, that he had overpowered and killed Walriq a few days prior in an argument. Evidently, the natives were too stupid to see any kind of contradiction between his only "one day" surpassing his mentor and having personally killed him so recently.

Ensharia waited until they'd stepped out of the room before speaking, which Silenos appreciated for the wise judgment call it was. She had no way of knowing whether they were being observed magically. Her eyes were not made of the same stuff as his.

"We can't get Walriq." She sighed. "But we can still track down Falls, right? If anything, he might be even better."

"Perhaps." Silenos hummed thoughtfully. Young casters were often capricious. The egotism and ambition that came so naturally to those of power tended to mix poorly, in his experience, with the hormonal chaos that was a body just barely out of puberty. Such an ally could be unreliable.

"He did kill his master," Silenos noted and found, pleasantly, that Ensharia was shaking her head.

"You think a magus would start an argument with someone they thought was stronger than them, or fail to recognize when they'd been surpassed by their apprentice? Further, you think that apprentice would go on letting a city full of men who think might makes right believe that he was only *eventually* going to be the better caster, if he'd already outgrown the strongest?"

A smile made itself known to Silenos, and he happily granted it space upon his features.

"Astute and logical deductions," he informed the woman. "Yes, we shall go and examine the apprentice in his cell."

Perhaps unsurprisingly, they met more resistance on their way to do so than they had moving for an audience with the magi. Accused murderers tended to be guarded well, Silenos knew, particularly when they carried the genetic material of a magical prodigy. The inconvenience of reaching Falls was nonetheless an opportunity to gather more information about him, and one he made the most of.

He was stored belowground, as might be expected of a wind mage, and behind heavy guards. Several doors of thick iron barred the sole corridor leading to his cell, manned by individuals whose bodies carried an innate magic of the same order as Ensharia's. Silenos had no doubt any of them could toss his own form around like a rag doll, such would be their strength, and made a mental note to study the phenomena responsible for humans being so passively imbued with power in this world. It was not known to the people of his own.

More iron doors, big, thick things. Slabs of metal that might have found use in House Shaiagrazni as shields against cannon fire. It made Silenos consider the order of caster who lay bound behind them. He wasn't considering for long. They soon reached the final door, stepping past, entering the chamber that held magus Walriq's supposed killer.

It was a young man, as Silenos might have expected. Seated against a far wall, and with the look of one who had been born handsome but recently withered in circumstance. His clothes were ragged, features unkempt, surroundings grimy and dirty in such a way as to seemingly infect him. He looked up to study Silenos with eyes colored an emerald green, tousled brown hair falling around them in greasy locks.

Silenos spoke first.

"Arion Falls," he identified. "Did you kill your master?"

The boy's face was tight with hostility instantly.

"Another interrogator?" he asked, then shook his head fractionally. "No, you're not local, and you're not working for the city either." He nodded to Ensharia. "Unless you had an exception made for you to be bringing the bitch along."

The paladin bristled but said nothing. A pity. Silenos would've found it rather amusing to see her temper run out.

"Answer the question," Silenos pressed. "I'm already bored, and should my boredom reach critical mass it—Ah." Of course, these savages had no concept of nuclear fission. "I am an incredibly destructive and dangerous person prone to mercurial violence when my patience is tested," he simplified.

Silenos saw the boy's eyes focus for a moment, then his pale skin went paler still. Had he . . . seen his magic? The gift of Sight was a rare thing to have naturally but not unheard-of. Not even among savages.

"I didn't," the magus said after a pause. "And people only say I did because they're jealous of me. They all know that, in Walriq's absence, there's no competition at all for greatest alive. It's just me, me, me, me. And without me, suddenly, that position is contested by about four others, any two of which would be hard-pressed to best me with both their powers combined."

An interesting answer.

"And so you would say your master remained superior to you as of his death?"

The boy snorted.

"He made magus at fifteen. I barely managed it at thirteen. I was more gifted, nobody was stupid enough to think otherwise, but the difference wasn't that big. He had sixty years of experience on me. I doubt I'd have beaten him one time in ten if we'd fought in earnest."

Silenos believed him. Such disparities were commonplace. Talent was two-thirds of magic, but age made up much of what remained.

"How did he die then?" Ensharia asked.

The magus stared at her as if she'd just drooled on herself.

"He was eighty," he said slowly. "How do you think he died? The old man's heart stopped while he was balls deep in some whore. I found the poor girl panicking next to his dead body when I came back half an hour later."

Silenos had once been told about Araquia the Great, one of the foremost casters of House Shaiagrazni. A woman of such power that she was able to split mesas in half with a thought and redirect entire rivers with a whispered word of power. She'd died when he was still in training. Autoerotic asphyxiation, as he had heard. Her safeguards had failed to act simply because it had, technically, been her own act that killed her. Such things were more common among masters of magic than most tended to know.

And the magi of Magira surely knew that.

There were other facts Silenos judged to be in Falls's favor. The second among a gathering of great powers was perhaps the least likely of all to challenge the first, in his experience. Such individuals were in a position to enjoy practically all the indulgences of the highest station and were the least often challenged. It meant those rare occasions on which they interacted with their superiors were far less grating, far more easily ignored. Some might have been impulsive enough to lash out regardless, and yet that seemed even less likely. Magi were patient, intelligent individuals, as most casters were. And Falls was the greater genius between him and his master. Had he decided to strike the old man down, he would simply have waited a half decade until he could be certain of doing so, not risked losing a contest to the death as he was.

All of that, and there were far less sloppy ways to kill a man sixty years one's elder. Silenos found himself more confident in the man's innocence with every passing moment.

"I believe you," he said at last, and Falls leaped to his feet, animated by a new vigor. It was like watching true life given to a fresh corpse. Silenos had to stifle his smile. "But it makes no difference," he continued. "You will be executed tomorrow regardless. Good day." He turned for the door, taking his leave without another word.

Ensharia was quiet behind him, face dark, eyes sad. Silenos recognized the primitive firing of empathetic synapses that had bound their species so tightly before sapience and knowledge had come to rule everything else.

"You dislike him," he observed. "And yet you are saddened by his death?"

She eyed him, confused, concerned. Thoughtful as she took her time in considering how best to answer. The more Silenos spoke with this paladin, the more he appreciated her habit of favoring silence over pointless speech.

"He's innocent, and I'm a paladin. I'm opposed to capital punishment at the best of times, and this is the worst of them."

He could understand that much, at least, however different his own people's customs were. Standing beside principle rather than emotional reaction was admirable.

"You're also worried that we're losing a powerful ally," Silenos observed, and Ensharia stiffened.

"Obviously," she conceded. "I'm not an idealist. I understand that there's more at stake here than one man's life. We can't free him?"

"No," Silenos replied. "If I had time, and a graveyard, perhaps, but I am not a direct combatant. Those magi we met, together, would be more than a match for me. However many other councillors of their level are in this city would further the gap, and then there would be several hundred more magi to contend with. It is impractical to free him." A smile creased his face. "But I have another plan."

Ensharia awaited it eagerly, and Silenos gave her the answer.

"I imagine Walriq has yet to be cremated, given how recent his death was. One day at least would be spared to examine his body, another to unlock whatever magical secrets may be held within. If we act quickly, tonight, I ought to be able to reanimate it, and unlike the drooling idiot you call a Dark Lord, I am able to bring back an individual with all the intellect and powers they held in life. When the situation calls for it."

A double-edged sword, always, but Silenos knew when a risk was worth taking. Walriq had impressed him. Ensharia seemed less thrilled.

"I suppose . . . it's for the best," she managed, sounding more to be convincing herself than acquiescing to him.

"Splendid. Then you will help me by being the one to execute Falls," Silenos announced, enjoying the look of shock upon her face rather a lot. "It will, after all, gather all the more magi to witness if he's killed by something as humiliating as a woman, hmm?"

CHAPTER EIGHT

Ensharia had not known the Savior for long, she realized. Under two weeks, in fact. She'd learned much about him in that time, however. And come to doubt much of what she initially assumed. He was callous, unpredictable, oddly cruel at times, all of which seemed at odds with his ends of halting the Dark Lord. His mind though had been every bit the force described in her people's stories, and he'd demonstrated the fact rather handily to her in how he convinced the Arcane Council to allow an outsider as Falls's executioner.

It had been like watching a man work clay, molding the magi with words instead of touch but wielding no less skill than an expert sculptor. They had bent to his suggestions, absorbed his ideas, twisted and worked his implications until each one seemed certain they had coined the ideas themselves. The entire conversation had lasted ten minutes or less, and by its end, all present were dancing to the Savior's tune.

She had agreed herself, of course. And Ensharia was smart enough to know that she'd almost certainly been manipulated just as seamlessly and completely. She was no genius, nor was she a schemer or politician. If the esteemed councilmen of Magira hadn't noticed themselves being subtly shifted along the currents of Silenos's consultancy, then she'd never have had a chance at all.

The day moved by, and Ensharia found herself getting a lot of looks from the inhabitants of Magira. She had not, of course, been permitted to actually stay in the university; rather she'd had quarters prepared for her a short walk away. A short walk provided one could clear fifty feet per stride, at least. She kept to herself for the most part, building her courage and resisting the urge to reinforce it with some wine. That was an increasingly difficult battle, these days. Every city taken by the Dark Lord was another whisper at the back of her mind to indulge, and her savior had only made things worse in that respect.

Her savior.

A fortnight had been too little time to become used to calling him by his title. It was a thing of folklore and mythology, made real only recently. And barely made real, at that. Silenos was brilliant, knowledgeable, and certainly powerful in all the ways he'd been imagined. But more and more, she'd seen him fall short of the heroic standards laid out by his preceding prophecies and promises.

She was going to kill a man she knew to be innocent on his command. It was for the greater good, Ensharia knew, but even that was not without direction. Her doing so was merely to give a distraction while her savior reanimated a man's corpse, enslaving it permanently to his will using magics so unnatural her order had been formed in part to battle them.

Compromise, sacrifice, pragmatism. It seemed to her that no three attributes ever mixed to so reliably create a moral degradation than those. But she'd have been lying to claim it was that that had her skin crawling.

He threatened to obliterate that man, just for doing his job.

Would the Savior have acted upon his threats and left that guard a corpse, had she not been so fast with their letter? She didn't know, couldn't know, and found herself hollowed out by the lack of knowledge. There seemed no point in asking him; he'd either lie or be truthful, and it was beyond her to know which was which.

Ensharia eyed the wine again. It was strong stuff. Magira tended to make all their indulgences strong, and she felt it drawing her toward it for one long, irresistible moment. Then she got to her feet and headed for the door.

She was a paladin, and a paladin was never without something to do. There were more productive, holy, and decent things to spend her energy on than self-pity. Ensharia headed back for the university.

Despite being recognized and known by now, she found her trip inside one of innumerable stares and sneers. Ensharia seemed only to take three paces in the average time between the barbed words thrown at her, insults, propositions, even just observations made of her body. Many were content to simply tell her she was a whore.

It had come to her attention that women *were* allowed within Magira—the particulars of magus Walriq's death attested to that much—there were simply few conditions in which it was permitted. The most common, apparently, was as a means of sexual release for its magi.

Ensharia passed a few on her way, all of them pretty, all dressed up like dolls. Their faces were calm, collected, dutiful when they weren't feigning lust and love for the eyes of a man. She'd seen such expressions before and felt a familiar stab of admiration for the strength needed to wear them in such conditions. Then her focus was broken as she came to the first of many iron doors separating Falls from his captors.

She was granted passage, the way people bearing royal seals tended to be, and had the entire walk down Falls's corridor to steel her nerves and master her wits. She was soon before him, eying the man through behind the bars of his cell, fascinated by the sight.

Fear had eaten even more of him, she saw. His face more lined, his body held tighter in the clutches of its fearful trembling.

"What are you doing here?" he asked, an edge to his voice, a touch of panic to his eyes. "Here to give me my last fuck before the end? Because I don't think I'm in the mood right now."

Ensharia was too mature a person to actually consider leaving for that, but it still took a notch out of her patience and compassion. She forced herself to calm for a moment before replying.

"I'm a paladin of the Order of Erogran," she told him coolly. "And, as such, I feel it is my duty to comfort you in your final hours."

He blinked.

"I just said I wasn't in the mood—"

"Spiritually, you idiot," Ensharia snapped. "I can—" She hesitated, spending *another* moment to control her temper, then continued. "I can pray with you, if you would like, or I can take confession of your sins. I can . . . advise you on making peace with yourself, or if you would prefer, I can simply . . . be here. As company, until the end arrives."

Falls stared at her, not seeming to quite comprehend what she'd said at first. Moments passed, and his face shifted toward shock, then . . . anger. She saw him begin to speak, a jagged, foul retort boiling up from his throat. But it died before reaching his lips. His face relaxed again, falling slack, eyes wide, helpless, staring. Then a tear began to slide down his cheek.

"Why would you do this for me?" he asked, voice already an unsteady croak, as was so common for the voices of those who cried without being used to it.

Years she'd been a paladin. And in that time Ensharia had done her work for hundreds. Delivering children, comforting orphans, fighting until her body digested itself from exhaustion and her urine was red with blood. But none of it was ever as hard as comforting the dying.

Must you die for the greater good? Would our savior tell me if you didn't need to?

She swallowed her doubt and forced a show of confidence.

"Because I am a paladin, and you are a dying man. I would not have your last moments in this world be any crueler and more painful than they need to be."

Falls broke down fully into tears at that, and she resisted the urge to violate security protocol by reaching out to take his hand through the bars. Once he had recovered, they began her work.

It was dark when the guards came, looking surprised to find Ensharia with the prisoner but clearly not caring enough to question it much.

"Time's up," one of them grunted, a towering man made of slabbed musculature and scarred skin. His face was cold and cruel in all the ways a good soldier's was. Ensharia nodded, standing as Falls was seized by one last trembling fit.

"Thank you," he whispered, and she only nodded, not wanting to speak, not wanting to accept his gratitude. It felt wrong to do so with what she was planning, perverse. Ensharia took her leave quickly and without meeting any of the men's eyes.

Magi had a sense of grandiosity in everything they did. Silenos had correctly predicted this, extrapolating the fact from the casters of his own world. Ensharia had seen it in the Savior himself too, by his choice of flowing crimson robes and gemcrusted lining.

She saw it more overtly now, standing in the center of their execution hall. A gallery lined one half of the great hemispherical building, seats made of smooth marble and filled with scores of magisters. Most with faces lined in middle age, some clearly well into the last decades of their lives, and a precious few bearing the talent to have earned their robes while youth still left their skin smooth and taut.

It had surprised her to find that most magi did not employ illusory magics to appear younger than they were, but Falls had explained it during their time together. It wasn't uncommon that a magus would do so; however, such spellwork was considered the height of ill manners within a gathering of other magi.

To her, that seemed an absurdity in such circumstances. They'd all gathered like vultures before a condemned man's death, mostly for the sheer novelty of seeing it happen in as humiliating a way as any of them could consider. How could such creatures care about something like manners? How could they care about anything at all?

Ensharia closed her eyes against the leering sights of the magi, whispering a prayer to herself as she stepped out into the room's center. A great chandelier hung high over it, illuminating a dais below in constant sterile light spewed forth by a dozen glowing crystals. It was upon this dais that Falls resided. His head was down, face pale, arms bound behind his back in thick runic chains that linked themselves to a fixture in the floor. Ensharia could feel the binding spells at work where they'd been woven into the metal. Powerful stuff, able to keep even a magus of Falls's caliber from drawing on his power. That was good, she decided. It would allow her to end everything in a single stroke.

Falls caught her approach quickly, eyes wide, questioning.

"You." He gasped. "They said it'd be a woman, but . . . Fuck, I should've guessed. So that's why you stayed with me?"

It was a struggle to keep her face from cracking apart and letting the emotion swell up from below, but Ensharia forced herself to manage it. This time, out of any, she would not betray herself.

"I stayed with you because it was the right thing to do," she replied, hoping that he heard the honesty in her words. "And I'll be the one to carry out your sentence for the same reason."

"Because my dying is right?" he hissed, hatred bleeding from him like ichor from a lanced heart. It was intense enough that even Ensharia found herself taking a backstep on reflex. Give her an undead any day, a demon, a vampire, a lich king even. Give her any abomination at all over the eyes of a dying man.

"Because it will lead to what is right," she replied quietly but found herself uncertain. She saw Falls's face twist from the corner of her vision, but in thought now, rather than rage. His voice rang out again, quieter.

"This is a diversion?" he guessed, and she looked up sharply. Just in time to see the triumph on his face as he realized his guess had been right.

"I see, but then that means I don't actually need to die, right?" the magus pressed. "How many more minutes do you buy by killing me? Not as many as you have already with the ceremony, right? Is my life worth so little that you'd spend it on that tiny measure of extra time?"

He was doing the most dangerous thing a person could: making sense.

A few extra minutes, not any stretch of time at all, really. Usually. But in battle, in a situation of death and danger, it could be all the time in the world. How much would she have done to win a few extra minutes during the siege? How many lives had been ended in those last few minutes before the Savior killed the enemy's general?

"I'm sorry," she replied quietly and watched Falls's face melt into horror, hate, and impotent rage as she hefted the axe high overhead. It was a simple thing, not a weapon she'd have ever carried into battle, but it was enough to do its work this night. With a paladin's strength behind it and the fragile tissues of a magus without magic, she could be sure it would do its work.

CHAPTER NINE

Ensharia swung down, sending the edged metal to bite hard into the chain connecting Falls's bound wrists to the great fixture by his feet. It was a thick thing, close to an inch of cold iron, but she drove the metal with strength enough that the axe broke apart on impact, and the robust links of chain followed suit. In an instant, the magus was on his feet, body aglow with power, air rippling around him as atmospheric currents danced and congealed in accordance with his will.

It took one second for the pressure to coalesce about his shackles, crushing and snapping them harmlessly from his wrists to fall empty. One more second saw a barrier of stone-dense air compressed around them, and it was the third second in which a sizzling lance of energy crunched into it, delivering power enough that Ensharia felt the hairs curl on her skin even as its heat was blocked feet shy of reaching her.

"Treacherous whore!" one magus roared.

"Teach us to let a bitch do a man's job!" cried another.

"Only thing you can trust them to cut is a fucking steak!" snarled a third. After that, the slurring came in such volume that Ensharia found it all blending incoherently together. Then even that was buried by the blasts of magic.

Ensharia found herself thrown to one side of the room and took a moment to realize it had been Arion Falls, the wind mage, who had done so. He didn't glance at her as she stared up at him, focusing instead on defending himself from the fusillades of magic still being thrown across the room.

Not one of the councilmen had stood to contribute their own power yet, and most of the similarly aged men appeared content to sit still and observe as well. Indeed, Ensharia realized it was largely the younger, and thus less trained, who were so vigorously throwing themselves at him.

But that did not give her new ally any sort of advantage, merely provided an explanation for why he had yet to be torn apart.

His barriers were like castle walls, but his enemies were like trebuchets. Arcs of propelled acid, shaped stones, metal barbs, and fireballs hurtled for him, deflecting and breaking on his shield to leave the ground around him fractured and glowing with molten agony. Even while magic was turned to solidity in their offense, others took less direct measures. Poisonous gases coiling about Falls, energies running through the ground beneath his feet and heating it to molten slag.

Ensharia was no magus, but she was a warrior, and she'd been in enough battles to recognize the tide of one when she watched it from so close. Falls was losing, and losing faster with every moment that passed. She got to her feet.

Closest to her was a younger magus, who fought by directing arcs of lightning at Falls. The static discharge seemed unable to penetrate its atmospheric barricade, glancing and deflecting off in all directions, blasting fist-sized chunks of stone from the ground in a dozen different places with every forked refraction. He didn't look up in time to see her close in, and Ensharia's mace caught him clean in the chest.

She held back, still a paladin, but a magus was not a warrior, and his body had not been rebuilt to a steely hardness by the same training hers had been. His ribs broke, and he fell, coughing blood. Ensharia moved on to the next.

There was magic on the air, war magic. Silenos could feel it. Magi were nothing compared to the named of House Shaiagrazni. Only the greatest of them would have even managed to progress that far within Silenos's people, but he sensed many turning their power to violence. Dozens, scores, perhaps close to a hundred in all. Such a sum of magic was more than even he could scoff at, even without any of the less modestly powerful councillors contributing to its sum.

Obviously, Ensharia had made a mistake. He reminded himself to chastise the idiot later as he advanced through the city. Provided she lived, of course. One couldn't take that prospect for granted with idiots.

Had Silenos been advancing through a city held by House Shaiagrazni, there would have been ample defenses to impede him. Fleshcrafted servitors of preternatural sensory potence and deadly combat effectiveness, runes and wards made to shatter upon contact with his magical presence and thus alert their casters. If nothing else, the occasional trip wire. Instead, he found very little to halt him.

That changed, however, as Silenos moved closer to his destination.

He flew across Magira upon great fleshcrafted wings, their substance made of keratinous compounds able to withstand the lifting forces generated by bundles of efficient, spring-coiled muscle fibers. The decades had long since made Silenos an adept at flight, but he still spent most of his airtime gliding, all too aware of the surprising volume generated when a creature of his mass held itself aloft through Newtonian principles.

Years ago, Silenos had enjoyed the sensation of flight. Enjoyed it like nothing else. He had since outgrown such juvenile sensations. These days the wind upon his face and moonlight on his back was of tertiary concern. His power was but a means, and he closed in quickly on the ends.

The magus Walriq's corpse was not stored in the university, as Silenos might have guessed, but rather in a more secure building just half a kilometer from it. The thing was of diabase, as much of Magira was, and constructed squat and stout for defense. Its outer walls were thick enough to stop cannon fire, threaded with barriers of magic that might turn away any attempts to transmute their substance, and guarded on all sides by more of the unfeasibly potent physical specimens who had lined the corridor of the holding cell.

None of which was quite sufficient to truly impede him, of course.

Silenos dropped down, reconfiguring his body as he did. He did not choose to take his combat form; such a shape was ill-suited for any degree of subterfuge. Eleven feet and four thousand kilograms of supermaterial tended to attract attention. Instead, he let his body fall into its standard form, having long since enhanced his humanoid visage as much as could be managed, and chose to engage his obstacles more magically than physically.

The first didn't even see him approach, simply felt the touch of Silenos's fingers on his neck, then dropped to the ground convulsing as his spinal cord was insulated past the point of transmitting nervous impulses. The second and third noticed Silenos as one, charging in to attack him, mouths widening to cry out a warning for the rest. It never came, for Silenos had already extended his focus to envelop them.

Fleshcrafting was a delicate art, and its range was limited. If a caster were to empower their magic enough to make the jump of dozens of meters, as was often done to target far-off areas with other forms, then the excess energy would destroy whatever fine precision allowed for the truly formidable uses of it. Silenos was not so distant as that, however, and his mastery allowed a degree of surgical sleight over the five or so meters separating him from his targets now.

He caused vocal convulsions first, letting neck muscles squeeze their own windpipes past the point of making any sound at all. Then he targeted his enemies' pineal glands, flooding their systems with the levels of melatonin that might be present from days without rest, while simultaneously purging them of any adrenal stimulants that might fight its effects. Both were unconscious within a minute and would remain so.

Silenos stepped irritably over them. It would have been far easier to simply kill the savages, but also politically inconvenient. It was customary for a caster and, he had learned, this world's magi to allow minor assaults to their retainers, but to destroy their property outright would be an insult too big to ignore. Silenos hadn't the time to be making grave enemies like that, and so he limited himself. Fortunately, no more guards stepped out to slow him as he slithered farther inside.

There was death on the air, clearly smelled, so close, and Silenos followed it. Soon finding the corpse tucked safely away inside. He hadn't a clue what the magus Walriq looked like, but he recognized the robes and age of him and didn't waste time humoring the idea that there may have simply been some other, unrelated senior caster killed at a similar time. The man was laid back across a stone slab of the sort that might have found use in some ancient-age empire. His clothing was identical to the others of his kind, dark robes signifying power and seniority, and his hands were folded over each other atop his stomach.

A beard flowed down from the magus's face, mixing above with long gray hair, framing a squat face covered with lines that told of much time spent frowning in his life. Silenos moved quickly, extending his magic for the corpse.

Fortunately, it seemed the savages of his city had possessed some knowledge of preservative measures for a dead body. Silenos detected no progressed rot within the lifeless tissues as he probed them. That was good. A desiccated or decomposed corpse could be repaired during reanimation, but doing so was difficult and time-consuming and would have added further points of failure to what would already be a taxing piece of spellwork.

Silenos felt a snag and ignored it. Easy to grow paranoid, to procrastinate, when working such a spell. He had to make himself act or else burn up what precious time remained for his distraction. Substituting fleshcrafting for necromancy, he flooded the corpse with his magic.

He should have used his arcane sight to examine the corpse. Silenos realized that the moment he felt his necrotic power touch the core of its target, for there was already magic within it, waiting, coiled up and doing its reanimative work in subtle silence. Walriq twitched, shifted, then sat bolt upright with a blast of over-pressure that left Silenos's teeth rattling. He hurtled backward, shoulders crashing hard into the stone wall behind him, vision blurring as he stared at the magus now standing up just ten meters beyond.

Wind coiled around Walriq, hurricane in its intensity, surgical in its precision. Great scything blades of pressurized air that scraped gouges into the stone floor like the clawing limbs of a great beast. The magus's eyes were empty, vacant, mindless, but the power within him was organic and without diminishment. Silenos recognized in an instant that he was staring down every ounce of magic the caster had managed to gather across his own life.

And he hadn't taken the opportunity to prepare his combat form.

The wind came for Silenos as a concentrated jet, powerful enough that he saw the air ripple with its intensity. His magic was immediate in answering, spasming muscles into throwing him aside far faster than mundane nerves could have managed, just barely letting him roll from the path of destruction. Where he'd been an instant prior, the stone wall surrendered into a foot-deep hole just as jagged and total as if artillery had impacted it. He was on his feet in an instant and running the next.

Silenos had been in this new world for weeks, and his transit to it had broken every one of the protective precautions that might stave off death were his physical body destroyed. Such things were complex magics, demanding months or longer to replace, and that time would not be available to him for a while. All that kept him from death now was the preservation of his physical flesh.

Soft tissues strong enough to halt a bayonet, bones of natural carbon fiber that might withstand a thousand times his weight, superconductive neurons and magical stimulation of muscular tissue to allow for reaction time beyond the limits of simple meat. It was all dust compared to his full might.

He was not a direct combatant, not without the precious minute needed to transform himself, and he'd let his battle begin without it. It took a very young or very stupid caster to die. Perhaps today would be the day Silenos proved himself the latter.

A pressure differential at his back warned Silenos of the wind current arcing for him, and he spun, transfiguring the oils and sweat of his body, the subcutaneous water within his arm, into a protean shield just in time to feel the current strike it. Energy transfer was near instantaneous, and Silenos flipped almost upside down before stopping against the far wall of his corridor, dozens of meters ahead of where he'd been.

Something sprained on impact, one of the vertebrae in his lower back cracked dangerously close to paralysis, but he was moving without even paying heed to the injury, taking advantage of his being launched to dive through the door.

Silenos knew he had seconds before the magus was back in pursuit and was still far from the building's exit, so he worked quickly. He could not create matter from nowhere, but he had sufficient waste material to be used for . . . something. Undigested food in his gut, flaking skin from his epidermis, plant matter growing beneath the stone underfoot. He took it all in, then reshaped it to a limb of elastic cartilage, affixing a block of iron-dense bone to a place at its top and binding the entire thing into the ground.

Walriq turned the corner, and Silenos stepped back to let the great flat wings protrude from his creation. The wind struck it, catching the broad planes of flesh as they billowed out like parachutes, concentrating all the attack into dragging the entire limb back against its own near-insurmountable tension. Force exhausted itself in the construct, kilonewtons transferred by the score until it was finally bent almost all the way back, the wind nearly completely subsided. That was when Silenos sent forth another wave of power, letting the construct loose.

It snapped back so quickly and violently that he heard the audible crack of supersonic velocity as its osseous fixtures released it right at the peak of their motion.

The magus was quick, for an outsider to House Shaiagrazni. His magic already moved to produce, then reinforce a barricade long before Silenos's creation could turn his own strength back at him, but there was nothing he could do.

A bow's power was greater than the arms needed to draw it, and so was this bullet of bone. Simple physics sent the projectile clean through Walriq's shield, hardened composition letting it survive the penetration intact to clip the man's side. Ribs shattered, jutting visibly out from his body as death moved past to obliterate a wall behind him. Silenos's follow-up was already prepared, a writhing jet of shadestuff.

But shadestuff was a physical material, once conjured just barely less dense than water and fluid in its composition. Walriq caught it with a jet of air that halted, then reversed its momentum, sending the deadly material right back at Silenos just as he had his enemy's wind. He dove aside, hearing the stone sizzle and scream where it was eaten by the magic, then rolled to his feet just in time to be blasted off of them again.

CHAPTER TEN

Somehow, in the midst of the chaos, Ensharia had found her back pressed against Falls's. The two of them stood together and faced the rest of the room, one clutching her fist tight about a war mace, the other clutching it tight just for the sake of clutching it. Around them, the magi had galvanized, and their power was thick enough that she could taste it.

They were like wolves circling a bear, able to guarantee victory with sheer numbers alone but rightly cautious about the attempt. There was a power advantage not to their favor, and Falls had made it clear that those first few to attack would be risking their lives with his retaliation.

Even so, there was murder on the air, and men did not remain terrified forever. Ensharia's paladin training was enough for her to recognize the currents of magic shifting as their enemies readied an attack.

Then the window high above them exploded inward, and whatever assault had been coming was interrupted as Silenos's body dropped fifty feet down to land hard between her and the enemy.

Instantly, the entire room fell silent. A hundred stunned eyes gaped wide at the fallen caster, as he grunted and pushed himself to his feet. Silenos Shaiagrazni did not appear terribly injured; however, he was clearly pained by one wound or another. Clothing ragged, body littered with minor cuts and bruises already etched across his bronze flesh.

A great pressure emanated from him that Ensharia recognized well, the pneumatic waste of his magic building to volcanic intensities and displacing the air around him. By the way they backed up and licked nervous lips, even as their elders got to their feet, the magi could sense it even more keenly. Here was a man who carried with him the killing might of an army, and Silenos looked in the mood to use it.

It was a testament to the pure terror at play that the newcomer managed to draw all eyes away from even that.

One surface, just above the window Silenos had been thrown through, came apart into flying, arrow-fast debris, chunks of mortar and stone hitting the far wall hard enough that they might have killed any men caught between. Before the dust had even cleared, a new figure emerged in its midst.

A tall man the magus Walriq was not. Ensharia recognized him nonetheless by the sheer force of magic surrounding him, wind currents whipping about so violently that the dust was dispelled from everywhere within a dozen feet of his body as if it were scared to go near him. The wind didn't remain by his side for long, however, lunging down for Silenos in a funnel of power so sudden and jarring that it didn't even give her a chance to wonder how her savior was being attacked by a dead man.

Silenos met the blast with a wall, some strange construct that looked like yellow-tinted bone and flexed upon impact. The wind broke against it, deflecting in all directions and sending magi to crash against walls. The rest of them panicked instantly and began fleeing from the hall.

Her own body was no heavier than theirs, but the magical Vigor that allowed Ensharia to move with the strength of a creature many times her weight also left her anchored to any less force than would be needed to move such a beast. She felt herself driven back a few inches by the deflected fraction of magus Walriq's attack that struck her, but a simple pressure at her heels let her hold herself still. The wind soon faded, and just as it did, she saw the Savior's arms raise.

Fluid gathered before him, the inky substance that had melted through siege towers in one hand, a more translucent liquid in the other. Then the explosion rang out.

Bombardier beetles had long since been an interest of Silenos's, and he'd taken the time to study their curious biochemistry, discovered the particular chemical formula of the deadly compounds their bodies produced and mixed to bring the power of incineration and detonation into biological matter. Then improved it. His own blend was just a hair weaker than nitroglycerin in mass-specific explosive power and notably denser. The armored plate he built into the palm of his hand was strained in absorbing the concussion of its ignition, and the shock wave forced his arm back.

It forced the shadestuff back too. And, having been placed between Silenos's own body and the necromantic material, it forced it back into a spray of high-velocity death arcing right for the magus.

Walriq had come to, if not impress, then at the very least enforce a healthy degree of *caution* into Silenos, and so it was no surprise that he shielded himself. The shadestuff would have eaten through any physical barrier a creature of his strength might have conjured, but it was unable to fully permeate the wall of wind that halted it. Force was not a thing; it was a stimulus that acted on things, and in taking on mass and substance, shadestuff made itself vulnerable to such misdirections. Silenos was finding this opponent particularly suited to troubling him and quickly dove from the path of his own redirected attack.

The paladin, Ensharia, surprised Silenos by charging for the magus while he focused on defense. Her speed was considerable, her determination more so, and yet the woman's strength had long since been evaluated, and he knew it fell far short of the sums needed to bring any measure of threat against something of their opponent's caliber.

At best she would be a mere inconvenience; at worst she would die, and he had far too much use for her to allow that.

Rather than attempt to stop the blows that soon aimed themselves for Ensharia, Silenos simply turned his focus onto capitalizing on whatever momentary distraction she caused. He shaped his arm, letting a long cavity form inside of it, then lining its interior with dense bodily minerals, prioritizing mass and hardness over all other things. At last he formed complex glands at the back, primed and ready to excrete another round of his blasting chemicals, before forming a projectile of yet more ossiferous tissue. Finally, he released the explosives.

Ensharia had already been forced to dodge twice, then finally swept from her feet and high into the air by the time enough moments had passed for Silenos's weapon to be fired. He saw then, however, that he had chosen right.

There hadn't been the time or available matter for a full-body combat-form transformation. His makeshift cannon proved deadly enough regardless. The blasting chemicals reacted with sufficient force that, even surrounded by the most unyielding and durable tissue he knew of, Silenos felt lances of pain run out from the point of their detonation. The released energy was strangled and intensified by confinement in his tight barrel, forcing the generated overpressure into extremes only measurable in gigapascals. Every ounce of this pressure found release only behind the bullet of bone placed between it and the exit far ahead, accelerating the projectile so rapidly that a sting soon alerted Silenos to his cannon being heated dangerously fast.

It all held though. Despite his decades without combat, despite it being a design Silenos had coined mere moments before, despite the dozen ways he'd already identified it falling short of idealization, the makeshift, prototypic weapon held, and it spat devastation from its mouth with such intensity that the air flashed visibly bright and hot for a moment.

Silenos's eyes and occipital neurons had been enhanced to the point of clearly perceiving the momentary spread of flame across black powder and seeing even the blinking of an unenhanced eye as if it were a sluggish, lengthy thing. Even he barely caught the flight of his projectile in its path toward the enemy, however.

Such was its speed. By the time he registered that it had left the barrel, it was almost upon the magus.

Air parted, then flesh and bone followed suit. The projectile punched clean through its target as if his body had been constructed of wet mud rather than solid matter. Blood fell in darkened, deoxygenated hues to spatter the ground beneath Walriq, and the reanimate was sent spinning backward. Silenos took the opportunity to alter his creation.

Fractionally thicker plating within the barrel, a membrane of frictionless lubricative mucus to avoid wear and tear, a tighter fit with the projectile so that he might make a more efficient gas seal. Despite it all, he was forced nonetheless to reduce the yield of his blasting fluids, but the next projectile was still supersonic. A fist-sized block of bone heavier than any equivalent volume of lead, smashing hard against the enemy shield once, twice.

By the third time, Walriq had moved to keep himself from being further assailed. Silenos was forced into another dodge, which only served to send him into the path of a second blast of wind, this one snatching his legs out from under him. He spun, hit the ground hard enough to shatter any bone not made with Shaiagrazni genius, and bounced a full meter back into the air before another jet came for him. He braced himself to be dashed against the far wall, then blinked as the air distorted in front of him, and the attack broke apart with nothing more than a few scrapes of pressure on his skin.

Silenos only needed to tighten his eyes for an instant to recognize that half the power before him was not the undead's. Arion Falls's magic was younger, less refined. All youth and passion and uncertain vigor, like a wildfire burning itself out. The innate power was something to be admired, however, and Silenos realized the boy wasn't entirely far from being a match for his own talent.

But he hadn't nearly his master's experience, and it was clear how a contest between the two of them would end. Silenos was quick in interrupting it.

Silenos took his time producing a secondary cannon, letting this one emerge from his other shoulder, and while he did, Silenos grew further plating around his sides and torso, serving as vents for yet more blasting fluid. He was done within ten seconds, firing within one, and this time his aim was truer by far thanks to the new stabilizing jets of pressure he could release from all directions to keep the momentum of his weaponry from spinning him like a leaf in the wind.

Walriq's magic quickly turned onto primarily defense once the volley began, buckling and shivering as the impacts racked it, while Arion Falls's own magic safeguarded Silenos from being attacked while he focused on breaking through. Finally Walriq's defense failed, but it was not Silenos's own attacks that struck at the weak point.

It was Ensharia's.

Ancestors only knew when the paladin had gotten it into her head that this was a fight she had any business partaking in, but her presence was actually of no small convenience. She struck, by instinct, fortune, or cognition, at the precisely perfect moment to slip past the gap in their enemy's defenses, latching on to the magus with a grip strong enough to crush most men to death.

Silenos saw the energies of wind magic wrapping about him, resisting her compressive hold, and realized that Ensharia's mace had been lost somewhere. Before he could even begin to doubt her odds, however, a glow began to build around the woman.

What the girl did next was something Silenos recognized only from stories and legends.

Holy magic, miracles, true faith—there were a thousand words for the curious phenomenon of otherwise mundane individuals gaining the ability to enfeeble and destroy undead. Naturally, such magics had long since been removed from his own world. House Shaiagrazni had utilized ten generations of careful eugenics to ensure it ceased emerging among the general human populace, but he was not entirely surprised to find it here. Witnessing its effects firsthand was an indescribably fascinating experience.

As a rule, magic was the act of changing the physical world through will and rarely anything more. Hers could not have been more different.

Silenos, with his Entity-granted perception, was able to see clearly how it functioned. The way the arcane powers conjured at Ensharia's will targeted not the physical world, but the undead's own magic, eating swirling colors of magical light and rapidly deteriorating their effect. He watched as Walriq grew sluggish, his wind less potent, Ensharia's iron grip closer to fully closing upon the reanimated corpse and crushing it to paste. Even still, it was a struggle for her to keep hold.

Walriq's magic was weakened, which in turn weakened the potency of his winds, but they were still a cut above anything the paladin was likely to muster in her lifetime. She had moments, at best, before being dislodged, and Silenos had seen enough to know all too well that she would not be allowed to even hit the ground before scything winds tore her apart.

CHAPTER ELEVEN

I t was clever of Ensharia, then, to let go first and take the moment to strengthen a new hold elsewhere on the magus. One hand entangled his beard, another closed around a spindly arm; both were vises. The two of them spun, Walriq desperate to shake his enemy off, his enemy more desperate still to deny him. Every moment saw them moved another dozen meters one way or the other, velocity such that a normal man might have died to the acceleration alone.

Ensharia simply withstood the strain, but Walriq's undead flesh was no harder than it had been in life, and Silenos was beginning to think his magic did not allow for protection of his innards the way others might. He saw blood begin to leak from the magus's orifices, veins popping in his eyes, heard the strain of bodily tissues against their own multiplied weight. Bit by bit, he was coming apart.

Finally, Ensharia's grip surrendered, but by then her enemy looked like a straw doll thrashed by the hands of a clumsy child. She had not cleared the man's path by so much as a meter before Silenos fired, loosing both cannons at once, and deliberately overcharging them past even their newly reinforced capacity for pressure.

Paladin magic had weakened Walriq's magic, paladin power had split his focus, and the wind magics of Falls raced ahead just before impact to further dash the magus's shield. When the projectiles hit, his body simply came apart. Like watching the straw doll struck by gunfire.

Giblets of pulverized flesh rained down while Silenos healed himself, restoring his body to its standard template, undoing the burned and ruptured flesh resulting from his excessive attack. By the time his ears had stopped ringing, the room's air still danced with the residual displacement of an impact akin to artillery this world would surely not know for another five centuries.

He looked around, seeing Ensharia slowly climbing to her feet amid crumbling mortar and dancing dust, then Falls standing and trembling as his eyes held themselves wide with disbelief. Aside from them, the chamber was empty. Silenos might have guessed. Casters were known for courage in much the same way that barbarians were known for their skilled rhetoric and complex philosophy.

"Walriq."

Silenos glanced back at Falls, who seemed to have substituted his trembling for a sort of dazed incomprehension.

"Walriq . . ." he echoed. "I . . . He . . . Fuck . . ."

The number of better things Silenos had to do than watch an idiot develop post-traumatic stress disorder numbered in the literal millions, and actually compiling and ordering such a list was among them, so he moved past the drooling primitive and headed for Enshaiia.

She was handling the conflict better than the magus, which shouldn't have been entirely surprising. Most casters, Silenos had heard, tended toward less stressful training methods than House Shaiagrazni. Indeed, from the stories he'd been told, some didn't even threaten their apprentices with vivisection at all. Such a coddling, patronizing environment could hardly have been expected to encourage the growth of strong spines as were needed to truly pursue magic, and so it was no surprise that the wind mage was a trembling wreck behind him.

Combat, evidently, had left the paladin's composition more hardened than that as well.

"We won," she breathed as he came to stand before her. The woman sounded actually questioning, so Silenos answered her.

"We won," he confirmed. "Mostly me, however. I would likely have won without help, but you accelerated the process of my victory, which was admirable in and of itself. Your courage in charging a superior foe is worthy of praise."

Surprisingly, her eyes seemed to glow with joy at that.

"I . . . Really?

Silenos decided to forgive the abject tedium of asking for confirmation and instead nodded.

"Yes, usually it takes hours of effort to carefully lobotomize a flesh construct into such an extreme of suicidal fearlessness. Finding a creature who possesses it simply innately is rare and extremely convenient. You will make a very helpful diversion in future conflict."

Oddly, the woman's face fell at that, but a new voice rang out across the room before she could say anything.

"Necromancer!"

Silenos turned again, growing rather exhausted with how often he'd been doing it recently. His eyes fell onto the first of many magi now piling into the room, eyes bloodshot with rage, face twisted with resignation.

"That was magus Walriq, resurrected. You did this, didn't you, you foul creature?" another one snarled. Silenos recognized the faces of them both, council members, and he recognized their flowing power even more vividly.

It was a taller magus who stepped forward, and Silenos needed only a glance to know he was stronger than any other present. His power fell short of Falls's, nonetheless, but backed by so many allies he would prove a threat, and his eyes were dangerously alert as he spoke.

"We've heard stories about you and your dark magics." He spat. "From Elkatin. Looks like they're all true, eh?"

As it happened, they were, and Silenos didn't see convincing them that it actually had been another necromancer to resurrect Walriq as a winning proposition. Particularly when his presence had already been sighted by the magus's corpse.

Slowly, subtly, he shaped what little remained of his body's redundant cells into a probing strip of nervous tissue barbed in nacre and wrapped in muscle, letting it burrow through the heel of his foot and deep into the ground. He spoke while it happened.

"Hold on!" Ensharia's voice rang out, interrupting Silenos's own and projecting a characteristic confidence and steel across the room. "The Savior is no dark mage, and this reanimation was not his doing."

"I would never be stupid enough to lose control of something I reanimated," Silenos added helpfully.

"So you admit to being a necromancer!" one of the magi near the back called out. He tried to see which one, making a mental note to destroy them for their stupidity if the opportunity ever arose.

"Of course not," Silenos snapped. "I am simply saying that *if* I *had*, then in that *hypothetical* scenario, my glorious intellect would leave no chance of such a reanimate attacking me."

"Surely you can all recognize his magical power and learning," Ensharia tried, nervous now. "You must realize that what he says is the truth."

"If he's so powerful, why is a whore speaking for him?" one magus called out.

"I heard he assaulted a guard," another added.

Silenos felt what was left of his emotional centers spasm in rage at that.

"If you wish for your subordinates to be free from assault, you should cultivate the power to protect them instead of whining to an actually competent caster for being your superior."

Their fury was quick, and volcanic.

"Enough of this!" The strongest of them roared. "Seize them and we'll—"

Silenos finished his fleshcrafting just as the man spoke.

The situation had been spiraling further and further from Ensharia's control, but it wasn't until the ground erupted into giant fleshy tendrils that she realized it was finally beyond salvaging. The Savior moved before anyone else, of course. Even aside from his impossible reactions and quick thinking, he was obviously the one engineering the eruption of meat, and he turned with a confidence that showed he knew exactly where and how they'd act without the need for anything so trivial as a glance over his shoulder.

She was not as knowledgeable, comprehending, or instantaneous as him and required a few moments to observe the situation.

Ensharia watched as the limbs thrashed around, each one easily twenty feet long and thick as tree trunks, making the entire floor shiver and sending jagged cracks along its stony face with every impact. None had yet killed a magus, and the entire crowd seemed instantly shocked and driven back by their gesticulations. It seemed obvious to her what was happening.

Behind her lay a diversion, hastily made and aimlessly cast. It was not made to kill or even wound, for Ensharia was sure it would already have done both had the Savior wished, only misdirect. She leaped on the chance quickly.

Ahead, her savior was already nearly to the wall, his arms loosing more of those faster-than-sight projectiles that had torn the magus Walriq to such efficiently separated particulates. They were no less effective against stone than flesh, smashing a man-sized hole in quick order, and she reached Falls just as Silenos exited through the opening.

The man was still staring, still stunned. It seemed that finding his master dead a second time had left him insensible, and Ensharia was just about to haul him out over her shoulder when he finally turned, sweeping his arms up in one gesture to conjure a mighty wind that cast both of them out of the building.

In only a few short weeks, Ensharia had found herself saved by a necromancer, been told to cook steak by the most gifted magi alive, watched men harassed by some tentacle monster, and beheld an undead strong enough to kill five of her having its head bitten off by a scaled monster the size of a smaller war elephant. She had, naively, come to think that nothing more existed with the capacity to surprise her.

That assumption did not survive the sight of her savior hovering, with both of his legs neatly gone, from the bottom of a great, slowly rising sphere of leathery meat.

He did not express anything at all upon seeing her and Falls come to drop down onto the stone, only called out with the same voice he always used, calm and mechanical.

"There are two more holds for the both of you. Grab on before the vessel rises beyond reach. Falls, you propel it away."

Neither of them hesitated in obeying. Ensharia supposed it was just that sort of day.

To her amazement, despite the Savior's warnings, the construct did rise. Slowly at first, then faster, until it soon drifted upward fifty feet or more with every passing moment. Falls was swift in providing their horizontal velocity, sending them shooting along faster even than his master had managed. Ensharia stared at him, awed.

Apparently understanding her confusion, he volunteered an answer.

"Don't need to lift us," the man grunted, clearly straining to sustain his hold while guiding the currents. "This machine is doing that. All that's required of me is pushing us sideways, not upward. And even that's easier with the winds already being so strong . . . Did you predict that?"

The last sentence was a question for the Savior, who nodded.

"Wind speeds increase with altitude," he replied. "Tubes will descend in front of your mouths. Inhale through them or you will lose consciousness and die."

As he said it, Ensharia found a cylinder of . . . meat lowering right before her lips. Burying her disgust, she did as instructed, finding breathable, if musky, air held within.

Perhaps predicting her questions, the Savior spoke more.

"The device around us utilizes complex biochemistry to synthesize hydrogen, a gas far lighter than air. This causes it to rise as it slowly fills the sphere above, which I imagine is nearing full capacity. We will stop our ascent only when the surrounding atmosphere is thin enough for our weight to equalize with the displaced mass. Another section is collecting air from around us and compressing it with muscular contractions to prevent it from being too thin to support your breathing. Any further questions, or can we move on to the more important issues?"

There were no further questions.

"Elkatin had spies within its council, with access to the list of Heroes," the Savior stated. "Otherwise the timing of Walriq's death and our arrival here is too coincidental. I should have considered it myself already. It was . . . an error."

She heard some actual emotion in his voice at that. A curious mutation of frustration that terrified her more than any previous lack of feeling had.

"We must hurry to the second Hero then," Ensharia replied, mainly to give herself some distraction in the speech.

Silenos was about to reply when Falls cut in.

"So my master *was* murdered?" he asked, voice coated in some tone she couldn't quite identify.

"Yes, yes," the Savior replied impatiently. "It happens more regularly than you might think, even more so than sexual mishaps, in fact. Moving on, we will actually be heading for the third Hero. Assuming this list was devised with some basic concept of travel efficiency in mind?"

Ensharia bristled at the implication of her people's incompetence.

"Of course," she snapped.

"Good," the Savior continued, apparently not caring about her tone. "Then we will head for the third. Whoever is moving ahead of us to kill them, they likely came from close to Elkatin. That is where the spies were, and with the speed they have shown, the agents must have been extremely nearby. Perhaps in the armies we destroyed, perhaps not. I did not detect any individuals of great power among them, but I *may* have missed one or two among such multitudes of scum, or our assassins may be substituting cleverness for power."

An air current ran over the vessel, sending cool needles to run along Ensharia. She heard Falls's teeth chattering suddenly, and the Savior sighed.

"I'll lower us," he said. "Magus, your heart rate is dropping alarmingly fast. Tell me if this happens again in the future. I do not want to be forced into the habit of scanning your biology to keep you from dying all the time."

Falls only nodded, apparently chilled past the point of retort. She couldn't blame him. Any temperature that could make Ensharia so much as shiver would be fatal for a normal body sooner or later.

When, at last, they touched the ground again, Falls had warmed a shade. Only a shade though. He managed to inform the group, through his chattering teeth, that they were five miles from Magira. Silenos seemed only mildly pleased.

"We shall have to cover more ground tomorrow." He sighed, speaking even as the vessel melted and flowed down around his body, congealing at the stumps of his legs to reform the limbs within moments. Ensharia almost vomited at the sight.

"For now we will make camp," the Savior continued.

"We need fuel for a fire," Ensharia noted. "I can look for some. It's dark, but—"

So close, she could just see the Savior as he knelt down and touched the grass and watched with horror as the blades around them all disappeared into the ground. His arm rippled, as if it were liquefied and flowing just as the previous construct had, then she saw matter drop out of it. One, two, ten, a hundred. Cuboids of wood all neatly stacked and perfectly formed.

It was the sort of firewood pile a person might make only after hours of perfectionism and an ample supply of unhewn branches, produced within seconds. The Savior straightened up.

"I am not familiar with survivalist skills," he announced, as if it were as idle an observation as the weather.

Ensharia snapped from her stupor.

"I am," she hastily noted, kneeling down and withdrawing her dagger. She had a few wood shavings ready soon, and some searching from the apparently night-visioned Savior yielded a piece of flint. In only a few minutes, they were all basked in the warmth of a fire, seated around it and sighing with relief.

Falls did not speak much before rolling over for sleep, apparently having come to terms with his new, nonoptional place in their group. Ensharia decided to let him drift off. Doubtless, he could use the time to process all that had changed. Doubtless too he deserved that small kindness. She hadn't forgotten the way he lunged forth to protect her so quickly after being freed.

"You did not kill him," Silenos noted once Falls's breathing had grown heavy enough to betray unconsciousness.

There was no accusation in the words, no anger or judgment, but Ensharia felt pricked by all three at once.

"And?" she snapped.

He eyed her coolly. Not for the first time, she wondered what thoughts were flitting behind this creature's gaze. She was left to wonder, for he betrayed none of them by speaking.

"I had not expected that," the Savior said at last.

Ensharia looked at her feet.

"There didn't seem any reason he needed to die. We'd not have bought more time in killing him, and if the plan had gone well, we could have just fled anyway with Walriq. In fact, we'd probably have had him then too out of gratitude."

The caster didn't nod, shake his head, or react to her words at all. Only looked into the fire, still thinking in thoughts too big for her. Everything was too big for her, these days.

"He's so powerful," Ensharia breathed, not even sure herself why she was sharing such troubles with the Savior. "So, so powerful and so young. I've trained longer than he has, I'd wager, but . . . I don't think three of me could beat one of him."

"You dislike your weakness."

She was so shocked to hear the Savior speak that Ensharia actually jumped, then nodded with a face flushing crimson.

"I hate it."

He paused a moment.

"What if I could help you alleviate it?"

Ensharia eyed him.

"You . . . know means of training?"

"I know means of strengthening a body, and you fight with a body—"

"No," Ensharia snapped, finding her temper hot again. "No, not that, never that. I will not be fleshcrafted."

The Savior studied her, still silent, still thinking. Then nodded.

"It is your choice," he said, in that way he had of saying everything that made her feel as if he were observing the world from a magnifying glass held far above it.

"Can you take the first watch?" she asked suddenly. "I'd like to sleep."

"I will watch all night," the caster said. "I do not require sleep."

She was too tired to do anything but lie down and enjoy the benefits of that.

CHAPTER TWELVE

Silenos had been left with much to do while his new companions slumbered, all of it pressing. He decided first upon lobotomizing himself. Only a little bit though. He didn't want to become *normal*, ancestors forbid, simply to redistribute the raw processing power of his mind somewhat.

Long ago, he had scraped his brain for the emotional and empathic centers, forcibly reconverting their neurons and synapses into yet more spatial reasoning, mathematical power, working memory. All the mental characteristics helpful for solving the abstract logic problems that assailed a skilled caster so frequently. This change had sat perfectly well for him for the last half century, but his situation had changed. He'd walked into an ambush for overlooking what his enemy's moves might be and how a magus of Walriq's strength might have been killed. That couldn't happen again.

Humans, people, socialization were no small blind spot to have. If he could not mirror the emotions and experiences of others, then he was denying himself the most important data stream with which to predict them. As much as it stung, Silenos got to work on optimizing his intellect.

It was difficult to alter a brain, and limited. Silenos could not increase the number of cells and synapses available to it—magic simply didn't allow such things. If it did, there would be no nonfleshcrafting Shaiagrazni, and the entire house would have long since stolen the magic of gods in their preternatural genius. A greater mind would find out how to make a still greater one, and the process would continue exponentially. The intellectual singularity. An interesting hypothetical, but not yet relevant to a caster of his people's limitations.

Hours passed before Silenos had finally done enough work on himself to be certain of neither dying nor violently convulsing the moment he withdrew his hand. Once that inconvenient grunt work was finished, however, he moved on to more intellectual problems.

Of course he'd have preferred to reason through such things with a complete mind, but that would doubtless take days, even weeks. Better to equip himself for survival as early as possible, even when the immediate task was weapon crafting.

Several issues had made themselves known during the recent altercation, all stemming from the same root cause. Silenos was not a warrior.

He could make war, conduct it, he could command and plan and strategize, even design the instruments of death with which conflict was carried out, but he was not a fighter. No more suited to brawling in the mud than any other general. That had to change, through simple necessity. General or not, men caught in a mud brawl through circumstance would either learn to win or die. He was far too clever to die.

The cannon had been promising, so Silenos started tweaking it. Reshaping his arm into the closest imitation of its previous shape he was able to manage, then working on his improvements.

Fleshcrafting was a powerful magic, but like all, it had its limits. Most of which were practical. The most fundamental was that it by nature involved the manipulation of structures too fiendishly complex for even an augmented human mind to fully visualize. Layers of misdirection and approximation were needed to manage it because there were quite simply too many cells in any sizable body part to be directly altered within a tenable time frame.

Even by keeping one's focus on the scale of organoids, however, sufficiently complex constructs took some time. Silenos had estimated around ten seconds passing before he'd finished his weaponry during his fight with Walriq. Such time could be fatal in single combat. The counter to this, of course, was through templates. Shapes that his magic had taken and retaken so often that they came with but a thought, reflexes filling in for focus.

But he had not produced more than two, had never found the need. A template was weeks of work, and Silenos always had more research to do, rituals to complete, summonings to manage. For the first time, he found himself forced into a more practical magic.

The newly reconstructed emotional centers of his brain quivered at that, oddly enough. Was it relish? Yes. He relished the challenge. Interesting.

Silenos altered and rearranged the weapon, adding a compressive gas drive to let him reduce the required amount of propellant—and thus allow for more shots. Finding a way to shape the projectiles more aerodynamically and mitigate their required size, further improving ammunition capacity. Ultimately, however, he found himself running into the same issue. A weapon that created and consumed materials would serve to reduce the amounts available in his body. Fleshcrafting did tacitly obey the laws of physics, and he could not create mass out of nowhere. Further, firing that mass away at supersonic speeds made it rather unfeasible to reabsorb afterward.

His solution seemed obvious. Silenos, for the first time in decades, began to alter the template of his natural, neutral body. Enlarging it, adding twenty centimeters more to the height and hundreds of kilos to its weight. He enlarged the bundled musculature, layered centimeters of keratin combat plate over his epidermis, thickened vascular walls. The process did not require much creativity; he'd already made himself a workable inspiration through his combat form. The only deviations from that came as necessary sacrifices for the boon of convenience.

Capillaries laced the lowest layers of his armor plating, supplying them with blood at the cost of room that might've been otherwise used for yet more armor. Enzymes and bioreactants oozed through his circulation, replacing additional oxygen in his veins to allow for maintenance that would sustain the body past its first hours of function. Its muscle fibers were adjusted to allow for more dexterity at the cost of brute strength, vision sharpened for contexts outside of combat, visage kept carefully human to avoid drawing unwanted attention rather than distorted into a thing of natural weapons and killing potential.

Silenos took several minutes to complete the changes in all, and once they were done, he took some seconds more moving, testing to ensure his newly altered body was functional. Then he reverted it, slipping back into his original form before restarting the process all over again.

That was the method of creating a template, be it for fleshcrafting or any other magic. Repetition, reflexive memory. One had to make the acts so constant and familiar that they were like breathing. He kept at it for over an hour more before finding himself interrupted.

"What are you doing?"

Silenos turned. It was the magus who'd spoken, Arion Falls. The man was clearly newly awakened and still groggy from the fatigue of recent events.

"I am improving my transformations for battle," he replied, turning his focus back to the deed. "You are familiar, at least, with the necessity of practice in magic."

"Of course," the magus replied testily. "I've gathered that your people, wherever you're from, are a bit beyond mine in knowledge, but Magira *is* one of the continent's magic capitals. We're not cavemen."

Practically, they were, but Silenos saw no point in insisting on the fact.

"That weapon of yours, it's like a trebuchet or ballista, yes? How does it propel things? Some . . . spring mechanism, made from grown muscle, stored at the back?"

Silenos glanced at him.

"A good guess," he conceded. "But no. My people have knowledge of incendiary substances that burn far hotter and more rapidly than charcoal or oil. It functions off of those." Hiding his smile, he waited for the boy to ask for further elaboration.

But he didn't, only stared, eyes widening in realization.

". . . And releasing heat that quickly causes the gases to lower in density, which exerts pressure if you give them too little room to do so. Oh! That's how you made breathable air on your flying machine too. You compressed the atmosphere until it was thick enough to inhale, right?"

"Arion Falls," Silenos said out loud, committing the boy's name to memory and ensuring he never forgot it. "Yes, that is all correct. Wisely noted."

"I'm a wind mage." The magus grinned, taking a seat closer to Silenos. "I already knew about the principles of compressing air. Truth be told, that's how we make our shields, but it hadn't occurred to me that there'd be ways of using the process in reverse with just simple heat. Still, a very rapid burn, yes?"

"Yes."

Silenos said nothing more, focusing instead on his work. Falls, however, appeared more interested in conversation than him.

"How long have you been doing that?"

He took a moment to recall.

"Seventy-three minutes," Silenos replied.

The boy hummed appreciatively.

"So your transformations are an innate ability? They don't require mana?"

"Oh, they do," Silenos corrected. "But this level of change is manageable."

"Manageable," the boy echoed. ". . . How much mana do you have?"

Silenos took a moment to study him with his arcane vision.

"Just under ten times the amount you do."

"Impossible," the boy replied instantly. "Nobody has that much. There hasn't been a magus in five hundred years who even equaled my reserves before the age of fifty."

"I estimate I had equaled them at fourteen or so." Silenos shrugged. A pause followed, and he turned to see a mix of skepticism and irritation on the boy's face. He decided to give further weight to his claim.

"You saw me summon half a dozen limbs of flesh, each weighing as much as ten of you, and two of the form I've been experimenting with now even at its heaviest."

Falls swallowed.

"So why don't you do that all the time?" he challenged. "If it's nothing to you, as it would be with those reserves."

"Because there isn't always the necessary matter. Animal matter is typically made of several elements, the most common of which, mass specifically, is oxygen, the rest of which are not often readily available. Usually, if I cannot absorb the biomass of other life through touch or near proximity, I am limited to whatever mass my body can supply, perhaps with a few dozen extra kilograms depending on local air composition."

The magus's face fell at that, eyes dropping to his feet.

"And here I was looking forward to surpassing Walriq," he breathed, then a tremble took him. Racking his body like a blizzard-born shiver. "Do you have a master?" he asked. "You can't be much older than me, or . . ." He frowned. "No, wait, you said you were as strong as me at eighteen, so . . . You're older than you look, or you have a way of increasing your mana?"

As it happened, both guesses were true.

"The former," Silenos said, deciding to hide his plans of gaining magic centuries in advance of his age. "I am one hundred and fifty years old, and to answer your first question, I do not have a master anymore. I ended my apprenticeship in House Shaiagrazni many decades ago."

"Are you the strongest of them?"

"I am not, though my abilities are not the norm either. I would estimate your master would have been at least roughly close to the average named of my household."

Falls was silent for a while, contemplative.

"Have you ever taken on an apprentice?"

Silenos felt a stab of irritation at the question.

"I have," he replied coolly. "And you are asking if I would instruct you?"

Falls narrowed his eyes, and Silenos turned back to his work.

"No," the young magus replied. "I've done all my learning already."

Silenos and his newly growing party came to the nation of Arbite merely two weeks after their forced departure from Magira. Their travel was uneventful and hastened by the use of magic to aid in transportation. The long hours gave ample opportunity for much progress to be made in personal projects and allowed Falls to properly integrate himself into the group.

Which was not to say there was any lack of tension between the magus and paladin. Silenos had been watching the two, careful to keep the friction already between them from growing. If nothing else, it had proved manageable thus far.

"Arbite is an ally of Elkatin," Ensharia declared as they approached the city. "With luck, that will mean we can expect a warmer welcome."

He examined the supposed ally and found himself tasked with not curling a lip at the sight.

The capital city of Arbite, Abaritan, was unlike Magira and not quite akin to Elkatin either. Far broader and more expansive than the former, far more jagged and angular than either. Its perimeter was lined by a towering wall of stone, curiously edged and cornered in such a way as to far more closely resemble the modern star fortresses of Silenos's own world than the circular structures more common to people of this one's technology.

Diabase was nowhere to be seen in the construction, and as they drew closer, he made out the telltale sight of mortar binding rock together in numerous irregular sizes and shapes. Clearly it had not been fashioned with magic, or else the stone would have been fused into its structure with far more homogeneity and precision.

A gate sat midway into it, covered by a portcullis that had been raised out of its sockets. The thing was mangled, iron twisted and warped by some great force in its past, fixtures broken apart. There was an abundance of guards around the exposed opening left while a new one was lowered into place, and their suspicion was scarcely thinned even after Ensharia revealed their letter of introduction and secured passage into the city.

Past the wall, things were hardly better. Silenos saw cobbled streets pock-marked with cracks and craters, small buildings nursing collapsed walls or fragmented roofs. Scared, dirty people scurried around, some carrying water or food, others blankets. Some carrying nothing but fear. All seemed far from pleased by the sight of his group, and him especially.

Subtlety had been one of the priorities of his new body, and so it wasn't nearly as intimidating as his towering combat form, but Silenos had raised his height to almost exactly two meters. Even if much of the keratin armor plating was hidden by clothing, and the rest difficult to make out as anything much more than a disfigurement, the lean musculature he'd built to support his heightened mass would have been a sight.

"It's a shithole." Falls frowned, lip curling with disgust much like Silenos's. "How do you even fuck a city up this much?"

Of course Silenos had yet to find a new-world city that was half the equal of one of House Shaiagrazni's, but there was a clear downgrade from Magira to Abaritan even if one disregarded the clear battle damage. Magic, it seemed, was as useful a construction tool in any world. Those few buildings that had more than one story in this city almost invariably remained limited to two, and the rare exceptions were far less proud and unweathered as would have been normal in the magus capital.

But it was the wounded and sick that truly caught his attention. Grimy, desiccated faces set with shriveled, hopeless eyes. They seemed of every age, though few were elderly, and all cowered in the streets.

"There are no healing magics in this world?"

Ensharia's face darkened at Silenos's question.

"There are," she growled. "And enough for all these people, I'd guess, but healers charge money. I'll need to come back here later and see if I can help."

"A foolish system," he noted. "When one allows a random child to perish or go without education, there is the risk of denying the full potential of a truly great individual."

The paladin's agreement was not as fierce as he might have thought. No doubt she found it blunted by Silenos's motive in his suggestion of health care, but she nodded all the same.

"And it would be all the easier if those magi in Magira would offer their aid, with fewer injured to begin with if they'd helped the world's cities defend themselves."

"Well, we have more important things to do," Falls cut in, clearly needled by the target their criticism had found. "The studies of a magus are manly things, you see, and require a degree of stoicism. Spine, even. We can't lose focus in progressing the sciences just because we hear a crying baby. That's what women are for."

"And why is it that House Shaiagrazni is so much more advanced when they allow women into their ranks with no conditions then?" Ensharia shot back. "Are the women of Silenos's land just different than ours?"

Falls smirked.

"Perhaps they'd have progressed even more if they put their cocksucking machines to more efficient use and gave their proper researchers some incentive."

The two began their bickering quickly and continued it intensely, rather reminding Silenos of the exothermic propulsion of his new cannon as they went back and forth. For the first minute he idly listened, finding his newly reconfigured mind oddly susceptible to the previously alien sensation of boredom, and eagerly seeking the break to his journey's monotony. Then he realized how much less interesting the arguments were to the many sights around him, such as dirt, cobbled roads, a cloudless sky, or the empty space of air.

CHAPTER THIRTEEN

Fortunately, despite the size of Abaritan, there was only so much distance that needed traversing. Silenos found no more than a half hour gone by before they finally reached their destination, the castle—or fortress—that made itself the city's crux and towered above every other structure, save the outer walls themselves.

There must, Silenos thought, have been some reason for the city to be guarded by such high stretches of stone. Perhaps to impede enemies of such a mass as to otherwise scale more conventionally sized ones.

Anything else would simply make it infeasible. He didn't believe that even savages of this world's stupidity would waste resources on vanity alone, and the relative stature of their castle confirmed to him that such scale was far from a casual investment.

It was efficiently shaped to turn away impacts greater than the mundane technologies of its world could muster, and as Silenos was escorted past the gates, he found the walls so thick that it almost felt like moving through a tunnel. Within the place was cold, frigid even, its exterior enforcing an unbroken stagnancy on the air inside that left his skin chilled enough that it might have shivered were any hand but his own responsible for crafting it.

Guards moved around the inside like ants inside a hill, chain mail clinking with every motion, spears held tight in strong grips. Silenos recognized more than a few magicians among them, casters of mixed, generally inferior power, all of which could have attacked him at once without causing an inconvenience. The real display came when they were taken to the office.

Behind a large, ebony desk there was a man. Seated, scratching away with quill and parchment, hooked nose housing a pair of delicate spectacles, dark hair neatly combed and maintained as it receded trigonometrically from his brow. His skin was darker than that of the people of Ensharia's lands, perhaps closer in tone to Silenos's own, and his eyes a beady green. He looked up at them with neither friendliness nor hostility. A simple weighing gaze that might be found upon an appraiser handed unspecified volumes of gold. Silenos could appreciate it, having donned it himself more than once.

"Greetings," he said impassively. "I am Eloran Khazh, the king's hand. I am aware that your letter of introduction specified a meeting with King Galukar in its request for an audience, however I am afraid that I will have to satisfy it in his place. My king, you see, is rather indisposed at the moment."

Silenos glanced at Ensharia, who in turn seemed entirely lost. Evidently it was not a mere lapse on his part, as an outsider to the world, that the king's absence would be found surprising.

"May I ask why?" she inquired, letting her confusion show without guarding it. The hand studied her.

"I had assumed you were aware already," he replied. "King Galukar is too busy to be meeting with even ambassadors of your caliber and has been for some weeks now."

"Busy how?" she demanded, and he shook his head.

"I am not at liberty to say."

"Not for a woman sent on behalf of Elkatin?" she pressed, and again he shook his head.

"Not even, you must forgive me, but—"

Silenos felt the precise instant his patience ran out, speaking over the man, letting it show.

"I have just spent weeks traveling across a thousand miles of countryside with the most irritating creature currently walking this world and the very type of human that most consistently activates him. I will not be denied my reason for doing so without cause."

The hand's eyes were like daggers.

"You are the Savior then," he noted. "I had expected one of a more heroic disposition."

"And if you continue to defy me, you will find you expected a hero of a less homicidal disposition too," Silenos answered. "What is your king busy with?"

The hand's fingers drummed upon his desk, once, twice, three times. Just before Silenos was considering castration as a means of encouragement, he spoke.

"Very well," the hand growled. "You, and only you three, may see King Galukar. But your meeting with him is to be held as the tightest of secrets, understand?"

"Of course," Silenos snapped.

"Thank you," Ensharia hastily added, nerves frayed almost past their limits. "Please, lead the way."

It was a longer walk to the king than Silenos might have expected, and that was, perhaps, a mark in the favor of his nation. House Shaiagrazni, and any league of casters, could appreciate the inherent dangers of ambush and assassination, and so the twists and turns totaling almost a quarter mile did not strike Silenos as particularly inappropriate.

They followed the hand farther into the fortress, along corridors that angled deeper gradually enough to almost escape notice. Silenos estimated that, by the time they came to the final door, they were already underground.

During their long walk, he had time to press his companions for information.

"You seemed shocked at the prospect of Galukar being unavailable," he noted to Ensharia, "Why is that?"

She kept her eyes ahead as she answered, but her worry was palpable.

"Galukar is said to be one of the finest warriors who ever lived," she said after a moment. "And the source of his strength is . . . his sword. It's a thing of . . . not magic, of miracle. A holy relic forged from a sliver of God's bone, harder than any steel—magic or otherwise—and able to imbue its wielder with a body mighty enough for most weapons to break upon him.

"Each of the precious few wielders have carved their names into history using its power, and Galukar is greater even than most of them. As I've heard, he's killed more of the Dark Lord's minions than anyone else."

It was an impressive summation but did not answer his question.

"So why were you worried?" Silenos pressed. She swallowed before continuing.

"A month ago, more or less, I heard that the king met the Dark Lord himself in the field of battle. The result of the actual conflict was that Abaritan's army won, but . . ."

"But you feared, upon hearing Galukar was not available to meet, that he had been killed and his death merely covered up for morale purposes."

She nodded, face tight.

"There hasn't been a wielder of the Godblade in a century," Ensharia whispered. "And it's known that all the king's sons were killed in that same battle, his sons who fought alongside him as personal guards and a retinue of elites, the only ones who could do so without slowing him down. With them gone, if Galukar really is dead, then . . . there is likely nobody alive able to wield the Godblade." Her voice was a thing of serrated despair. Falls chose that moment to cut in.

"And there will never be one again. Magic is advancing by the generation. Any day now, we'll unwrap the secret to your stupid mysticism, and from then on the weapon will be nothing more than the relic of a bygone age. Your god can follow soon after."

Ensharia said nothing at first, only kept her eyes on her feet.

"I do so hope you're right," she whispered at last.

Finally they reached a stop, standing and waiting before the most hilarious door Silenos had ever seen. It was not composed of iron, nor even mundane steel, but a curious metal he could not quite place the substance of. Its volume glowed with magic strong enough to leave little doubt of it weathering more than one shot of Silenos's new cannon, and perhaps an assault from his combat form. Covered with locks and glowing runes, it hummed in response to the hand's touch, then trembled for a few moments before finally sliding open.

"The king lies beyond," he said redundantly. "You will treat him with the respect and reverence that is due to one of his station. Call him His Majesty, sire, or liege; make no sudden or threatening movements; and thank him for his time." The man hesitated then before continuing. ". . . He will not be as you expect, no doubt. You will have heard tales of the towering warrior king able to spark flints against his musculature and toss twenty times his weight around like straw dolls. I am warning you now . . . Temper your expectations."

A solemn, considering pause followed. Then Silenos was moving in to find the man without delay.

Past the door lay a chamber of unexpected comfort. A thick, warm carpet, a crackling fireplace, padded chairs, and a crystalline decanter lying beside a ludicrously large bed. Atop that bed, there sat a man. Or what was left of him.

His face was lined, sagging, and hollow. Eyes sunken, bones showing beneath loose skin. His limbs were so spindly that Silenos believed he had actually reanimated year-old corpses with more muscle, and the hair atop his trembling scalp fell down in scraggly strips.

Above it all, his newly opened senses found a bottomless sorrow in the man's eyes. Inky black as shadestuff and infinitely dense. Silenos did not meet his gaze, finding himself suddenly too disquieted to do so.

"The king has been like this ever since he met the Dark Lord in battle," the hand said from behind them, closing the door as he did. "The rumors, I imagine you have gathered, are true. They truly did engage in single combat, and the day was, in the end, the nation of Arbite's. But there was a cost. My liege, would you . . . please explain?"

For a few moments, Silenos thought the monarch might well be too far gone to do even that much. He only jerked his head around, eyes flitting about in panic and paranoid delusion, face twitching as if he were on the brink of tears. Then he spoke in a voice that sounded somehow infant young and ancient at once.

"He . . . came down upon wings of nighttime, and a dozen lichs writhed at his feet. We clashed with them, my sons and I, and blood fell in sheets. Every one of us was a blade master, you understand, quicker, stronger, tougher than other men. My sons had each been trained by my personal hand, and though none had the necessary gift to wield the Godblade, any of them could have been a lesser king's champion. We hacked the lichs apart, then moved on to the Dark Lord himself. One by one, my boys were killed. Bodies broken like dolls before his mace, until only he and I remained. I fought him like I've fought nothing else, but in the end, even I was too weak to leave more than a single crack upon his breast-plate. I lost consciousness before he left, but when I awoke I . . ." The man's face split apart into a sob then, and a cry of utter agony escaped him. "My sword! He took my sword! He had no reason to. It is useless in any hands but mine, and yet he took it just to shame me!"

Silenos looked about the room, finding Ensharia's face first. Her eyes were oceans of sympathy and warmth. Beside them the hand's were cool with resignation. Only Falls demonstrated a contemptuous apathy.

Only Falls, including even himself. Silenos felt the nascent circuitry of his brain's emotional centers spark at the story, flooding him with intuition, insight, and . . . Yes. And pity.

"Thank you for sharing that, Your Majesty," Ensharia blurted out. Her eyes remained low for a moment, then rose. Silenos could see the difficulty she felt in lifting them to meet the king's. "I understand it must have been difficult for you to revisit that, the loss of your swords, your sons, everything. You did an amazing thing by fighting against the Dark Lord. Nobody else can ask anything more of you, nor could they have even asked what you've given already. Thank you."

Silenos was surprised to see the king's eyes grow wet with tears, his lips tremble as emotion took him. He didn't say anything, just nodded tightly as the hand stepped forward.

"I think you had all better leave," the man advised. None argued with him.

CHAPTER FOURTEEN

There were advantages to having left all his treasures back in his own world, and Silenos found that ease of departure was among them. He had virtually nothing worth packing, and thus virtually no delay between him and his moving on from the city of Abaritan. Nothing, save for Ensharia's whining.

"You're leaving?" she pressed, eyes wide with a mix of disbelief, betrayal, and fury. Silenos only nodded.

"Our work here is meaningless. If the king has lost his combat power then he is of no use to anyone, and we would be better suited in hurrying toward the next Hero on our list."

While Ensharia's face tightened and throat warped in preparation for an argument, Falls cut in. He leaned against a door, grinning that smug grin that seemed perpetually upon him since they'd left Abaritan's palace.

"I agree with the caster," he declared. "Anyone spineless enough to collapse after one battle was never going to be worth anything to begin with."

Silenos felt a stab of irritation. It was of no particularly empathetic nature, mere offense taken at the brazen *incorrectness* of what Falls had said.

"The effects of trauma upon a human brain are complex, unpredictable, and varied," he replied, letting his displeasure show. "A lack of comprehension regarding this fact, an insistence that they are evidence of mere weakness, is one of the most common markers for a primitive society."

Falls's face fell. Clearly, he had expected Silenos to indulge his stupidity, while Ensharia looked utterly thrilled to see him contradict it. She didn't let the relief keep her from speaking more, however.

"What I don't understand is why the Dark Lord has kept quiet about taking the sword."

Silenos paused, considering the words himself.

"He wouldn't," he said at last, thinking the matter through even as he did. "This would be an immeasurably large morale victory, a humiliation and neutralization of a deadly enemy. Any skilled general would have it demonstrated for all the land. And yet no stories have come of the Godblade being paraded across the world?"

"None." She nodded, seeing clearly that Silenos was back to pondering the matter. No doubt she considered that her chance to rope him into staying, and now that she'd broached the mystery, he couldn't say she was entirely wrong.

"We're staying," he announced, earning a grin from Ensharia and a groan from Falls. The look upon the magus's face needled Silenos a shade, so he continued speaking to rectify it.

"And the two of you will be searching the city for the Godblade. I believe it is still somewhere in Abaritan."

There, much better. The look of utter dread replacing Falls's annoyance was vastly more amusing.

"Why?!" Ensharia frowned, clearly not an enthusiast of the idea.

"Fuck you!" Falls snapped, clearly even less so.

"Because I have more important things to do," Silenos replied. "And attempting to use my glorious mind with the two of you following me would be like—Do your people have an understanding of brain tumors?"

They paused, and Ensharia slowly shook her head. Silenos sighed.

"It would be like attempting to think with a large deadly growth slowly spreading through the meat of my brain." He made a note to educate the two on more advanced sciences so that they might better gasp his rapier wit, then began for the door. "Now get to work. We haven't long."

Arion watched the caster stride out of the room as if he owned the place and felt his blood boiling again.

There hadn't been many positives to his master's murder, but the largest by far was that, finally, he'd been able to claim his birthright as the greatest caster alive. No decades of waiting to surpass his power or years of waiting for his aged heart to give out. He'd finally reached the front of the line and sat down in his vacant seat. Then the Shaiagrazni had arrived to ruin everything.

"Unbelievable," the bitch grumbled, interrupting Arion's thoughts as she glared at him. "Leaving me with you."

"Sorry, am I distracting?" he asked, flashing her his second-most-charming smile. She was a good actor, he had to say. Her look of feigned repulsion and loathing almost convinced even him and betrayed not even a trace of the lust he must surely have inspired.

"He must have a good reason," she pressed, turning away from him, face curling in that adorable way Arion had learned it did whenever she thought particularly hard about something. "He can be eccentric, *is* selfish, but he doesn't waste time without cause. He'll be doing something important."

Arion had rather thought that past the requirement of pointing out but decided to let the bitch have her petty victory

"So you're going to do as he says," he guessed. She rounded on him at that, glaring.

"*We* are, unless you want to take longer leaving this city than is necessary."

Arion, at that, found himself caught between the twin evils of agreeing with a woman and leaving himself trapped in the shit-smelling warrior's city. He took his time in thinking the problem over.

"Fine," he conceded at last. "Let's go."

It was irritating to admit, but Arion found the female far more useful than him in navigating their search. He supposed that was one of the major advantages to being a paladin, getting used to finding one's way around foreign cities. That, and her womanly instincts were probably helping to home in on the sword. They were rather good at finding things, he'd heard.

First, the two of them directed their efforts toward just asking random soldiers if they knew anyone who'd been present during the battle, which turned over a few names but not any that were within reach. Their next plan was to try following the actual Godblade itself, moving off to find the city's underworld.

"When something valuable goes missing, you can think of a city's gangs as one big safety net to catch it, should it slip out of everyone else's hands," the bitch had explained.

"And you know all this how, exactly?" Arion noted. "You don't strike me as master of the criminal mind."

She didn't strike him as much more than a giant ball of sugar and honey actually, but that was neither here nor there. However bitchy she'd become since, Arion still remembered her kindness when he'd been faced with execution, even if it had probably been motivated by her being the one scheduled to behead him.

"I wasn't always a paladin" was all the bitch said.

Arion noticed the obvious there; she was leaving something unsaid. He considered whether to press for more information or not but decided there were better things to do. He could always needle it out of her later or just fuck her until she let it slip in pillow talk whenever she finally caved.

"You're leering at me," the paladin growled, trying, and failing, to look intimidating rather than cute. Arion smiled.

"I prefer to call it appraising."

"Everyone else calls it leering. Stop."

She turned away pointedly, and he actually felt his smile waver. Arion had known women who enjoyed playing hard to get, but this one was taking it to a ridiculous extreme. She almost didn't seem interested.

Arion had never actually interacted with gangs before, his knowledge of them being entirely theoretical and gleaned from books or stories. They were quite disappointing. They didn't sing and dance, for one thing, and they demonstrated no plans to erode aristocratic society and destroy the world. He failed to spot even a single baby being eaten, and not even one of them was being puppeteered by a demon. Nonetheless, they proved the most useful source of information so far, particularly with the bitch's rather well-aimed questioning.

One group led them to another, who directed them to a smuggler, who volunteered his contacts, one of which was a man famous for collecting weapons of a magical inclination. They headed straight for him, finding themselves at a large, if unassuming, building. It was made of solid stone and mortar, a rare feature in cities as primitive and unmagical as Abaritan, and Arion took a moment to let a strong breeze sweep over the surrounding vicinity for a few moments, coiling through alleys and under crevices.

"A dozen men hiding nearby," he noted, feeling the shapes and movements of their shivering bodies as light resistance against his magic. "Not sure how armed they are, but . . ." He focused on dimensions, shape, size. "They're probably commoners, by their shortness."

It was more than a little satisfying to see the bitch staring at him with the mix of awe and considering weariness she usually reserved for Shaiagrazni. Arion was careful to hide his tiredness as he soaked it in.

Small breezes were one thing, but he'd spread that one over everything within a hundred feet horizontally and fifty vertically. He'd probably shifted close to ten thousand stone of air as fast as a jogging man, and even he'd been pushed close to his limits in doing so.

But surprise attacks were the bane of any caster. Arion put his worry aside and stepped into the building alongside the paladin.

The first thing he noticed inside the place was that it was tight and cramped. Not good. If a fight broke out, any caster would be disadvantaged in such circumstances, and a wind mage more than even most others. The second thing that hit Arion was the smell on the air, an odd, sanitary scent of careful cleaning and perfumed surfaces that felt entirely at odds with its function.

It seemed not to deter the bitch because she just hurried on into the place without a moment's hesitation, forcing Arion to increase his own pace so as to not be left following a woman. The interior was no more spacious once they headed deeper into its bowels, walls of wood and brick closing in like strangling fingers around him. The thought of a fight became more concerning to Arion with every new step. His worry only grew as they came to a central room in the place.

Half office and half bunker, it was another structure of stone rather than wood and seemed made to withstand a trebuchet. Arion had seen far more robustly built places. The University of Magira had held chambers that would've weathered weapons capable of skewering five of such rooms in a row, but he had to concede it was impressive enough for the work of duns. Those without magic were not *entirely* helpless, he supposed. Particularly when they could hire others who didn't share their disabilities.

Seeing those duns in person though had Arion feeling a shade less sympathetic of their limitations. The ones around him now were all broad, hard, and mean looking, bodies encased in armor varying from simple hauberks to full steel plate with articulated mobility about the joints. The sole exception was a man lounging on a sofa at the back of the room, whose gaunt face framed a pair of eerily clever eyes.

"Please, let yourselves right in," he said, sounding more amused than affronted at their unannounced entry. "Random strangers are always welcome in my home."

"Your shop," the bitch countered. "Or do you not do business in subtly acquired goods anymore?"

He grinned.

"Subtly acquired. Ha, I like that. Who the fuck are you?" The shift in tone was so sudden that it sent Arion back a step and had his fingers twitching with fraying nerves. His magic was just a hair beyond reach, and he had to fight not to call on it. It wouldn't help their cause if he tore their leads apart before extracting any answers.

"We're the people who are going to turn you over to the hand if you don't hand over the Godblade," the bitch retorted, seemingly oblivious to the men stiffening and half drawing blades as she said it. Arion found himself suddenly less confident as he eyed the size of them, but she remained unfazed.

"Funny," the beady-eyed man sneered. "Kill the—"

Arion had always been quick, and so his winds were already squeezing down the nearest man's throat before the order to fight even came. He'd compressed with close to the full capacity of his magic's power, having prepared the move well ahead of time, and yet this opponent was one gifted with a rare physical power.

He received nothing more than a shattered neck, bits of jagged bone erupting out from torn skin where the air pressed. Arion had meant to behead him completely. Not a bad bodyguard.

CHAPTER FIFTEEN

One of the other men, faster than the first, was coming for Arion before he could ready another attack—the distance between them, paired with his preternatural speed, almost too much to contend with. Almost. Arion's magic had hardened air into another barrier just before his cudgel reached him. A big, heavy thing made of ugly, tortured iron that visibly cracked as it bounced off the barricade, then fell from its wielder's fingers as the barrier shifted and crushed the attacker against a far wall. Two more came, both dropping to the floor in multiple sections as Arion reworked his barrier into a number of scything winds that cut through chain mail and meat about as easily as each other.

When he looked back, the bitch had already laid another man out with that mace of hers—though failed to kill him—and was lifting the couch dweller high in a single-handed grip. It was an impressive sight, for sure. Arion had seen men three times her mass without the strength to do as much as that, even when not weighed down by paladin plate armor.

The man she held now was not three times her mass. Nor, indeed, was he even equal to it. He writhed around like a strangled rat, legs kicking beneath him, fingers desperately clawing at her wrist, though managing only to rip their own nails bloodily out of place. The bitch's face was a mask of cold iron as she glared up at him.

"Do you have any idea how easily I could snap your neck?" she asked, voice low, quiet, and dangerous in a way that certainly shouldn't have been arousing, but rather was. "One squeeze, that's all I'd need. One squeeze, a quick crack, then you're dead. Only movement in you would be your legs kicking a few more times, and maybe some waste running down your leg as you soiled yourself."

He was still now, the sofa man. Still in that way only true terror could ever make a person. Arion recalled freezing like that himself. The day he'd been scheduled to die.

"I won't kill you if you tell me where the Godblade is," the bitch spat, and Arion knew then, in that moment, that two simple facts were immutably true. The first was that she genuinely, sincerely hated this man. And the second was that, despite that, she was telling the truth.

Perhaps drawing the same conclusion, the slab of human scum in her grip desperately nodded toward a wall at one far section of the room. Arion's fingers twitched, sending a jet of air toward it.

It wasn't diabase, that much was obvious. He smashed through the inch or so of stone with the magical equivalent of a flexed biceps, then banished the resulting dust cloud with another twitch of his fingers. Light spilled into a hollow space within the wall that revealed their prize, and the bitch dropped sofa man to take it out.

"You can go," she said distractedly, taking the sword in her hands and eying it thoughtfully. The man went.

Even Arion hardly noticed him leave, however, finding his focus drawn to the sword. If the men watching outside were equal to the ones waiting indoors—and that was unlikely already—then they'd be of no real threat to him. The sword though was interesting.

"It's heavy," the bitch noted, though she seemed to move it around without issue. It was, indeed, bloody heavy. Arion could tell that much just from a glance. The thing was ugly, its blade about two inches at the widest and stretching out easily five feet from the guard, with an oddly dull coloration and a jagged, irregular rhythm to its shape. As the bitch turned it in her hands, he got a glimpse of it sidelong. Arion was shocked by the depth.

"Must be a good inch of iron at the thickest point," he observed, noting the bitch frowning as she nodded.

"I'd expected more . . . sophistication," she replied, sounding almost disappointed. He let a smile grow.

"From a two-thousand-year-old sword."

She glared at him. "It's a miracle."

"A miracle that this slab of pig iron hasn't snapped in half yet, yes." Arion snorted. "Come on, whatever unknown magic—"

"Divine power," she interrupted. "Granted by God to arm his chosen warriors."

"Yes, yes." Arion sighed. "Whatever imaginary power is responsible for making it so effective in battle, the physical sword was still made by human hands and human minds. And the humans of two thousand years ago were still carving runes on their casters' faces to let baby-eating gods recognize them in the afterlife. Your miracle sword was not made by smart or knowledgeable people, I'm sorry to say."

"Well, we have it now," the bitch snapped, and Arion enjoyed seeing a point so clearly scored. "Let's just take it back to Silenos before word gets out that we have it."

Sobering, he nodded.

"Good idea," Arion conceded, heading for the door. He hesitated before stepping through, then sent the wind churning outside once again.

Always irksome to do that, but rarely smart not to. Arion took a good few moments examining the sensation of resistance against his magic, using it to feel out the area around them. Sure enough, the number of men awaiting them *had* changed.

It had, of course, dropped down to zero. There wasn't a single humanoid within a hundred feet. He allowed himself a smile at that.

"Clear," he noted, striding out of the room. Sometimes it was awfully convenient to be the most ingenious caster in all human history.

The bitch did not seem to share his enthusiasm.

Silenos had found more than one source leading him to several of the surviving warriors present upon the battlefield the day the Godblade was taken. Fortunately, all were within reach once he took a few moments to fashion himself a means of flight. Such an approach would have been impossible to enter a Shaiagrazni arcology, which were sealed on all sides by thick sheets of metal, but the primitives of this new world seemed content to leave themselves open to any wise and powerful enough to claim the skies.

Easier to travel a hundred miles by air than three by land, he'd always found, and that remained true as he swooped down into the city's noble district, over hostile walling and alert guards. Those few who spotted him were easily neutralized.

He had learned from his fiasco at Magira and since devised a means of producing potent intoxicants able to render a normal man unconscious within moments.

Silenos extended a spinal tail from himself, barbed with a sharp injection mechanism at its tip, and dosed men and women whenever they laid eyes upon him. Some had been remarkably strong, bodies magically strengthened in what seemed to be the way of this world's residents.

He'd even needed to squeeze noticeably hard when emptying his toxin glands into one.

The first name on Silenos's mental list was one Lord Valdaryre, a noble of some prominence who lived in a building that had clearly been fortified with magic, but sadly not nearly enough. Silenos, being in the hurry he was, decided to save time by merely smashing one wall down with a jet of blasting oil, then striding inside. Guards swarmed him and achieved as much as any could hope against a being of his majesty, and soon enough Silenos had the noble before him.

Valdaryre was half dressed in plate armor, having equipped a breastplate and greaves. The metal hummed with no small measure of magic, and the man's musculature was clearly imbued with power too. The most impressive thing, however, was his instantaneous surrender. Recognizing Silenos's overwhelming superiority was a rare quality in this world.

"You want money?" he asked desperately. "I can—"

"I do not want your pitiable currency," Silenos interrupted. "Doubtless I will still be alive long after it has been replaced by whichever set of barbarians conquers your people. I am here for answers. You were present when Galukar lost the Godblade. Explain everything you saw. Lie and I will know."

That, itself, had been a lie. House Shaiagrazni had yet to discern a reliable way of telling truth from deception or forcing a person to veer from one in favor of the other. Being thought to possess such a skill, however, was often almost as valuable as the ever-sought-after ability itself would have been.

"I . . . I saw the Dark Lord take the Godblade after defeating Galukar. He hurled the king's body to the edge of the battlefield and flew off upon wings of night, weaved between ballista bolts and spells, rallied his forces for a fighting retreat, and disappeared over the horizon within a minute. That's it."

The man had grown more fearful, then paused before answering. Silenos placed a hand upon his head, with no particular measure of force.

"The Dark Lord flew back over the horizon. What happened before that? Answer quickly."

The man frowned, blinking, sluggish.

"He . . . rallied his forces—"

"And immediately before that, what happened?"

Another hesitation. People struggled, Silenos had found, to recite a false story backward. When rehearsing them, they invariably did so in chronological order. Those recalling real memories found it much easier to swap the sequence of events than those reciting manufactured accounts.

He let his magic seep into the man's spine, fraying the nervous fibers that connected it to his legs. He dropped into a heap instantly, the panic on him barely a moment later.

"What have you done?!" he demanded. Silenos ignored the question. There had been a strange amount of resistance in changing this one's body. He supposed that was a feature of the natural magics imbuing it. Better to find that out now, rather than in the attempt to weaponize his fleshcrafting against an enemy of sufficient power to threaten him.

"Tell the truth of what happened or I shall remove the use of your arms, then ask again. If you fail to do as told the third time, I shall leave. Without killing you, without restoring the use of your body. I will warn you, however, that my skills are rather more precise than any healer you can likely reach, and irreversible to casters of their power."

By the horror in Valdaryre's eyes, Silenos knew he'd been believed. And he found what the man said next to be truthful too.

As he had implied he would, Silenos took a single instant to restore the man's legs. It would be dangerous to gain a reputation as one who could not be relied upon to uphold his word.

Then he flew from the building as fast as his wings could manage, hurrying for the king's fortress. Hurrying to outpace the disaster.

It was almost surprising how quickly the hand reacted to Arion and the bitch's call for his attention, but then, sending word that one had obtained one of the most powerful and valuable things in the world tended to hurry people up. Arion barely had the chance to sit down before he was whisked away through the fortress, deep, deep, deeper still, until he and the bitch were ushered into a large, expansive chamber with walls of . . .

Yes, steel. Even he was surprised at the sight. Steel wasn't really *hard* to make, of course, but the process of properly doing so was lengthy and resource consuming, even with magic. To line an entire room with it, let alone one as big as the fifty-foot hemisphere he now waited in, must have cost a fortune. Or several. If the walls measured even half an inch thick, they'd have held sufficient metal to equip a thousand men with plate armor, chain mail, and polearms. Perhaps with some bard thrown in for good measure. Even the door had been made of the stuff, and by its sheer thickness, the hinges upon which it hung would have held against a troll being lynched from them.

"Impressive, isn't it?" came a voice from one end. Arion turned quickly to see the hand making his way in through the entrance behind them, smiling thinly. "Galukar's eldest son had it made, back when the Dark Lord was only just starting to really threaten things. A last defensible position was the idea, a funnel of steel able to force enemies to attack slowly and in concentrated areas, to be held by the royals."

"A choke point with no escape," the bitch finished. "To die with as many dead enemies around them as possible."

The hand smiled again, sending a chill down Arion's spine for some reason.

"Inspired by the old tales from the eastern hoplites, said to have held a pass against tens of thousands with only three hundred of their own. Such stories are the backbone of Arbite's culture, I suppose. We have been a warrior's nation since our founding a century ago." Something flitted across his face for an instant, too fast to examine, and then he continued in a different tone. "Galukar's family is not a particularly optimistic one, I must say, but . . . perhaps they ought to be."

His eyes fell upon the Godblade and practically glowed as they beheld it.

"No need to verify," he said. "I know the real article when I see it. Hand it over and you'll get your reward."

The bitch stepped forward, doing just that, and Arion found himself frowning. Why meet them in a place like that? He studied the door. It was a wide thing, but not so wide that he couldn't imagine five or six men holding it without being flanked. Five or six, not two.

"We didn't do it for a reward," the paladin noted as the hand grunted. He strained at the sword's weight. He forced a smile through his exertive grimace.

"No, of course not. Forgive me, Dame Paladin." He let the blade's edge hit the ground rather than hold it more awkwardly and turned. Moving to the door now. Arion saw the great slab of steel swing wide as the hand approached it and felt his heart sink at what lay beyond.

Knights. Dozens, all standing tall and armed in glinting armor, all moving as if their sixty pounds of protection weighed as much as a thick shirt. They parted to let the hand move in between their ranks, eyes all affixed on Arion and the bitch behind visors that betrayed as much emotion as the sockets of skeletons.

"And you must forgive me for this too, Dame Paladin," the hand called as he disappeared between his men. "But I cannot cede control of my city to that family of imbeciles again."

The knights charged.

CHAPTER SIXTEEN

Arion should've seen the trap coming a mile off, but he realized the cause for his missing it. Out of all the places within Abaritan Castle that he might have found himself ambushed, few were worse than the late prince's safety room . . . for the people doing the ambushing.

Fifty feet was cramped compared to open air, but it was far more room than he'd had back in the gangster's shop. Arion didn't waste a moment in using it, throwing himself back and high up into the air, holding his body just ten feet shy of the ceiling as he gathered more winds farther down below.

They were knights attacking them now. The best of the best. Not one man in fifty had the capacity to become one, even among the better-nourished and -trained upper classes, and those that did were trained even better than the rest. Arion had heard accounts as verifiable and trustworthy as any records in the world tell of armies numbering in the thousands falling to just a few dozen.

And there seemed to be about that many attacking him now. He acted quickly.

His first wave of air caught four knights at once, sending them crashing back against the rest of their comrades and giving the crowd pause, for a moment, as its constituents stumbled and fought to right themselves. They weren't held for long though, and so Arion tried concentrating his next blast onto just one, letting that unlucky individual take as much power as could be focused against his body's surface area.

Three hundred pounds of knight and steel were lifted from the ground and dashed against the far wall, rebounding on it and spinning head over heels no less than thrice before finally landing once more in a heap. Arion saw blood oozing out from under the knight's helmet and gorget, and there was no more movement in his limp form. One down, perhaps twenty or so remaining.

The bitch was doing her best, bless, but she was only keeping herself from being surrounded by backing off. She was faster than the knights, certainly stronger, but she'd not had a chance to don her helmet, and she was rapidly running out of space at her back to retreat into. If she was attacked from all sides, she'd lose fast. Arion moved to take care of that, reaching out with more of his winds, sending an arced blast to sweep along the front row attacking her. They all stumbled at once, and she seized the advantage lightning fast, bringing her mace down hard on the back of one's head.

Better to have an anvil fall on him than that, Arion thought. The knight dropped like a stone and didn't move again, but more were soon focusing themselves upon the paladin, forcing her focus to split itself four ways as they struck from every angle they could. Arion decided to try a different approach than just scattering them, wrapping currents of air around both the fallen knights' weapons, then hurling them into their allies. They struck like arrows, and with their mass such an impact was far from trivial. Metal ruptured, blood flew, and in an instant the paladin had just a bit more breathing room.

Most might've used that to try to remove themselves from the fight, but she turned it to more practical means. Taking the chance to down another knight with her weapon and lunging into the space he'd been occupying, furthering her space.

Arion typically preferred to be front and center in a fight. That was where all the opportunities for showing off his impressive magic lay, but the knights were stronger an enemy than he could afford to be so dismissive of. He hung back, letting the bitch take most of their aggression, focusing his powers on shielding her when necessary, and crushing another foe or two when the opportunity presented itself. Between the two of them, it didn't take long for things to end.

Standing and panting at the center of strewn-about, unconscious knights, the bitch was clearly worn out. Even Arion himself felt a shade drained from the combat, having exerted himself more than would likely have been needed had he been in an area with heavier projectiles to leverage with his magic.

The room was silent, save for her panting, and that silence let Arion recognize their latest problem instantaneously.

"The hand," he noted. "Fuck."

However shortly they'd taken care of the knights, it had been long enough for a sprinting man to get far. Even carrying twenty pounds of iron.

Silenos had made the decision to retract his wings and reabsorb the excess matter into his body upon entering the castle. It was no great tedium to do. A caster of his excellence was able to manage it while running with no distraction, and the benefits to removing such inherent a vulnerability as the lightweight and thin structure required of flight-performing limbs were well worth it. He soon found himself regretting the decision, however.

For three minutes and nineteen seconds, he roamed the building, navigating through the perception of his arcane sight. Had he known how incandescently the Godblade registered to such things, he might well have tried searching for it by simply flying over the city, for there was an intense flare of magic he could only deduce was coming from the relic, its source deep in the fortress and moving through it at a more than manageable pace.

Manageable enough that it did not take Silenos long to find himself face-to-face with it.

Of course, it came as no surprise to set eyes upon the hand. Silenos had hurried back only after learning independently that the man was responsible for the Godblade's disappearance. What ran through him upon locking eyes with the traitor was a dull concern.

"Where are my companions?" he asked calmly. Silenos had learned, in his month or so in the new world, that warriors of Ensharia's caliber required the combination of talent found only in one among every thousand with well over a dozen years' training. Casters the equal of Arion were, of course, rarer still by a factor of several hundred times. Neither one was an acceptable loss.

The hand froze, stiffened, stared at Silenos for a good long moment. He could see the simple thoughts flashing around behind the man's eyes, primitive machinery of his cognition racing as fast as its shoddy construction would allow. Eventually, inevitably, it led him to perhaps the only conclusion it ever would have.

He turned and ran. Instantly, men were behind him and before Silenos, barring the path between them with their own bodies, raising weapons and narrowing eyes. He walked through them, barely even noticing what he did to the fools as he bypassed their defenses: liquefying flesh, crumbling bone, fusing limbs into unnatural fixtures, and boiling the fragile meat of their brains. The hand had barely gotten a further five meters by the time Silenos was done, leaving less than twenty separating them. And it was then that he tested his new body's capacity for sprinting.

Silenos closed in on the hand, surprising even himself with the sound of wind howling past his ears. He reached the man within a half dozen strides, seizing him hard by the back of the neck and snatching his body up off of the ground. Unsurprisingly, the man tried to swing his stolen Godblade around at Silenos's head. The weapon didn't even make it halfway, simply falling from his grip as fatigue and poor leverage dragged its weight down more fiercely than he could compensate for.

"You need to let me keep it," the hand tried, words spilling out of him fast enough that they almost interrupted one another. "I can do great things for this city. I can make it the world's crowning jewel. All you need to do is—"

Silenos halted the signals running from the man's cerebellum to his spine, then deftly lifted the sword up to make his way to Ensharia and Falls, stepping over the convulsive traitor with a curled lip.

He didn't take long to decide where his presence was most needed; it was obvious. There had been only one reason for his coming to Arbite in the first place, after all, and now he had the tool needed to make it worth doing. Silenos made his way for King Galukar.

CHAPTER SEVENTEEN

Perhaps predictably, the door to the throne room already had Ensharia and Falls hovering around it, eying the slab of iron as if uncertain how to get past. Their eyes lit up as they turned and recognized the sword in Silenos's hands.

"You got him!" Falls noted pointlessly.

"Step aside, both of you," Silenos instructed. Both hurried to do so.

Silenos felt a new, alien feeling as he shaped the last few cubic centimeters of material needed to turn the insides of his arm into his newly designed cannon. He realized the anomaly came from within. He'd not experimented with the full destructive power of his weapon, not with his emotions restored to some approximation of human normalcy, and the thought of seeing its limits was a captivating one.

Steadying his aim and bracing his body, he fired.

Iron was not such a feeble material. Even House Shaiagrazni found use in it to armor their battleships and other such constructions. But it was weaker than steel, and certainly weaker than any material potent enough to be equipped by a real named entering into battle. The door surrendered quickly.

Scraps of mangled metal and cracked stone fell from the structure, and Silenos stepped over it all without a word as he headed into the room. He found Galukar trembling, as might have been expected, and staring upon him with wide eyes. Silenos greeted him by dropping the sword down just in front of the man, watching as its great weight deformed the king's mattress. Recognition sparked in Galukar's eyes.

"Your sword," Silenos explained, just in case the savage didn't understand what was happening. "Grab it, reclaim your power, then repay your debt by helping us in our quest."

The king shook his head, staring at Silenos as if he were some ferocious creature lurking in the shadows.

"No," he croaked.

Silenos felt his eye twitch with fury, then seized the sword. It was not so heavy as to make him struggle with it, though its length left it unwieldy. He nonetheless managed to stab it into the stone floor.

"Take it," he insisted.

"I can't," Galukar replied, not meeting Silenos's eye, nor any other's. "I've lost the will."

"The will," Silenos echoed, feeling his disgust congeal. "The *will*?!"

How he wished to kill this man, this pitiable, writhing insect. Ensharia spoke up before he could think of a suitable torment.

"Why not, my king?" she asked.

Galukar's eyes remained low.

"Answer now or I shall activate every pain receptor in your body and remove your ability to adjust," Silenos informed him. The king hardly even seemed moved by his words, taking his time in replying even under threat of eternal torment. He raised his withered hands, staring at splayed fingers as if they were attached to something more foreign than his own body.

"How could I?" Galukar asked helplessly. "I've betrayed everything that sword stood for. Strength, courage, heroism. I'm not a warrior anymore. You're best finding someone else to try and win it."

Silenos felt tendrils of icy disgust run through his mind as he gazed upon the pitiable creature before him, then turned for the door and marched out.

He passed the slain humans on his way out, noting their corpses strewn about the hallway just where he'd left them. Some guards turned to the sight of him, seemingly on the verge of questioning the scene, then simply falling silent and scattering instead. Silenos considered resurrecting the corpses. It would be no great undertaking, doable with a single flick of his mind, but . . . perhaps inconvenient.

Rumors of his necromancy had traveled far enough from Elkatin to Magira and caused plenty of issues. There was no point in spawning more, not in exchange for a mere dozen undead as weak as what could be made from such bodies. He moved past.

Silenos was long gone by the time Ensharia had finished trying, and failing, to comfort Galukar. She was almost pleased by the fact. Talking with the Savior was taxing, particularly when his apathy was spiking. Bad enough she had to follow him around keeping his iciness from starting international incidents; bad enough he'd no doubt realized she would and thus began to let more of his civil veneer fall away. She couldn't deal with him when her mood was already foul.

"Well, this has been a nice waste of fucking time." Arion Falls sighed, not even trying to hide his irritation, nor his blaming gaze as it shot for Ensharia. For once, she met it in kind.

"You do not get to complain about wasted anything," she snapped. "For years, you were one of the most influential men in Magira, and you didn't lift a finger in motivating it to aid nations like Arbite. This is your fault more than it is Galukar's."

He rolled his eyes, and Ensharia shut hers. Taking a moment to pray, letting God's wisdom fill her as she reminded herself of decade-old teachings and long-finished meditations upon scriptural ethics. Smashing a man's face in was generally not in line with those ethics, at least not when it wasn't in the name of self-defense.

"You're a pig," she told Falls, then started down the hall. Their walk was cold and silent, and that was just fine with her. Ensharia was beginning to fill up on cruelty and coldness, beginning to fill up on this entire endeavor. There were surely paladins better suited to it than her. Perhaps she could find one—or several—to replace her.

Silenos would have headed straight for a carriage, Ensharia knew, and so she went the same way. Falls trudged along beside her, as disinterested as ever, and her temper slowly unraveled while they moved. Her grim mood and broiling thoughts were interrupted only when a figure caught her eye moving ahead.

It was a man, she saw, and a vaguely familiar one. She couldn't quite place him, but could have sworn she'd read his description somewhere. He was tall, wiry, his body clothed in a long coat that seemed almost similar to the robes of a magus, his mouth mustached with needle-thin hairs kept carefully brushed and in place. Sharp eyes peered back at her from his sockets, and the intense focus of them told Ensharia in an instant that the man was here for her. He started forward.

"Wait, I know you!" Falls gasped. Ensharia glanced over to see him shifting where he stood, body falling into a defensive posture as his hands raised. "Kraika the Toxicologist."

Her blood ran cold. That had been the second name on their list, the one they'd skipped over for fear of the Dark Lord's spies beating them to it just as he had Walriq. And Ensharia could see only one reason its owner might be here in Arbite and heading her way.

The toxicologist broke out into a run, hands raising, and Ensharia felt her battered armor creak as she moved with combative speed to respond.

It was not hard to procure a carriage, though Silenos still found his irritation mounting as he did. In the lands of House Shaiagrazni, a named of his power would simply travel to and from a city as he saw fit, flying under his own power or fleshcrafting a mount more enduring and swift than anything evolution could produce. Such things would be reviled as an act of evil here, and the more he did it, the farther rumors of his doing so would follow.

Like the days before House Shaiagrazni's founders carved out their territory, he was in a world ruled by ignorance and stupidity. Silenos suddenly felt tired at the fact, his new emotional core registering it more deeply than purely cerebral logic ever could.

Perhaps it was that that dulled his senses, slowed his reactions. Let precious milliseconds slip by before the sudden attack caught his notice.

Silenos whirled just in time to see the undead descending upon him, catching the scent of its putrefying magic long moments before impact. He lunged to one side and heard the stone crack where he'd been standing, rolling to his feet, then jumping again as another pricked his arcane senses in the attempt to strike him from behind while he focused upon the first.

He jumped, extending focus to the internal mechanisms of his arms and feeling no slight amount of satisfaction at how quick the process of shaping one into its cannon form was. Silenos had the weapon ready just as he reached the peak of his altitude and fired it an instant later.

No projectile came free; rather he allowed the explosive propellant to launch nothing but boiling gases and overpressure through the barrel. Silenos felt the familiar force throw him back, and he fired a dozen more times to propel himself before twisting. His memory had served well, letting his feet come down first as his body reached the nearest building, and he turned again to sight the enemies.

Obviously he'd surprised them, for they were reorganizing, and that alone betrayed something of their construction. These undead were capable of independent thought to some limited degree, else they'd all have been coordinated instantly by whichever singular intellect was controlling them. It was testament to a semiformidable hand in crafting the things.

Silenos's observations were cut short as the enemy finally galvanized, then flooded after him.

He'd noted the two that attacked him clearly enough, recognizing the magic and movements of mid-level undead. Around them there now swarmed a horde of lower-class creatures, though still ones of considerable craftsmanship.

The act of reanimating an undead was one of imbuing an object with power, just like any other magic. Most stopped at the first step, blindly flooding an empty vessel with the means to begin moving once more, letting energy and force flow down accustomed channels and mindlessly restart mechanisms that had once been active. Such methods did not create a servitor worth using, by Shaiagrazni standards.

Now though, Silenos recognized the sight of magic flowing in excess. Carefully woven and directed, ensuring that every muscle fiber was reinforced in both contractive power and, perhaps more importantly, physical resistance. The amounts of energy at play were not considerable, but the fact that they deviated from the norm meant a lot for his approach.

Ordinary undead would break themselves upon him. These ones, at the very least, surpassed the basic threshold required to wound him.

The mid-level undead were upon him first, of course, reaching the base of the building and scaling it instantly. Behind them, others shuffled out crossbows, clearly drawn with a force not possible to ordinary humans. Made in preparation of their wielders' advanced strength then. Well prepared. The volley of bolts was no great concern. Silenos simply covered the gaps in his armor and allowed them to harmlessly bounce from the keratin-goethite plates. Below, the greater enemies were approaching the halfway point of their five-meter climb, which gave him just a moment to attack.

He used it well, aiming his cannon, conjuring the dense mass of its projectile, readying it. Then gasping as something struck him from behind.

Of course, he had jumped before, flown even, during the siege of Elkatin. No ambush would be readied for him with careful preparation that did not account for Silenos's battlefield mobility. He turned and caught a glimpse of his attacker, even as the agony at his back intensified. It was a torture he knew well, remembered, even from half a century in the past, like the clawing nails of a nemesis.

Shadestuff. He had been struck with shadestuff. It was not so potent as his own, but easily enough to tax the density and tensile resilience of his armor. Silenos landed hard, body bouncing, rolling, barely rising to its feet before the enemy were converging from all sides.

Atop the roof, he caught a glimpse of the one who had cast him down. She grinned, black skin catching the light, eyes glowing with the unquestioning egotism of one who had no shortage of power.

For the first time since gaining his name, Silenos Shaiagrazni felt the numbing animal touch of fear reaching his heart.

CHAPTER EIGHTEEN

Alchemists were not warriors, nor casters. But they were not to be trifled with. Ensharia had read up on them well, during her training as a paladin, for they were second only to rogue casters and conjurers as a source of necromantic research or experimentation into the dark sorceries of fleshcrafting. And they were dangerous, whatever others thought.

Things could be done with alchemy that even the magic of magi could not achieve, and never any more easily than on the alchemist themselves. Invariably, the best of them learned their own bodies on the most intimate level possible, studying every fiber of their substance and quantifying every facet of their existence. From there, it was all too easy to improve them. Drugs and concoctions, mutagens drip dosed over the course of years, tweaks and improvements made by the inch, all eventually creating an immune system and physiology able to withstand combinations of imbibement that would kill a warrior dozens of times their strength.

She'd heard the stories, and now she saw the truth of them. Kraika the Toxicologist was faster than any man of his frame and clear inexperience ought to have been.

He came at her like a fired arrow almost, sidestepping one swing of her mace, then replying by emptying some vial at her face with the flick of a wrist.

Ensharia just barely turned away in time to feel the pungent liquid splash against the side of her helmet rather than the front, and the sizzling of digesting steel reached her ears instantly. There came a great shiver in the air as winds buffeted the toxicologist backward, then yet more hit the side of her helmet and halted the sizzling. She saw droplets of lilac fluid spatter the ground around them, eating it with frightening speed.

"We can take him." The magus grinned, stepping in eagerly, fingers flexing. The corridor was long and wide, a far more advantageous stage for him to unleash his powers than their ambush site. Ensharia found herself almost tempted to go along with the idea.

But she resisted it.

"We need to retreat," she insisted. "He's as powerful as your master, or close."

For one terrifying second, Ensharia thought the magus might refuse. Then she saw a trickle of fear and caution color his eyes. He nodded, seeming reluctant but decided.

An instant later, the toxicologist was on them again. This time he prioritized Falls as his target, clawing for him with fingers suddenly boasting curled talons like the limbs of a falcon. Ensharia saw the air ripple, then give as they bit through her ally's shields, but the thickened atmosphere slowed them enough for her mace to come in for Kraika's temple. The alchemist ducked, backing away, then leaping as another jet of wind shot for his belly.

Ensharia was ready for him when he came down, swinging just right to ensure that the mace was centered on his body from every direction. He moved left, lurching aside just the instant before impact and moving too little to fully escape its path. His heels left the ground, then the wall became his ground as he struck it sidelong and devastatingly.

It had been Falls, of course. Ensharia's arms lacked the strength to hurl a man so hard, and the magus demonstrated his own capacity a second time as he sent the alchemist sprawling far along the floor dozens of feet from them both. Turning back to her, his eyes were wide as he spoke with a growl.

"Run, now."

She didn't need telling even that once. Ensharia and Falls backed away together, making a hasty path for the nearest exit. In their case, a window. As she recalled it was a steep fall to the ground outside, a hundred feet perhaps. She'd hit the ground hard from a height like that, but not hard enough to be injured unless she was unlucky, and with Falls following suit, the odds of harm would be slim indeed.

Footsteps shook the world behind them, and Ensharia risked a glance. The alchemist was in hot pursuit, body now coated with thick scales, legs now bulging with unnatural vascularity. It didn't take more than a glance to know he was faster than either of them and would be on them soon. She conveyed as much to Falls.

"Take a pause. We need to ready ourselves to fight him off again," she advised. "He'll be fighting quickly. His body can't take his drugs forever, so if we buy time, we win."

Falls glared at her, face twisting, but nodded. They both stopped, turned, and readied themselves to fight the man back.

Four times they succeeded in turning him away. Falls kept Ensharia warded with thick walls of air, while she focused on attacking and taking the brunt of their enemy's attacks. An alchemist could not match the physical potence of a true warrior, not on average, and so despite the exceptional difference in experience and power between them, her physicality was not so far inferior to his. With magic and might combined, they had a chance. Of escaping, if nothing else.

But it was Falls again who ruined their rhythm and broke their cycle. On the fifth attack, Ensharia ordered him to ward her while she went straight for a swing. The magus refused with a snarl.

"Enough of this. I'm not following some fucking woman's orders. Sit back and let me take care of it." Her ears popped from the atmospheric distortion as Falls called on every scrap of his magic, the kind of power she'd been trained not to fight against with anything less than a dozen other paladins helping. It might have been comforting, but Ensharia had seen too much of Kraika the Toxicologist to feel anything but dread as Falls reared his magic up to meet the man ahead of her.

Wind came down like a guillotine, and Kraika dodged. It shifted to a horizontal attack, which he leaped over, then continued into a roll as rubble that had been broken from the walls during the previous misses was accelerated at his back. Obviously there had been some sensory enhancement to the man, for he seemed impossible to surprise.

Falls backed off, and Ensharia closed to support him, but there was no stopping what came next. The magus's barriers were smashed apart, his body caught almost directly by a vicious punch, and even from feet back, Ensharia could hear the sound of his ribs breaking clear as day.

Silenos's cannon blew a visceral hole in the swarm of enemies closing in and allowed him to lunge through it to escape their ranks. By the clear lack of anticipation, they'd not heard about his weapon. That told him that they hadn't had any further surveillance in Magira to gather word of his battle with Walriq, and that they'd not been informed by either of his companions. It was not, however, particularly useful in the moment.

He resisted the urge to scan the surrounding area for the necromancer, knowing he'd not catch sight of her until he was near to death. Wielders of death magic were less suited for direct combat than even fleshcrafters. It was always better for them to construct others for their fighting.

This one had done a good job of that, for still fifty undead pursued Silenos too quickly to be avoided for long. He managed a single shot more, aimed at one of the stronger but missing and splitting a lesser foe in half, before they closed in.

Axes, polearms, clubs. Dozens of crude weapons came down on him from dozens of shifting directions. Silenos did his best to cover himself, letting his composited plate weather the impacts while he sent a tendril of nervous tissue shooting out, probing around until it found what was left of the mangled corpse he'd made moments earlier. Then he extended his magic to it.

Despite their superhuman strength and heavy weaponry, these enemies were not so deadly as to quickly hurt him. Only the mightiest of them could even scratch his newly armored body, which meant Silenos could afford to work slowly and carefully.

Within reason. The necromancer herself could use shadestuff; no doubt she'd do so if he remained unalert and stationary. Even in an amateur's hands, nothing but his war form could withstand such destructive magic for long.

He drew the mass in, converted it to his nitrous blend quickly. Undead were animated by magic, but that magic required certain anchors, most typically internal organs. Silenos had heard of a people to the northeast of House Shaiagrazni's land who removed the organs before reanimation, storing them in enchanted pots and thus creating a servitor that could not be killed with mere injury. These enemies were not made with such measures.

Sixty kilograms of biological matter was more than enough for him to produce an explosion of his requirements, and Silenos used the excess to form a shield around himself. The blast went off like the largest of any he'd ever seen before, and as he let his keratinous cocoon fall away, Silenos looked around at the results.

Everything within ten meters had been, more or less, completely destroyed. The strongest of the undead might have withstood the blast near the edge of that perimeter, which had barely been sufficient to break stone, but both of them had stood directly beside Silenos when it occurred. In all likelihood, considering the inverse square law, each had been subjected to overpressure in the range of megapascals or more. He saw traces of them scattered about: an arm here, a scrap of armor there, all ruined beyond repair. There was no sight of the weaker ones, but he would have wagered that they were constituents of the reddish-gray mist swirling around the area on rapid currents of disturbed wind.

Silenos took a step, finding himself weary. He was in the center of a crater, easily four or five meters at its deepest, his cocoon clearly having been driven directly downward. The incline was not easy to traverse with his sudden fatigue.

Forty kilograms of nitrous explosives were, apparently, approaching his limit. The chemical formula was complex, and Silenos had been rushed in assembling it. He wasn't at the end of his mana, not even close, but if forced to do that more than once, it would be a risk he'd have to consider. Reaching the crater's edge, he glanced around again to find that every building within dozens of meters was no more, primitive mud and wooden construction surrendering easily to his glorious power.

It was this fact that made it so easy for Silenos to sight the necromancer.

"How old are you?" he called out, not truly expecting an answer, but receiving one.

"In my twenties," the woman replied. He examined her. She certainly looked that old, but that hardly proved much. It was uncommon for those of House

Shaiagrazni not to perpetuate their own youth well into their centuries. Her black skin made it difficult to make out the slight gradations that might come from natural ageing, but her green eyes and sharp features were aligned into the sort of conceited grin that was rather rare among those accustomed with adulthood.

Twenty, fascinating.

"Your talent is impressive," Silenos told her. "I've only encountered ten, perhaps a dozen, who are its equal. One of which is me. How would you care to be taken on as my apprentice?"

A stab caught his guts, and he buried it. Apparently the memories of Adonis still stung, whatever had happened since.

What stung more, somehow, was the look of derision plastering itself across the necromancer's face.

"I don't need the tutorship of a petty conjurer." She snorted. "I was trained by the Dark Lord himself. Your powers are nothing to his."

His eye twitched, something Silenos was beginning to learn tended to happen when his regrown emotions were pricked.

"And what basis do you have for that? If you'd prefer a demonstration, I can give you one with just a few moments and a corpse."

The woman smiled, more smug than amused.

"I think not. You've already fallen right where I wanted you."

Silenos heard the scraping of metal against stone and risked a glance to one side. He saw more undead, of course. Larger, better armored, shambling toward him with a near-human dexterity and glowing with more magic than any of the ones he'd just bested.

"Knights," he noted, recalling what he'd read of the new world's martial elite. And the great battle just one month in the past.

"Quick, aren't you," the necromancer noted. "Yes, knights. No battle of that scale can have all its corpses found and cremated, when you're dealing with armies in the hundreds of thousands . . . Some will slip through the cracks. Double when both sides were eviscerated so completely."

It would not have been hard to find corpses littered about too far and inconveniently for retrieval, and simply on a statistical level, with tens of thousands dead, no small number would have been elites.

Silenos counted ten knights, no, eleven. Each one humming with more power even than their living counterparts bore. Their armor was crusted with dirt and buckled, looking very much as if it had been pushed through a vicious fight already, and the wearers moved around as if its weight was nothing at all. He had no doubt they would have an easier time harming him.

His options were few. Standing and fighting once more was a losing proposition. No doubt the initial assault had simply been a means of finding out what powers he possessed. Trying to flee entirely was better, but Silenos wasn't certain of his ability to outrun creatures as powerful as these unless he took the time to fleshcraft himself a body better suited for escape.

He could buy time by running, however. And time was a commodity he had precious little of. Silenos turned and broke out into a sprint while the enemy were still some ten meters away.

It was not so far to the castle, a kilometer or slightly less. Silenos was quite confident his new body could cover such distances in under a minute. He was also confident that the enemy would match or exceed that pace, and they seemed unwilling to even wait until they'd caught him through speed alone. Projectiles began to whip by him quickly and jaggedly, taking chunks out of walls and trees where they missed him.

Arrows, made of solid metal. Silenos wasn't certain what propelled them and was not left to ponder it long before one caught his shoulder. It bounced harmlessly from the composited plates but left him stumbling nonetheless, allowed the gap to shorten between him and the enemy. Made their next shots easier to land.

CHAPTER NINETEEN

Withstanding such impacts forever was a losing proposition, and being downed entirely was death. Silenos did not intend to permit either. He fleshcrafted as he ran, producing venting ports on the sides and back of his body similar to the ones he'd used to stabilize himself during his early cannon experiments. The process took only a few moments, and once finished, he put them to use instantly.

His first detonation of blasting oil sent him fully two meters ahead. The second sent him sidelong, with a third maintaining his momentum. A volley of projectiles missed him entirely, and Silenos made further use of his new trick.

Stride by stride, explosive leap by explosive leap, the castle drew nearer. Silenos was soon hurling himself inside and hurrying through the halls.

Evidently, the place's defenses had been largely expended on trying to kill his companions earlier because there was little resistance, attempted or otherwise, as the undead pursued him through its halls. He followed the path indicated by memory, drawing himself at last to the hall in which he had first encountered the hand and the Godblade. Luck was on his side because the mangled corpses of the guards who'd tried to halt his pursuit remained.

Silenos put them to good use.

Reanimation could be done in many ways, but a caster of his caliber needed only touch and focus. At least for bodies as weak as these. Silenos estimated he had perhaps twenty meters separating him and his enemies still, which did not leave time for dallying. He extended cords of nerve tissue from his hands, impaling each of the scattered corpses as he did, fleshcrafting their bodies back into functionality even as the necromantic energies flooded into them.

Likewise, he split his focus. Searching the abyss for suitable forces with which to imbue them.

It was very, very rare for an undead to be inhabited by their own previous soul, and House Shaiagrazni had learned that some souls were stronger than others. Silenos searched now for those of killers, of saviors, of heroes and pit fighters. He scraped the abyss for congealed warfare and emptied it out into the hollow vessels of the dozen or so carcasses lying at his feet.

By the time Silenos's undead were rising, twitchy and spasmodic, to a stand, the enemy was already upon him. His cannon screamed, blasting a hole the size of a fist through one of the undead and leaving perforated entrails to spill out over its legs. It kept coming, however, and Silenos recognized more would be upon him before he could ready another shot. He fired the blasting oil from his back ports, surprising the enemy with a tackle that left bones breaking against the keratin of his shoulder plates, then aimed again and decapitated the foe before it could recover.

One dead enemy was a start, but he saw his battle was going poorly even with that advantage.

An undead knight was sent stumbling as a fist caught its head, impacting with such force that the knuckles broke and the steel buckled. It replied by cramming its polearm through the enemy's chest, then twisted it free. Another one was being wrestled by two of Silenos's undead at once, skull slowly popped from the socket of its spine by brute strength while it failed to free itself. Elsewhere he saw one of his reanimates deprived of a head in one hammer swing.

Equipment and armor made the difference here. Silenos's side had the numbers, and they certainly had more raw physical prowess, but such things were easily overcome by their being either unarmed or wielding weapons too fragile and shoddy to withstand their users' power.

Silenos was quick to turn his own power into helping. He fired his cannon again, this time aiming for legs and heads, closing in to shoot from the shortest distance possible and maximize his odds of a hit. Where the projectiles found undead flesh, they ruined it. One, two, three enemies disabled in twice as many shots. Even still, the flow of the battle moved against him.

The rotating skull finished its movement with a sharp crack; another enemy knight was paralyzed by a stolen polearm crunching down into the back of its head. Meanwhile, Silenos's dozen servitors were hacked apart. By the end of it all, he stood alone once more, surrounded by five reanimates and a smirking necromancer.

"I overprepared." The woman grinned. "I came here expecting you'd unleash that form you used in the siege, the one that could bite off a belladonnan puppeteer's head and weather the strikes of dullahan. I planned to delay you, at best, and here you are at my mercy." As she spoke, more undead funneled in from behind her, a third trap that would never be sprung simply because Silenos had been too weak to make it necessary. He saw the magic in these ones, recognizing them instantly. Two lichs and three necrotic gladiators, any one of which might have been a test for his dozen reanimates alone. It almost distracted him from following the implication of her words.

So she had been at the siege, and Silenos had doubtless destroyed the undead she'd spent more time on during it. That explained why she'd come to fight him with only the ones crafted from local corpses, caution about losing the remainder of her prepared forces.

"It seems a necromancer is still a necromancer. You should have taken more measures to protect yourself." Her hands raised, shadestuff coiling around them. Silenos felt himself taken by a new emotion.

Impotent, bitter fury.

Ensharia had come to find that the Heroes were not as unstoppable as she'd once believed, and that discovery was, perhaps, responsible for the shock that took her at how easily Kraika the Toxicologist overpowered her.

He was toying with her, she saw. And that alone already conveyed much. Cats did not play with food larger than mice; humans did not amuse themselves in a battle with their lives on the line. That her enemy could afford to take her so lightly, despite his clear experience, demonstrated an insurmountable separation of power between them.

But she was a paladin; fighting against such gaps was what her people did.

Ensharia's mace flew like a falcon and missed like a blind man's swing. Kraika was under it, then he was beside her as she tried to reposition, lashing out with some curiously shaped dagger with an oddly thick blade and a hollow tip to its edge. The blade missed her, and she saw liquid flick out of it, realized in an instant that the weapon was a delivery system for some poison or drug, then felt the air leave her as a heel crunched into her broken breastplate.

Her back hit the wall. She dove aside as Kraika jabbed at her again, then rolled to her feet. Ensharia was swinging, dodging, even screaming after a moment, limbs animated by something bestial and terrified.

Then he clipped her wrist. It wasn't a deep gash, barely a cut, but she felt the toxic fluids enter her in an instant, then her fingers were seizing up. The mace fell from Ensharia's hand, her arm dropped to her side, her knees began to tremble, and drool started leaking from her half-open mouth. She tried to retreat, couldn't. Tried to hit the toxicologist and failed to even lift an arm. She tried to remain standing but found herself drawn inexorably closer to the ground underfoot, body surrendering in spite of the silent protests of will and intellect.

Kraika's brown eyes were like empty pits as they met hers, his face a needle-sharp mask of bemused cruelty and malice. Ensharia could barely even breathe, so deeply was the poison seeping.

"I should've used a weaker blend." The man sighed. "I'd expected to fight two people on Falls's level. A paladin that strong would still be moving."

His words were a sharper and deeper wound than any Ensharia had yet felt today, and they brought tears of frustration to her eyes. She couldn't even lower her gaze, paralyzed as she was. Only watch as the knife slowly moved for her throat.

"Might as well finish things now then and link back up with my master," the man—the undead—breathed, then pressed the knife's edge against her neck.

"Stop."

The voice came out without any strain of a shout to it, but the sheer volume was enough to instantly snap both Ensharia's and Kraika's focus to the source. And it was certainly a source to behold.

At first, she did not recognize King Galukar. He had grown to be an inch or two taller than even Silenos's newly increased height, standing bare-chested and clad below the waist only in sleeping wear. His exposed skin was not wrinkled and withered, however, but rather smooth and glinting, pulled taut by the subdermal press of muscles that now bulged quite unlike any she'd ever seen. His hair spilled down to his shoulders like a black mane, his eyes were narrowed for battle, and his face was every bit as strong and handsome as the noble knights from a story she might have heard in her childhood.

In the king's right hand, he held the Godblade. Ensharia took a moment to recognize it, for the weapon almost looked normal sized. Galukar's fist was the size of a boulder, closed tight about his sword's handle, and the five-foot length of iron erupting from its guard was hardly unusual compared to the proportions of his form. He moved forward, twisting his wrist, bringing the weapon around as if it weighed nothing at all. Ensharia had an instant to marvel at the strength involved before his first swing came.

Easier to see a crossbow bolt in flight than to catch the movement of his weapon in the air, and easier to halt the crumbling of a cliff face than withstand it. Kraika did the only thing he could have, leaping back from the swing.

It was a near miss, even still, and Ensharia saw the toxicologist desperately drawing a new vial to toss at his enemy. Galukar sidestepped it, bringing the Godblade around in an arc so wide it threatened to intersect with the ceiling. Ensharia almost warned him of it, certain she was about to see the man's blow interrupted and body caught in the resultant opening. Instead, the cold iron cleaved right through the stone above it like a normal blade carving through thickets. It was barely even slowed as it came down on Kraika, this time catching the man's outer calf as he threw himself from it.

Ensharia had seen glancing blows from sword swings before, but the Godblade was no normal sword. Through sheer weight and breadth it tore a jagged gash down Kraika's leg and left the ugly wound weeping a putrid reddish-black blood in a long trail as he scrambled farther back. The display seemed only to draw Galukar in faster.

Acids spilled out of some strange ventilator on Kraika's person, forming a deadly mist that the Godblade dispersed with a single wind-shearing sweep, then Galukar was marching back after him. This, Ensharia realized, was the battle of a warrior and an alchemist in close quarters. No sort of true battle at all.

Obviously Kraika realized it too because his scrambles for escape only grew more frantic. He seemed to hurl every little thing on his person as he backed away, until the hallway was alight with chemical reactions and his feet were fast and blurry under him.

Galukar pursued, like a hunting hound after a rabbit. His musculature moved in great rippling waves with every step, hair whipping behind him as his pace accelerated, and the two had disappeared around a corner almost before she knew what was happening.

Silenos readied himself for the finishing blow, a mass of shadestuff that, imperfectly conjured though it was, would likely have eaten through an iron door. He was tense, coiled, ready to leap aside even while knowing that he'd be bowled over and held by the woman's servitors to ensure her attacks hit. Curious. Would he have given up had his emotions still been absent? He couldn't know.

And he didn't find out what his last moments with them would be like either because before the attack could come, he heard the sound of thunderous footsteps on the stone behind him. The genuine surprise upon the necromancer's face was near impossible to fake, and so he turned to follow her gaze at the risk of an attack from behind.

An undead was sprinting toward them, though new. By the flawlessness of its body and the ease of its movements, Silenos could tell it had been reanimated almost at the exact moment of its death. The thing chasing it, however, was closing in, nonetheless.

Galukar was recognizable only by the Godblade clutched in one ludicrously sized hand, and Silenos's own preternatural reactions scarcely gave him a moment's warning before the chase was upon him.

Everything happened with remarkable speed after that. The newly arrived undead rushed past him, while the necromancer abandoned her attack on him and chose instead to tear her way through a wall before slipping through it. Her servitors followed suit as one, but despite the exit being barely large enough for a normal man, Galukar wasn't impeded by it at all.

"Wait," Silenos called out jaggedly. The giant paused for only an instant. "I'll accompany you."

Before Galukar could reply, footsteps rang out along the hall for a second time. Silenos looked over to see Ensharia hurrying over.

"Falls," she gasped, seeming to wrestle herself for every word. "He's . . . injured. Silenos, you need to help him."

They needed to take care of this enemy now, before she could beat them to the fourth Hero. Each one she found first would be another powerful enemy alongside her, and one less ally on their own side. Silenos found his decision quickly.

"Lead me to him," he ordered, and the paladin sprinted off to do just that.

CHAPTER TWENTY

She had understated things, Silenos found. Falls was dying, and yet the particulars of his demise were grizzly even measured against the deaths Silenos himself had seen over the years.

He was no stranger to the breaking down of human tissues. Most of his knowledge had, after all, come from human experimentation. It was uncommon for a Shaiagrazni fleshcrafter *not* to hone their skills by testing enhancements or toxins upon the bodies of prisoners before risking their own well-being. Still, the fate befalling his companion now was transcendently gruesome.

Ribs were broken all down his left side, fractures severe enough that shards of bone made themselves visible where they protruded through the meat. There was little bleeding visible on the outside, but Silenos had long since mastered enough of human anatomy to know that the man's ichor would be spilling and clogging tissues beneath his skin. And that was the least of his concerns.

The boy's veins were turning black as whatever esoteric toxins he'd been stupid enough to let inside him did their work, already emulsified throughout his blood and acting quickly to assassinate cells wherever it was carried. There was no time to stop the spread. Blood could circulate a human body in only twenty seconds and had doubtless carried the venom to every inch of Falls's already. Silenos had to counteract the substance itself, or his companion would die.

"I . . ." Silenos glanced up, surprised to see Falls's lips moving slightly, his eyes staring unfocused out into nothing, his throat convulsing with the effort of turning breath into words. "I . . . don't . . . want to die . . ."

A tear rolled down the boy's cheek, fearful, disbelieving. Silenos was reminded by that single milli-scale volume of bodily fluid how young the magus was, how raw the world must have felt to him. Had he ever been inexperienced enough for fear of death to hit him as such a primal force? Silenos could hardly remember.

"You won't," Ensharia whispered, reaching out to take the magus's hand without a moment's hesitation. Silenos appreciated that; it distracted the writhing slab of meat attached to it from moving around in response to his ministrations and made what would come next easier.

The first thing Silenos did was fray the delicate nerves responsible for carrying sensations of pain through Falls's body. Those would be his biggest obstacle, and he'd not get another chance to remove them other than the momentary distraction Ensharia was providing. His subject spasmed in responsive agony to the pain of having so much destroyed so quickly, but that pain was the last he would feel.

Instantly, Silenos felt an unexpected resistance, and it took his arcane sight to realize why. The toxins in Falls's body defied identification, but more than that, they defied even the blind organic deconstruction that all fleshcrafters could apply to living tissue even ignorant of its nature.

There was a potent magic interwoven within them, intensifying their effects and keeping them from being opposed by external powers. Silenos had seen such things used before, usually by necromancers, sometimes by other fleshcrafters. He'd yet to encounter it in the new world.

A smile threatened to form across his face. He did so like a challenge, on occasion.

Silenos's mind came for the toxins as a horde of locusts, eager and hungry for the crops growing from Falls's life force. They transfigured before he could devour them, shifting to camouflaged lizards awaiting his probing power to draw it in. He became a bird, razored eyesight picking the enemy out and talons skewering them like kebabs, and then his prey became a den of gargantuan arachnids, snatching his diving hunters in thumb-thick limbs and digesting them to death amid a hail of squawking and disconnected feathers.

Magic was not a thing of pure rationality, however much knowledge could help its application in the real world. Silenos had not practiced the art of such wholly arcane wrestling in an age, and he felt rusty synapses fire off with a new vigor as he sharpened himself even while doing so.

The birds became snakes, crushing the arachnids, which turned likewise into mammals of skin so loose and constitution so hardy that venomous fangs yielded no threat at all. His snakes were felines then, gnashing apart throats, and then they were met by still greater ones. Tigers, muscled and terrible, then, as if to anticipate him, captive-bred ligers of hybrid strength and gigantism.

But Silenos's enemy had betrayed himself in such an escalation, for though this toxin of his was clever, it was as ignorant as all other savages of the new world. There were deadlier things than any beast.

Silenos's will became a virus, submicrobial and voracious as it infested the toxin's metaphysical blood and consumed cells from within. He detected a pause as the foreign magic attempted to adjust, too simple to realize that it simply lacked the will and cognition to comprehend a war on such scales as was being conceptualized. Silenos took the chance to bypass it while it still wrestled with his knowledge, splitting his focus to extend their war onto a physical, purely biological front.

In that regard, it was still remarkable. The venom was not a killing thing, not wholly, which was doubtless the only reason Falls's merely human immune system had withstood it for so long. As far as Silenos could tell, it was a neurally targeted construction made to maximize pain and suffering, stepping past mere physical agony, though there was no small portion of that involved, to induce a sort of delusional depression in whomever it affected. He actually took notes as he worked to denature the crudely worked proteins making up its structure, finding himself rather admiring the cruelty involved in its manufacture.

Cruelty was not a substitute for skill, but there was plenty of that too. Just not enough to stave off the intellect of a man trained by House Shaiagrazni.

Once Silenos was certain he'd extricated every scrap of the toxin from Falls, he turned his focus to the damage left in its wake. There had been surprisingly little, another testament to the intent of its creator that he be left to suffer an extended death rather than perish quickly, but Silenos still hastened to fix what little remained. He didn't leave it at that, however. There was an opportunity there.

Humans, as a general rule, disliked having their bodies changed against their will, and Falls had seemed similarly reluctant as most of the new world's residents to have his form be made more efficient by Silenos's hand. Which meant that anything done would have to be subtle.

He focused on genetic alterations rather than physical ones, changing the fundamental blueprints of Falls's body to ensure that it would simply re-create itself over time. Organically woven ceramics to replace bone minerals with substances an order of magnitude stronger, lengthened myelin sheaths along nervous tissues, muscular fibers altered into twisted, compressive shapes with a far greater contractile distance. None of it would be immediately apparent, but over time Falls's cells would be replaced and his body reworked by all the processes that allowed for exercise or excess to produce changes of their own. Silenos added a finishing touch of select proteins added into the fibers of skin and soft tissue.

Given time, his companion would be more durable than any normal human. He could only hope that made him last a shade longer the next time he was stupid enough to fight something in such excess of his own power.

"It's done." Silenos sighed, leaning back and finding himself overcome by a sudden . . . weariness? No, he'd not been focusing for so long, and hardly bored in doing so. Perhaps it was simple irritation. Whatever the emotion, it left him strangely hollowed.

The sensation was curiously mitigated by Ensharia's eyes, practically inflating as she stared at him.

"He'll live?" she asked, hope brimming from her as might sulfurous fumes from the pit of a volcano.

"He'll live," he confirmed. "And won't be so long in recovering either, though there may be some long-term effects. I had to take certain measures to heighten his resistance against the toxin, or else risk him succumbing to it."

A blatant lie, but not one Silenos imagined Ensharia would ever possess the arcane or biological knowledge to recognize.

She nodded, seeming to swallow it easily enough, then gently scooped Falls into her arms.

"I should take him to . . . rest. He needs rest, yes?"

"Yes," Silenos confirmed. "Go and find one of the guest rooms, I suppose. If someone challenges you on placing him there, direct them to me."

He'd expended a bit of biomass in the fighting and already made use of forbidden magics obviously enough. Silenos might as well take the opportunity to replenish himself before leaving the castle if it was there.

Once Ensharia was gone, however, he found himself called on. The sheer novelty of such things had worn off rather quickly after his entrance into the new world. Monarchs were prone to the habit after all, but Silenos found himself no less curious at the latest instance. It was, after all, a summons from the famous King Galukar.

The man received him in his throne room, and Silenos had to admit he cut an impressive figure. Great statues adorned the far walls of the room, though did not succeed in fully dwarfing their owner as he seated himself upon a great chair of hewn stone. Beside him was the Godblade, which Silenos now took the chance to properly study with his arcane sight.

As expected, its magic was a force. Not beyond his, not quite, but considerable, nonetheless. He knew of perhaps three Shaiagrazni casters with the skill and power required to make such an artifact, and possibly only one whose work would have retained that much potency for millennia. The king seemed a match for it, and upon closer inspection Silenos saw that, despite his not touching the weapon, no small fraction of its magic was flowing through him, hardening and strengthening his body like piezoelectrics stiffening in answer to a current.

"Caster." The king's booming voice rang out, bouncing from the far walls like cannon fire. Silenos nodded but did not bow. He held his silence, waiting to hear what the king had to say.

Galukar stood up before speaking and began to talk only as he started down the steps leading up to his throne, closing in on Silenos one loping stride after another. Just as he came to within arm's reach, he struck.

Silenos had done fine work on repairing his body after the battle ended, restoring the integrity of its composite exoskeleton. It was for this reason that he felt an indescribable shock run through him at the feeling of those same thick plates cracking apart beneath the king's knuckles. His feet were snatched from the ground, and the wind ran in his ears faster than if he'd ridden a steam locomotive downhill at full throttle.

His body found a stone pillar to impede its flight, and for one moment he actually thought the bone-chilling crack that rang out came from him rather than the inferior architecture he'd impacted.

The floor caught him, and Silenos groaned while his head spun and chunks of rock rained down upon him from the torso-sized dent left in the surface above. The king was standing over him before he could rise.

"You resurrected my men." He spat. "Using your foul magics. Your *necromancy*. The paladin has spoken well of you, and you continue to draw breath on her good word alone, but let me be clear right now when I say that if I ever catch you doing such a thing to my subjects again, I will tear the head from that scrawny neck and crush it like an egg between my hands."

The head in question was alight with thought, conclusions being drawn before King Galukar had even finished speaking, and Silenos considered each one as carefully as he'd spent his decades learning to.

CHAPTER TWENTY-ONE

He was being threatened, which itself told Silenos that the king was preparing to cooperate. One did not give such ultimatums to a man one had no intention of further interacting with. That he'd had a hand raised to him, however, could not be forgiven. Any man fool enough to strike a Shaiagrazni would find the limits of human cruelty extended before him. That had been the case for millennia before Silenos had even been born.

But he did not now live in the lands of House Shaiagrazni, and it was not a normal man who had struck him.

If Silenos fought King Galukar, he would find himself disadvantaged. In close quarters, without his war form, there would be a scarce chance of victory. He could certainly buy time enough to flee and absorb the necessary external biomass to meet his enemy with all his power, and yet even that would cause issues.

Galukar was a proud king, a warrior king, and such kings would only be further enraged if retaliated against. He was considering Silenos a potential ally, and that might be changed if he had his pride crushed before him.

Threats were another option, a simple demonstration of power, and yet that too ran the risk of causing a prick of the ego and an escalation of the conflict. Silenos ran through one option after another, trying to find some way of asserting himself without compromising the alliance he'd come to Abaritan in search of.

He found none.

Silenos swallowed, both the salty blood in his mouth and the bitter fury mounting in his throat. It was an irksome compromise that he had to accept the emotional stabs in order to enjoy the intuitive empathy that had served him so well in his assessment.

"Understood," he replied after a moment but did not look away from the king. "You will be accompanying us as Ensharia asked then?"

Irritation sparked upon Galukar's face. Silenos let himself enjoy it; however disadvantaged he'd found himself by circumstance, he could at least remain certain he'd find little intellectual rivalry in this world.

"I will be accompanying you." Galukar spat, literally spat, though not at Silenos. "My hand was left alive, I noticed. Did you do that on purpose?"

Silenos said nothing, and the king's lip curled.

"Casters, you're all snakes." He sneered. "In any case, he'll be remaining in control of Abaritan in my absence. He's a traitor, and I'm having him whipped as a traitor, but . . . He's the only one besides me and my sons who's established enough in our city to take command without disrupting things. And my people have suffered enough already."

Silenos saw a flicker of half-buried emotion at mention of the king's sons, but there was otherwise no chink in his armor of idiocy besides that. He tucked all the information briskly away into his memory, nodded to show he'd comprehended, then stood.

"Will that be all?" Silenos asked, enjoying the seemingly perpetual fury upon Galukar's face.

"Yes, damn it," the man growled. "It will be all."

Silenos took his leave without another word, finding himself rather eager to be out of the giant, fist-throwing barbarian's presence. He was beginning to grow tired of being ambushed, beginning, almost, to regret his pursuits of magic. Beginning to look forward to the day when he'd have the luxury of preparing his forces the way he had for House Shaiagrazni.

But his pondering was interrupted as he stepped out through the doors and found Ensharia awaiting him beyond them, her eyes on the floor, her arms folded with hidden nerves. Her armor as ruined as it had been when she'd first brought news to him of Falls.

Any other time, Silenos might have expected another lecture from the paladin, but she seemed somehow past such things now. He weighed her in silence, deciding to simply wait for her to speak and see where it took them both.

"I would like you to . . . improve my power," Ensharia said at last, mumbling the words so quietly that even Silenos's augmented ears strained to pick them out. He didn't let his gaze waver.

"And this will not be something you change your mind on later?" he asked, rather eager to avoid the inconvenience of having her commit suicide in a dysphoric frenzy. She nodded, then raised her eyes to his.

Silenos could see a certainty burning behind them, the one that seemed to imbue all other things Ensharia did. He knew there would be no second thoughts on this one's behalf.

"Very well then, but I must attend to something first. Meet me beside Falls's resting chambers."

The matter demanding Silenos's focus was securing a rider, and he was careful to threaten the hand into getting him the fastest one possible. It did not take too long. Necromancers had a way of intimidating the new world's denizens that went beyond any tangible power.

With that seen to, he met Ensharia in their agreed-upon place and found the woman in the room beside Falls's. Her armor had been removed, and much of the clothing beneath that, revealing a body of hardly cleaved musculature covered only by her undergarments. He could tell she was embarrassed at the exposure, which begged a rather important question.

"Why did you remove your apparel?"

She blinked, stared at him, then stared at the wall as her face slowly began to turn red with pooling blood.

"You need to . . . It's like a medical procedure, right? Like a chirurgeon's treatment?"

"No," Silenos told her. "I just need physical contact, and I can observe every facet of your body at once. Would you like to—"

"Turn around," she demanded, standing and reaching for her discarded clothes where they were neatly piled beside her. Silenos did so, waiting patiently for her to finish clothing, then turned back around.

Ensharia looked rather like she'd just found out what sexual intercourse was from her parents, while watching a demonstration. Silenos wished he had less pressing issues and fewer grim moods concerning him. Any other time, he might have enjoyed the emotional distress. Instead, he just started forward.

"Sit," he advised. "This will take some time."

She did not flinch as Silenos's hands came down upon her shoulders, nor as his presence probed the insides of her body for points of improvement. That made things easier. The process of a large-scale, permanent fleshcrafting always started with a proper survey of the body in its original state, for good reason. The human form was a fiendishly complex machine, however inefficient it was, and there were thousands of potential points of failure that an ignorant, hasty, or stupid fleshcrafter might trip upon to ruin their work.

He mapped each one out, making notes of the places in which Ensharia's proportions differed from a conventional human form, then got to work. His first focus was the muscle fibers, and it was here that Silenos found one of his hypotheses confirmed. Though he extended more than enough power to improve Ensharia's body, reshaping the tissue just as he had Falls's, he found the changes coming slowly, awkwardly, and tediously.

The magic that made her stronger, faster, and more durable than would otherwise have been possible clearly had the secondary effect of interfering with efforts to fleshcraft her. Silenos took a moment to acknowledge the issue, then compensated for the resistance by simply flooding Ensharia with mana.

She gasped, quivered in shock, and he felt a stab of annoyance.

"Hold still," Silenos instructed her. He sensed embarrassment in the woman's voice as she replied.

"I'm sorry, but . . . it stings. Like sitting next to a bonfire."

"It's your own fault for having a body that interferes with the application of my genius," Silenos replied calmly. "Now hold still and stop interfering more."

He could sense her annoyance, but it did not go so far as to manifest as further inconvenience. Ensharia slowly stilled as he continued his work.

"The next Hero, tell me about them," Silenos instructed, just as he moved his work onto the woman's nerves. "It seems there is a considerable chance we will be meeting them in combat, and I would like to ensure we do so with prior knowledge of their capabilities."

"Of course," Ensharia answered, seeming to have calmed somewhat as the procedure continued. "His name is Swick the Swift. Or, rather, that's the name he's most commonly known by, at least."

"His powers, capabilities, resources?" Silenos prodded.

"A translocator," Ensharia replied. "I don't know if you know—"

"I do," Silenos noted, finding himself suddenly less confident in their mission. Translocation magic was more than just known to him; it was one of the most infamous and challenging kinds that had ever existed. The power to disappear and reappear elsewhere within an instant had been known to only a handful of House Shaiagrazni over the course of their history.

Ensharia sounded hesitant as she spoke next.

"Are you okay?" the paladin asked, and Silenos found himself redoubling his efforts, irritated. He'd been concerned, thinking back to his last encounter with a translocator, and it irked him to have her notice something was off so quickly.

"It's a difficult magic to contend with" was all he said.

"But a useful one to get on our side," Ensharia noted. Silenos paused, then hummed, acknowledging the point. It concerned him slightly how his emotions were affecting him these days. It was quite unlike him, and very unbecoming of a Shaiagrazni, to spend so long concerned over a potential enemy rather than plotting to seize the potential asset.

That it was worth considering the advantages of Swick's aid did not mean it was worth jeopardizing their mission to obtain it, however. In all likelihood, the necromancer would reach him before they did, given her seemingly superior travel speed.

Silenos moved on to Ensharia's bones, replacing the fragile minerals with the same ceramics he'd sustained Falls with, reworking the marrow to produce antitoxins, then adding a dozen other small advantages that might make the difference between life and death.

"What does he do then? You have told me of this Swick's magic and abilities but not of his profession, allies, skills, or anything else."

She told him shortly. A sky pirate, furthering the recurring trend of new-world names being loathsomely uncreative, and one of some renown. Swick was famously fast, famously cunning, and infamously crooked. Along with his crew. He had all the markings of one who would be more than a little tedious to track down.

Yes, better to pursue the fifth on their list rather than him.

"I am finished," Silenos finally said once he'd completed the delicate process of encasing her brain stem and spinal cord in a somewhat thicker protective bone.

Ensharia pulled away, standing with a thoughtful look as she flexed her fingers and tested her weight.

"I don't feel much different," she noted.

"That is by design," Silenos told her. "I altered your nervous system and motor cortices, essentially adding muscle memory designed for this level of physical potence. Your body has changed in many ways, most slight, some large. It will take time to relearn, but I have given you a head start."

Only a head start. The human brain was too complex for any precise manipulation of motor neurons to be applied. For now. Ensharia still had many hours of practice and adjustment awaiting her.

"I would suggest you find someone substantially more powerful than you used to be if you wish for a sparring partner," Silenos advised. "And, on top of that, make sure you hold back. You are several times your previous strength."

The paladin looked caught between displeasure and excitement, settling for a dutiful, severe nod. If nothing else, she had a healthy respect for power.

"Thank you," she replied, and Silenos dismissed her with a gesture.

"Begone. I have my own work to do."

She quickly made herself scarce and left Silenos with nothing but his own company. Perfect.

His second direct confrontation had exposed yet more weaknesses, and this time Silenos's enemy had escaped being killed. They would almost doubtlessly fight again, and he began preparing his countermeasures with outright relish.

CHAPTER TWENTY-TWO

The first and most apparent of Silenos's shortcomings during the ambush by the necromancer had been a lack of massed killing power. His cannon was a devastating weapon against singular targets, but its rate of fire was too limited to be functional against larger crowds. Even five or ten enemies at a time were beyond its efficiency. He experimented with several hypothesized fixes.

Creating an automatic firing mechanism was beyond him. Silenos could, after some time, intuit the ways in which his own world's Gatling guns functioned of course, but those held particular issues for use with fleshcrafting.

To chamber several rounds at a time, each one propelled by its own portion of blasting oil, Silenos would need to synthesize chemicals and substances with a combination of subsecond speed and millimeter-scale precision. On top of that, he would have to exactly position each newly crafted bullet within a scaled-down Gatling mechanism that had been made small, and thus space sensitive, enough to fit within the meat of his arm. On top of everything else, he would be doing so while accounting for the fact that the barrels and chambers in which he was carefully placing his projectiles and propellants would all be rotating at high speed, which itself would almost certainly be made variable based on the amount of pressure attached to the walls of the rotating mechanism by surrounding muscle.

Other options presented themselves, and most were flawed in different ways. A multibarrel mechanism eventually proved an inferior prospect entirely, as Silenos realized shaping one would force him to spend precious seconds de- and reforming his arm if the need arose for him to switch to larger, anti-individual shots. What he needed was a weapon that could fire both powerful armor-piercing projectiles as well as smaller, more numerous ones for crowd control, with no long delay between them.

It was an archaic idea that finally struck him, but that did not make it a bad one. Silenos shaped the end of his cannon to give it a protruding bell shape, then made minor tweaks to the rest of its structure. The keratinous material he'd made it from yielded better than steel, and so having it spread outward by a few degrees was no great exertion. Silenos was ready to test his new design in under a second.

Sure enough, it worked well. Silenos fired off one shot after another, experimenting with area coverage, velocity, and projectile mass. Soon enough he settled on bullets of a spherical shape, as the barrel's width and dimensions removed the acceleration advantages typically gained from a longer configuration.

Around Silenos, the room was made of steel. It had been Ensharia who had told him of the place, and he'd quickly headed down to find that she'd spoken true when describing a chamber fit to test all but his most destructive magics in.

Dents appeared where organic matter met steel, the metal proving its inferior construction by surrendering easily to Silenos's work. Fissures centimeters long and deep appeared where the finger-wide projectiles struck, sparks flying as kinetic energy bled into the thermal range.

The blunderbuss had been invented for a reason, he supposed. Silenos felt a stab of appreciation for the genius of his ancestors. He had always climbed upon their shoulders to pursue his research, wielding the knowledge of Shaiagrazni ancients both living and dead, and now he'd explored yet another facet of his great inheritance.

All the doubt, the fear, slowly oozed out of him. He'd scarcely even noticed it, but now it was shrinking even from that insubstantial quantity. Silenos had nothing to fear from this world of fools and animals, not when he wielded the knowledge of minds greater than their entire race had yet yielded.

His next challenge was mobility, and that was an issue half solved already. Silenos had proved to himself the benefits of propulsion—proved them enough that he almost regretted not further lightening his new body to make it more effective, in spite of the increased effect his cannon's recoil would thus have—but what he needed was a means of guiding himself. Yet more velocity in his directional launches would hardly hurt.

Blasting oil was an excellent means of eviscerating otherwise sturdy targets, but it was hardly the only explosive he knew, nor the easiest to use for simple locomotion. Silenos experimented with various other formulas tucked away in his memory, dredging up recipes he'd learned so long ago that he cringed at the inferior mnemonic methods utilized in storing them. The one he landed on was another hydrogen compound.

It had a low detonation velocity, which suited him perfectly fine, and was near effortless to produce. A simple blend of hydrogen and oxygen, substances readily supplied by water, let alone the spectrum of atmospheric elements made available to him with every inhalation. More promisingly, he realized its total energy yield was remarkably high.

By compressing the chemicals prior to detonation, Silenos could ensure that as much of their chemical energy was turned to kinetic discharge as possible. The speed at which this energy would be released removed any threat to his body's integrity, and the volatility made even the effort of igniting it a point of cost-reduction.

Soon enough, he was lurching from one end of the hall to the other without even straining his magic, conjuring kilograms of the explosive at once and feeling the wind hit him like a wall as it tossed him around. Silenos made a note to properly test his limits of distance in a more open area and focused on guidance.

That much was easy; nature had long since coined means of gliding once velocity had been obtained. Silenos added crevices to his armored plates from which sheets of protein-woven tissue could protrude, bound to ceramic frames and maximizing both area and lightness to catch the winds. It was far from perfect, but with but a half meter of protrusion and a few dozen potential points for his guiding fins to emerge, he was confident he had rendered himself capable of almost swimming through the air. With practice, of course.

His mind and magic being capable of engineering such a thing did not give his body any inherent mastery over its use. Stronger casters than he had learned that lesson at the cost of broken bones and leaking veins.

Indeed, he had learned such lessons too. Twice he'd contested an enemy he was ill-suited to beat, and on the second occasion, he'd already had one chance to know better. Named of House Shaiagrazni did not make mistakes often, and should he make one he'd already suffered from before, there would be many of his peers calling for his immediate suicide. They would be right to do so.

The hydrogen compound's energy was released largely as heat, which was why it yielded so little kinetic energy outside of gaseous compression that allowed its thermal discharge to be converted into atmospheric motion. That had other uses. Silenos took a while longer experimenting with combinations of carbons and silicon before eventually finding a suitable mix.

Of course there was an issue; carbon was not nearly so abundant in the air as the elements he'd been previously using in his explosives. Silenos took a while to consider searching for some substitute, however unlikely he found the prospect of stumbling upon one. Then paused.

Sometimes, even after fifteen decades of life, he could be an idiot beyond description. Virtually all soils had some measure of carbon within them, even those too infertile and barren for life to possibly blossom. Silenos stepped out of his steel chamber and extended a nervous tendril down through the stone of the floor, stopping only as it embedded itself in the dirt beneath the castle. Within moments, he found himself able to extract more carbon from it than he could possibly need and quickly shaped it into the blend he required.

After a second of thought, he assembled a target for himself too. A block of solid keratinous armor just as tall as a human body and twice as thick. Experimentally he fired his cannon into it, finding the smaller crowd-controlling projectiles bouncing harmlessly from the material, then watching as the larger shot ricocheted violently across the room. By the time its kinetic energy was exhausted, the target had been forced back against the far wall and left with a good handful of cracks. Save for a centimeters-deep crater, however, it remained undamaged.

That was when he unleashed his newest weapon.

It was not so hard to adjust his cannon's internals to its blunderbuss configuration, which already resembled a nozzle more than enough. The hydrogenated propulsion served Silenos's new purposes perfectly, for a supersonic muzzle velocity would only diffuse his new attack more than was effective, and the additional heat served to ignite his carbon blend as it was fired at just the right velocity to both remove itself from his person before releasing the full extent of its deadly flames and travel several dozen meters before gravity and air resistance forced it to a stop.

He watched as his newly made flamethrower engulfed the statue with adhesive, viscous fuel. The substance clung to it like tar might and burned so brightly he knew his eyes would sting to behold the flames were they not long since polarized against such photonic excess. In mere moments, the target started to crack as it absorbed thermal energy.

Sometimes Silenos pondered the idea of life: where it began, at what place the line in the sand was drawn for his magic to determine something as being either within or beyond the confines of its powers. The incendiary devastation he now bore witness to was not one to beg that question. Its construction was purely inorganic, and thus not something his powers could simply devise directly. Fortunately, indirection was something any good caster became well acquainted with.

He had worked various bodily cavities within him into glands and organoids capable of forcing the kinds of conditions needed to synthesize his new compound naturally, and the raw materials they required, largely glucose, were things his fleshcrafting was more than able to provide. It was not as fast as if he made it directly, and thus his new weapon was far from as functionally limitless in ammunition capacity as his cannon, but it was, at the very least, a new *kind* of attack. Such things were worth developing. One never knew when an enemy might be unexpectedly resistant to any single one.

Before him, the keratin statue cracked further, quivered, then collapsed. Bathed in flames just shy of melting iron, the material could hardly have been expected to last much longer. Silenos was almost tempted to take the time to conjure some of the kinds he used in his personal armor but decided against it. Blends as perfect as that took time and energy to make, and he'd long since verified his own defenses would stave off iron-melting heat without failure.

It was good enough, for now, to know that he could reduce men in plate to mere puddles. That its cohesive properties would let it cling to anything it struck, and that even water would be unable to extinguish it short of completely submerging the stuff and denying it breath. With luck, he'd soon find something deadly enough to expose further shortcomings in the weapon.

House Shaiagrazni valued innovation and progress above all other things, after all.

Silenos was interrupted as he left the hall by a face that he likely should have expected. Arion Falls, looking much like a man who'd recently spent several hours in a coma.

"May I speak with you?" the boy asked. Silenos considered it well, weighing the infuriating experience of speaking with the primitive against the minuscule chance of missing something worthwhile by not doing so.

"You may." He nodded.

Falls was not slow in speaking, thankfully.

"I heard you healed me," he volunteered.

"I did. You are valuable to our mission."

Falls nodded, weighed his answer, looked for a moment like he'd say more, then just nodded again and turned. Silenos did not call him back as he left.

CHAPTER TWENTY-THREE

It was a cool morning when they set off, rather than a cold night. The delay came from the newly acquired King Galukar and his tedious aversion to all things fleshcrafting.

Silenos had spent the night resting in his room, as had they all. Given, however, that he had long since transcended the mortal requirement of actually sleeping, his own methods of rest were rather more productive.

His flying machine was a primitive thing, and not truly his own design, but there were already several areas in which it could be improved without its complexity becoming impractical. Silenos saw to these quickly. More secure harnesses to hold its riders, a propeller powered by a ring of coordinated muscular convulsions built at its back, wide wings to stabilize it for slightly sharper turns. By the time he was finished, Silenos was not entirely convinced the vehicle would not be outrunning any living land creature.

That it was the fastest transportation that existed in Abaritan was no reason for Galukar to accept it readily, however, and it was only after over an hour of cajoling that the king agreed to travel by the "filthy" magic. Which more or less sealed their choice on bypassing the fourth hero entirely. Silenos wasn't certain how the necromancer was traveling, but he could think of a hundred ways someone of her abilities could cross the continent with otherwise impossible speed. Which meant she could probably think of at least three.

"If we're skipping the thief, then Oltick will be our next goal," Galukar noted confidently. "A real warrior, him. Probably better to prioritize his help over some damned sky raider's anyway."

Silenos was not entirely certain the man had buried whatever trauma kept him from wielding his sword at first, and it was replies like that that kept him guessing. They seemed, to him, an unnatural answer born from the desire for a veneer of strength rather than its true presence. He resigned to watch the warlord carefully as they traveled.

Wind currents posed an interesting factor in their journey, and Silenos found himself modifying the vehicle as they flew to avoid being thrown off course. Falls, now risen and recovered from his injuries, once again provided the magical propulsion to their journey, yielding a far greater speed now that the vehicle had been constructed to more efficiently catch his conjured winds. They made great progress in crossing the landscape, arriving to descend upon their new destination within only a few days.

They came down together a good horizon away from their destination, all aware that riding in on a fleshcrafted construct was a poor way to start negotiations with a man known for chivalrous piety.

Around them the land was rather rockier than when they'd set off, full of boulders, cliff faces, sheets of gravel or slate. It seemed one could not walk a dozen meters without coming onto another stone protrusion, none of which seemed entirely natural.

"Never seen Helgra's Grasp?" Galukar asked, apparently taking note of Silenos's interest.

"I am a magic caster from another world, dragged between the fabric separating dimensions through the use of magic so mighty and potent that men with twice your intelligence and ten times your mental sturdiness have gone mad attempting to comprehend but a single fraction of it," Silenos replied. "No, I have not seen the part of your countryside with slightly interesting rock formations."

The king looked somewhat put out at that, eyes narrowing a shade.

"Well forgive me for assuming the great and mighty magus had some passing knowledge of the place he got himself stuck in." He started walking without another word, leaving Silenos to eye the back of his head and ponder how difficult it would truly be to kill the giant brute when his usefulness finally expired.

Not as easy as might have been hoped. Silenos resolved to have at least a few grotesqueries with him to be completely sure of an effortless victory.

They made good time on their walk, three of them with the superhuman speed made possible by innate magic and fleshcrafted anatomy, Falls by simply assisting himself in the journey with levitating winds. By the time the castle came within sight, conversation had already moved on to its owner.

Neither Silenos nor Galukar was expecting much to come from the meeting with him.

"Sir Oltick was given his position guarding Castle Edmari years ago, and he's kept to it without failure," the king noted with a touch of pride to him. "He's a man of steel and duty, not one to turn away from a task. Not even for a quest as important as ours. Arbite born, you know. As anyone could tell by his valor and chivalry."

Silenos had gathered that it was surprisingly common for those of magic to be exchanged between nations of the new world, even outside of the magi who so often served kings as scholars and creators. Arbite in particular was famous for its exports of trained, magically gifted knights, gaining wealth and prestige by having them claim patches of land in neighboring kingdoms to defend them on behalf of the nation with which they were transacting.

"I've heard of Oltick," Ensharia added. "Is it true he bested five hundred orc berserkers single-handedly?"

"It is." Galukar grinned proudly. "I dispatched him to do so myself, actually. It was a few years ago now, maybe . . . God, ten in fact. He'd still been Arbitan at the time and it was at the Battle of Grimskull Cove."

Silenos had read something of that occasion. It had been an attempted invasion from the orcs spurred on by a perceived weakness in nearby human military presence, inspired, of course, by the Dark Lord's warpath elsewhere.

Five hundred men being killed by one was not unheard of in this land. The magic that infused muscle and bone made that much easy to see. It was, however, impressive. Orcs were a great deal larger and stronger than most humans, and mildly magical themselves.

"And you say this man is unflinching in his duty?"

Galukar eyed Silenos as if the very question were somehow an affront to Oltick. "More so than any I've met before."

More so than the hand then, at least. Silenos did not say it out loud. Nor did he voice the rest of his rapidly congealing thoughts.

It was not noble to stick so unerringly to an order, regardless of circumstance. If a Shaiagrazni retainer behaved in such ways, Silenos would have fleshcrafted them into a sentient piece of furniture.

The place called Helgra's Grasp seemed to be grasped ever more as they continued, stony protrusions growing more common with every step closer they drew. Their destination was in sight soon but viewed only through the gaps between natural monoliths and rocky spears.

Ensharia gasped, Falls frowned, Galukar gawped, and Silenos hummed as recognition ran through him. Castle Edmari was not a match for the architecture he'd seen elsewhere in the new world, and he'd have recognized its millennia-spanning age at a glance even without being told of it beforehand.

"This area," he began. "It used to be hotter, drier, yes?"

All eyes turned to him, some confused, others impressed.

"Yes." Falls frowned. "How did you . . . know?"

Silenos studied the castle. It was an angular thing of boxed proportions, several cuboidal structures linked together by walls, all built both into and around a large outcropping of stone. The structure was a bunker as much as it was a construction, the sure sign of a people whose masonry and architecture had not yet advanced enough to transcend the whims of terrain. Those parts of it that were erected entirely of stone built around the hill, he could see, were considerably younger than the rest.

"Because this architecture is very similar to a kind once used by my own people," he explained. "I am not a historian, but all of House Shaiagrazni received some knowledge of the finer points regarding dating and historical engineering. It is not hard to extrapolate a climate from the techniques and priorities apparent in this structure."

Oddly, none of Silenos's company looked any less impressed. Which was entirely appropriate. He'd have expected savages such as them to have less appreciation for inductive reasoning than they did impossible prescience, but a pleasant surprise was no less enjoyable than a pleasant prediction.

"Did your people use similar magic?" Falls asked instantaneously. "Castle Edmari can fly, but no one knows how it does or how to replicate it in other buildings."

Silenos had heard as much. It was, apparently, part of some international agreement that only one man may guard the castle at any given time, for fear of its secrets being studied, unlocked, and replicated enough to forever enhance the art of war. He examined the structure again, this time looking at the arcane rather than the physical.

He was not beyond surprise—not even Shaiagrazni centuries past his age could claim that much—but after 150 years, he had found true, soul-shaking shock to be a rarity. The moment Silenos took in the magic of Castle Edmari, he found himself treated to the scarce delicacy it had become.

Whatever people had crafted the magic of the place, they'd done so with a knowledge of supernaturalism that far exceeded their mastery over the mundane stone and rocks of their world. Silenos found a bonfire of power billowing skyward before him, great enough that its volume far exceeded that of the castle itself, dense enough that even in spite of the sheer scale he found it clearly visible in his sight.

Silenos made a note to study the place more later on, as every new moment of examination yielded yet another fascination.

"We did not," he said, not even bothering to hide his excitement. This was new, foreign, novel. Yet there was a logic to it. He could clearly see the workings of genius in how magic was inlaid and ordered about the place and knew that it would have been explicable to a mind only half his equal. It was power shaped by science, not instinct. And science was the domain of House Shaiagrazni.

Despite the joy of his new discovery, Silenos soon found himself forced back into the focus of an imminent mission. They reached the gates, allowing themselves inside as Galukar singularly forced the great doors apart, and entered to find an interior kept lit by well-maintained torches but eerily absent of human habitation.

"Oltick was always stationed alone," Galukar observed. "Looks like that hasn't changed. Looks like . . . like nobody else has been here. That's promising."

"Promising appearances are a crucial component to any good trap," Silenos observed, noting that Ensharia was nodding along with him.

"We're dealing with a necromancer," she breathed. "Directly now. And one who overcame"—her eyes flickered to Silenos, but she found no irritation or pricked ego in him—"who overcame the Savior."

It was a fair thing to bring up, true and accurate. An enemy who could defeat him through ambush, and almost do so again on another occasion, was not to be taken lightly.

"We're dealing with a necromancer who'll be heading here quickly if she's not arrived already," Falls noted, his recently off-kilter tone returned to some semblance of normalcy as he applied his mind to the purely logical problem it now faced. "We need to split up."

"Into pairs," Ensharia suggested. "That way we won't be entirely vulnerable if this actually is a trap, and if anything, one group can help free the other should they trip it."

"That is logical," Silenos noted before the ape-man Galukar could add his own input and poison the conversation. "Time is of the essence, as Falls said. Let us move." He started walking as he spoke and had already cleared five paces before the conversation's end had fully settled into those taking part. As he'd hoped, the speed with which he'd moved put a premature end to any continuation.

He resisted the urge to turn even when he heard the footsteps of someone joining him, keeping his eyes forward and holding his silence until he'd turned a corner and was certain that the suggestions had been properly accepted. Then, at last, glanced around to find the face of Arion Falls peering back.

"Something told me you'd be better than Galukar, even in tight conditions like this." The magus shrugged. Silenos turned back away from him.

He was not exactly wrong.

CHAPTER TWENTY-FOUR

The lights did not continue past the first few corridors immediately adjacent to their entrance hall. Silenos considered that an unpromising sign but not a necessarily damning one. He could envision a man that might leave his entrance illuminated but neglect less-used walkways elsewhere in the place, though such a man would by necessity be unlikely to dwell within the dark areas.

"Think the lights are gone because the necromancer beat us here?" Falls asked, proving his wits once again by considering the possibility barely seconds after Silenos.

"It's likely enough to be wary of," he told him. "Keep your magic ready and stick close to me. My body is sturdier than yours by no small degree."

Falls swallowed audibly but seemed to remain calm enough. They took only a few more steps before he spoke again.

"Silenos—"

"Call me Master Silenos, Esteemed Fleshcrafter of House Shaiagrazni, Keeper of the Auburn Flame, Conductor of Arts Most Ancient, and Lord of Hara'lguanta."

Falls swallowed irritably, then nodded.

"Right, apologies. I was asking though whether you think you can teach me necromancy."

Silenos glanced at him.

"How do you destroy water?" he asked.

Falls frowned but was not stupid enough to voice any questions. Obviously Silenos would not ask him something without cause, and Silenos could see the boy struggling to think through why even as he considered an answer to the challenge.

"I don't know," he said at last.

Silenos eyed him.

"You didn't think to boil it? Freeze it?"

"That doesn't destroy it," the magus snapped. "Just changes its form."

"And what of having it absorbed into dirt or sand, creating muddy sludge from it?"

"The water's still there, just trapped in something else. Is this stupid question supposed to prove something—"

Silenos struck Falls hard and watched as he took a step back, eyes wide with alarm.

"Apprentices of House Shaiagrazni do not speak to their masters in such a way," Silenos told him calmly. "You will have earned that right only on the day where you are a being whose strength makes my taking a hand to you too dangerous to be considered."

The magus stared, and an entire ecosystem of emotion flitted through his face. Rage, assassinated by calming pragmatism, giving way to spine-rending uncertainty, eaten by a confliction of panic and hope, turning all the way back into rage. But he was a clever man, and so inevitably, the apex predator proved to be rationality and cognition.

". . . So I'm your apprentice now," he noted, proving his wits and will at once. Thus passing Silenos's second test.

"You are," he informed the boy. "Congratulations, and good luck. Only one has ever survived my tutoring for more than a decade before."

His lip curled. The one in question would spend a thousand years dying for what he'd done after, but not today.

"So what was the question with the water?"

Silenos blinked, dragged back to the frigid waters of the present by Falls's demand. He turned to him, considered striking the magus, then decided against it. He couldn't be bothered.

"It was to see whether you have the instincts necessary for necromantic study. An imprecise test, I will admit, but one with a considerable reliability given how quick it is. It has successfully predicted four of every five failures I've witnessed."

"How?" Falls frowned.

"Life, true life, is like water. It cannot be destroyed, only changed from one form to another. Moved, altered, absorbed, or boiled. But never destroyed. This is the primal truth that makes necromancy possible. The vital spark that animates an undead is no different from that which animates a human or animal. It is merely . . . less precisely placed."

Falls took a moment to think before replying to that. His answer betrayed everything.

"Is it possible to keep from dying, forever?"

He'd been shaken, then, by coming so close to the grave. It was a common enough motivator for those seeking to master necromancy.

"No," Silenos explained. "But it is possible to come close. I have known necromancers who lived for millennia, some for so long that their birth pre-dated any coherent records of history existing at all. My own master was a woman whose mastery began when humanity first learned the smelting of bronze."

"And she never died?" Falls asked hopefully. Silenos hesitated.

"She did," he told the boy. "As I recall, a century ago she choked to death on another woman's bra after removing it with her teeth, but she had long since installed precautions to keep such ends from being permanent."

Falls frowned.

"There's someone powerful enough to order your master to remove another woman's bra?"

"She did it voluntarily, for . . . recreational purposes," Silenos replied, having never quite understood the appeal of sexuality himself. Falls seemed only more confused.

"Wait, so . . . Two women, with no man? Why would they even bother?"

Silenos decided the conversation had outlived its utility.

"It's almost hard to believe," the paladin girl said abruptly. "We have you, the Savior, and now we're in the castle of Sir Oltick himself. Plus the . . . other advantages we've gotten. I . . . I actually think we might manage to win. To defeat the Dark Lord. We might finally be free of his rule."

Galukar eyed her as she spoke, her gaze open, her face glistening with youth and innocence. Had he ever been that naive?

Yes, he must have been. Once. Many years and many sons ago.

They'd come to a dark section of the castle, which left little to guide their path save intuition and the noise of footsteps reverberating from walls ahead. Galukar felt a chill at his spine that he'd felt a thousand or more times before, the sensation of danger. He drank it in, searched for that familiar excitation that had threaded his arms with steel and filled his gut with fire on so many battle-fields prior.

It was nowhere to be found.

"Your Majesty?"

He snapped his head around at once to meet the paladin's gaze and realized he'd been asked a question while his thoughts were elsewhere.

"Apologies, my dear," he replied hastily. "I was listening for danger. Could you repeat that?"

She smiled, that way women always did when they were trying not to blush, and nodded.

"Of course, Your Majesty. I was just noting that you can actually recall a time before the Dark Lord's rule, can't you? What . . . was that like?"

God, had it been so long already? Long enough that grown, fighting women could risk their lives without ever even knowing the sort of world they were bleeding for? Galukar's heart would have broken had it not been sundered beyond recognition already.

"It was not as peaceful as you might be hoping," he told her honestly. "People still raised armies, learned to fight, sent their forces against one another. We still fought over much the same things, for that matter. Our territories were just invaded and stolen by other monarchs rather than some insane necromancer king."

Her face fell a shade, but she pressed on. Paladins were not known for abandoning a cause.

"My order speaks of how we used to patrol the world. We can't do that anymore, not without being singled out and assassinated, but . . . we were peacekeepers once. Protectors of the innocent."

That was a half-truth. Like all good things, the paladins had mostly been enjoyed by those closest to the world's capitals, and thus most weighed down by its wealth. But, on occasion, they would gift some off-the-path settlement with the privilege of true justice. Provided one was particularly theological in sentiments.

"My kingdom used to be a creator of warriors and a proponent of chivalry." Galukar smiled, knowing full well that his words were empty. "Once this is over, I hope to see it in such a state."

In heaven, he would. He could only hope to end up there once he'd died putting the Godblade through the Dark Lord's throat.

"Wait, what's that?"

Galukar paused at the sudden edge to the paladin's voice and turned to see her eyes glinting in the dark. Affixed on something ahead.

"There's scrapes in the stonework," she breathed. "Looks like . . . a struggle."

The Godblade was in his hand instantly, grip tightening. The power was always with him so long as the blade remained close by, but Galukar never felt its sheer intensity quite like when it sat in his palm. Once it had been thrilling, glorious. Now it was just a weight upon his shoulders.

"Stick close by," he advised the girl. "There'll be trouble here."

What kind of fool could lose so much of his family while wielding a power like this?

"I will take the front," Galukar continued. "Can you use healing miracles?"

What kind of coward could hesitate to wield a weapon like this when his people were at stake?

"I can," the Paladin replied. "But not strongly. I was always a better warrior than healer."

What kind of delusion could motivate him to hold sacred a God whose holy relic had failed him once already?

"That should be enough." Galukar nodded, forcing a grin like the ones he used to make. "With you to knit me back together, I'm sure I could defeat the Dark Lord himself."

Even at just the mention of his name, Galukar felt the strength leave his heart.

"A struggle?" Falls asked. His annoyance betrayed his ignorance. The boy clearly was still not used to being only the second-most-knowledgeable caster present.

"I see it in the magic of this place," Silenos replied. "But it is . . . difficult to make out details. Imagine a drop of red dye upon a shirt colored like a rainbow already. This castle's power is interfering with gathering any particulars."

Falls's wind magic was felt as a light pressure in the air, currents obeying him as if his nerves ran through them.

"But you can tell it's not magic inherent to the castle?"

"It is not," Silenos confirmed, readying his cannon. "And it's recent too. A struggle, as I said."

He turned, grabbing Falls and dragging him in his wake, heading sharply down the corridor and moving at a jog rather than a mere walk.

"We must leave," Silenos declared. "If the knight was the victor of whatever fight came here, we would have found the place readied in some way for more. Well lit, barricaded, not simply abandoned." They turned a corner, then another, flying down the halls faster than a sprinting man as he talked. "Instead, we find nothing but—"

Just as they came for the doors through which they'd entered, Silenos saw a great force run through them, closing them hard and letting them shiver as magic churned and writhed to hold them fast.

"You were sloppy, necromancer," came a voice, sourceless and unseen, echoing through the place like wind in an aged house. "You were hasty. So desperate to snatch another Hero that you didn't stop to consider I might think of skipping the fourth as well, that I'd beat you to this one and ready a trap."

Silenos saw Falls stiffen, fractional trembles taking the boy's body as primitive adrenal glands readied him for battle. He did not seem to be freezing or weakening with his trauma, which was a much-needed advantage.

"I hope you enjoy my preparations," the necromancer continued. "It took me ever so long to prepare them."

Silenos readied his magic, stiffened his back, and squared his chin. Despite his best efforts, his grin almost escaped.

He had spent weeks finalizing his own preparations too, and he was more than a little eager to finally see them unleashed on the woman they were made for.

After all, she'd already fallen right into his own trap.

CHAPTER TWENTY-FIVE

Castle Edmari did, in fact, fly. Silenos felt the inertial shift as it lifted itself from the ground, the sudden horizontal weight against him as it accelerated diagonally skyward. His balance threatened to break for just a moment before he adjusted, while Falls just lost his footing entirely and rolled back to hit a wall.

"Stand, idiot," he demanded, shifting his gaze up and down the hall, anticipating an attack.

"Where are the others?!" Falls asked, scrambling to his feet, currents of wind coiling around him with the same restless energy that now animated their controller. "We need to regroup. Splitting up was a mistake."

"Down that way." Silenos nodded, turning to the doors and unleashing his cannon. The rattle of compressed air shot out across the room just as its projectile hit the surface. There was a flash of magic in Silenos's arcane sight, suddenly denser by far than anything else the castle had mustered, and he watched as the supersonic block of ceramic tissue simply rebounded on impact.

He watched the magic diffuse itself once more, spreading out across the rest of the structure the moment its attack ended. A remarkable enchantment, concentrating so much power so instantaneously into whichever site happened to be attacked in the moment. Remarkable, and incredibly inconvenient for him. There would be no escaping it.

Footsteps hit Silenos's ear, rapid and closing fast. He looked up just in time to find a man approaching with all the speed and unerring trajectory of an arrow. The toxicologist, he realized quickly, closing in just as he had some days prior, except now there was no sign of Galukar to help stave him off. Behind the reanimated Hero charged more undead, each one humming with magical presence of the highest order. He responded quickly as they closed.

Silenos let one blast out from his cannon as single shot, watching the toxicologist try to lunge from the path of the projectile and feeling no small amount of satisfaction as it succeeded in gouging a chunk from his shoulder regardless. As the blast forced him to the ground, he transfigured his weapon again.

By the time his body had finished changing itself, the row of undead had drawn in and were separated by only a handful of meters. It was as devastatingly close a range as could have been wished for. A dozen balls of mercury-dense death were spat from Silenos's weapon and bit into the enemy, drilling through armor, rupturing the putrefied meat below. Three fell in the first shot as black blood filled the air in ropes and flecks. He was reloading just as Falls unleashed his own magic.

Wind blasted out like an avalanche, snagging each of the remaining undead, slowing them, almost forcing them entirely to a stop. They kept advancing, strength enough to overcome the resisting pressure, but it bought Silenos time enough for another shot. This one destroyed two.

The toxicologist was up a moment later, flying over the heads of the other undead and tossing something before him. Silenos watched Falls adjust his winds too late as the glass vial broke itself against the ceiling before it could be thrown back, spilling its contents out and letting the stone above them begin to erode and weaken. He leaped back, Falls a moment after him, just as tonnes of rock dropped down to fill out the space between them and the enemy.

Even before the dust had cleared, the toxicologist was scaling the pile of boulders, and more vials were flying. Falls tossed up a wall of air that caught them both, but this time the fluids inside detonated upon their breaking, shock wave throwing the magus off of his feet and leaving Silenos standing alone as the remaining undead charged in. All of them were armed with heavy armor and blades, close quarters fighters without question, and at their proximity there would be little time to force them back.

So Silenos didn't; he merely doused the pile of rubble with his flamethrower and made them all scale a mound of white-hot fire to reach him. By the time the first of them had overcome it, their armor was glowing cherry red with thermal transfer and came apart in an instant as it caught the blast from his cannon. The second and third attacked as one before he could reload, but Silenos had already prepared a lance of nacre similar to the one he'd once used in his combat form. His weapon ran fully through the first of them, propelled by his own lunge as he vented detonating air from his back and shoulders. The second of them sidestepped, paused, then turned to flee. Kraika the Toxicologist, he saw, joined it.

Silenos fired as they moved, but the flames he'd cast before him ruined his aim by exhaling thick smoke out in all directions, and they were gone within a few moments. He turned to Falls, finding the boy trembling but unhurt.

"That was incredible." The magus gasped. Silenos felt a smile.

It was almost disappointing to have won so easily and denied himself the chance to find and remove further flaws in his weaponry.

* * *

Fighting alongside King Galukar was nothing like Ensharia had expected. In the stories, he had been a man without mirror, a peerless warrior. Two Heroes in one, dashing enemies with every swing of his sword, towering over every soldier around him, and proving his prodigious strength with each and every stroke he made.

In reality, it did not feel like fighting alongside a man at all. More like an engine of war.

They'd been attacked by a horde of undead, each one as fast and strong as a dullahan, all clearly made by a necromantic genius. Ensharia would surely have died or lost within moments had she not been gifted a new body by the Savior. As things were, she fought them with a greater ease than ever before.

Her mace took heads off with one or two hits, her body twisting aside from blade strokes. Her armor, destroyed in Abaritan, had long since been replaced by a suit made of the same pseudo-organic plates that Silenos used in his own body's protection. Lighter and stronger at once, turning aside the impacts of dark weaponry even as Ensharia focused on crushing their wielders.

But she was still the weaker, when measured against King Galukar.

Where he moved, things died. Where he stood, blows rebounded from whipping steel. Sparks and viscera trailed after him like an afterimage, and the corridor shook around them each time he broke an enemy down with his strength. Ensharia was so awed by his power that it almost distracted her from her own fight. She'd never seen a man move like him, not as fast, as graceful, and certainly nowhere near as strong. She doubted there was a paladin in the world who even rivaled him.

An undead reared up before him, feet taller than even Galukar and almost as wide. The stone floor rattled where its boots came down, and in one arm it wielded a sword even bigger than the Godblade. That sword came for the king's head like a sling bullet, catching the iron edge of his own weapon and making the air shiver as both blades ground against each other. Ensharia saw strips of steel fall where they made contact, the metal shaved from her enemy's blade by the divine power of her ally's, then Galukar's feet shifted, arms twisted, and in another instant he'd buried the Godblade in the undead's chest.

Light exploded from its eyes, obliterating and solar in its intensity. Ensharia had barely a second to appreciate the sight of God's own wrath channeled through his weapon, then the undead fell as a charred heap, and King Galukar was whirling around to hack the head from another one's shoulders. She fell in to guard his back.

Undead were abominations, less than mere beasts, less than the most vicious of monsters. To see one was to be exposed to an evil so distilled that it left only instantaneous combat to the death as the logical response. And yet, surrounded on all sides by that same taint, Ensharia smiled. She could be of use like this. With muscles forged by House Shaiagrazni and nerves carrying thoughts faster than any regular matter, she could make a difference.

The thought lasted Ensharia as long as it took her to swing her mace twice more. Then a new presence washed over her, pricking instincts like the sensation of hot breath against the back of her neck. She looked ahead to see an undead smaller than most of the others, but unmistakable in its danger.

Sir Oltick was not hard to recognize. He'd been famous for his crystalline plate, which the reanimated monster he'd been reduced to still wore as it stepped forward.

One hand was closed around the handle of a flanged mace, the other about a broad tower shield of solid steel. He—it—moved with the unnatural ease common to all creatures whose strength was great enough that their weight no longer even registered.

He did not say a thing as he approached them—it, damn it, always an it. However many legends and myths were weighing down across the shoulders it had stolen with necromantic evil, that thing was still an it. And it remained silent, but the one responsible for inflicting her magic upon the Hero himself did not.

"I see recognition in you, paladin. A study of Oltick's legends, were you?"

Ensharia did not panic, nor did she let the creeping paranoia reach her. Instead, she merely observed the fact that clearly this necromancer was able to observe and speak to her from somewhere else in the sprawling castle, then tucked it away for later use.

Her focus was well needed because Oltick came on like a lightning bolt.

Silenos wasted no time, but Falls did. Or tried to. The moment their enemy was gone, trauma set in to the magus, freezing him up into useless spasms and locking his feet where they rested.

"We need to try to leave again," he croaked. "Did yo—"

Silenos slapped him harder than he had before, and Falls almost fell to the ground before mastering himself and turning to glare daggers at him.

"Our best chance is regrouping with the others and consolidating our power," he told the boy, already moving in the direction Ensharia and the king would have gone. "Come, unless you'd rather stay by yourself."

Unsurprisingly, Falls turned out to not prefer staying by himself. The two of them made quick progress down the first corridor, then paused as they came to a fork in the path. Silenos frowned.

"The floor is scraped," he observed. "And recently. Scraped right along . . ." Yes, an arc in the ground, the very sort that would have been left by a wall shifting its position. He considered blasting through the offending stone but decided he hadn't the time, nor did he intend to let his presence be so easily triangulated. Silenos followed the new path, eyes peeled.

With luck, he'd be moving down the same pathway that Ensharia and the king had, and without it . . . Silenos had consulted Galukar about the floor plans on their journey. He knew there were only so many places a man might be redirected on the lowest levels of the castle. He had nothing to lose but time.

He could only hope he had enough to spare.

One turn, another. Sharp corners and short corridors. Silenos powered down the hall for close to half a minute before he heard the scraping of movement running down it. A glance over his shoulder revealed more undead, and behind them was the toxicologist. He shifted his arm to the scattershot, murmuring a warning to Falls, then looking ahead just in time to see yet more undead closing in before them.

No, not undead. Armor. Suits of steel plate armor, enchanted with durability, locomotion, animation. He'd been told about them, part of Castle Edmari's defenses, a way of circumventing the agreed-upon rule that only one man could be custodian at a time. They clanked and clattered as they shot for him, faceless and unhesitating, numbering close to a dozen.

Silenos thought quickly, then turned. He blasted himself almost to the ceiling as his cannon shifted form again, took careful aim, and fired. The blast went clean through Kraika the Toxicologist's chest, erupting out through his back in a spray of hot viscera. Silenos landed just in time to begin the fight.

As ever more armor closed in, he found himself certain it was a doomed one.

Oltick's sword met the Godblade, and the knight was sent stumbling before his former king. Galukar closed to press the advantage, swinging low and just barely missing as the castle's custodian sidestepped, then retaliated in kind. The two men fought at a speed even Ensharia's new body couldn't have managed, one wielding more power than perhaps any other Hero alive, the other having his own already exceptional gifts bolstered by the reanimating powers of a necromancer.

Her own fighting was less glorious and far more supportive than Galukar's. Ensharia focused on keeping the rest of their enemies from overwhelming the king, fending them off like rats beaten from a grain store. She struck until her arms grew weary, until her spit tasted of acid, and then she struck some more. Galukar took great chunks out of the knight's armor, letting dark blood seep from the wounds he left beneath steel, but it was Ensharia who let them down. A mace caught her head, and then more swings followed in the moment of her unbalance. She was soon pinned down beneath several undead at once, watching as yet more fell upon Galukar.

Even his preternatural strength was overwhelmed by such a concentration of power, and the last thing Ensharia had the consciousness to perceive was King Galukar being wrestled to the ground alongside her.

CHAPTER TWENTY-SIX

When Silenos awoke, his body was bound in great sheets of steel. Head, neck, shoulders and ribs, all four limbs, as well as every other joint attached to him. It was the sort of restraint that spoke of ridiculous, excessive paranoia. Or a healthy familiarity with the powers of a Shaiagrazni senior.

From his position in the bindings, Silenos's head was just barely angled to let him catch the sight of Falls by straining his eyes to one extreme of their sockets. The magus was pinned against a wall, like him, by bands of metal that did not seem quite so thick but would nonetheless do well enough in holding him.

"He's awake," came a voice. King Galukar's. Silenos heard the anger in it just before it continued. "Great idea, magus, having us all split up like that. Really, we ought to put you in charge of this whole expedition."

"I *am* in charge of this whole expedition," Silenos informed him, despite still being unable to actually catch sight of the man. He tuned out the king's petty arguments to the contrary, focusing instead on seeing what he could glean of the room around him.

It seemed to match the architecture he'd observed in Castle Edmari, save that, unlike the bottom floor, there was a window within his view. Silenos peered through it to find a dark landscape flitting by far below them. The altitude and speed confirmed that he was still in the castle, at least, but the look of the lands below . . .

". . . The Dark Lord's territory," he guessed out loud. "We're there, yes?"

For once, for a single, rare moment, Silenos let a shade of hope build before he was answered. By Ensharia this time.

"We are," she breathed, sounding as defeated as he'd ever heard any human sound at all.

"Correct," he heard a new voice ring out, less familiar than Ensharia's, but not hard to recognize all the same. "All of you are making your way there as we speak, captured and bound, perfectly prepared to be slain and reanimated by the Dark Lord's glorious power!"

It was the necromancer, who now strolled into Silenos's line of sight with . . . Yes, an undead. A belladonnan puppeteer, in fact, dancing with it like the two of them were in the middle of some ballroom floor.

She had changed her apparel since last Silenos saw her in person. No longer did she wear combat-practical attire made to permit swift movement and wide extension; instead her body was covered by some trailing black dress that would not have been out of place on a woman awaiting her wedding. Or Silenos's own master, for that matter.

"Admiring my beauty?" she asked, surprising Silenos by addressing the question to him. The woman spun in a circle as she spoke, grinning from ear to ear, practically giggling as she gesticulated with more joy than he'd seen in a long time. It was rather revolting to behold.

"You remind me of someone" was all he said. "What would it take for you to release us?"

The necromancer laughed, striding toward him with the gait of a predatory cat that had been struck with the urge for expression through dance while it toyed with its prey.

"What makes you think you can offer anything that would interest me? I have everything I want already." She grinned.

Silenos did not find his confidence chipped. That she was answering him at all provided an opening.

"You've fought me twice now, and both times it was with all the preparation and situational advantages on your side. You've seen how quickly I've improved the shortcomings in my armament and combat capability."

That wiped the smile from her face, if only for a moment.

"I'd expected an easy victory," the woman replied stiffly. Silenos took no small degree of satisfaction in that. Oh, he'd lost, and lost without question. Even now, his body stung with the bruises and broken bones lying beneath the skin—injuries that he was fixing even as he spoke. But he'd obliterated numerous suits of enchanted armor and high-grade undead before being felled. His only regret was that the necromancer had sent too little of the latter for him to enter his combat form. That would have put an end to the question of his supremacy.

"You'll have a harder victory every time you fight me again, even assuming this isn't your last," Silenos replied. "And I can augment you to make your own enemies have harder ones still. You noticed the power of our paladin, I assume, compared to last time."

The necromancer's eyes flicked toward Ensharia, just as Galukar's voice rang out.

"What did you do to her, you abomination of a caster?"

Silenos did not even dignify such a drooling question with a response, merely kept his eyes on the necromancer.

"You're considering it," he observed. "Thinking about what you could do with a body capable of matching a seasoned knight and, I imagine, thinking about whether you might also learn the skills needed to create such things yourself."

Her eyes hardened with conviction.

"You overestimate the appeal of your offer, I think," the necromancer replied. "I already serve the greatest caster to ever live. Your petty hedge magic does not interest me in the slightest." She turned, and Silenos felt a stab of haste touch him.

An idea struck him then, and he directed fleshcrafting energies down into his chest, weaving the tissues there into newer constructs. A springy, coiled mass of muscle to twist and extend like a piston, then yet more around to rotate one way and the other like an oscillating drill bit. At the tip he wove the same nacre-like composite used to create his deadliest weapons and let the construct get to work.

It began eroding the steel bit by bit, limited only by range of motion and the need to go unnoticed. As flecks of the binding around Silenos's chest began to fall away, he let nervous tissues catch them, assimilating them into his biomass. Iron for goethite, carbon for keratin.

Fleshcrafting was an art of destruction as much as creation, and the harder its target material, the more resistant to strain and destruction, the longer it took to break down into its constituent elements and absorb for biomass. Solid steel was not dirt, with its components easily extracted and processed. Silenos would have to hurry in his work, even while buying himself more time.

"King Galukar," Silenos called out. "Tell me, how powerful was the Dark Lord, as someone who's fought him in combat directly? A firsthand account seems an appropriate contribution to this discussion."

Silenos felt his confidence grow. A few white lies, the occasional stretched truth or understated fact, and this conversation could be turned 180 degrees to his favor.

"The Dark Lord was the most powerful creature I have ever fought, seen, or heard about," Galukar replied, and Silenos barely managed to keep from letting the choking sounds audibly leave his throat as his own tongue threatened to suffocate him. The necromancer's smile was smug and incandescent but fell as the king continued. "However, his power is not limitless. Had there been two of me, I would have tested him. Three and I would have wounded him. I cannot imagine him withstanding five Heroes of my strength or above."

Stiffening, the necromancer turned on him.

"And how would you fare against him and his armies? If he wanted to, the Dark Lord could concentrate every undead under his command into the same location and render himself unstoppable. But he has grander ambitions."

"And, I would imagine, too little skill to coordinate them in such density," Silenos noted. He'd absorbed close to a full kilogram of carbon already, and fifty times as much iron. Progress, but slow progress.

"Do you recall the grotesquerie—the towering undead—that I conjured to crush the first army attacking Elkatin's capital?" Silenos challenged her. "I imagine your Dark Lord has never produced one as potent as that."

Her eye twitched.

"Because he can't fleshcraft them together like you did."

Clearly, she would not believe Silenos if he told her he could have made a similarly powerful reanimate through other means, so instead he concentrated on the point of what she'd seen him manage.

"It would appear that my knowledge makes my necromancy superior to your master's then," Silenos pressed. "And it could similarly benefit you."

"Enough," the necromancer snapped, her good mood diminished but restoring itself shortly.

"You are my prisoners," she repeated slowly, calming with every word. "Mine. I will present you to the Dark Lord, and I will be rewarded handsomely for handing him such powerful reanimate fodder. Perhaps, even, by being made his wife. This is my victory now, and there's nothing any of you can do to—"

She was interrupted as the skyship crashed into the side of the castle.

Even Silenos hadn't expected that, despite it being he who had sent word ahead to Swick the Swift, using the fastest means of communication available to the hand of Abaritan, that they would require his help. He'd spent no small amount of effort after learning of the flying Castle Edmari to calculate where it might go if it were to be taken and moved toward the Dark Lord's lands, then factored in projected travel times as he sent the predicted trajectory on to the captain ahead of time.

It had been a tedious thing to prepare, but seeing the great mass of enchanted copper and wood that made the vessel's face breach through enchanted stone only vindicated him in having taken the time to do so.

Dust filled the air within an instant, then became a hurricane in an instant more. With the outer wall breached, the castle's extreme velocity was clearly felt as intense currents of wind scraping through the interior. They doubtless left the eyes of all else present wet with tears, but Silenos's had long since been treated to resist such things. He focused, letting airborne particulates into his mouth and lungs, breaking the molecules down to add their constituent carbon to the reserves he was already amassing from the steel bindings. With the sudden volume, he'd increased the power of his drilling and already taken in a hundred kilograms more.

He needed half a tonne more to enter his combat form, and Silenos had it by the time his restraints were completely removed.

Silenos worked the fleshcrafting he'd gone so long without drawing on, feeling an uncharacteristic cry of triumph escape him as his body swelled with power and mass. More than a meter added itself to his height and width as centimeters of composite plating swelled to form along his epidermis. The musculature below was woven so tight and dense that its waste heat would cause tissue damage given too long, and talons and fangs replaced nails and teeth.

While he transformed, the bodily alterations taking long, sluggish seconds to fully complete, Silenos aimed his cannon at Galukar. The king remained in his towering muscular form. Which was good, as the shriveled thing Silenos had first seen sprawled across his bed would surely have died when his cannon's single shot caught the steel bands wrapped around his body.

The bullet smashed against the metal, cleaving hundreds of cubic centimeters to ruined scrap, and before Silenos could even fire again the king had already torn the bound arm free. His fist came down on the strap about his chest, denting it slightly, and Silenos fired on the same spot. This time the band was thicker, but with Galukar's free arm working to widen the gash left by Silenos's weapon, he did not remain trapped for long.

Before the king was free, however, Silenos saw undead descend upon him. He realized their motives instantly. Galukar was easily the greatest threat that still remained bound and was moments from freeing himself. One did not allow that to happen if one had half a brain. The king would be either killed or restrained before he could bring his full strength into the battle, and likely before Silenos was able to fire on his attackers.

It was not Silenos, however, who saved him. A man appeared behind one undead, lancing it through the neck with a knife the size of Silenos's untransformed forearm, then disappearing before the rest could turn their blades on him. The instant he bought was enough for Silenos to remove one of their heads with his cannon, aiming it to ensure the projectile slammed into one of the king's leg restraints after ripping through their body. It came free just as the chest band did, and Galukar was straining his torso and two of four limbs against the remaining bonds without any hesitation.

He ripped himself from the wall just in time to evade the stabbing swords and crushing hammers, rolling back from his enemies, and Silenos took the chance to fire a bundle of nerves far across the room, stabbing them into the body of the slain undead.

That provided the final ingredients needed for his growing combat form to be completed, precious missing elements drawn from the three-meter reanimate and added to Silenos's own body. All that was left was for him to shape them.

While he did, the world erupted into chaos.

CHAPTER TWENTY-SEVEN

Ten seconds into his transformation, and Silenos estimated he had eighteen remaining. He'd gotten faster. That was interesting, and logical. He supposed he'd never practiced fleshcrafting at any great speed before, never felt the need to grow better; there had always been other Shaiagrazni to buy him time or fight in his place. It was promising to know he'd be less reliant on such guards with time. But not immediately helpful.

Seventeen seconds remaining, and Swick the Swift, the translocating man Silenos now realized had freed Galukar, made a second appearance. This time he lunged; the man's knife came down with a furious haste upon the shackles holding Arion. Those, Silenos saw, were by far the frailest, focusing on simply immobilizing the magus's arms and fingers. Without those, he could not focus his magic, and thus cast. It didn't take long for the metal to be eroded by the newcomer, and he was leaping from the wall amid a wall of thrown air, scattering several nearby undead that had not yet turned to brace themselves.

Twelve seconds, and Swick the Swift had disappeared again. Galukar was backing away from a trio of towering undead, fending off weapons with his bare hands, wincing as trickles of blood wept from every finger-deep cut left in his meaty arms by scraping blades or rebounding maces.

The king had impressed Silenos, in regard to strength alone, but even his might was not inexhaustible, and without a weapon there was little he could do against three enemies of such caliber simultaneously. His fist caught one, tossing it back with a dented helm even as the remaining two marked his body yet again, and Silenos's eyes were snatched to Falls by his latest idiot apprentice's scream.

He was running, the imbecile, toward Ensharia. She was of course the last of them to remain bound, and her restraints looked perhaps as thick as King Galukar's. Even with three limbs free, Silenos was unsure she'd break them. Falls had come within a few meters of her when he caught the sight of necromantic magic build-ing from the corner of his eye.

It was the necromancer, of course, and her power was flowing from where she hid behind a pair of enormous six-limbed reanimates clad in black plate armor. The distilled darkness of shadestuff congealed between her palms for just a moment before she cast it after the magus.

Falls was still running, his hands held together and gathering magic in a way Silenos knew must have spurred on the enemy's attention. He turned just as he came to stand before Ensharia, revealing his face to Silenos a moment before the shadestuff impacted.

He had expected to see terror, panic, fear. Instead he saw only victory. Arion Falls projected his wall of air out at a sloped angle before himself, letting the shadestuff impact, then splash just as Silenos's had when he'd cast it at Walriq. This time the substance was deflected into Ensharia's binds, at least one globule hitting each band of steel and melting them through like piranha solution being doused over meat.

Nine seconds, and Ensharia's bonds were breaking as Falls redirected the Mach 0.1 winds from the breached wall into cleaving blades bouncing jaggedly from what was left of the metal. She dropped down, landed hard on her feet, then turned as the necromancer's bodyguards joined the fight. Their master was leaving, and Silenos missed his hasty attempt to destroy her with his cannon before she could turn around a corner. The room was nothing but undead and allies, at that.

Eight seconds. Ensharia had seized a piece of steel from her destroyed bonds, perhaps five centimeters wide, three thick, and thirty or so long. It was not jagged enough to be a knife, but the sheer weight made it a serviceable bludgeon as she swung at the enemy, backing off from them while Falls provided aid with his winds. Jets of air knocked them from their feet, blocking swings, occasionally channeled from the breach to add power and speed to his magic. It was clear, regardless, that their fight was a losing one.

Six seconds, and Silenos expanded his arcane sight to search the castle, des-perately peering past its ambient magic for any sign of that inexhaustible power he'd seen in Galukar's hands. The Godblade made itself known quickly. Their weapons, of course, had been confiscated upon their capture, but if Silenos's guess was correct, the "divine" weapon that gave King Galukar his strength was likely stored along with the others. He called out its location, just before his throat fin-ished reconfiguring past the point of speech.

Three seconds, and Silenos saw the others reacting to his words, turning. Falls managed one step toward the door that led to their weaponry, Ensharia four, Galukar five. There was no sign of the captain, Swick the Swift, until an undead looked to be in line to intercept Ensharia. Then he dropped beside it, knifing the thing just as unexpectedly as any others and disappearing before it could retaliate.

One second. Silenos had to fight the urge to move now, knowing his body's reforming state would be delayed and prolonged if he exerted any great force upon it prior to its finishing.

Ensharia was at the door first, Falls second, Galukar third a moment later. The three of them disappeared down the hall pursued by one undead after another. But only four managed to actually follow; the fifth was slammed against the wall as Silenos's combat form finally reached completion and he lunged forward like a striking viper.

Almost ten thousand kilograms of keratin and muscle pinned it in place, crushing metal plates inward and bursting the undead's body like a grape between molars. Then Silenos spun, his whip twisting around to take the head off of another as it hurried to strike from behind. While the weapon reared back, he raised his cannon, letting its bell-shaped multishot exit in a spray that eviscerated two more undead. From the corner of his eye he saw animated armor spilling into the room, suits charging him by the dozen.

Good, he thought. All the more enemies to finally vent his true power against.

Leading the suits of armor was a figure that practically glowed with magic, most of which was not necromantic in nature. The reanimated Sir Oltick, he imagined, moving in with a two-handed sword that came for Silenos like a guillotine blade. He didn't even bother blocking, just let the metal bite into his shoulder.

Back in the lands of House Shaiagrazni, Silenos's war form would come into battle equipped in armor made by other named more specialized in metallurgy and crafting. Alloys able to weather the screaming heat of a star's surface or mountain-cracking detonations. He could not make them himself, but in their absence, Silenos's combat form would be charging into battle naked. He had put the six thousand additional kilograms of mass suddenly freed up by that to good use.

Eleven centimeters of keratin composites caught the sword, leaving its edge stuck fast. Silenos dragged himself to one side, forcing the undead to twist and turn as his weapon was dragged along behind him, then suddenly reversing his motion. The nacre lance engulfing Silenos's right arm ate the metal around Sir Oltick's right side, barely missing the reanimates' innards as it dodged back with all the speed of a whip. Suits of armor closed in around them as the undead knight retreated. Silenos had no time to be dealing with them, and certainly not pinned down. He crouched and jumped, firing jets of explosive gel beneath him as he did and managing to propel himself almost to the five-meter ceiling. When he landed, it was like an artillery impact.

Steel was not a match for the kinds of forces his reunion with the ground induced, and Silenos saw several of the animated suits actually topple over around it. Balance broken as the ground shook. The knight was back, however, and well-timed in his return. Leaping over his shoulders, grabbing the handle of his sword and wrenching it free in one swing. He dragged its edge across Silenos's back armor thrice before even landing, then lunged back out of range before Silenos could turn again.

More undead came in to replace him, cudgeling and striking in a frenzy.

He ignored the impacts, less than pinpricks against his armor. Easier to breach the hull of an ironclad warship than Silenos's combat form, easier to kill its crew than wound the mind beneath. Everywhere Silenos swung, another enemy was disabled. His cannon belching storms of bony projectiles to rip apart bodies and detach limbs, killing a half dozen enemies with every other second. Whip, lance, sheer muscularity all proving weapons deadlier than any other present.

And then the bolt of lightning struck him.

Silenos stumbled, mass somehow sent off-kilter by the sheer exothermic impact of electricity bleeding into heat and pressure against his shoulder. He did not feel pain, but his fleshcrafting senses had been deeply infused through every cell of his body, and he was well aware that centimeters of his armor had been charred and sheared from the point of contact.

Lightning was a deadly thing. Unlikely to kill in nature, largely for the fact that most who were struck by it did not catch the main, inch-wide fork of plasma that composed the stuff's body. When something did, the results were spectacular. Burning keratin filled Silenos's nostrils, and he sensed the proteins denaturing around where he'd been struck. Heat in the order of twenty thousand kelvins was bad enough; the fact that megapascals of pressure were induced immediately around it as air was forcibly displaced only worsened things.

Righting himself, Silenos exerted his will and forced muddling thoughts into a state of coherence. The knight, Oltick, was charging again, and Silenos considered his other enemies. The belladonnan puppeteer he'd seen dancing with the necromancer was clearly the one responsible for the lightning; no caster short of that could conjure such a potent bolt, which meant that he likely had a good few moments before being struck again.

A morning star caught the plate he'd felt struck by lightning, and Silenos spun to snatch the wielder's unlife. It was out of reach by the time he did, then a sting caught him. Sharp, intense, not the mere cerebral alert of damaged armor; his actual body had been wounded. Silenos found the knight's enchanted blade lodged between sheets of keratin about his leg, and once more Oltick was back before he could crush him. Silenos waited for the knight to retreat farther, then unloaded his cannon. It missed but took a satisfying chunk of metal and meat from one shoulder.

Then the second blast of lightning came. It was aimed perfectly, and timed even better, striking the exact same place as the first. Silenos felt the armor burned and crushed until it was so thin that he felt the heat upon his skin beneath it. More undead, more armor, and the knight. They struck from all sides, and more than one caught the new vulnerability in his body. He killed and killed, then killed some more. Conjuring shadestuff to melt apart several at a time, dousing more with flames and watching as they fell apart under their own high-speed movements, even simply bifurcating one when it avoided his swing by one moment too little.

Silenos fought so violently that it fully slipped his mind he was merely buying time.

King Galukar let his presence be known by taking off Sir Oltick's arm from behind, Godblade cutting so forcefully that sheer strength compensated for the bluntness of its edge. Before the limb had even hit the ground, its owner was kicked and launched high overhead to clatter down at the far side of the room. Before he could rise, Swick the Swift was dropping down once more upon him, knife thrust through his eye slit and making short work of the enfeebled enemy before he blinked out of sight again.

A gust of wind was thrown from the outside, knocking several more suits of armor down, just as Ensharia fell upon an undead and staved its knee in with her mace. Silenos took the opportunity to conjure another wall of shadestuff and let it drop down over several more, watching them disappear beneath the abyssal touch.

Within moments, the room had been deprived of most that formerly inhabited it, and those that remained did not look like they would for long. Silenos took one step toward the puppeteer, readying his whip to strike the head from its shoulders, and then Castle Edmari tilted.

He had moments to realize what was happening.

He studied the surroundings, recognized the ambient magic thinning as it drained away, and concluded that their flight had turned into a fall. Silenos thought back to their altitude, did the necessary calculations, and hurriedly transformed his throat even as he unraveled his armor into a sheath of fiber.

"Oo mah!" he roared, words garbled by the abominable hybrid his half-transformed vocal cords had become. Fortunately, their message proved coherent enough for his allies to close in on him just before the sphere of tissue could close. Silenos hurled them to the breach, almost jumping as the sky pirate ran into the folds of his exit strategy, then the last point of it was sealed up.

With a sphere spanning several meters filled with air, he could only hope drag force would slow their impact enough for all present to land after the castle.

If they were caught beneath the million-tonne ruin as it struck the earth, there would be no surviving.

CHAPTER TWENTY-EIGHT

Venka had been hesitant to believe rumors of an asteroid impact, let alone investigate. It had been his casters who had convinced him, sensing a scent of magic upon the wind that, so they claimed, was greater even than that of the Dark Lord's own power. Such a claim demanded investigation, verification, and if appropriate, punishment. It was this that motivated him to lead his war band several miles off course until they came upon the wreckage.

"General, would you like us search the runes?"

It had been Chtun who spoke, one of Venka's officers. He turned to the orc, finding a stab of irritation at the near-monosyllabic grunting escaping the colonel. Venka considered sarcasm for a moment but knew better. Orcs were dull creatures, closer in cognitive prowess to mere apes than they were to humans. Sarcasm had a way of confusing the poor beasts.

"I would, yes," Venka replied. "Sweep the perimeter first though. Send in a . . . Hmm, send a company of heavy infantry first. Surround the ruins; make sure nothing gets out."

Chtun nodded, turning and shambling back to the rest of his savage kind without another word. Venka watched him go. Orcs were a disturbing sight, even after long years of proximity to them. Though they were no taller than the average man at first glance, Venka had long since discovered their heights were actually a good half foot or more above what they first appeared as due to the species' apparently inexorable urge toward slouching. No doubt a product of their natural predisposition toward ill manners and savagery.

Their bulk was beyond human, and most of it was muscle and bone. Behind their low brow and sloped forehead, the orc's underdeveloped brain controlled a frame of four hundred pounds, close to three hundred of which was muscle. More than a slight amount magical, this robust body could typically raise double its weight fully overhead using shoulder strength alone. And that was only to speak of the average specimens.

The orcs under Venka's command, however, were nonetheless a well-trained group. Led by individuals among their kind that could at least *remember* more complex orders and serving under a human general. He watched them shift around the ruin, thousands of thirty-stone behemoths organized so tightly, they almost behaved as humans.

It did not take long before the survey was complete and Venka himself, finally, safe to close in and examine the site personally. It was an illuminating study.

As it was, flattened against the ground and obliterated into scraps of broken stone scarcely bigger than a man, it was no wonder Venka had not immediately recognized the legendary Castle Edmari where it lay cratered and diffused across the landscape. Once he did though, it recontextualized everything.

Venka had never actually seen the ruin, of course, but he'd made a study of it. All good generals had, and most of the mediocre ones too for that matter. The prospect of a flying fortress large enough to hold thousands was rather an important thing to consider when planning the movement of armies across the countryside.

He tightened his eyes, focusing them into that ever-imprecise esoteric sight that had marked him as special from his birth. Studying not the physical presence of stone and debris littered out a horizon's width before him, but the wisps of remaining magic that still clung to it. Venka's eye for magic was not something that could be taught, and that would forever remain a tragedy. It revealed so much to those who inherited it from birth that the world would surely have changed were it to spread across humanity as a whole.

There was no small amount of magic to be seen, of course. One would be foolish to expect anything else when studying the ruins of Castle Edmari. Nonetheless, Venka found plenty of useful clues to go off of. By the state of arcane decay, he could tell the wreck was close to a day old, for one thing, and mixed in with the mangled magic of the structure itself were less physically anchored remnants. Magic of density and intensity that let it stick out even among the sea of ambient power around it.

Necromancy. That much was visible and might have been even at a glance. It was thickly seen and concentrated all around the same rough area. Dark, in that ephemeral way that energies untouched by light could be colored at all, and churning like the currents of a storm-driven sea. Necromantic magics tended to look like that, inherently vicious and destructive as they were. The thrashing around of all that invisible power almost distracted Venka enough to let the other presence slip his notice. That would have been a humiliating mistake because its intensity was almost impossible to believe.

What was it?

"Prepare a vanguard," he ordered. "And close the circle around that mound over there." Venka gestured to some visibly jutting stone about where he'd seen the magics, knowing that none present shared his gift. "I wish to examine it more closely."

The orcs obeyed instantly, proving yet again the effectiveness of Venka's civilizing influence.

Venka made his way through the rubble at the very pace he'd spent so long drilling his troops to sustain, more than most humans could withstand. More, in fact, than *any* could, without the assistance of passive magical energies suffusing their muscles. He soon found the site in question and, upon studying it closer, found a great more to boot.

Not the specific style of magic that made up the second kind, however, remained a mystery. Venka had simply never seen its like before . . . No, he had, once. The Dark Lord had had wisps of it around him, and it was found in even slighter traces about the bodies of growing orcs. Beyond that, he had no basis of what it could possibly be.

But the scale of power that had been unleashed was without a doubt. Venka turned his gaze from that to see if he might find other kinds.

Had it not been for the physical wreckage of the skyship, Venka would not have even noticed the fractional difference in flavor between the propulsion and levitation magics woven around it and those around the ruins of Castle Edmari. Once seen, however, the picture painted was easy enough to interpret. There had been an air battle, perhaps even a collision, and at the ridiculous speeds aerial vessels could manage, it was not hard to imagine that it had been responsible for the descent.

Mangled undead lay around them, but many had the telltale wounds of death to weaponry of the largest and most devastating kind. Clearly there had been a battle on board before or after the crash. No, before, without a doubt. There was not nearly enough blood spilled on the ground for it to have been after; whatever veins had been emptied, it had happened in the air and then had the evidence distorted by the collision.

Venka peered once more at the magic, comparing the ambient necromancy to that infusing the undead and then once more to his memory. The conclusion he drew was not difficult to formulate.

Sphera, then, eh? It was you. You got your nose stuck in this.

He wasn't surprised. Easily the youngest of the Dark Lord's generals, Sphera the Necromancer had fallen into the trap that so many natural prodigies tended to. She had become intoxicated on the drug of her own power. Everything was about magic and strength for her. Even her service to the Dark Lord himself, Venka suspected, stemmed only from a desire for more might.

Ordinarily that was not such an issue, for it motivated her into further excellence, but Venka had long since feared the girl would overstep and bring ruin upon herself. Or worse, upon her side. He saw now that she had made such an error.

Sphera's body was nowhere to be seen, though there were several human corpses among the rubble so mangled that they could scarcely be recognized. All were, nonetheless, undeniably male. He was not entirely sure whether it ought to have been relieving, knowing that Sphera still lived.

Venka studied the place further until he found evidence of additional magic, far from the wreckage of Castle Edmari, and once again ushered his orcs on after it. More of that mysterious kind he'd seen used amid the castle. Not as powerful but there, visible as ever. It was a mercurial thing, slippery, transmutative. As if someone had crossbred the principles of megalomania and mathematics, then somehow blended the resulting offspring with poetry. A hybrid concept that could only ever have stemmed from magic. He committed it to memory.

Tracks led away from the site, which he followed farther and scrutinized hard.

"What can the trackers smell?" he asked aloud. It did not take long before orcs rushed to bring forth their fat-nostriled scouts and hunters. The beasts hurried ahead, throwing themselves down onto all fours and drinking in the air around every track in the dirt, snorting whatever imperceptible scents remained. He followed them slowly as they grunted to one another, then fed their input to an interpreter. Venka had long since learned to assign some of the quicker-witted and more civilized of his orcs to translating the verbal sludge of their lessers; oftentimes humans were barely better at recognizing the intended meaning of regular orcs than bloodhounds.

"Six humanoids," he murmured once the information had been conveyed. "Two women." Venka saw a trail of necromancy that, upon further study, he recognized as Sphera's. Then he thought.

Despite his concerns, Sphera had been ever reliable in sending reports. The last word he'd heard of her work in the field had been that Elkatin's so-called savior had allied himself with a paladin and the magus Arion Falls. He had heard word himself of King Galukar's departure from Arbite and even Abaritan. That left only one individual possibly unaccounted for.

The pilot of the skyship, perhaps? He paused, turned back to the ship itself, and resumed his examination, more detailed. Venka could discover no identifying marks or sigils despite searching for close to half an hour and withdrew himself from the task only reluctantly. It would not do to tie himself up in scrutinizing the wreck for nonexistent details, not when a trusted champion of the Dark Lord was being hauled farther from him with every passing moment.

He paused again, thought harder, then made up his mind with the same military precision he tended to place into all things.

"Men, we will be changing course slightly. Assume marching formation double time and prepare for a brisk pace. We'll be making up for lost days."

As the orcs shuffled and reorganized, Venka considered his decision. He was on his way to a siege, with weaponry that might well alter its course. His presence was a grave thing to be delayed on any battlefield, and doubly so under such circumstances as these.

But his forces were elites in all, and the speed they could sustain over land was greater than almost any other army on the continent. They would, he wagered, be catching up to their prey quickly, if stride size was any indicator.

And that prey had the second-most-potent necromancer to draw breath within a thousand years. Every day she remained deprived from the Dark Lord's side was a loss equivalent to a thousand orcs or more. Her death would be the equal to a million.

"Forward!" Venka called out, hauling himself back onto his mount and urging it on. Around him, orcs shook the ground with footfalls that came down into the dark dirt like hammer blows, and they headed for the horizon.

Headed for whatever enemy was stupid and unfortunate enough to be lurking just beyond it.

CHAPTER TWENTY-NINE

Silenos had gotten used to traveling with improvized fleshcraftings. Sluggish, inefficient things that lacked the native speed and power borne into House Shaiagrazni's more traditional transportation by millennia of refinement and improvement. He considered himself unfortunate to have had to do so, considered the circumstances that had forced his hand bothersome and unacceptable. He had not realized how much worse things could get.

The Dark Lord's land was not simply ugly to look at and was not a region of mere discolored soils or grim weather as he had mistakenly believed when glancing down upon it from the skies above. The entire place was, for want of a better word, simply cursed.

Below the diffuse black sands that seemed to cover every inch of it, Silenos had been carefully probing the terrain with every rest they took, letting threads of nerve bundles permeate to the greatest depths he could manage, branching off into treelike structures that sifted through dozens of cubic meters at a time. Despite it all, he found nearly nothing.

No free elemental matter that might be consumed for his fleshcrafting, no abundance of microbiological life that might be forcibly converted. Not even the skeletal remains of creatures that had once been made from the same materials he now sought to do his work with. It was, for the first time in Silenos's life, a total and absolute scarcity of biological material.

Clean water was yet another absence they'd had to contend with, though Silenos had found means around that simple problem. Water was fortunately made of far more rudimentary molecules than other substances, and he had been able to generate it within his own body by simply utilizing photosynthetic principles. He might have found other ways to do so too. The air was far more humid than it was occupied by life, and the same went for the ground.

A water mage would have been quite at home, as would an earth mage, or any one of a dozen other kinds of caster. Just not one who relied upon living and dead flesh. Silenos was beginning to suspect the circumstances of his travels had somehow been arranged by the Entity.

Starvation was more of an issue than thirst, however. The landscape around them was predictably barren for a place with such a laughable scarcity of biomatter to be found within it, and neither Silenos nor any of his situationally convenient traveling companions caught sight of another living thing as they moved.

Save for the necromancer, of course. Sphera was her name; they'd gotten that much from the woman, and little else. Besides that, she was rather determined to be anywhere but under their custody.

Within the first half hour of emerging from the wreckage, Silenos's new group had been pressed with two issues, only one of which had been related to her. The other had stemmed from their unlikely savior. The sky captain Swick the Swift.

He was a tall man of dark skin, darker even than Silenos's. His hair was bound in thick, long dreadlocks that reached down to the man's broad shoulders, and his body, though scarcely armored in loose leathers, was well-built and scarred from numerous altercations left in his past. By the patterns and make of their damaged tissues, it was clear that the man's body healed unnaturally well. Silenos had seen such things already in the new world. Apparently those gifted with Vigor and innate superhumanity tended to recover more quickly too.

Well, all present had benefited from Ensharia's healing as well. Even Falls, whose body was no tougher or more enduring than any other sedentary scholar's. Silenos had benefited most of all, despite not requiring her aid to physically repair his body. He'd gotten to see it work at last.

As far as Silenos could tell, the paladin's healing was certainly magical, but of a curious kind. Rather than physically alter the flesh directly, simply reshaping and rearranging it as his own powers would have, it rather infused the target with energies that allowed the body to repair itself, enhancing physical processes in much the same way it enhanced the muscular strength or durability of its user.

That had been his first observation, and disastrously, Silenos had almost left it there. Upon closer inspection, however, he realized that the paladin's healing actually targeted the magic within her patient, not their body. Just as Ensharia gained immense superhuman prowess through arcane energies naturally built within her body, so too did even the most mundane of humans have lower levels of magic lurking within them. Typically these amounts were too limited to do anything of note, but at her touch, Ensharia had enhanced them in all present. The results had been explosive, impressive, and revolutionary.

Silenos could think of many uses for magic that affected other magic. It only increased his irritation to be stranded so far from his laboratory.

"I think I'll need to rest soon," Falls breathed, sounding almost embarrassed. Even using the wind to help lift part of his body weight and move himself along, he lacked the stamina that came so naturally to those whose bodies were reshaped or augmented by magic. His words drew a harsh glare from the lumbering King Galukar, who eyed him over one shoulder while the necromancer remained strewn across the other.

"We're in the Borderlands," the king growled. "Ten, maybe fifteen miles in. There's a town ahead, I know it, just a few more miles away."

"I can't walk a few more miles," Falls insisted. "You're asking me to push on for another half hour."

"I'm asking everyone to," Galukar replied coolly. "You're the only one complaining."

Silenos cut in at that, finding the stupidity too much for him to tolerate.

"And he is telling you he physically cannot. You can tantrum against reality itself, if you'd like, but that will not change anything about this situation. The world is not going to conform to your will no matter how long you've grown used to wearing a crown."

"That's rich, coming from you," the king fired back. Silenos frowned.

"What in the world does that even mean?"

"It means that out of us all, you're by far the most prone to insisting that everything be just how you want it. Or are you too delusional to have noticed even that?"

Silenos was just about to explain the finer differences between impotently whining about things and factually vocalizing plans to change them when it was within one's power when the pirate began his own contribution to their debate.

"For one, I'd quite like to know what's waiting for us in whatever town we're heading toward," he declared. "Because, and pardon me rightly if this is a bit too blunt, but I'm not so sure I won't have my head chopped off if I'm recognized."

It was his turn now to weather the glare of King Galukar, and he did so with an admirable lack of fear.

"Perhaps you should have thought about such things before deciding to make your life's work stealing, pilfering, and raping," the king replied, his eyes like lances, his words like a charging warhorse. Both bounced right off the pirate.

"We all have to do what we have to do." He shrugged. "You should know all about that, considering your choice of company."

He glanced toward Silenos at that, ridiculously. It was clear enough what he was referencing. Early after the crash, Silenos had suggested they all head back to the wreckage and reanimate the slain crew of Swick the Swift's skyship. They had been left on board when he made his assault on the castle, and thus killed instantly when the entire structure struck the earth. Apparently, their being mindless, lifeless blocks of useless meat was not justification to actually do something with their remains.

Silenos had to take a moment to swallow his fury. It was getting harder, the emotion strengthening each time he was afflicted once more by its cause. How long would he spend trapped in this land of cavemen? He'd already been here for months. Would years more pass before he escaped? Decades?

Would it possibly even be centuries? Silenos couldn't know, and that uncertainty gnawed at him.

Minutes passed by quickly, then a few more passed more slowly as Falls's complaints picked up. Finally Galukar caved and permitted the group to stop without more of his incessant urges onward, and they all seated themselves to make camp.

Silenos did not feel the lack of any fire; his body had been insulated to keep heat in just as it had to keep it out, but he could see Falls and the necromancer were not quite so fortunate. The latter seemed to be doing a good job of hiding her displeasure, having it betrayed only as Silenos grazed her shoulder to scan the woman's vital signs, while the magus was taking rather a different approach to handling his issue.

"We ought to huddle together, for warmth," he suggested to Ensharia, who looked no less disgusted by the proposal—or proposition—as might have been expected.

"You ought to keep yourself distracted from the cold," Silenos cut in. "With your studies."

The look of fear, of horror, sprawling across the face of an apprentice when they were called to practice was a joy he had never quite grown beyond appreciating, not after rewiring his brain for pure logic and mnemonics, and not after spending decades becoming used to it. It was particularly amusing on the features of Falls. The more pampered and privileged a student, the more they could truly bask in the misery of his methods.

Reluctantly, the boy shuffled over to sit before Silenos, head lowered.

"I thank you for this opportunity, Master Silenos," he said mechanically, "And I look forward to growing ever mightier from it."

The official, proper terms of opening for their sessions had not taken him long to memorize at least. His mind was nearly as impressive as his magic, after all.

"We will be starting with the practicum," Silenos told him. They had had only one session before, and it had not been a long one. Exhaustion had kept Falls from dedicating much time to it, though with the rate at which he assimilated information, it had almost been introduction enough. The boy was somewhere beyond genius, and not entirely far from Silenos's own gift of nature. Three, maybe four Shaiagrazni had surpassed his raw talent that Silenos knew of. All of which had been far in excess of his own idiot apprentices.

Save for Adonis.

"Am I going to learn reanimation?" Falls asked, interrupting Silenos before his temper could implode on itself once more.

"No," he replied quickly. "That would be an inefficient use of our time. It would take years for you to learn enough to reanimate corpses in amounts that would meaningfully add to the multitudes I can already bring forth."

"Of course. Don't desecrate the dead because it would be inefficient," the king snarled. Silenos ignored him, just as he ignored the pungent odor reaching his nostrils from the wind.

"I will be selecting lessons more suited to leveraging your preexisting strengths," he concluded. Falls considered that.

It was not impossible to learn more than one form of magic, but it was rare. Each new field a caster dedicated himself to mastering was longer, harder than the one before. Silenos was a rarity even among House Shaiagrazni to have come close to mastering two before his second century, and even with the new world's pathetic standards of mastery, the general principles remained in place and ensured that most magi used only one kind.

Which meant the prospect of gaining a second would have given Falls quite a lot to consider. He landed on the obvious conclusion quickly enough.

"Wait, my strength of wind magic, right? So you mean . . ."

"Yes." Silenos smiled. "You will be learning how to conjure shadestuff. That ought to improve your destructive potential a touch."

CHAPTER THIRTY

Early the next day, they caught sight of the town King Galukar had spent so much time promising them. The giant oaf seemed to think himself vindicated, despite it appearing entirely too early and westward, but Silenos was in no mood to burst the delusional bubble keeping his temporary asset in such an agreeable mood. Instead he maintained focus on approaching the distant settlement and peering ahead to see what might be gleaned of it from afar.

"Do you know the name of the town?" Ensharia asked, succeeding in diminishing the grinning idiot's pleasure with just that simple question alone.

"I don't," Galukar replied testily. "But we can learn that easily enough."

"What about its loyalties?" Falls added. "I don't want to step into some safe haven only to get lynched."

The king snorted.

"Oh, they're traitors here to a man. All of them under the Dark Lord, have been for years. They'll be well used to it I imagine."

It was Ensharia's turn to frown at that.

"Won't they crave freedom? Won't that make it that much easier to inspire them into revolt?"

The king eyed her, almost pitying.

"No, paladin, it won't. Freedom isn't a dream that survives being unfulfilled for long. They'll be more tired than angry."

Silenos could agree with that much; he'd held plenty of cities using just such a concept himself. So long as things did not worsen for people, and they were held tightly and forcibly while given time to adjust, the urge to fight back against their conquerors would dissipate surprisingly quickly. It was what had made House Shaiagrazni's territory so easy to expand back in his own world.

But it did beg one important question.

"If it's loyal to the enemy, we might run the risk of capture heading into it," he observed. "I advise that we send some of us in first, those of a less distinct appearance."

His eyes flitted across the group, though hardly needed to. It was more of a focusing aid than anything.

Galukar was close to 210 centimeters tall, weighed almost as many kilograms, and had one of the most famous faces and names on the entire continent. Even to say nothing of his being as subtle as a brick dipped in nitroglycerin. He, obviously, was out of the question.

Silenos himself was a few centimeters shorter, but he hardly looked entirely human. His clothing had been torn badly enough in the fighting that patches of keratin armor were visible through the gaps, and his own height was still far in excess of the new world's norm. His accent would be further evidence of his foreign origins.

Ensharia was an option, however. And, surprisingly, so was Swick the Swift. The sky pirate looked distinct enough but likely had better firsthand knowledge of the region than anyone else present, and with her previous paladin armor destroyed and replaced by Silenos's fleshcrafted substitute, Ensharia had high odds of at least looking the part of a foreigner of no particular loyalties or inclinations.

The only real question was whether he ought to send Falls in with them, which Silenos eventually decided against. Putting aside the boy's ridiculous lack of firsthand experience regarding the outside world, he was now an apprentice of House Shaiagrazni, and one of the most gifted who'd ever lived. Silenos would burn nations to the ground and scatter their ashes across the winds before allowing harm to befall him.

"It will be Ensharia and Swick," Silenos informed the group, interrupting Galukar in the middle of what looked to be a promisingly horrible tirade. "They have the most required blend of physical indistinction and actual social skills, not to mention worldly knowledge."

The king glared for a moment, then nodded. Seeming almost annoyed to have been given a logical idea.

"Makes sense," he conceded, turning to the pair. "Alright, head on in. We want to know where we are, get a map, if possible, and above everything else find some food and water. Horses too if you can manage it."

The sky pirate eyed him at that, seeming rather affronted.

"I have a couple of silver," he noted. "Not gold, silver. Horses are out of the question. And I'm not sure why I should be getting food for the rest of you as well. It'll go further if I just save it for myself."

"Because you'll still be holding it when I throw you as hard as I can," Galukar replied calmly. "Which, believe it or not, would actually bring you quite close to clearing that horizon."

Silenos did not inquire as to how the brute knew that, simply spoke up to add his own, less idiotic means of persuasion into the mix.

"And it would also mean you'd be making your way through the Dark Lord's territory with no assistance, and no chance to collect the debt you've sown in us by providing your aid during the battle in the castle."

He'd had a feeling that it would be the appeal of wealth to sway the captain, and it proved correct. Swick the Swift did not take long to change his tune after Silenos aimed his words at greed and pragmatism, soon nodding, though still looking reluctant enough as he agreed. Good, that would, with luck, leave him more cautious.

The captain's eyes narrowed after a moment.

"Someone must've found the rubble of Castle Edmari by now," he noted. "And you must've known that. Are you by chance trying to fuck me?"

Silenos met his eye, keeping his face level.

"I would rather obscure our real numbers for when whoever may or may not be pursuing us reaches the town to ask about any suspicious outsiders," he replied, preferring not to lie when unnecessary. "I did not feel the need to mention this because I had assumed the rest of you had drawn similar conclusions."

He glanced around, found varying levels of disbelief greeting his eyes, then Swick the Swift sighed.

"Bloody casters. Alright then. Let's go." He started for the town quickly, and Ensharia hurried after. Silenos watched the pair go with an odd disquiet sitting in his gut.

The air smelled of sulfur, Ensharia thought. Sulfur and the strange, sickly sweetness of infected flesh. She'd studied such scents during her time training as a paladin and knew them both well. They were the telltale signs of necromantic corruption in a landscape.

Normally such a state did not take a place instantly, which was good. When the lands turned dark and twisted like this, they became anathema to life of any kind. Attracted undead from across the continent, like the smell of flesh did scavengers, and strengthened and sustained those that dwelled within. Crops withered, water turned putrid and toxic, and, apparently even the deep roots and burrowing insects, and the very matter that usually nourished such things, were reduced to such an extent as to deny Silenos his fleshcrafting.

The Savior had said, insisted, even, that the Dark Lord's necromancy was amateurish by the standards of House Shaiagrazni. She'd believed him once, found the revelation a source of hope and strength, but Ensharia had seen the man's flaws demonstrated with far too much regularity to just take him at his word any longer.

Could he have underestimated their enemy in such an excessive and extreme way? Perhaps, perhaps. Ensharia didn't think Silenos Shaiagrazni would ever misjudge a caster who had stood before his eyes, but he'd still not encountered the Dark Lord in person. Until he did, his arrogance may well have been what motivated his conclusions.

"Bloody hate necrotic lands," the pirate breathed beside her. Ensharia glanced over, pulled from her thoughts by the momentary assumption he was talking to her, then relaxing slightly as she found him staring ahead. Just thinking out loud. Ensharia's concern blossomed again as she studied the man.

Swick the Swift had become famous for his piracy, in more than one way. Mostly, the stories told of his cunning. He'd escaped from more prisons than most pirates with twice his experience had even been thrown in, stolen perhaps a full tonne of gold, made himself rich in the dirty work, and then made himself poor with how he spent it. By all merits, he was a man of staggering intellect and ridiculous impulsivity. She'd been ready for that.

What struck her now though was the sheer calm about him. He strutted along the dark, grimy soil as if it were a red carpet, looking almost bored at their surroundings, irritated at their circumstances. But not shaken.

He had rammed a prized skyship into perhaps the most valuable building on the continent, destroying both, and lost each and every one of his crew in a failed attempt to keep them out of the fighting.

Had Ensharia suffered as much misfortune and loss, she wouldn't have been able to even stand, and yet mere days afterward, Swick the Swift was striding away as if the fact weren't even occupying space in his head.

It irked her, and she spoke up to let him know as much.

"Does it not bother you, that all your men are dead?"

The man turned, eying her as if she'd just asked if he wanted to drink a puddle of cow urine.

"Ray of sunshine, you, aren't you, love?" He grinned, revealing two teeth that had, at some point, been knocked from his mouth and since replaced by ones made of gold. Ensharia shivered at the smile, returning her eyes to the space ahead of them.

Fortunately, with Falls and the prisoner no longer in their company, she and Swick were able to make far faster progress along the landscape than their entire group had earlier, each stride eating up well over a yard of space and coming faster than would be sustainable for less trained and Vigorous individuals.

Ensharia almost wished they'd been moving slower soon. It would have given her more time before her eyes took in the withered settlement awaiting them.

It was not a small thing, nor was it particularly large. A town that likely held a few thousand, at first glance. As they entered through its outer wall, however, Ensharia found the streets far too thinly populated for such numbers to possibly be true. It seemed very much as if a typical settlement had had one out of each three of its citizens removed, and those who remained were terribly thinned by hunger and fatigue.

With a few exceptions, which Ensharia had to fight herself not to attack on sight. The soldiers of the Dark Lord were perfectly healthy and well maintained as they walked around, looking as if they were enjoying rations of rare and exceeding quality for the soldiers' lives they'd chosen. The scum.

They weren't undead, as was common for those servants of necromancer tyrants who policed civilian areas rather than marching to battle. That just made things worse. Oh, humans could be relied upon not to eat or slaughter those they watched over, but that was because they were thinking beings. People. It was not mere mindless nature that compelled them to act the way they did or obey orders with a singular savagery; they could choose. And these ones were choosing evil of their own volition.

One of them shoved an old woman and sent her hitting the ground hard. It happened just a few yards ahead of Ensharia and her companion.

"You owe nine," the guard snarled, clutching what looked to be less than nine copper coins in one fist, while the other closed tight about a spear at his side. "Are you trying to rob His Majesty?"

The woman couldn't have been a day younger than sixty, and Ensharia feared her aged body might have given in from just that single shove alone before she rose to her knees, looking up at the soldier with pleading eyes as gray hair spilled over her face.

A hand closed around Ensharia's wrist, and she turned to see it was Captain Swick's. His face had grown serious, eyes hard and determined.

"Careful," he warned. "We're here to gather information and travel supplies, and we need to keep a low profile."

"The sentence for theft, woman, is flogging," the soldier continued up ahead, turning Ensharia's face back around to watch as another man drew a vicious-looking whip out from his belt. "And since you stole from the Dark Lord himself, we'll be delivering your sentence in public."

One man moved to expose the woman's back while the other prepared his instrument of torture, and Ensharia tore her arm from the sky pirate's grip.

She took one step, then another. Forcing herself to turn away from the sight and leave, knowing that extrication from the situation was the only way she had of ensuring she wouldn't cave in. Knowing that the impulses of justice and righteousness would kill far more people than one old woman if she were to obey them now and jeopardize her mission.

The woman's screams came out, each one of them landing in Ensharia's ears like a whip strike itself. She weathered them.

CHAPTER THIRTY-ONE

The paladin, Ensharia, tore her arm from Swick's grip, and he readied himself for the worst. From what he'd seen, she wasn't quite as strong as him, and nowhere near as fast, but her armor was a damn sight heavier. If things got violent, she'd have slim but greater than zero odds of beating him. Better to just translocate away if she looked to be on the verge of doing something stupid.

She didn't though.

Instead of charging over to start splitting open heads and tearing off limbs, the woman turned, then started her march *away* from the atrocity unfolding just twenty feet ahead. Her strides were almost reluctant, as if she were wrestling herself just to make them. Swick recognized the disposition of a woman at war with herself, but though the conflict was clear, he didn't see any doubt. Given the same choice, she'd make the same decision. She knew she'd have to.

He followed after her, taking only a moment for his shock to finish running through his system. Swick found his mood brightening somewhat as they avoided what could easily have been a very annoying problem.

The paladin had surprised Swick by turning away from the old woman as her lashes came down, and that surprise had been quite a pleasant one.

In all honesty, he'd not had his own skin on the line. If she'd insisted on fighting the guards, he had no doubt she could have handled two; between them both—or perhaps even by herself—they likely could have killed however many hundred more were dotted around the rest of the settlement, even at once. And at worst, if there had been some nasty surprise awaiting them like a particularly strong undead or three, he could have simply translocated away.

One particularly loud cry actually made Swick jump, and he found himself glancing back at the old woman's punishment, wincing before it. A screamer, that one. With lungs like those, she'd probably make it to eighty before going toes up. Shame about the flogging.

Surprisingly, the paladin proved quite skilled at navigating the town, though not quite so much as Swick. He supposed her lot were probably taught all about different customs and regional cultures, on account of their job being wandering around them cudgeling brains out of things. Still, she must've had most of her life eaten up fighting the Dark Lord rather than policing the world, and nothing beat experience in Swick's view.

They focused on simple foods, light and filling. This region, apparently, was one that either grew or—more likely—imported rice, which was excellent for weight efficiency in their travel rations. Water was harder to come by, but not impossible. Apparently this town was one that had learned to ration its drinking water out because buying the stuff privately was damned expensive. By the time they'd finished with it, Swick's reserves of coin had been reduced to under half.

While the water merchant headed back to retrieve the product, Swick was left standing beside the paladin. The two of them had the company only of each other and silence. He eyed her while it stretched on.

She was not crying, nor had she been. That didn't surprise him as much. Swick had been around more than a few times in his life, and he'd seen enough to be more than skeptical of women as the emotionally fragile whiners plenty of other men tended to know them as. More to the point, this one was tough, and more than just the way most paladins seemed to be.

But that didn't mean her sadness, and the wrathful bitterness feeding off of it, didn't strike him like a hammer to the chest.

Swick tried to just ignore it, but the seconds dragged by, and the merchant kept on doing whatever the hell she'd been wasting so much of their time doing in the back. Eventually something had to give in, and it was Swick's nerves.

God, he needed a drink. He couldn't deal with people while he was sober.

"What we saw back there," he began, choosing his words carefully. "You, uh, you did the right thing in walking away from it, you know. World doesn't have a lot of heroes, but it's got plenty of dead idiots who tried to be one. There was nothing you could've done except make this mission more dangerous for the rest of us. It's just the way of things."

She turned, and the look in her eyes made ice seem warm.

"Is that why you didn't so much as shed a tear over your dead comrades?" she snapped. "Because it's just the way of things?"

Swick felt a jab of irritation at her retort and had to resist firing back one of his own. The headache was pricking his thoughts, brain slathered in acidic pain by its dehydrated, alcohol-deprived state. It was all he could do not to tell her to shut up and nap right then and there.

"They knew what they'd be getting in for when they signed up for their jobs," he explained, trying to make the mudwalker understand. "It'd be an insult to mourn them when they died in something they got themselves involved with of their own volitions, and I'd be insulted if I found out they mourned for me were our fates reversed."

"You're serious?" she asked, not seeming to even believe him. Shock had to be an improvement over derision, at least.

"Deadly," Swick growled. "We're pirates. Sky pirates, at that. We have our code, just as you paladins do. Treat a man like he's soft and you're insulting him; take a look behind you and you're insulting everything in front."

"Unbelievable." The paladin stared. "That you'd even compare such a barbaric code to the tenets of my order. What, do you honor your men by drinking? I saw you guzzling away from that canteen the other day. It's like you were kissing it, and you've been blinking fifty times a minute since it ran out. Is the boozing part of your code?"

"No," he replied, feeling a stab as her words touched something more sensitive than he'd expected. "The boozing is just fun."

At last the merchant returned, and not a moment too soon. Had she left Swick alone with the paladin for much longer, he half suspected she'd have started taking that mace to him, or trying. Purging the world of criminal scum like him was among their horribly lengthy set of vows, if he remembered right.

"Much obliged, darling." Swick grinned as she handed his coins over the counter. "Much obliged. Tell me, uh, if it's not too much trouble I mean, my companion here and I could use a bit of directional advice. Not quite used to navigating a landscape as black and death-y as this one, you understand."

She smiled back, apparently swallowing every word easily enough.

"Oh, of course, sir, of course. What would you like to know? I'm not as well traveled as some of the merchants here—the older ones mostly—but I've ventured out beyond the walls more than a few times."

Swick maintained his grin and did his best to hide the strain that threatened to imbue it as he moved on to the real reason for his asking her.

"How exactly, if we were so inclined, would we cross the border and exit the Dark Lord's territory?"

The change was instantaneous and pronounced. Within the span of a single heartbeat Swick saw the woman's face fall, friendliness withering and dying like a rose under desert heat, openness disappearing as whatever cracks he'd managed to widen in her guard were rapidly pulled shut. She was a wall of steel before he spoke again, but not yet fully sealed, not yet impossible to reach. He'd have to move her quickly, before she clamped up completely.

"You understand we're just looking to move on," he noted hurriedly. "Tell us what we need to hear—as, I assure you, plenty more merchants will—and you'll never have to hear from us again, eh? Just one trader to another."

She shifted slightly but still didn't meet his eye.

"It is forbidden to leave the Dark Lord's lands," she whispered. "All of His Majesty's subjects are required to aid the Great Work, any who leave without his permission are deserters, and desertion is a crime that carries the penalty of death."

He might have expected as much. Swick had traveled enough that this was far from his first time in the Dark Lord's territory; borders in general didn't mean much to a sky captain, after all. He'd met plenty of people with similar levels of fearful loyalty, and all of them much closer to the border and more recently conquered. This far into the Dark Lord's land, with well over a decade of history under his rule, there were people over the adult's age of sixteen that wouldn't have ever known anything else.

This one didn't look as young as that though. By Swick's guess, he had a chance to sway her.

"Lots of things are forbidden by the Dark Lord," he noted. "There's a big difference between what he can announce and what he can effectively police, eh?" Swick affixed his most winning smile. "Come on, help us out, please? You might be our only chance to actually find a path back home to our families."

She hesitated, an agonized look washing over her face at his words. Swick could see how torn the woman was, and it filled him with an adrenal shot of anticipation. A torn barterer was halfway to a convinced one.

Just as her gaze stiffened and she looked to be on the verge of refusing, the paladin's hand came down on hers, and the woman was absorbed in a stare so heartfelt and honest that even Swick almost blurted out everything he knew about their route back home.

"We know we're asking a lot, that this would be a betrayal, but it would mean the world to us," she whispered, squeezing the woman's hand gently for emphasis. "We'd be in your debt—I'd be in your debt—forever, and . . . you might well be saving our lives. Can you do it for us, please?"

Good Lord, Swick had seen quite a few strumpets in his day, but none had ever managed to make their eyes inflate quite like this paladin did. It was remarkable, almost wasteful, really, that she'd chosen to use her talents on smashing undead heads open with a cudgel.

And it revealed rather quickly why his own persuasive methods hadn't worked. By the sudden flush across the merchant's face and the swift movements of her tongue lolling over both lips, her interests swung in another direction entirely to any man, even one as handsome as Swick the Swift.

"I don't know anything concrete," the merchant whispered, looking rather more at the paladin than jolly old Swick. "But I've heard rumors about the city Kaltan. You've heard of it?"

Swick saw incomprehension in the paladin and figured that was about right. Mostly they learned about nations, not cities. Far more efficient when they were being educated on a thousand other matters to travel around doling out justice that mostly wasn't city dependent anyway. Sky pirates like him, however, tended to get a more nuanced and detailed view of the world.

"I've heard of it," Swick volunteered. "The rebel's city, right? Overthrew their nobility and started lopping off heads a few years ago. Twenty or so, I think."

She nodded.

"That's right. Well a great deal fewer years before now, they fell under the Dark Lord's dominion. But there've been whispers that there's a man within their walls offering safe passage from the Dark Lord's territory. They call him Silhouette."

"Silhouette," Swick echoed, while the paladin busied herself with thanking the shopkeeper. He moved the word around in his mouth as they left. Silhouette.

Yes, it did sound quite like the sort of name he'd come up with while drunk.

CHAPTER THIRTY-TWO

Sphera had not been having a good week, all things considered. There'd been a few ups early on. Besting the pretender Silenos had been fun, seeing the limits of her undead had been positively *thrilling*, and corrupting Castle Edmari through its Hero master may well have been the highlight of her service to the Dark Lord. Things had deteriorated, she decided, around the time of her being tricked, overpowered, and hauled off as a captive. Such events as that did tend to have a marked impact on one's happiness.

At the moment, she was seated by the rebel group's campsite, if it could even be called that when they lacked the means to make fire. She was tied up, of course, fingers forcibly splayed and held out apart from one another by the special cuffs made by that damned necromancer, body kept still and stiff as she lay face down with nothing to do but glare, bask in the growing aches of her unnaturally sustained position, and of course, glare some more.

Today, the subject of her glaring was the king. It was he who by chance had ended up within her line of sight, and so it was he who absorbed the unrelenting barrage of her fury. Sphera did not make the rules; she only obeyed them.

"Stop looking at me," the giant said without even glancing up. His voice was so deep it sounded more like something that would exit a bear's throat than a man's. Sphera had to keep her surprise that he'd noticed her attention from showing.

"I have nothing else to do," she replied and glared even harder. If he was bothered by the fact, it didn't show on his face. But Sphera felt the breath leave her as his eyes turned to hers.

King Galukar's power was not something truly felt from any perspective save the one that was seeing it focused upon itself. She almost soiled herself then and there at the sight of his withering gaze.

"I am going to turn you to face another direction now," the king told her. "Attempt to move against me in any way and I will rip your head off. Doing so will take me no more effort than uncorking a bottle would you. Perhaps less."

Sphera believed him, and so she stayed very still while the man moved her. He turned her quite roughly so that her eyes were falling upon the pretender and his student, then moved away without another word. Sphera wondered for a moment whether he'd done it on purpose, then stopped her wondering. Of course he had, the hateful bastard.

"The abyss," she heard Silenos Shaiagrazni continue. "It is the source of necromancy, and death itself."

Her breath caught in her throat, and despite herself, Sphera leaned in. He was speaking about the metaphysics of their art. That, Sphera knew, would be worth listening to.

"Do all magics have a source?" the student asked, and his master frowned.

"We are not certain entirely. My people know much more of phys—natural philosophy than yours. Yet the more we learn, the more discrepancies we find in how the world behaves normally and how it behaves when magic is considered. It is possible that the very requirement of sources and beginnings, of time and causality itself, does not apply to the force."

Falls frowned in the way little boys or puppy dogs might, then nodded.

"That makes sense," he breathed. "We're made of mundane matter. It'd be too convenient if we could intuit magic as well as natural law."

His teacher was expressionless but nodded.

"Now," Silenos Shaiagrazni pressed. "The abyss. It is best explained through a philosophy of life held by some people within my land, likening the world to one great ocean. Individual lives, in such a universe, are waves. Born of forces acting on water, shaping it, moving it, giving it momentum and velocity, conducting its substance into a pattern that will never quite be replicated entirely again. Then the wave exhausts its energy, falls back down into the ocean, and is assimilated into the mass of water. In this scenario, the vital sparks that animate our bodies are the waves. The abyss is the ocean."

Falls nodded along as he listened, waiting patiently with a question. Sphera had to admit, he was a good student.

"So what is that shadestuff substance you conjure? Soul energy?"

Shaiagrazni did not look impressed.

"Shadestuff is raw abyssal substance, and it varies in nature. Much as the pressure of the ocean . . . Ah, you don't know about that, never mind. Within the abyss everything is shadestuff, except for the vital sparks, the 'souls' as you put it, that exist within. Different parts of the abyss house different grades of shadestuff. It is always destructive and unrelenting in its interaction with physical matter but can be more so if you extract it from a deeper part. Observe."

He held out two fingers, and two identical spheres of shadestuff formed from each. The man's face was instantly seized in concentration, as was proper. Only an idiot could ever be *relaxed* while handling the deadliest force magic had to offer.

Without warning, Shaiagrazni dropped both the globules of shadestuff and let them fall into the dirt. Their reactions were instantaneous, eating through the matter like boiling water dropped onto ice. Within a second, both had vanished, and in their place a pair of hemispherical craters rested in the ground. One was as wide as a man's finger, the other almost as wide as a fist.

"Neither of those reached the limits of shadestuff I am capable of conjuring, but the second would have been equal to, perhaps, the Dark Lord's necromancer officer we fought the other day."

Neither of them glanced over to meet Sphera's glare, which somehow made being used as a measuring stick even worse. Fury bubbled in her breast as she watched the smug bastard explain what he'd done and how to replicate it.

He talked of the methods through which shadestuff was conjured, the way one might extend their consciousness to touch the abyss, the sensations of plunging a head underwater and holding one's breath. The dangers, the risks, the rewards. Sphera searched his words for any faults and found none. Her irritation only grew.

Clearly, this one was skilled when it came to teaching the fundamentals; that was a mark to his credit, at least. Perhaps he could have become one of her lieutenants, or a bodyguard, more likely, given the potency of his other magic. Sphera reminded herself to try to uncover how he'd broken his bonds in the castle. More even than the skyship collision, that had been when things began to turn sour.

Sphera found herself suddenly sick of the sight, grunting and snarling with effort as she forcibly turned her body again. The pained sensation of hard dirt scraping against the underside of her body was worth not having to watch any more of that smug bastard's teaching.

For all the tedious, punishing effort, Sphera soon found her decision a stroke of luck. Just as she'd started settling into her position staring out into the distance, something caught her eye. It was subtle, quick, but all too familiar. Orcs.

Just two of them, moving along the ground faster than most humans could run, eying their surroundings as they shuffled ahead with wind under their feet and fire in their legs.

Scouts. Venka's scouts, surely, because Venka was the only human general on the continent to use orcs in such a way, and certainly the only one who trained his orcs to move like that. As she looked harder, Sphera made out the bulk of armor about them, and not the kind that orc barbarians produced around the Steppes.

There was a lot for Sphera to consider, but one of the few, perhaps only, advantages to being held hostage was that she had nothing but time on her hands, and so she put it to good use. Considering the implications.

If Venka's orcs were nearby, then so was Venka. He had never trusted the creatures to act outside of his immediate supervision before, not without a tight line of communication, which was only sustainable over smaller distances. If Venka was nearby, then . . .

Then he was near because of her, searching for her. Sphera's heart fluttered with triumph, and she checked her reasoning, all too wary of the trap that was false hope and wishful thinking. Venka was an offensive general, an attacker. He did not hold ground as often as take it. Moreover, they now stood within one of the more loyal and secure regions of the Dark Lord's territory.

Sphera thought, trying to recall any local regions that might be contested in the Dark Lord's conquest. There weren't any close by, but one or two could be reached by taking only a minor detour. Would Venka send himself off course in such a way to retrieve her if he thought she was missing?

Without question, yes. He was ambitious above all else, convinced he was the greatest genius to ever live, and rescuing one of his peers would be an undeniable mark in his favor.

And a mark against the peer being rescued, she realized, but that was a concern she didn't have the luxury of considering.

Her suspicions were confirmed soon enough. The scouts were followed by marching columns. Humanoid and bipedal, but broad in the way only orcs could be. The figures were clad in thick, dark metal that Sphera knew from experience was the armor of heavy infantry—particularly brave and violent specimens Venka had singled out as shock troops and turned into certifiable siege engines by covering them in half an inch of wrought iron.

They were not as subtle as the scouts, which were in turn less subtle still than well-trained human ones. Sooner rather than later, they'd be spotted. Sphera strained harder, faster, more painfully even than before to quickly turn herself, this time trying to keep the entire group of her captors within sight at once.

She'd not get another stroke of luck as big as this one, that much was certain. Sphera would be damned if she let it go to waste. Figuratively, and very literally. She needed a distraction from the approaching army.

"I wasn't there when your sons were killed," Sphera began, addressing her words to the king. "But I was there when they were . . . worked on."

He stiffened, then slowly lifted his gaze to eye her. It was a hell of a thing, lying in the midst of that stare. Like facing down ten armies at once. Like staring into the mouth of a volcano. Casters had magic running through their nerves, if not their muscle and bone. Sphera was confident she would see the king moving if he went for her. She was more confident still that those plate-sized hands could close around her head so powerfully as to liquefy it before she'd even felt the sensation of her own death.

It was the sort of observation that dried a tongue and tightened a throat, but she made herself speak in spite of it.

"Necromantically, you understand," she continued, forcing a smile. "They were very, *very* powerful. Really, each one had the strength of several knights. You must've been proud to call them your blood. I can only imagine how impressive they are, now that they've been further infused with the strength of the abyss."

She did not, in the end, fail to see King Galukar move. But she failed to react to it. One moment she was mid-word, then a hand was around her neck, and her body was suddenly straining the soft tendons with its own weight as she dangled in his grip. Sphera choked, legs kicking in instinctual search of ground that was a yard too low for them to reach. The king's eyes were harder than ever.

"You will not speak of my sons," he told her, as if she were a subject to be commanded. No challenge, no rage, just a single, simple statement of fact. Sphera had to admit, she was awfully tempted to let it be so. The king dropped her with no great measure of care, leaving her to land knee first in the dirt.

The king took his steps away, and Sphera waited, catching her breath, hardening her nerves. Readying herself.

"It was odd," she gasped through her half-crushed throat, "how much they moved. Most corpses are still while being reanimated, but your sons danced like puppets."

King Galukar's sword was moving for Sphera like a bolt of lightning, and it took just long enough for her to realize her error before it was upon her.

She'd gone too far.

The Godblade swept past Sphera, missing her shoulder by mere inches as a strong wind struck her in its proximity. The dark iron dug itself feet deep into the ground by her feet, and only once it had done so did she realize that Falls had knocked the swing aside with a blast of wind.

It wasn't buried for more than a second before rising again, but by then the necromancer, Silenos, had stepped in to place a hand on the king's arm and wedge himself between him and Sphera. The two stared at each other, separated by mere inches in height and distance, yet seeming to her the picture of a man facing down a giant.

"Do you think your strength will resist mine?" the king growled. "That even your abominably remade flesh can even press hard enough for me to notice any difference between it and that of an infant?"

"I have no doubt at all that it cannot," the caster replied. "But I do not care." His hand was instantly filled by the abyssal black of shadestuff. "This is not a fight you can afford to start over a few hurled barbs."

The king's eyes narrowed.

"I'm an ally," he growled. "You're stupid enough to wound me?"

"If you kill a hostage with valuable information because you decided to tantrum after hearing your pathetic children insulted, then you will have proved yourself too unstable and unpredictable to be of use. Better to kill a mad dog like that before it can turn on me."

The necromancer's voice did not quiver in the slightest as he spoke, and Sphera found herself struggling not to drown in his bottomless, empty eyes. It was like staring into the depths of a sea, and the vertigo it induced forced her to look away.

Which was why she heard the king's concession rather than seeing it.

"Watch yourself, abomination," Galukar grumbled, striding away. Sphera didn't notice much beyond that, subtly turning herself one last time.

As she glanced over at the settlement, this time, she caught no sight of orcs, soldiers, or anything hopeful at all. A grin split her lips.

That meant the enemy wouldn't either.

CHAPTER THIRTY-THREE

Ensharia was just about ready to be done with her and the pirate's little outing, finding herself driven to the edge of her tolerance by more or less every word from him. Her oaths forbade wanton violence, particularly in anger, but breaking them was made more appealing each and every time she heard him smack his lips or murmur about a yearning for alcohol.

Just a few more minutes, Ensharia, just a few more minutes to get the rest of our supplies and you can leave.

The mantra was of some comfort, but her nerves still kept on eroding. Right up until the people around them started moving.

Ensharia didn't need to ask why the town's citizens were suddenly slipping along the street like some human river; she found her answer shortly.

"The general Venka is calling a town-wide ounce-ment!" came a voice, dull and heavy as a hammer blow, loud as the sound of a trebuchet striking castle walls. Ensharia barely even noticed that the speaker was an orc, barely even took a moment to glance at the unholy creature. Her mind was occupied by the name sitting in the midst of it, searing a hole in her thoughts.

Venka.

Venka. General Venka, the butcher. The orc wrangler, the man responsible for putting a dozen cities to the torch and ordering so many hangings that all the world's scholars had yet to fully uncover, record, and count them. Her blood boiled at the mere mention, hands curling into fists so tight they'd have crushed stone caught between their fingers.

She turned to look at the pirate, suddenly struck by a great curiosity of what his reaction might have been. It did not surprise Ensharia that Swick's emotions on the matter were limited to no more than surprise, concern, and a dull, subtle worry.

"We need to leave," Ensharia told him, doing everything she could to keep from screaming the words out, then following them with a hasty attack on the nearest orc.

"We need to head with the others," the pirate replied, and Ensharia wore her stare openly.

"Are you mad?!"

"I'm smart," Swick shot back with unexpected venom. "Trust me, the most suspicious thing we can possibly do now is leave at the precise moment we found out about some big, town-wide meeting. We follow everyone else, blend in, and leave when we have a chance to do so by walking in the *same* direction everyone else is."

Ensharia tried her best to find a flaw in the man's reasoning, but it proved stubbornly insistent on yielding none. With an exhalation of breath heated almost to scorching by her temper, she nodded.

"Fine, lead the way."

They both headed onward.

Around her new, Shaiagrazni-made armor, Silenos had hastily conjured and wrapped cloth constructed from various "materials" within his form. Apparently the issue of food had been less demanding of his redundant armor plating than the issue of disguise.

Being told as much had certainly annoyed Ensharia, but now she couldn't be gladder for the draped fabrics hiding her abominable armor from sight. Orcs were dull, but it would take only one enemy human taking notice of them for the Dark Lord's finest general to be brought word of her presence.

That made something else occur to Ensharia, and she turned quickly to Swick.

"Won't you be recognized?" she asked. "You're a Hero, right? Even the others had heard of you, and they didn't study . . . outlaws. Your name's spread halfway across the continent, and you're a particular issue for the Dark Lord, considering you possess the means to travel through his corrupted lands without ever actually encountering a reanimate or monster."

He smirked at that, in a way that left Ensharia somehow rather disconcerted rather than reassured.

"You ever heard of a witch?"

Her irritation soon replaced the worry.

"Of course I have," Ensharia snapped. "What does that have to—"

"Five hundred gold, more or less," the man cut in, eyes still ahead, smirk still in place. "That's how much they usually charge to erase the memory of my face and appearance from the world, provided only a few people see me at a time."

Ensharia was speechless.

Witches were rare, and feared. And both for good reason. Theirs was a miraculous magic, incomparable in power and versatility, yet terrible in practice. Every instance of its use, whether a parlor trick or grand working, cost them a little piece of their lives. Aged them that tiny bit more. The paladins used them only sparingly, and with great reverence, and most barely had any understanding of even their own powers for fear of wasting their lives by practically training with them.

Finally, she found her voice.

"How could you do that?" Ensharia demanded, anger rather than curiosity flooding through her. Life was sacred; time was sacred. To use a magic that demanded its price in both so casually was . . . It was beyond evil.

Swick merely shrugged.

"Cost them a few weeks, or months, and over the years it's probably kept me alive for just as long in total. You don't live long in my position if you're prone to being recognized. I might have been held down and killed by orcs already if I were."

"And you didn't think to simply not be a pirate and anger people into wanting to kill you instead?" she snapped. Swick grinned that infuriating Swick grin that never failed to make Ensharia want to pick him up off the ground and hurl him as hard and far as she could manage.

"Seems to me like that's the major concern here rather than what I pay witches to voluntarily do as part of a mutually beneficial transaction."

He was right, in the practical matters at least. That wasn't all that Ensharia cared about, of course. It wasn't all that any paladin cared about, but it wasn't a disagreement she had the time to push in their current situation either. For the moment, practicality would have to reign supreme.

It seems that every moment has been one of those moments, of late.

The people were ferried along the streets by yet more orcs, and in following them, Ensharia was able to gaze at the creatures more closely than she might have liked. They really were repulsive, like things made by Silenos's magic. Musculature bulged so broadly and sharply that it seemed almost edged, where it wasn't covered in thick layers of linen gambeson or hidden behind sheets of ugly iron.

"Don't stare," Swick whispered. "They aren't as stupid as people say."

Ensharia whipped her head around quickly, feeling her face burn. She was getting corrected a lot, it seemed, by this one. Perhaps he had been the wisest choice of company.

Soon enough, the river of flesh reached its mouth, a large town square with a statue placed in the center and surrounded by cobbles instead of the dirt roads that marked everywhere else in the settlement. Standing at the statue, standing on its very head in fact, was a man Ensharia could only imagine was General Venka.

He was shorter than in the stories she'd heard, which Ensharia had found was an eternal constant common to all generals. His skin was of a pale northern shade, like hers rather than the darker-fleshed necromancer they'd captured, and a pink scar ran over the brow and lid of his left eye, reaching just through the cheek.

Venka's hair was black, like Silenos's, but far shorter, carefully cropped and carefully held in place with such attentive scrutiny that Ensharia found herself wondering whether it might have been encased in molten tar. It was his eyes that struck her most though. More than the cruel twist to his lip, more than the towering orcs standing at the base of his perch, and more than the creaseless attire covering his body, which looked to demand the work of a dozen servants in its maintenance.

The general's eyes were fierce and inexhaustible in their search of the crowd.

"Good people, I offer my greetings to you all on behalf of our master, the Dark Lord."

Heads lowered, eyes shifting to avoid meeting his, bodies trembling slightly as the crowd recoiled in mere mention of their dominar. The general continued.

"I am sure that many of you must be startled and disturbed by the presence of my forces in your town, and for that I can only apologize. It is not my intent to spread upset or distress among any of you, nor any other citizen of the Dark Lands. These are hard times we are facing, plagued by war on each side of our borders, and I am well aware that the demands of taxation and rationing will already be gnawing at your livelihoods. You have no need of further concerns added to that, and yet, I am afraid, I have no choice but to burden you with my presence. For among your settlement is a man, woman, or group who are working to act against our great nation and all that it stands for. Among you, there are, I believe, enemies. Rebels, terrorists acting against the people of His Majesty's empire. I am here to extricate them from among you."

Ensharia's mind raced. The general, obviously, was talking about them, but she wasn't certain how he could have followed them. Silenos hadn't been using magic outside of the crash site, none of them had, and they'd specifically watched the necromancer to keep her from doing so.

They were, however, at the nearest town to the site, just a few dozen miles from it. If someone wanted to track them, they'd not need much more information than the simple direction they'd been moving. Was that what the general had been operating on? How could he have gotten even that much?

They turned as the crowd dispersed, hurrying for the edge of the city. So far only a few orcs had made themselves known, and all were armored in the way of General Venka's heavy infantry. So elites, too few, Ensharia hoped, to fully encircle the settlement's perimeter.

Mud streets were dented by their footsteps, so hard did they make their way for the town's edge. Dirt cratering and spattering outward with each stride. They reached the edge in a mere minute, and that was when Ensharia's heart sank.

Orcs waited for them, not heavy infantry. Mere footmen. Numerous slabs of hulking muscle, lined outside the settlement with sneering faces and cruel glints in their eyes. Tusks and fangs split their mouths into perpetual grins, and each one held an ugly weapon tight within their fist.

They started coming for them instantly, having already seen Ensharia and Swick moving for the edge, and doubtless having been told to seize anyone who did so. The general had hidden the bulk of his forces to encourage any traitors hearing his announcement to flee quickly and daringly, an elaborate trap that Ensharia had been just clever and stupid enough to trip.

"Halt," one of the orcs growled as a dozen more followed it in marching over to them. They moved in a wedge formation, an oddly complex position which Ensharia imagined said far more about their general than it did them. Each held a spear, shafts thick enough to be driven through stone without breaking, tips as dark and dense as all their other metal.

Obviously, halting was not an option.

CHAPTER THIRTY-FOUR

Ensharia turned to Swick, eying him with a silent question and finding the man with no answer. Ensharia half expected him to translocate elsewhere, but he remained. She couldn't think why. Perhaps his options were limited, and he couldn't muster the distance to travel far enough to reach true safety. Perhaps he'd been covering up some additional limit in his power that she had no idea of. Either way, he readied his fists instead of his magic and prepared himself for a fight. It appeared Ensharia, if nothing else, would have a Hero as an ally.

The first orc came on so fast Ensharia almost felt like she was fighting a knight. No, faster, as fast as a dullahan even. Its spear was like the lance thrust of a mounted rider. She slapped it aside, feeling the sensation of wood shivering against her knuckles, wincing even as the weapon went wide. She was unarmed, unprepared, vulnerable, and lucky enough not to have met something harder than her bare hands already.

Obviously, the orc was not expecting to lose a contest of physical power, and she gave it something else to worry about by driving her fist out to smack into its chest. The wrought iron made a thick cushion against Ensharia's strength, but it wasn't steel, and she wasn't the woman who'd once struggled in battle against magical enemies clad in plate. The material surrendered with a grating, shivering groan as its wearer was knocked flat, legs twitching in agony where it lay in the dirt.

Ensharia did not wait to consolidate her advantage, merely turned and ran, desperately running around the remaining orcs. A light pop beside her warned of Swick the Swift translocating in without her needing to actually look at him, and the two of them were heading toward the town's edge faster than Ensharia had ever headed toward anything at all.

They were unarmed, which was never a good way to open a fight. Ensharia was glad she'd insisted on bringing her armor, if nothing else, but it would be poor protection against weapons and enemies as big as those orcs. Just a quarter mile ahead of them was the city's outskirts; beyond that it wouldn't take them long to catch the sight of their teammates. They'd have a chance from there, but everything hinged on escaping.

Ensharia tried to find the confidence she so desperately wanted, settling on determination instead.

Three hundred yards to the outskirts, and more orcs closed from the sides. There must have been an entire army around them, Ensharia thought, to have men so far out as to reach her sidelong where she was already. And reach her they did, crushing in like the jaws of a bear trap.

Ensharia caught one orc across the jaw with a punch and felt the bone snap. Another grabbed her from behind, but she merely forced its grip apart with a flex of her arms, slammed the back of her head into its face, and moved on to strike another as the creature fell convulsing and groaning at her feet. Blades came, great big machetes and blunter cudgels aside them. Those that actually hit left little etches in the impossibly hard material of her armor. None did true damage.

It didn't matter. The danger here was losses of time. Ensharia knew an army of this size would have at least a few elite soldiers; she'd already fought one herself. If a handful more orcs like the one she'd knocked flat attacked simultaneously, there wasn't a hope in hell she'd win. Not without her weapons.

And then there was the general.

Ensharia threw an orc down over her shoulder, snarling as something crunched into the joint between her arm and torso. The armor there was thinner, more vulnerable, and she actually felt it give before something sharp bit her skin. She rounded on the attacker instantly.

By the dent in its chest, the orc she'd laid flat at the altercation's opening was the same one who'd just cut her. It didn't hesitate to try drawing more blood, flailing its oversize weapon one way and the other like a leaf caught in the wind. Ensharia stumbled back, forcing herself not to rely on any of the old parrying reflexes she'd spent so long developing. They'd only fail her here.

Swick the Swift, however, did not. Ensharia actually blinked as the block of stone came down upon the orc, smashing its helmet in and sending the creature to drop face down into the dirt. The pirate didn't hesitate over it for an instant, simply dropped the makeshift weapon and seized the orc's own. Ensharia took the chance to do likewise. Following after him, waiting for him to kill, then taking the hammer from his fallen enemy.

An orc went low, then fell as she cudgeled it. Three tried to attack at once from different sides, showing Ensharia how high she could jump as she found herself leaping into the air and clearing all their heads, then laying waste to the confused enemies from their back. One after another, a score after a dozen, they fought and moved at once as they came closer and closer to freedom.

It was when they'd just come to within a hundred or so yards of the city's limits that Ensharia heard a voice ring out and felt the sudden pressure of orcish assault let up.

"Back off. These two are far beyond the likes of you."

She turned, panting, but barely needed to. Venka's orcs did back off as they were ordered, and she knew there was only one man alive capable of commanding those soldiers. The general approached, strolling down the street as if he were on the parade ground, fingers resting on the handle of a saber held at his side.

He did not wear much in the way of armor, but he walked like a man covered in it from head to toe. He didn't seem armed with anything more than his sword and his body, but he moved as if the Dark Lord himself were standing behind him. General Venka's face was like a hawk's as his eyes fell upon Ensharia.

"Who are you?" he asked her.

Throat tight, she took a moment to think. He cut in before she could answer.

"The next question I ask, you will answer instantly, or I will attack and kill you where you stand. You'll have no time to lie here."

It was as stunning a verbal blow as any physical one she'd ever received, knocking the wind from her lungs and the thought from her mind. A simple, devastatingly effective tactic that seemed to leave no reason at all for the contrivances of counterplay or strategy. Which was, of course, the point.

Ensharia couldn't even blink before he spoke again.

"What are you doing in this village?"

"Buying food," she replied instantly.

"For whom?"

"For myself."

"Why did you attempt to flee without any after hearing my announcement?"

Her heart seized, and Ensharia *almost* delayed that single, precious moment that would have cost her life itself.

"I've heard of your reputation, of your infamous brutality and cruelty, and thought that you'd be likely to decide any foreigners were enemies of your lord."

"And are you?"

"No," Ensharia replied, but he was speaking again before she could elaborate.

"What brings you foreigners to our lands?"

"Trade," she replied, blurting out the first thought to enter her head.

"You have trade caravans then? Goods?" the general challenged. Ensharia almost cursed. Every answer she gave locked out possible others, left her ever more tightly held within his voice of deduction. Her panic was mounting with every moment that passed.

"We were robbed," she replied hastily. "On the road." Ensharia found herself elongating the lie without even realizing what she was saying. "We, uh, we saw something fall from the sky, something absurdly huge. And when we went to investigate it there were . . . these people, moving away from the place we think it landed."

"How many?" The general asked. "What did they look like?"

"Six," Ensharia replied. "A tall man of brown skin and black hair, a giant hulking one with a sword so big it looked heavier than me, a woman with black skin—she was being carried by the largest of them—a man in magus robes with green eyes, and a . . ." She couldn't describe Swick accurately; he was standing right there. "A sky pirate, I think. It must have been. He talked about crashing his ship, and he had the sort of accent they usually do. All guttural and common. They . . . They robbed us, killed my friends, stole our goods."

Ensharia could only hope her look of pained frustration was convincing enough.

"Interesting," the general replied and began to pace as he spoke, taking long, easy strides. The sword swayed by his side, hand still resting atop it. "Very interesting. Your story does seem consistent with other facts I have gathered. I know of the great falling object you speak of, of the people you claim you encountered. It all lines up rather well."

The sword was out before Ensharia even saw it, thrusting through the gap between backplate and pauldron, digging in and leaving blood to fountain from her wound. Whatever its edge was made from, it wasn't steel. Steel could not survive such forces being exerted through it. She staggered back.

Ensharia whirled, but the sword did not fly for her again. Only twisted where the general held it.

"Intriguing," he breathed, studying its edge. "You're oddly well armed for a merchant. But then, you're actually the paladin Ensharia Zeriqua, are you not?"

Her blood ran so cold, Ensharia thought it must have expanded to ice in her heart. The look of victory upon the general's face almost thawed it instantly.

"If you're wondering, King Galukar was with your group. I deduced that much myself before arriving here. That you failed to mention one of the most famous men alive by name rather than simply physically describing him betrayed your deception. It was, however, not a poorly made one besides that."

The praise seemed genuine, bizarrely enough, and it was followed by another sword swing. Ensharia was watching General Venka this time and saw clearly that he moved faster than any man she'd ever seen. Faster than her, Silenos, faster than Galukar himself. The man's sword was like a streak of mercury as it came for her, biting into a pauldron before she could react. The force of it sent her fabric attire flying free, exposing the armor beneath as Ensharia slid backward five, ten, then fifteen feet. She stopped only as she crashed into an orc, knocking the beast flat.

Swick the Swift was living up to his name, dancing back from Venka's blade for almost three entire steps before it caught him. Cleaving the shoddy knife he wielded in half, sending its remnants to scatter away, then arching back around to cut an equatorial gash from his shoulder to hip. The pirate didn't even make a sound as he fell, just silently inhaled, in shock and seized with muscular convulsion. Venka examined him for a few moments, and so did Ensharia. She found a flutter of relief as she saw the subtle rising and falling of the pirate's chest. Venka only relaxed his face a shade, clearly invested in taking him alive, but not by any great degree.

Not a great enough one to delay him any more than an instant before he was charging once more for Ensharia.

She tried. She really, truly tried. But a rat could try just as hard and just as long against a cat; some results were simply immutable. Ensharia's hammer was cut in half, then the handle of Venka's sword caught her between the eyes. The general was not as strong as King Galukar, not nearly, but he didn't need to be. Not with a blow as cleanly delivered as that.

Before the flecks of light had even finished dancing in her vision, he brought the flat of his blade down hard.

That was when her memory cut off.

CHAPTER THIRTY-FIVE

It really was rather promising, how quickly Falls was picking up the art of necromancy. The boy had learned more in four hours than most did in fifty, and Silenos suspected he would hit a learning curve on top of that within the next few lessons. If all went as planned, he was in the process of training one of the most gifted and powerful necromancers to ever live. If all went as hoped . . . he may well, eventually, produce his own equal in the art.

That begged a great many questions, however. Too many to ignore. Silenos, like all the most recent generations of House Shaiagrazni, was the product of some four thousand years of constant, painstakingly executed eugenics applied across a population of millions. His talent had been scoured from numerous well-educated, -nourished, and -developed humans, who had all had all their needs and requirements met to grow as completely as they could. All to ensure that House Shaiagrazni extracted its named from the most ideal genetic stock possible. On a purely statistical level, when measured against a more conventional human populace, Silenos's talent was one in quintillions, perhaps less.

Falls was not his equal, but he was still an anomaly. Finding him, naturally occurring, in such a backwater world was no different to finding a strip of perfectly alloyed factory steel among a vein of iron ore inhabiting the wall of some cliff face. Not impossible—very few physical occurrences were *truly* impossible—but so vanishingly unlikely that it almost defied calculation.

And that was to say nothing of the *other* too. Silenos glanced over at the necromancer Sphera. She wasn't quite the equal of Falls, but her gift of nature was still sufficient to leave statisticians baffled. What was it about this world that yielded such magical talent?

The better question, he imagined, was what sort of reward would await him for being the first of House Shaiagrazni to discover and absorb it for the rest of their use?

Silenos's plotting was interrupted as his eyes came to focus upon the woman's features, and he found something very, very wrong in them.

The woman's typical glare was nowhere to be seen, not hers and not the more general expression that remained in place atop the expressions of all who found themselves held captive and dragged along miles of countryside. She had stopped her fidgeting, no longer scrutinously glanced at every minor thing around her in silent search of an opening. Indeed, everything about her was . . . not content, but patient. Waiting.

He thought back to the inexplicable outburst of taunting she had hurled at King Galukar, and everything clicked into place in an instant.

"Falls, go and check on the other two in town. If they're in trouble then fly back to us as quickly as you can manage."

"Are you just screaming at phantoms now?" the necromancer asked from the side, confirming all Silenos's suspicions at once.

"What's going on?" Falls frowned.

"I believe our companions have been ambushed," Silenos told him. "And I want you to verify that. If we can help them, we will. But we need to know what we're dealing with first, and time is of the essence. Now hurry up and make your observation."

He was careful to control his temper, all too aware of how angered demands tended to leave men freezing up with indecision and worry. Falls, fortunately, was moving into action quickly.

"I can do this," he replied. "You can rely on me, master."

The boy was rushing off without another word, and Silenos found a strange sensation building in his chest. Actual approval of something his apprentice was doing?

Stranger things had surely happened, but for the life of him he couldn't recall any off the top of his head.

Arion's heart was a drum, beating so loudly he felt certain it would attract the attention of whomever or whatever he was hoping so desperately to avoid. As luck would have it, it did not. Not even as its volume rose to exponential heights upon his reaching the town's outer perimeter.

There were orcs, not in front of him, fortunately, but all hurrying along and around the town to reach some point at its far end. Falls took the opportunity to slip by them even as he drew the obvious conclusions about why so many heavily armored monsters might be moving at once.

Falls found his first source of answers in a woman, however limited such things were.

"You there," he demanded. "What's going on?"

The poor thing seemed rather confused, apparently not grasping that he was an outsider for long moments before she answered him.

"You've not heard? The general Venka came, said he'd investigate us for, for traitors, for spies. Then within a quarter hour, he ordered all his orcs to rush in on one side of the town. Most reckon he's found one."

Arion felt an ache appear within the depths of his stomach, mounting and convulsive in its intensity, like holding hot magma in his belly. It made him want to vomit, to scream, to run away with both arms flailing over his head and his bowels emptying themselves down his leg. Why was it that he could never go anywhere, or do anything, with Silenos Shaiagrazni without some new complication emerging that threatened to kill him?

Why was the world so desperate to ruin his life?

He resisted the urge to flee like a terrified animal, instead forcing himself to stop, wait, and think things through. Enshaila and the pirate had been gone for a few hours at most. That wasn't enough time for *much* to happen. They were almost undoubtedly still in the town, at least, and that meant there might just be some means of reaching them still.

Of course, his major issue was in actually gathering the information. Arion knew about the town, knew about its history, knew about most of the world's facts, he often thought. But he'd never lived there, spoken to its people, or actually interacted with its culture in any meaningful way. He could pass a quiz on the place a hundred times before figuring out how best to ask for directions to the nearest inn.

Which was inconvenient but not something he had the luxury of humoring. It was another half hour to his master, at least, and bringing in the rest of their group with an enemy army in the city would only risk capture for them all. Whatever Arion found himself doing, whatever solution this latest disaster had, he was on his own in resolving things.

Something oddly freeing about that. Arion had often been on his own before, for years during his tutoring, in fact. Walriq, may he rest in pieces, had always been a great teacher but never a good mentor. Arion could handle doing things by himself.

Could, or would. There really wasn't any choice besides one of those.

Arion was in the town for about half an hour before he was confident he'd gained enough information to act without being instantly exposed and clubbed to death by giant, angry orcs. Fortunately, his skin seemed to match the tone that was most common in this region. That would make any subterfuge go over a shade easier.

His questions didn't seem to garner much suspicion, which he'd been banking on given the overall excitement with spies and imprisonment the town seemed to hold, and Arion was soon pointed to a rather large building near the town's center. He headed for it with a weight of fear upon his shoulders.

The building wasn't a fortress, that much was clear. Perhaps it had been some barracks once or a storehouse. A large stone thing constructed sturdily enough that it might have weathered a trebuchet. For all of ten minutes. Arion saw no small number of orcs standing outside its front door, guarding the interior with a focus and patience he'd rarely heard attributed to their kind in the scholarly articles he'd consumed about them.

Arion, as subtly as he could manage and from the widest berth available to him, scanned the building for potential points of entry. In yet another stroke of cosmic misfortune, it appeared the enemy had done a fine job of covering them. Orcs stood guard around each and every doorway, as well as even the less convenient entrances through windows.

Had he been anyone else, it might have spelled trouble. Fortunately Arion was Arion, and wind mages tended to dislike the ground in any case. He looked around for a few minutes, locating a washing line hung just a street and a half from the warehouse, then conjured the strongest wind he could and diffused it across the area.

It took a moment of focus to rip the large blanket from its place along the wire and a moment more to ready himself for its slow flight over to the space just above his head. Arion jumped, then caught his body with a conjured wind and lifted it high, carefully manipulating the sheet to be between him and any surveying eyes that might watch from below.

The flight was blessedly quick, taking only seconds before Arion came to drift over the warehouse and could let himself drop down. He didn't land particularly gently, but the wind gave its helping hand for that too.

Around him was the roof, less cramped than might have been feared, and fortunately unguarded. Arion took a few moments to study it before deciding on his next move. There was a hatch that didn't strain him to lift open, unlocked fortunately, and led down into the building's guts. He followed it quickly.

The building's size was considerable, but it was not at all difficult to extend his magic throughout it and press at the air. Just a shade, not enough to conjure some gale-force wind, merely the minimum amount required to draw tactile sensation from his surroundings. Arion felt more orcs, a dozen maybe. He felt jagged walls, iron plate, patrolling guards. Then, after a few moments, he felt a familiar form. Ensharia.

She was deeper than he'd have hoped, as deep as a smart captor would have had her placed, but Arion swallowed his fear and forced himself down after her regardless. Every step was a victory, and he got the feeling that each one would only bring him closer to defeat.

At the deepest point of the warehouse, there was a cellar. Arion knew without even checking that it was where Ensharia would be, but he gave it a quick survey with his magic just in case. It wasn't good to read the air too often indoors; people tended to notice the minor atmospheric shifts it caused, but a second indulgence didn't seem disastrous to him.

Not unexpectedly, he felt the same things he had before. An unoccupied room save for two figures, one of which matched his companion. Arion moved down into it and found a stab of relief almost cutting his speech off as he laid eyes within it.

There was a great cage in the room, thick bars of iron sealing one half of it off from the other. It was within this cage that Ensharia and Swick the Swift dwelled. Both were in a poor state.

Ensharia, the least obviously wounded, was covered in minor and larger bruises. Her armor had been cracked at several points, which was terrifying given the sheer resilience of Shaiagrazni engineering, and a cut seemed etched across her skin with every few inches of it one bothered to look at. There was an undeniable fatigue to her face that left Arion's question as to the lack of guards answered, and even still she was in a better state than the pirate.

Swick the Swift had been bleeding, and bleeding a lot. Most of his clothes were fully soaked through with his own ichor, dark and clotted, scabbing and congealed. His black skin seemed to have grayed somewhat with the exsanguination, and he was shallowly breathing in as deep and inexorable a sleep as Arion had ever seen.

His studies of the pair did not take long to be interrupted. Ensharia soon noticed him, looking up and speaking with a sharp fire in her eyes, managing only three words before realizing who it was she was addressing.

"What do y—Oh . . ." Her eyes widened, first with hope, then panic. "Arion, what are you doing here?!"

He was hardly less concerned than her, being honest.

"Rescuing you," Arion whispered, resisting the grin that tried to take over his face as he said it. "And the pirate, I suppose. Now come on, stand and get ready to leave. I'll take care of those bars."

CHAPTER THIRTY-SIX

Iron was harder and denser than stone, and by no small amount. There was a reason it had been the material of choice in the construction of Arion's own cell back in Magira. His winds were powerful, powerful enough to cut through steel plate armor, but they'd need to cleave apart an order of magnitude more material here. Could they do it?

Yes, of course they could. The real question was how quickly. Arion wasn't certain about the answer to that.

"Wait," the paladin snapped, her voice a jagged thorn lodged deep through his thoughts. Arion turned to her, confusion blossoming. "You need to leave," Ensharia whispered.

Anger flared up in him at that.

"I'm not leaving without you," Arion snapped.

"You have to—"

"No," he growled, interrupting her with an anger that surprised even him. "Twice now, you've saved my life. I'm not leaving you to lose yours. I'm getting you out of here, then we're heading back to the others and escaping this shithole of a town."

The woman's fury grew to match his own, and Arion ignored it. Just kept on examining the bars for some sign of a weakness. He found it, fortunately. A great, thick lock made of iron or steel. Even on a boulder, it would have been the strongest part. To conventional trauma. Around the surrounding obstacles, it left Arion sighing in relief at how much easier his task had become.

"Falls, leave. There's no point in bringing me. I'm too weak to move myself. I can't fight. I can't even run. You're only endangering yourself."

Arion tuned her out, concentrating on the lock. He felt its interior, in the vaguest sense. He couldn't glean enough information through the touch of his air to know exactly how to unlatch it, but he had other options in any case.

His will infused the air within the lock, expanding and hardening it like a growing bubble underwater. The pressure around it grew by the moment, iron straining against magic. He was growing close to breaking it, that much was clear. Solid metal was one thing, but the delicate mechanisms of a lock were no match for the most gifted magus alive.

Second most gifted. Bugger.

Noise reached his ears, running down from the rooms above. It was Ensharia who reacted first, speaking in a hurried, strangled tone that spoke of primal fear and haste.

"Arion, someone's coming. You need to fucking *leave.*"

It almost gave him pause, hearing her swear. She never had before. Perhaps it was ridiculous, that *that* of all things conveyed the severity of his situation, but one couldn't choose one's own wake-up call.

What he was doing was insane, beyond dangerous. Perhaps even suicidal. So why did he feel so right in doing it? Why did every nerve of Arion's body scream at him to keep going?

He was a thing of magic unrivaled, and he'd been told from the first moments of his memory that that made all the world's luxuries his due. But why?

In House Shaiagrazni, a man's magic earned him power and privilege only because of how he could use it to help the collective. Somehow that made it all taste better. Somehow, Arion realized, he found himself wanting to be more than just a pampered trophy. He kept working.

"Listen, even if you get me out now, you'll need more than just your own power to fight a path out. General Venka is here, and his soldiers—the elites—they're stronger than you'd believe. We need help. Get the Savior, King Galukar, come back later. Just don't try to fight this fight by yourself."

Arion hesitated, and in the moment he spent thinking more footfalls rang out from the space above them. He cursed, feeling all his strength and courage evaporate at once. Was it just pragmatism? It was a convenient excuse, one way or the other.

"I'll be back," he promised her, and Ensharia nodded.

"Go," she insisted, voice as soft as a summer breeze. "Go to Kaltan and find the Silhouette. They can help you out of the Dark Lord's lands."

Arion went, hurrying from the room like a panicking rat and scrambling his way back out through the building. He'd memorized his path in and didn't need to exert much of his intellect to reverse the directions in carving an exit. His mind was good for handling information, it seemed, just not doing anything righteous or worthwhile with it.

Up the stairs, down the hall, three lefts and a right. Then Arion was closing in once more on the hatch he'd come through. That was when he heard the footsteps behind him, rapid, terrifying. Sending a shiver down through skin, muscle, and into the very marrow of his bones. He didn't dare look back at whatever was causing it, just hurried on in his flight from the building, teeth chattering all the while.

On the roof, he finally turned. Slamming the latch shut, then slamming down a wall of air atop it. He felt the stone ceiling creak, crumble, then collapse entirely as tonnes of rock rained down to fill in the cavity below it. Arion was already running farther away by the time he heard it start to happen, rushing for the ledge.

A gust caught him, as they always did, and flung Arion far into and through the air. He'd seen rocks hurled at lower speeds by catapults and felt less pressure from the attacks of amateur wind magi than he did from the wall of air breaking against his face. His time in the sky was closer to a minute than a second, ending as the streets below began to close with a terrifying speed.

Arion was not Walriq, not yet. Flight, even levitation, was power denied to him by the demands of time and experience. But he'd always learned half as fast again as the old man, and he'd worked at few things as hard as mastering the skies.

When the ground came up to meet him with its crushing embrace, he wrapped himself in a cushion of pressurized air that deformed and decelerated him while he was still yards from the ground. His body's weight still kept him from breathing while he bounced, and it took all of Arion's focus to stabilize himself once he was flying from the point of contact. He just about managed to turn his flight into a rapid sprint without falling.

Had almost anything in the world been chasing Arion, he'd surely have escaped. Dozens of yards cleared in mere seconds, and a sprint started faster than any man could manage, then sustained farther by the continued press of wind at his back and stabilizing pressure at his sides, he would have bet money on himself outracing a horse, let alone a biped.

Once more, the urge to turn was on him. Arion resisted it just as he had in the corridor, but it only grew stronger now that there was no potential escape awaiting him within a few strides. If he'd gotten his directions right, and a wind mage of half his competence could not have failed to, then he had a good few hundred yards to reach Silenos. Ordinarily, he'd have been confident of clearing such a distance. Not now. Whatever was chasing him, it seemed well equipped for pursuit.

Arion finally risked reaching out after himself to feel the presence and almost vented his fear out as a verbal groan as he did. It was humanoid, cold, covered with metal, and moving in on him like a bloodhound. He didn't need his book learning to tell him it was an undead chasing him, nor did he require his newly gained worldly experience to realize that there was a second one falling in beside it.

He churned the mud up in his wake, creating a great wall of clotted air and debris to try to distract them, then sent heavy items flying from nearby. Buckets, carts. Arion found his panic growing as the enemy came closer and closer, and then a sudden, inexorable sort of calm washed over him.

If he simply kept as he was, death would catch him before he reached Silenos. Arion cooled his wits, gathered his focus, then plucked himself from the ground once more with wind.

Nine times out of ten, such a move as that was devastatingly dangerous for him. He'd not yet mastered the art of vectored aerial thrust, not yet managed the hundred tiny little subtleties that kept a person both aloft and stable at once. Arion could never have turned a corner, let alone evaded a strike. Not in the air.

But he didn't need to. All his magic did as he called on it was throw him, lifting him and hurling his body like the stone from a whistling sling. He moved so quickly through the world that he scarcely felt a part of it, faster than before, faster than he'd ever gone. His few moments in motion were well needed to wrap himself in decelerating coils of pressurized air, then the ground met him.

Arion had thought he'd landed hard before, thought he'd been hit hard once or twice in his life. What met him in the dirt proved the ludicrous delusion of both beliefs. He broke the ground, so hard did he strike it, and bounced several of his own height back up skyward before hitting it again on the return stroke. Spinning, ears ringing, blood dragged to all the wrong ends of him with the accelerative forces of his rotation, he barely had any wits left in his head by the time he finally came rolling to a stop.

Groaning, twitching, gasping. He stood. It was an effort done more with magic than muscle, for every fiber of Arion's body screamed and trembled like a battered dog. Even the arcane struggled to heed his calls, mind left blunt and clumsy by the concussive disruption of his impact. Arion glanced back over his shoulder as he lurched on, finding some sliver of satisfaction at the hundreds of yards he'd cast himself across in mere moments.

Finding a much larger lance of fear as he saw something else.

There was a crater some handful of dozen feet behind him, no doubt the point of Arion's initial impact. It was wider than he was tall and almost as deep, the sort of ruin left by an impact that would leave no room for survival. Had he not shielded himself, his body would be a sack of blood and floating flaked bone fragments. But it was the sight beyond that truly brought about thoughts of his mortality.

Still coming, still faster than charging horses, the undead he'd felt earlier were powering on. Moving with that lifeless gait they all did, carrying a dexterity and grace born from muscles moved by nerves too dead to tremble. Arion swallowed his fear and surged on away from them.

Every second of movement was a new torture as body parts ached and groaned at the exertion. Muscle, bone, even tissues so deep he thought they must have been close to the median points of his torso. Every pause he took was worse, a stabbing, damning moment of progress he'd allowed his enemies to make in hunting him.

Stride by stride he neared the hill, the one he could only hope was right in his memory as hiding Silenos and Galukar. Chain by chain the enemies closed, halving the distance, then passing the crater, then halving it again. Soon enough they were within fifty yards of his back, and mere seconds away. Arion roared, turning himself around and mustering all the power he could manage.

He was going to die, fine. He'd hurt the fucking monsters responsible before he did. Dent that black armor, smash the necrotic bones beneath, leave rotting juice to drool out through whatever gashes he managed to make. There was nothing of a magus in his will as he waited for the towering plate-clad figures to close. Only raw animalism. Perhaps that was what he needed to make the most of his last few moments.

The rain of fire was all the more of a shock in his bestial frame of mind, snapping Arion from his savagery and leaving him gawping. It was not like any flame he'd seen before, almost a liquid as it dripped down in broad sheets, clinging to the ground around and atop the undead, burning so hot and bright that there was scarcely any sight of them within it. Arion took a moment to recognize the magical fire his master had conjured, only just doing so before Silenos Shaiagrazni dropped down beside him.

"We must leave," the caster said instantly, hoisting Arion over one shoulder as if he weighed nothing, then taking off at a sprint. His head still left facing the undead, Arion got a good, long look at the inferno continuing to scream around them. No figures emerged, though he had no way of knowing whether they'd perished. If nothing else, they weren't being followed.

It did not take long to reach their new safe haven. Naturally, Silenos chose a different hill from before, and Arion wasn't surprised to find King Galukar seated behind its crest. The necromancer was lying down beside him, thoroughly gagged and glaring daggers.

Arion couldn't imagine the fury she must have felt, knowing her allies were within shouting distance, knowing she couldn't shout. He hoped it was worse than he was picturing. The bitch deserved it.

"What happened?" his master asked, interrupting Arion's thoughts with his usual tact-shaped vacuum.

Turning to him, Arion made a concerted effort to focus. Silenos must have gotten tired of waiting after a moment, for the caster lifted a hand to his head and extended magic to his flesh, banishing the throbbing pain from his skull, then quickly moving on to work at the rest of his body.

Arion took the moment of clarity to speak.

He told Silenos of all he'd seen, all Ensharia had said. Told of his endeavors, his failures, her position, and his flight. Silenos was finished with the healing before Arion was with his account and eyed him in much the same way he did whenever observing a mistake made with magic.

"You were foolish to remain as long as you did, almost getting yourself killed. Nearly threatening me, even. It was pure luck that saved you. Had I not heard the impact of whatever caused that crater—you, I can only imagine—I'd have not known to come and meet you on your way back."

"I wasn't going to just leave her there," Arion growled. "Now that we know where she is, now that I have you too, we can go back and—"

"And do nothing," Galukar interrupted, voice like a needle. "I'm sorry, magus, but we can do nothing. An army of thousands, with elites in the area of power you've described . . . And a Hero on the enemy's side . . . That is too much, even for us."

Arion felt like the sky was falling down and leaving his shoulders alone to bear the impact. He glared at his master.

"And you agree?" he growled. "You're Silenos Shaiagrazni. How can you not even try—"

Silenos hit him, a blow just fractionally harder than most he tended to discipline Arion with. It sent him to the ground, left his ears ringing as they received the words that came after.

"I cannot try because I cannot muster my full power," he replied, and for once Arion heard none of the iron-cast calm in his master's voice. "Because I have found myself in a world of simpletons and savages, grunting like apes and beating their chests in aggressive, fearful anger when they see sciences and magics they do not understand.

"I cannot try because I have been traveling with one such primitive." He glared a venom more concentrated and corrosive than any Arion had seen at Galukar, then continued. "And am thus now without an army of my own and fewer options as a result. We will go to the city of Kaltan, we will contact this Silhouette, and we will see if something can be done about Ensharia's capture. That is all."

Nobody said anything after that. Not even Galukar.

CHAPTER THIRTY-SEVEN

Finlay bloody hated crossbows.

Oh, they were convenient. Easy to use, simple enough that an idiot could become competent with a fraction of the training one might give to a good longbowman. But they were loud too. Louder than a bow, which was already a damn sight louder than most tended to guess. All well and good if you were assembling a conscripted force to stand on a hill and put bolts into whatever tried to push them off it, but useless for the types of work he tended to do.

Today, as on so many other days, Finlay was leading his rangers on a night raid. Quiet, precise, rapid. A lightning strike of an assault meant to gouge the eyes out of their enemy's force, then lance the heart of its body while it still spasmed in disorientation. It was the sort of operation that required coordination, hard-drilled protocols, men of talent, fierce training, and experience all at once.

It was not, by any measure, the sort of thing for which Finlay would have requested five hundred fucking crossbowmen to try to help with their blunt, flaccid penises for fingers. But it was also one skirmish of many in a war that grew more desperate and doomed by the year.

He'd make do. He had no choice.

Finlay moved over the hilltop as quietly as any creature he'd ever encountered, insects included. There were many magics in the world, many powers. Some people could uproot trees and use them as clubs; others could've set the hilltop he was so carefully crawling across ablaze with barely even a few seconds of thought. Finlay wasn't anything so flashy as that.

Indeed, Finlay's power was assassinating flashiness itself. And he did it better than any he'd ever met.

He slithered, moving with the unbreakable certainty that he was beyond notice. Any eyes that happened to drop their gaze upon him would see it slide off like water on stone, and unless he decided to enter a coughing fit while breathing down the sentries' necks, there was little chance of them paying any more heed to whatever sounds he let out.

Fomors, six of them. He recognized the abominations quickly. Not undead, not alive, some wretched halfway point. Each was over seven feet tall but no broader than a normal man, rapier thin and paper lean. Their skin was gray, yellow, or crimson, their eyes black or glowing violet, with mouths filled by jutting razors for teeth and scalps coated in stringy, matted thorns for hair. One had an axe blade for a nose, the tiny scrap of steel catching moonlight whenever she turned. Another's legs were made from stalactites. The third did not look so unremarkable. With luck, it meant the blood flowed weaker in him.

Of all the things leading the enemy, fomors were perhaps the worst. Finlay felt his mouth dry as he studied them, the dozen or so dullahan around them, then the handful of thousand orcs still around them. This was going to be a nasty, brutal, and hard-fought fight.

Pulling out his bow, tightening his focus, Finlay nocked an arrow. His weren't made the normal way; there wasn't a scrap of wood in their structure. Just solid sharpened steel running a few feet from ass to head and boasting a nasty point on one end. It gave them more mass, a smoother path through the air. Most importantly, it gave them bodies that could withstand impacting things as hard as his bowstring tended to launch them. Finlay drew the string back.

It wasn't strength that let him do so, not entirely. Finlay's power felt the tensile demands of the string and lowered them. It hummed around the air adjacent to it, stifling sound before it could even begin, and when he loosed the arrow, it flew with no more noise than a punch might have.

Both were misleading features because it moved as fast as an arrow could do without giving away Finlay's position with a supersonic whip crack. The length of steel caught one fomor perfectly, guided mid-flight by Finlay to adjust its course by precious inches and plow right into the vulnerable point between breastplate and helmet. He watched the creature fall in a spurt of blood, already drawing another arrow before it even hit the ground.

By the time he fired his second, the remaining fomors were scattering. It didn't matter. Finlay managed to skewer a second through their neck before they could fully remove themselves from danger. The attack came just as the third escaped his field of view.

Finlay had spent years training his rangers to be living instruments of death, and they proved his success within moments. Coming out of seemingly nowhere, opening up blood vessels and skewering organs as they fell on the orc guards before their hapless enemies even knew a fight had found them. With his night vision as potent as it was, Finlay saw the air turn crimson with spraying arterial blood as five-hundred-pound bodies thudded harshly to the ground, watched the enemy's ranks begin to tremble in exertion. He swallowed his anticipation, focusing only on the job.

A dullahan's helmet ruptured as Finlay cast another arrow through it, then a towering orc reared up, calling out words of galvanization and encouragement to its men. He got that one through the eye. Every time he released a projectile, another enemy died, and he made sure they counted. Killing officers, killing elites, killing anything that might have the ability to restore order to the chaotic cancer spreading through their forces, or individually challenge and kill any of his rangers.

The carnage could not have taken more than half a minute, but by the time it ended, he'd already emptied a full quiver of thirty into the other side.

Finlay saw orcs roaring and flailing in confusion, campfires rapidly extinguishing, braziers emptied out into the dirt. He saw officers snarling at their sudden loss of control over the ranked men in their forces and undead lumbering one way and the other in search of something to kill. It seemed to him about as chaotic a state as the enemy was likely to enter and, like all military chaos, a sharply temporary state. It was his moment.

Calling out, Finlay gave the order for the rest of their men to advance, then began to draw on his second quiver. He took off an orc's arm before the first of their conventional soldiers crashed into enemy ranks.

He hated crossbows, he really did. But there were times when it did help a shade to have a few hundred idiots throwing their contributions into the giant, convulsing monster of combat. Finlay saw orcs falling en masse as volleys of bolts tunneled into gray meat and let blood to spurt out in their wake.

Finlay saw his rangers congealing, forming the lance formation that would cut to the heart of whatever counter their enemies managed to hastily construct against the main body. He hurried to join them.

It took only seconds to reach the group, but those seconds were enough for the fighting to intensify. Men flew head over heels as orcs launched them one way and another, gambesons splitting open along with their wearers beneath the guillotine swings of dullahan. Finlay came into the weakest flank, his bow discarded in favor of two longknives. He started putting them to work on one of the black-armored undead without a moment's pause.

The dullahan swung back at him, its broadsword outranging Finlay's knives by well over a foot and forcing him to hang back. He dodged, sidestepped, kept at bay and forced to evade rather than parry. In a contest of strength, he didn't think he'd lose, but his physicality wasn't so great that he could push back a blade that heavy with ones as small as his, not when a dullahan was on the other end. Eventually though, his chance came, and Finlay leaped on it like a bloodhound upon a fox.

He drove one length of steel deep into a gap between pauldron and cuirass, then twisted. The chain mail blocking his blade was thicker and heavier than could be worn by most humans, but it didn't last long against the enchanted metal grinding against it, not with the amount of strength Finlay had at his disposal. He tore apart ligaments and joints, then wrenched the knife out and stepped in, placing another one through the dullahan's eye slit and mangling the brains beneath.

Another dullahan moved in beside him, readying a sword stroke that might have killed Finlay on the spot. Had his men not moved faster. Two of them, rangers both, one snatching the undead's arm with both of his own, the other sliding his own knife along the most fragile areas of its plate. Properly made armor didn't have many true openings, but wielding a weapon with the strength of twenty men caused a lot more functional gaps to appear. And all Finlay's boys were well trained in finding them.

One dullahan dropped, then another, and then all that was left to fight were orcs and undead. The former had strength, the latter a near-inexhaustible endurance, but neither characteristic provided much aid as limbs started to detach beneath slashing blows. The only hitch came when one ranger was sent flying high, blood arcing away from him as a spinning limb flew from his body in the opposite direction.

It was the fomor, the last one. Finlay saw his men backing away, the momentum of their crushing assault quickly evaporating as terror seeped in. It entered his mind too.

Fomor were neither undead nor living, things of demonic blood and esoteric magic. Just to behold one was to stare at an entity more instinctually terrifying than death itself. Even his rangers couldn't overcome such a fear easily; there was simply no training to do so. It took innate, immutable will to manage something like that.

Finlay's hands tightened about his knives as he closed in for it. Had he been a man lacking in will, he'd have died in the gutters he came from.

The dagger scraped along heavy armor, leaving a deep gouge in the steel as Finlay leaped back. His enemy's spinning arm came fast as a striking viper, missing him by inches. Finlay made sure to snag the wrist with another knife as it went past, not missing the chance to leave another gash in his enemy.

It was not the sort of wound that typically felled a normal man, let alone a fomor. The monster was rounding on him again when the first of Finlay's rangers fell upon its back, the second and third following soon after.

He saw his chance, shoving while the abomination struggled for balance and sending it to the ground, then all of them fell upon it. Their knives found every vulnerability there was to be found, drawing acidic black blood in great rivulets and puddles as they skewered the piece of monstrous meat at their feet. By the time they were done, a crater had been eroded beneath the minced enemy.

It was then that Finlay stumbled back, panting for breath, feeling the adrenal frenzy of battle finally slow enough for thought. He surveyed the state of his men.

Many wounds, some dead. The vast majority of casualties had, perhaps expectedly, come from the regular soldiers he'd been granted, their bodies less sturdy and swift than his elites. A few rangers had died too, though. That made him truly hurt. Each of those was a man possessing talent found in only one among dozens, then trained for years to hone it. They were not easily replaced.

And the ones lost today were not the only casualties of their rebellion.

Finlay climbed to his feet, forcing himself to think of other matters before his thoughts could turn once more to Collin. His son would not be freed from the Dark Lord by simply agonizing over his capture, nor would any of the men now under Finlay's command be served by finding their leader's mind elsewhere. He buried every scrap of distraction, weakness, and humanity he had to.

His men needed him; his people needed him. Kaltan needed him. As the city's governor, that had been something he'd made peace with years ago. What Finlay hadn't known accepting the job was that the entire world would one day demand he do it well to boot.

But that was the least among his concerns, leading a rebellion against the Dark Lord. And yet more larger ones would soon be added to the pile. They always were.

CHAPTER THIRTY-EIGHT

Arion's the name," the boy explained, beginning his lie with an admirable ease. Such aptitudes were a sign of personalities that went well in House Shaiagrazni. "Arion Hawk, merchant, trader, entrepreneur . . . You may have heard of me? No matter if you haven't. I'm just passing through for a bit of bargain hunting, you see."

The guard did not verbally reply, only peered at Silenos and King Galukar in silent question. It was an understandable concern, of course. Silenos knew full well that both of them cut an intimidating enough sight on their own. He stood a full two meters in height, and though he was far leaner than muscled, his body would nonetheless have been correctly assessed as physically potent even were it not for the genius of fleshcrafting that gave it such macromolecular strength.

King Galukar's physicality was more apparent even than that. Beyond the handful of centimeters he towered over even Silenos by, his musculature was quite frankly in defiance of Shaiagrazni biology. No man in a preindustrial world ought to have been able to sustain it, nor even could any animal natural selection engineer it at all. Between that and his sheer scale, Silenos estimated the barbarian king to weigh even more than his own quarter tonne.

A single flexed biceps on that king's part was enough to quickly snap the guard's eyes back to Falls, who used the resumed attention as well as Silenos had come to expect.

"My bodyguards," he explained, grinning. "These are treacherous lands, you understand, if you don't happen to be a dark magus or such things."

The man nodded in empathetic understanding, then sent his gaze expectedly to the next sight of note. The largest point of failure in their entire masquerade.

Sphera, the petty necromancer officer of the so-called Dark Lord, was no more compliant in their deception than she had been in their journey.

"They're lying," she snapped, glaring from one of them to another, then staring at the guard with a desperation that would have been enjoyable to witness at any other time. "That one's a magus. He's a dark caster. They're just trying to get entrance without giving you their true identities—"

She trailed off as Falls hit her, perhaps a shade harder than was necessary.

"Shut it, whore," he snapped, then turned back to the guard, feigning apology. "You must forgive me. That one's a slave, and she's rather recently captured. Still haven't finished breaking her in, if you understand, so she'll be a bit unmanageable for a while."

It had been their one great concession. Finlay Baird, governor of Kaltan, was famously a man of progress and liberation.

He despised slavery almost as much as a slave might and had all but outlawed it within his own city before being redirected in his efforts by the Dark Lord. Traveling with one openly behind his walls was not a way to go unnoticed.

But they could not have risked leaving Sphera behind outside, not without the risk of her escaping whatever bonds they encased her in, and there was simply no other way to bring an openly held prisoner within. Gagging her would only have conveyed all that binding her already had, as well as making it apparent that they did not wish her to speak.

It was possible the guard saw through their facade, as imperfect a concession as it was, but if he did there was no hint of the fact in his gaze. He only nodded, slowly at first, then more earnestly as he watched the hateful glares Sphera sent at Falls.

"You're aware of the governor's opinion on slavery?" the man asked wearily. Falls shrugged.

"Nobody's perfect. I'll take a bit of abolitionist sentiment if it means doing my business in the only undead-free city within fifty miles."

The guard snorted, then stepped aside to allow them unbarred passage through the broad gates.

"In that case, by all means, go about your business and please accept my apologies for keeping you so long in the first place."

With a few more tedious moments of feigned smiles, they moved past the man and into the city. Silenos felt his expression relax into its usual sensible mask the moment he was certain it could no longer be scrutinized by the guard.

"Arion, you stay with the prisoner," Silenos ordered his apprentice. "The barbarian and I shall investigate this place alone. We can walk faster and easier than you and are more intimidating."

The latter would be useful in extracting answers from otherwise unwilling containers, while the former would simply allow for more ground to be covered within the same span. Perhaps even Galukar understood as much because he gave little in the way of protests before following after Silenos.

It was an uneventful day for them both. Grinding sluggishly past them in lengthy patches of nothing, punctuated by the occasional bout of insubstantiality. It was easy to grow frustrated as their continued efforts proved uselessly applied, but Silenos found his temper a simple thing to control. Perhaps he had merely been unpracticed in regulating the primordial idiocy of emotion, given his century of freedom from its touch. Perhaps, more disturbingly, he was growing accustomed to being denied his will. That was an unacceptable thought. Seniors of House Shaiagrazni did not get accustomed to such things.

However wrong it was in the ethical sense, reality did not seem to care. The people Silenos probed with questions were of invariably little help. Refusing to answer, turning back in fear, or even meeting him with overt confusion. Those few who knew something, they all knew the very same fact. And it was a tedious thing to squeeze from each and every one of them despite its insignificance.

Only one fact emerged with any consistency in their search: that the governor, of all people, knew of the man named Silhouette, going so far as to even publicly claim he had met the man. Galukar's face darkened to a rather grim mask as that much was made clear, his eyes sharpening with rage.

"This was a fine city once," the king growled. "I knew many of the people who ruled it. Good, decent people. Then Finlay the Butcher staged his little coup and painted the streets with red. I'd sooner surrender the world to the Dark Lord than work with that upstart little monster. I say we wring his neck before taking our leave and find some other way out of the area."

Silenos really was getting tired of the local idiots of this new world. Really, he'd never seen a class rebellion that hadn't been deserved. It was ludicrously easy to keep the common people held underfoot. Ordinary humans were a remarkably docile bunch. Anyone stupid enough to be *overthrown* by them deserved it.

And that was without considering the simple fact of Finlay's success in holding the city. As Silenos had heard it, half of the settlement was going to be ceded over to the Dark Lord by its inept rulers before his coup. No doubt that had been the inciting incident for it. People tended to lash out against foreigners substantially more readily than they did starvation or tyranny.

One citizen after another, regardless of rank, they all gave the same responses. Either nothing of any real substance or a direction toward Finlay himself. King Galukar grew angrier by the answer, his blood pooling with rage intensely enough that it actually showed beneath his bronzed skin. Silenos found himself wondering whether the giant oaf might burst a blood vessel if it continued. Found himself hoping he did. Such a thing would be trivially healed, and unspeakably amusing.

Silenos's own annoyance mounted as they continued their questioning, eventually becoming clear that there was only one man they had anything to gain by investigating. He asked, more specifically, about Finlay.

* * *

Arion had gotten a cheap inn, given the state of their funds, and found himself mortified to realize that it was striking him as some sort of luxury. The walls were thin and marked by numerous holes. Floors rough, unvarnished wood. The beds were two in number and rickety, with the ceiling being low and the entire place smelling faintly of human flesh and alcohol.

But it was not the wilds. Not a charred wasteland of black necromantic dirt. The ceiling was better coverage than unbound sky; the walls were better windbreaks than empty air. Good God, he was going native. What a revolting thought.

The necromancer, Sphera, was with him still, of course. Arion didn't intend to let her out of his sight for an instant, leaving her bound against the far wall, glaring back at him as he glared likewise. She was powerful, he had to admit. For a woman.

No, just powerful in general. The more Arion actually saw of women in the wilds, the more skeptical he found himself of how the other magi regarded them. If nothing else, there were exceptions to the general rule, and he was holding one of them prisoner. A dangerous exception.

She was older than him by at least a few years, and as far as Arion could tell, her talent was superior to Walriq's. The difference wasn't small either. In raw power alone, she was likely the equal of a lesser Hero, more than a match for Arion's own. She was bound tightly though, carefully immobilized and kept from conjuring shadestuff to free herself. More importantly, she was a necromancer without reanimates. Arion had already seen just how a fight like that went when his master spent those days struggling so dangerously while weaponizing his fleshcrafting.

"Thinking of how you'll fight back if I escape?"

Her question came abrupt and staggering as a cavalry charge, whipping Arion out of his own mind and back to the present. He turned sharply to the necromancer, half expecting to find her already free and readying an attack. Instead she remained as she was, bound to one corner, but smiling now. Looking altogether too confident for his liking.

"Why would I bother thinking about that?" Arion shot back. "You don't have a chance against me, and we both know it."

He briefly considered breaking an arm or leg to make sure but decided against it. The noise, and the injury following the noise, might attract undue attention. Even in a city not actively filled with the enemy, caution was needed.

"I had a chance against your master." She grinned back, speaking of her killing the great wind mage as if . . . Well, as if it were the killing of the great wind mage. "And I didn't have a hard time tricking you about it either. Dead to a heart attack mid-fuck, eh?"

Arion felt his jaw tighten with rage. Hers, meanwhile, grew lax with amusement.

"Oh! You didn't recognize me? Come now, how little attention do you pay? No wonder you magi never get anything done. Too busy thinking about sex and food to even notice what's right beneath your nose, hmm?"

Arion couldn't know whether she was telling the truth or not. He didn't remember the girl he'd found standing over his dead master, couldn't even recall the color of her skin or hair. For all he knew, the necromancer really was being honest.

"Couldn't think of a better way to get him alone than by fucking him?" he noted, deciding to be safe and simply turn things around on her. "A woman is still a woman, I suppose."

He saw the necromancer's eyes narrow for a moment, turning jagged with hatred at his jab. Arion found that interesting. He'd struck a nerve, it seemed. She didn't let it remain exposed for long.

"And how about the woman in your group, that paladin. Still held captive by Venka, I'd guess?"

Arion's blood curdled as she threw the verbal lance his way, feeling it sink in deep. Her smile only widened at the sight.

"Oh, yes, I know it was him she got snatched up by. You've heard of his reputation of course, yes?"

"I have," Arion snapped, but she just kept on talking as if he'd said nothing at all.

"Cruelty is the main thing. Though having met him, I wouldn't say he's exactly cruel. More . . . hard, sharp. Doesn't take uncooperative prisoners lightly. He does his duty in the hopes of one day ascending in rank as reward and won't let anything get in the way of that. Your friend should be fine as long as she gives him what he wants to know during interrogation."

He wanted to vomit more with each new word past her lips.

"We'll get her back," he snapped, glaring at the woman, feeling his hatred foam over. "Or she'll escape. Ensharia's smarter than you'd believe. She—"

"She is not getting past several thousand orcs and the most gifted fencer currently alive." The Necromancer grinned. "But it's adorable that you have so much faith in her. Perhaps it will prove well placed. If she's particularly resourceful, she might make it out of whatever cell she's in and manage to get killed in the attempt of fleeing by her guards rather than strapped down and peeled like a grape for information."

Arion was storming toward her before he knew it, hand raised and cocked back in a fist, ready to strike her. He was interrupted by the door's opening.

Silenos Shaiagrazni strode into the room as if his every step were something to be celebrated, and behind him King Galukar ducked down beneath the low frame to squeeze in after. The door closing behind them. Both men affixed Arion and the necromancer with thoughtful looks. Galukar seemed approving of what he'd been about to do, Silenos indifferent. Neither bothered to remark upon it.

"I have decided our next move," Silenos declared, moving to the single chair resting against a wall in their room, then pausing. He remained standing rather than taking it. Arion would have done the same. The caster was far heavier than he looked, and such a fragile thing would surely have perished beneath his weight.

"What is it?" he asked his master, eager for the distraction of planning.

"We require the aid of this city's governor," Silenos explained. "And to get that, we need an audience. If an audience of thanks and gratitude on his part, then so much the better. We are going to break his son out of prison."

CHAPTER THIRTY-NINE

The first thing General Venka had done when Ensharia was finally taken from her makeshift cell and marched alongside his men was to shackle her. He'd used big, thick bands of iron to do it. Things large enough that a normal woman wouldn't have been able to raise her arms against their weight, strong enough that she might have struggled to break them were she unbound and armed with an axe.

He needn't have bothered. The day before, and the night after it, she'd spent virtually all her time healing the pirate. Ensharia was not a true healer, not even a true cleric of her order whose power was focused exclusively on such things rather than equipping its wielder with physicality and potency. Her ability to restore a man's life and strength was stretched almost to its limits in treating Swick the Swift. Almost.

Now, the pirate shuffled along just ahead of her. His feet were bound in shackles of leather fixed to thick rope, like Ensharia behind him and like the man behind her. Slaves. Captured and sealed, dragged along in the wake of General Venka and his gray-skinned engine of war. Ensharia felt rather sick at the very thought.

Orcs were among the slaves. That fact had surprised her when she'd first learned of it the day before. It seemed absurd. Orcs were the soldiers, they were Venka's warriors, and yet the more she considered it, the more sense it made. Humans were her warriors too. And they were the Dark Lord's. There was no reason a species could not be cast into two roles at once.

Soon enough, they stopped, and their work began. While some slaves set up tents for the officers and pickets for defense, others, like Ensharia, were put to work in more manual roles. It was their job to provide the campfires.

Apparently the black dirt of the Dark Lord's lands could be burned; it simply required the right treatments first. One of the major steps was compressing it. Such knowledge was known well in advance of Venka's expedition, had been for years, and so the forces had hauled several purpose-made wooden molds to do so. She'd been confused, at first, by the metal bands around the sides of the molds. Then the work had begun.

In making the black dirt useful as fuel, one had to squeeze it to an absurd degree. Ensharia was taught to fill the containers up roughly three-quarters, leaving the dirt piled up to a line drawn just a hand or two from the top, then press down an iron top, drive a lever through a side slot, and start drawing it back to crush the stuff.

Easy work, at first. Then harder. Ensharia eyed the lid of the thing, knowing that she was permitted to call each batch finished only once it had reached the median point of the container. Every inch closer it came, the effort required for the next shift grew ever more. She started looking at the other workers for some example of how she might improve around the 60 percent mark.

Most others, she realized, were working in teams. Five, even six orcs at each lever, all gripping and grunting, sweat building against their skin in great globules. Ensharia's body was still sore, throbbing, and at any other time it might have been heartening to see so many great brutes needed to match her own work.

Now, she just found herself dwelling on how similar their roles had become. She was an orc in function, and lesser even than most of the orcs present.

Certainly, less than the humans were.

Ensharia's work was finished soon, despite her injuries. That much she could thank Silenos for. The Savior's fleshcrafting was growing on her by the day, proving itself well worth the moral compromise each and every time she put it to work, and the free rest she gained from using it so was valuable. It meant more time to spend recuperating, and more strength to use once she'd finished her recovery. All that was left was finding the best way to use it.

Her much-needed observations were not given much time to be completed, however. A voice soon rang out in her ear, interrupting whatever surveillance she might have managed and almost making Ensharia jump.

"I was half drunk when I got Shaiagrazni's message."

She turned, half expecting some orc or even Venka, realizing what the words meant—how many possibilities they eliminated—only as she finished turning. Swick the Swift was seated a foot or two beside her, still chained just as tightly, still bound to the orcs working away not three yards ahead. His face was almost unrecognizable. The man's broad grin was gone, his unbroken cockiness shattered. The sockets of his eyes seemed deeper than before, the eyes themselves bloodshot, and by the texture of his skin and hair, he seemed to have aged halfway into a corpse.

Ensharia took the sights in while digesting his words, taking her time before replying to them.

"I thought you were always half drunk," she noted testily. He didn't react to her response at all, simply moved past it as if he'd not even noticed.

"Half drunk, fully stupid," Swick murmured. "They were my men, my crew, and we'd sailed for years. A decade, some of them. Seizing entire galleons, snatching home tonnes of gold. Literally tonnes! Another few years and we'd have been rich, all of us. I'd have watched some of them retire with wealth to make most nobles jealous and made some of the others my captains. Always wanted my own fleet of ships. Admiral Swick the Swift, king of the sky pirates, dominator of the winds . . . Aye, that always seemed good for me."

She didn't say anything this time, only watched him speak. Listening with a sickening satisfaction. Ensharia wouldn't have expected the display she saw now, not from a man half as proud as the captain had been. She wondered what the cause was for all of a second before it became apparent.

"Ah!" Swick winced, clutching his head. "Shit, the headache."

Ensharia had treated her fair share of drunks and knew the sight of withdrawal all too well. It could get nasty in most men, as bodily functions either shut down or went haywire, mind sending its vessel into spasmodic frenzy as if to compensate for all the hours spent blunted and dull. That didn't happen to Swick the Swift. Such things were difficult to inflict on a man of his native physical prowess, but it almost felt like he'd have been struck by a mercy if it had.

"You took a risk," she said hesitantly. "They all knew what they were in for. You told me that yourself."

She had been ready for more drunken self-loathing or hatred. The fire he directed at *her* as she said that left her taken aback completely.

"Don't speak on things you don't understand," the pirate snapped. "They didn't sign up to be thrown into suicide by some drunkard."

Tears were threatening to form upon the man's features, and Ensharia felt whatever animosity or disgust she'd been overcome with earlier bleed back into simple pity. Perhaps it was weak of her.

It certainly wasn't kind because Swick the Swift didn't so much as glance back at Ensharia after that. Just remained locked in his own agony. She found herself reassessing the man, watching him blubber and weep.

Ensharia decided he really did need a drink, after all.

A day passed, and Ensharia used it well in learning even more about the circumstances around her. Some of it was rather promising and good; other things, most things, were terrible. It was, she supposed, the sort of ratio one might expect from information gained while held chained and imprisoned amid a horde of orcs.

The orcs were what soaked up most of her studies, and for good reason. It was taught among paladins that they were simple creatures. Clever enough for tool usage and primitive ambushes but never any form of complex society. When more than a few hundred joined together, they would invariably collapse and schism through infighting. What Ensharia was seeing around her now though defied it all.

Venka had managed to forge a military glue capable of binding even the most savage species of all into one block, and the more she observed, the more she understood how it worked.

Each orc was motivated not by loyalty, or a yearning for status, but by fear of becoming like the ones beneath them. The basest soldiers acted to keep from being made slaves, the officers acted out of desperation to keep themselves removed from the common ranks, and Venka's most trusted orcs each worked tirelessly to retain his favor. It was a brutal system, leaving countrymen pitted against one another, and yet it held the orcs chained into their stations remarkably well.

Ensharia's appreciation for it only grew the more she saw of their casual savagery.

Brawls were common, and terrifying. The strength an orc could unleash in battle was sufficient to send another of their kind flying and rolling as if they weighed no more than a child. Ground was churned up and dirt cast in all directions whenever two of them fought, and on the occasions where they snagged the slave's binding rope, it would drag several to the ground. Each time, Ensharia was pulled from whatever thoughts occupied her and reminded of the monstrous company she was trapped among.

Her one reprieve came briefly as she passed a flower. It wasn't anything big. A small, fragile strip of crimson petals mounted on a withered stem, hunched and desiccated amid the ocean of black dirt around it. She couldn't have explained why, if pressed, but the sight of it left a tear welling in the ducts of her eyes even still. It was hope in a land of ruin.

Ensharia made herself look away from the flower and focus back upon their march.

Her body still ached, despite the time spent recovering and healing, and it would continue to ache no matter how long she was given for it to mend. That was Venka's doing. The general had not been satisfied with what Ensharia had told him, which was almost fair enough, given that she had lied and feigned ignorance without exception. He had called for her torture, one day and then the next. Ensharia had felt her skin peeled back from muscle, flesh burned and tortured by hot iron, had a molar torn from her mouth and a steel-tipped whip strike at her back and buttocks with such force that it would have flayed a tree of its bark.

Through it all, she'd surrendered nothing.

Venka had surely not expected her to because he didn't seem the least bit surprised. Ensharia might have hoped he would grow tired of the torment, that she might be spared further agony the next night, but somehow she doubted it. General Venka did not strike her as the sort of man to stop doing a thing just because he grew weary of it.

Something moved in Ensharia's vision, drawing her eyes back across to the site of the flower. She felt a stab of urgency take her at the sight of an orc kneeling down beside it, reaching to the dirt and plucking the plant free.

Her fury was instantaneous and instinctive, sending her surging on for the savage with such force that she toppled several of the beasts still tethered to her in doing so.

It looked up just as Ensharia came over to shove it, sending the orc flat against the floor, eyes wide and face tight with sudden fear as she stared down at it.

"Why did you do that?" she snarled, temper almost blinding her. "That was the only living thing anywhere in this awful place. What made you so incapable of resisting its destruction? Do you just hate life?"

The orc stared up at her, and to Ensharia's surprise its face was twisted more by confusion than hate or fear. Carefully, slowly, it took an arm out from under itself and raised it out to her. The fist was curled, and she took a half step back from it, fearing an attack. When it unfurled, however, Ensharia found nothing within. Save a crimson flower, resting along the palm.

It had been spared any damage at all, despite the orc's heavy fall. Preserved delicately and perfectly amid the gray flesh.

"Sorry," the orc mumbled, not meeting her eye. "Flower prit tee. Human like flower. I . . . wanted make hap pea."

Something twisted in Ensharia's breast, and she reevaluated the information. The orc hadn't been destroying the flower, Ensharia realized. He'd been picking it. Picking it for her.

Forcing herself calm, swallowing the blend of guilt and regret, Ensharia slowly reached out to take the delicate plant. Eyes wide, heart breaking as the orc flinched again. He hadn't meant any harm at all.

"I'm sorry," she breathed, speaking slowly and clearly for the sake of understanding. "I . . . didn't realize what you were doing, I . . . This is a lovely flower, thank you." She took the thing, raising it up to her head and gently pushing its stem into her hair. It was all tangled, knotted, and greasy from unwashed travels, but that only made the flower hold its place easier.

The orc's eyes brightened a shade as Ensharia helped him up.

CHAPTER FORTY

Ensharia was tortured the day after. And the day after that. After a while she almost grew accustomed to it, which was disheartening in its own way. Paladins were trained to resist interrogation, however, and she found herself kept calm and solid by the very same breathing techniques and mental disassociations she'd spent so long accruing all those years ago in training.

It helped, she knew, that despite the sheer brutality inherent to any act of torture, Ensharia's body had not been broken or crippled in any way that surpassed its ability to recover.

She'd been confused by that, at first, but quickly realized the motive behind it. Unsurprisingly, it was not the general Venka's mercy.

Ensharia, and Captain Swick the Swift, were both to be presented to the Dark Lord himself. Her heart had almost stopped with fright when she'd first realized that, and then her thoughts had further accelerated into a frenzied, panicked mess at the implications. One conclusion was very clear, indeed. She would not be surviving his presence.

They'd kept her body intact because they planned on reanimating her as an undead after whatever interrogation the Dark Lord had planned was finished. Or, possibly, they didn't plan on getting any information from her at all. Perhaps the sessions of torture were merely a pretense to keep her body enfeebled and weak, to prevent escape without letting her know she'd already been consigned to death. Either way, Ensharia didn't plan to find out on her enemy's terms.

She'd not been sure how long it would take for the group to reach their destination, but it couldn't have been long. Her days were numbered, and with no way of knowing what that number was, Ensharia had thought quickly. Gathering every scrap of knowledge she could, scrutinizing General Venka's entire convoy for whatever weaknesses might be exploited.

It was yet another mark in the inscrutable commander's favor that she managed to find so few.

Ensharia turned quickly to Swick, asking the man about whether his magic might manage the deed. His response was pained and bitter.

"Not a chance," he grunted. "I can't translocate without bringing whatever I'm touching with me."

She frowned at that, recalling the way he'd seemed always to step back from an enemy before using his power.

"Including the slaves bound to us?"

"Including them," he confirmed. "And before you suggest it, I can't just bring them along with us. The distance I can manage is limited enough usually, a quarter of a mile on a good day. It drops, and the fatigue of reaching it rises, as I need to carry more and more mass along on the journey. I also can't travel to any place I haven't splattered with my blood either."

Ensharia glanced back down the row of their fellow prisoners. They weren't all bound together—such a thing would be inconvenient—rather they'd been separated into several dozen rows of perhaps a hundred or so. One hundred people was one hundred times the captain's own mass already. One hundred orcs though, as so many of the prisoners seemed to be . . . She could imagine the strain it would impart.

"What's the largest thing you could bring?" she asked, considering a way they might free themselves from the rest and translocate away once the connection was broken. Swick just sighed.

"Something small, I'm afraid. A suit of armor, a young child. Not an adult, definitely not one of your . . . size. Sorry."

It was almost funny that he thought she'd be bothered by a perceived slight against her figure or weight. Almost. But nothing could have truly amused Ensharia in such a time, not if every fool in the world had tried at once. Perhaps she'd have cracked a smile if one of them had broken off her chains and doubled Swick's powers first.

She took a mental step back from her current predicament, assessing her situation in more general terms. What did she know of Venka? Of his army, his plans, his methods? Reassuringly, quite a bit.

The man's plan was to link up with another, larger force of orcs in order to prepare a besieging army with which to attack Kaltan. Such tactics were commonplace among human forces; it was, after all, far easier to send ten forces of a thousand through land than one force of ten thousand. What was exceptional was the fact that Venka dared to do it with orcs.

But then, Venka had done so much else with the creatures. Ensharia had been studying the hierarchy of his army, and everything she learned just left it ever more impressive in her mind.

Hierarchy was the secret at the center of everything, a strict and irresistible hierarchy. Rather than being valued for strength, as many general's men were, or wits and intellect, as were the bannermen of many lords, Venka's soldiers seemed to gain promotion and status based on nothing more complex than good behavior. Good behavior. It was like the man was training dogs rather than thinking people. Ensharia had seen the results clearly enough.

At the bottom of his ranks were the slave orcs, almost all of which were newly captured and newly conscripted into the forces. At the top were those that had learned to navigate Venka's preferences of manners and etiquette, most commonly the orcs that had been among his men for the longest.

It was one of the former kind, not the latter, that Ensharia headed to next.

Garutan was sitting down as Ensharia approached him, one who had an appreciation for taking his life slowly, she had learned. The great orc stood almost a head taller than even most of his kin and had perhaps enough bodily mass in bone and musculature that even she might have felt its resistance were she to try moving him. He looked up at her approach, face splitting into a broad smile the way it always did when she came to speak.

"Enshar!" He grinned. Ensharia smiled back.

Garutan had been the orc responsible for handing her the flower she now wore in her mottled hair, and she'd spent no small stretch of time speaking with him over the past days. At first she'd thought him to be a savage animal. That perception had not long survived knowing Garutan.

He was not an animal, not savage, and certainly not a cruel beast as many of the stories might have claimed. True, he was not as clever as a human, but that was hardly the orc's own fault. He'd brought Ensharia the flower because he'd thought she looked pretty and nice, and having known him for just a few more days, Ensharia had found him to be simply one of the sweetest people she'd ever met. Less a giant animal, and more a giant, loving little boy.

"How are things going?" she asked, taking her own seat. Garutan answered as eagerly as ever, seeming thrilled just to have had the question posed to him. He was always one to enjoy talking and sharing, but more than that, Ensharia had found, he enjoyed having an interest taken in him.

Garutan excitedly talked about the sights he'd seen, mostly clouds and mountains, but occasionally veering into a revelation of curious behavior from his fellow slaves or guarding soldiers. Ensharia listened, committing it all to memory as usual, and interrupted only as a harsh voice called the orc off to continue his work elsewhere.

"Sorry, Ensha," he grumbled, storming off with his misery dripping from him. It made Ensharia's guts twist to behold. She watched him leave until the rattling of shackles and scraping of binds told her Swick was coming back to sit beside her.

The pirate had changed, over the days, and not for the better. Face infested by scraggly, messy stubble, eyes sunken ever deeper into his sockets. He had looked half corpse before and since made the transition further to at least three-quarters. She felt nothing but pity as she gazed upon him.

"I'm going to die here," he grunted, sounding like a man holding his own blood-slick entrails in the midst of a battle. "I killed my men, and now I'm going to get myself killed right alongside them."

"Don't say that," Ensharia growled, speaking with a venom that was perhaps disproportionate to his words. Whenever he spoke of such things, it made her think of them. Squeezed those last embers of hope in her mind almost to the limit.

"Have you come up with any plans?" the pirate countered, looking at her with a blend of emotion Ensharia couldn't quite identify. It was hard to be truthful, but she forced herself to.

"Not yet, but even if I think of nothing at all we still have hope. We'll be heading to Kaltan soon, yes?"

The pirate eyed her, frowning, then nodding.

". . . Yes," he conceded. "You say that as if it changes everything."

"It does." Ensharia grinned. "Silenos and the others will be heading to it as well. Arion came to try to rescue us while you were unconscious, and I told him about what we learned of the Silhouette, that they can find a way of leaving the Dark Lord's lands there. If they end up there, they'll doubtless find out about the city's conflict with the Dark Lord and be roped into helping defend it, or even find out Venka himself is marching on it and stay deliberately to wait for us."

"How will they know we'd still be with him?" the pirate challenged. Ensharia felt a smile grow, a genuine one for the first time in days.

"Simple calculation. If Venka is there within the time frame he'll arrive in, then he will have had to forgo dropping us off with the Dark Lord or any other forts. Otherwise . . . Well, we'd be there already. If they have access to maps or decent scouting, they'll draw the same conclusion. And if we can't be brought to a powerful necromancer, we'll be kept alive to ensure we're reanimated in as fresh a state as possible, given our combat power and magic."

Swick considered her words with slow, subtle nods. Ensharia had expected—or hoped—to see some new flash of resolve across his features as she explained her optimism. That didn't happen, but there certainly was a change behind those glassy eyes. It was an unnerving one rather than reassuring. Gnawing at her confidence and leaving her uncertain.

"What are you thinking?" she challenged, finding the ludicrous question escaping her out of sheer, sudden desperation.

Swick eyed her levelly.

"I'm thinking that I'm sorry," he replied, as if he were a headsman and she the condemned criminal. Swick turned away from Ensharia before she could process his words, heading to an orc. One of the guards, not the slaves.

"I have information your general might be interested in hearing," he told it, speaking with that loud, confident voice that best maximized the odds of being understood by their kind. "Secrets, from traitors, and enemy plans. Take me to him and I can share it."

The orc took its time in processing Swick's words, but not as much of it as Ensharia did. By the time she'd truly realized what was happening, that she had been betrayed, the pirate had already been unbound from the other slaves, firmly grabbed by both arms, and hauled away to speak with the general.

Leaving her alone once more.

CHAPTER FORTY-ONE

There hadn't been much for Collin to do of late. But he supposed that was one of the states one could expect to enter when one happened to be confined within a cell.

His little room was a hard one, that much was clear. Bars of iron were mounted over the window, which itself was barely larger than his head. Through it, he could estimate the walls to be over a foot in thick, and solid stone all the way through. Diabase, of course, no doubt the work of some very gifted magi. The fuckers. He wanted to find those magi, then slam their big, ancient tomes down onto their scrota. Collin bet he'd outright burst the things, started wondering how wide the blood spatters would end up.

It was not a particularly productive train of thought, he had to admit, and even more so, it was not the kind his father would have encouraged.

You're a Kaltan boy, Collin, he could practically hear him saying. *People expect the worst of you. Everything you do will be criticized and scrutinized just because of how you talk. It's not fair, and it's not right, but it's the way things are. So put on a show they can't find fault in.*

Fat lot of good such teachings had done him, in the end. Collin hadn't found much use for them in the field of battle. He'd not found much use for anything there. Save his skill, his power, his quickness. And even they had been of limited help. As evidenced by his being trapped in a fucking cell within the enemy's lands.

Collin got to his feet, making his way across the room and nearing his window. He jumped. The thing was built about seven feet off the floor, so if he ever wanted a decent look at the world outside, he had to elevate himself a bit. It wasn't hard, fortunately. His training may not have kept him out of prison, but it'd made a fathom-high jump no issue at all.

He caught the ledge of the window, holding his body up with the strength of his fingers and peering out. The angle wasn't ideal; thanks to the sheer thickness of the wall, Collin could see nothing within half a mile of the tower's shadow. But he saw enough.

Black dirt, dunes of corrupted sand. Putrefying air. He dropped down a moment later, then moved back to a corner, sitting. It had been a mistake to remind himself where he was.

What he'd do for just an hour outside. Just a minute. One minute, one bow, and fifty arrows. He'd have fired each one and killed as many of the Dark Lord's bastards before the time had expired, that much Collin was certain of. Even one would be something. Even one would be more than his weeks of worthlessness. In his cell, there was little to do save focus on keeping his strength from waning.

Collin's musings were interrupted when the door blew up.

It was rather an abrupt thing, abrupt enough that he just sat and gasped at the ruined, mangled heap of smoldering metal rather than move to do anything about it. Fortunately, it wasn't an enemy responsible.

The man was not one Collin had ever seen before, and his foreign features were apparent at a glance. Hair the color of coal, skin like copper, eyes a vibrant glare that somehow rang empty as they fell upon him. No more invested in what they might behold than a butcher studying a slab of meat. The stranger was ridiculously tall, closer to seven feet than six, and lean as a duelist. His skin had a curious texture that took Collin a moment to identify as similar in appearance to the exoskeletal armor of an insect, all hard and ridged. It shifted slightly as he moved farther into the room.

"You are Collin Baird," the man said. Said, not asked. He did not seem to doubt the fact at all, but Collin nodded anyway.

"Are you here to . . . You were sent by my father?" he asked, finding his shock abating as he spoke, hope finally flaring up like an inferno in his chest.

"Yes," the man replied, as if the matter was of no more consequence to him than the weather. Collin supposed imprisonment did tend to carry less significance for those outside the cell.

"What sort of forces do we have?" Collin asked, realizing only then that he'd heard no combat outside. The walls were thick, the spaces in them few, but even so he'd have certainly caught wind of armies clashing outside the fort. Clearly this was a stealth mission, which meant the destruction of his prison door had alerted every enemy nearby. There'd be fighting soon.

"None," the man replied. "I am here alone, save for a single companion. I believe he should be finished now."

Before Collin could speak, could do anything more than panic at the thought of being swarmed by enemies, a new figure emerged at the doorway. This one was bigger even than the first, almost too broad to fit through the opening. His shoulders were like those of a draft horse, hands like dinner plates. On his back there hung the biggest sword Collin had ever seen before, a great slab of ugly iron that dwarfed even its gargantuan wielder.

But all the size in the world was little help against a force of undead thousands strong and led by fomors.

"You found him," the giant grunted with a voice so low and rumbling it sounded almost like the marching of armies itself.

"We need to leave!" Collin snapped, finding himself almost stunned at the sheer stupidity of these men. "The enemy will be on us any moment. We have to—"

"Enemy?" the giant asked with a grin. "You mean the ones outside and throughout the fort, yes?"

Collin wavered slightly. Clearly, there was something known to his rescuers that he'd not been enlightened on.

"Yes," Collin snapped. "What are—What have the two of you got planned?"

"Nothing much." The giant shrugged. "We're going to march back on foot, nothing fancy. But the fort's occupants aren't an issue anymore. We killed them all."

Collin looked from one man to the other, scrying their faces for sign of the joke. He found none. The first man, the leaner, smaller one, looked more impatient than anything, as if human conversation were a mere inconvenience he'd learned to occasionally tolerate. The larger one seemed to be in rather a good mood, grinning broadly like a man who'd just been handed a particularly enticing barrel of wine by a particularly curvaceous woman. Neither expression struck Collin as that of a person waiting for crushing defeat to descend upon them.

"My God," he breathed. "You're . . . Both of you are serious, aren't you?"

"It never ceases to amaze me how simple your kind are." The smaller man sighed, turning for the door. "Let us go."

The giant followed, glaring at his companion with more hate than irritation.

"You keep saying that. You keep being stuck here with us," he spat.

"And I draw closer to doing something drastic with each moment that remains the case," the younger one replied. "While you continue to speak as if you have not already been extended more liberties than most men could earn in a lifetime."

Collin did not really have much to do, which he imagined was an experience common to many weeks-long prisoners. For the most recent stretch of his life, days had been divided into time spent exercising, time spent eating, and time spent throwing punches into the cell's outer wall in hope of eventually breaking through. The latter had so far achieved a dent only fingers deep and less than a foot wide.

Outside, he found the air almost driven from his lungs. The hall outside Collin's cell was something he'd seen only once before, ever. He was kept clean and sanitary. Sterile might have been the best word for it, really. Exercise had never been a priority for his jailers, and so he had only a weeks-old memory to compare to the sight of carnage he was met with.

Bodies were broken apart, both skeletal and fleshy. Rotting brown blood-stained floor, walls and ceiling in seemingly equal volumes, while broken and bent weapons were littered around the place. The devastation was such that Collin couldn't even hope to count the number of enemies left strewn across the corridor. He recognized some of the types though. Basic reanimates, stronger dullahan . . . and a fomor.

Instantly, his eyes were back on the duo, heart racing.

"Who are you both?" Collin demanded. These two men were strangers to him, but not the world. One could not walk the earth with even half their power and not leave a legend behind.

The slender man seemed as irritated by the question as all other things, the broader one only amused. Neither slowed their stride as the second of them answered.

"You will not know my . . . companion," he replied, referring to the other man as if even referencing him tasted foul. "But you may have heard my name. I am Galukar, king of Arbite and—"

"Wielder of the Godblade!" Collin gasped, realizing then where he'd seen him before. King Galukar was a foreign monarch, a distant one at that, but his name was one to transcend any border on the continent. Collin had seen a painting of him once, at a party. He barely seemed exaggerated by the paint.

"The very same." King Galukar nodded, smiling now. "And, of course, we already know who you are, Sir Baird."

Something strained in the king's eyes as he spoke Collin's name, and it wasn't hard to guess what. His father was not a popular man among the world's royals and aristocrats. Such things were hard to even consider, however, when measured against the weight of reputation now standing before him.

No bloody wonder the fortress's garrison had been scythed away so effortlessly. If even half of what Collin had heard of King Galukar was true, and the slender man was so much as one-third his equal, then he was following perhaps the deadliest pair currently walking the world. They might have flattened the entire building itself within a few minutes, if they'd really tried, let alone killed all the monsters inside.

His pondering was interrupted as the smaller man halted, raising an open hand in silence. Despite the obvious friction between them, the larger one caught his meaning before even Collin, freezing himself, then holding Collin still with one giant arm.

"New enemies," the slender man whispered. "They are few, but powerful. Dullahans numbering one or two dozen, a handful of those fomor creatures . . . Yes, a lich is with them. There are maybe two hundred well-armed orcs to boot."

King Galukar nodded gravely, speaking quietly but somehow still rattling Collin's bones as he did.

"We can take them together," he grunted.

"It is not worth the risk. Baird is too fragile, and this may well be an assassination squad designed to cut losses in the event of his escape. Their timing is conveniently inconvenient."

There came the slightest pause, then, impressively quickly, the giant nodded again.

"Very well. One of us must divert them."

"I can," the smaller one said instantly. "Take the boy. It is best if he is not . . . present."

Another pause, then a great tightening of the giant's face. He finally sighed, as if conceding to something, and took Collin by the arm. His grip did not feel in any way exertive or strained, but it still sent a dull throb through Collin's musculature and into the bone. How easily could this man have crushed the limb entirely had he wished? Collin was whipped along behind him before he could ponder the thought.

Their strides came fast and rhythmic, but not so much so that he was kept from glancing behind him. Just before they turned a corner, he caught one last sight of the smaller man.

Collin couldn't begin to guess why, but for some strange reason, there seemed to be thin tendrils of some curious substance shooting out of him, stabbing into the fleshen bodies of fallen enemies. They were gone before he could glimpse what came next.

CHAPTER FORTY-TWO

Collin heard explosions thrashing the building around him as he ran. He'd read about them, of course. Typically things born from that weird, black powder made in the east, but more commonly the work of a particularly strong magus. He wasn't surprised to find such ability in the lean man, but to feel it unleashed on the fortress was another thing entirely.

The floor shook, the walls creaked, and the sound of crumbling mortar and crashing stone was impossible to ignore. It felt more like being in a castle under attack than simply hearing a distant battle, and apparently King Galukar was not immune to his concerns.

"Damned fool is going to bring the place down around us," he grumbled. "Pick up the pace. I'd rather not have to dig us both out of stone."

He didn't make it easy for Collin to pick up the pace. Rangers like him were trained for speed, able to outpace a warrior without even reaching the limits. Most of the time. Collin was no Hero though, and clearly King Galukar was a man to match the stories shared about him. Within a few more moments, sweat was running down Collin's body in thick rivulets as he strained himself just to near the king's velocity.

The corner was turned sharply, first by Galukar, then Collin. As Collin himself rounded it, he found the king locked in battle with a fomor of all things, a giant. The gaunt beast reared up to more than a yard over even the foreigner's incredible height, its powerful limbs whipping at him to tear the flesh away with barbed points. Like a man being attacked by an entire den of snakes at once.

Galukar did not seem to struggle with such a thing.

In an instant, the fomor's tendrils were tight around Galukar's forearms, squeezing them and straining to drag them apart, exposing the man's chest to further attack. The king's lip curled as he eyed the beast.

"Please," he scoffed.

With one move, he broke its grip, tearing his arms from the fomorian hold and flexing the fingers as he did. The creature was sent forward, overbalanced by the movement, and quickly turned its stumble into a desperate lunge for the warrior. Collin understood why; the man had yet to draw that beastly sword of his. Attacking now, while he remained unarmed, seemed the best chance for victory.

Galukar moved too, however. And Collin saw in that single motion that victory had never been within his enemy's reach to begin with.

The king slammed a shoulder into the fomor, sending it flat against the ground, then he came down atop it, pinning the creature beneath his body, holding its flailing, thrashing form in place. With one hand, he reached up to the blade mounted at his back and drew it, raising the sword high, then turning it and thrusting downward in one great motion.

Collin had seen kebabs skewered with less ease than that fomor, seen the juicy stock of cooking meat let to ooze free in more reluctance than the black blood in its veins. The sword stabbed the monster so violently that it broke through the back of its skull and sank several feet into the stone below, pinning it in place to flail and scream.

But not to die. Fomors took a long time to die, even when hurt enough to die properly. Collin watched this one fail to lose its life and felt a stab of satisfaction.

King Galukar ruined it by dragging his sword free, standing, and swinging down. His second strike split the thing's head open completely, his third took the head from the fomor's shoulders, and by his seventh the abomination was in more pieces than could easily be counted.

Collin stared blankly as the king finally straightened back up, glancing to eye him thoughtfully.

"You're unhurt?" he asked.

". . . Yes," Collin breathed, barely finding the words in light of what he'd just seen. Galukar nodded, seemingly heedless.

"Good, then let's continue. Do as you did this time for any more enemies we encounter. We need you kept safe."

Collin almost thought he was being mocked for a moment, then realized that to this man, his regionally famous combat power was simply not a factor to be considered. Not entirely sure how he might respond to such a truthful slight, he merely nodded and hurried to follow the jogging king.

Their pace continued, and the combat continued with even more violence. Soon enough, Collin found cracks beginning to diffuse along the stone walls, dust raining from the ceiling. King Galukar seemed more annoyed than angry.

"What is he doing?!" the monarch growled. "Does he not know anything but damned blasting magic and heresy?"

Many things had been drilled into Collin over the years when it came to dealing with the doings of magi, and chief among them was to ensure he was as far away as possible when one of them started hurling magic. Being inside the same building certainly went against those tenets, and so he was rather tempted to just continue walking as they came past the armory.

Tempted, but he didn't cave.

"Wait," Collin barked. "In here. My weapons. If I get them, I'll be able to defend myself."

The king seemed half tempted to argue but ended up just gesturing him on.

"Hurry up," he growled.

Collin did so.

The armory was not shaped in the same way that any he'd ever encountered had been, but there was a certain inexorable logic to the organization of any storehouse that made it navigable to one familiar with what it held. Collin soon found the bows, then his bow, taking the weapon with the sensation of power and lightning running along his arm. A purely phantom sensation, most would say, but he knew better. Limbed with flexible steel and strung with metal wire tense enough to hurl arrows over a horizon, it was a weapon that had served Collin even beyond its physical faculties. A thing of luck and old magic the likes of which only fighters could understand.

His arrows were located nearby, or ones able to serve as arrows, at the very least. Lengths of worked iron heavy enough that a normal man might have used them as smaller javelins.

Collin resisted the urge to take his time in admiring the finds, simply stuffing as many arrows as he could manage into quivers, binding as many of those as he could manage across his body, and taking flight. As he exited the armory, he found Galukar locked in battle again. This time, it seemed a more testing contest.

Two fomors were already attacking the king, whipping at his body with their wiry limbs, drawing blood on direct hits and gouging great clefts out of the surrounding diabase upon misses. The king himself fought back well, but his focus was split between the two greatest undead and the numerous lesser beasts striking from other sides. Dullahan, numbering perhaps a half dozen, and a magic caster hurling jets of flame and spears of ice as if they were Collin's own arrows.

Collin got to work quickly, overcoming his shock and shaking off the weeks of rust from his old killing machinery. He was in a corridor. A wide one, it had to be said, but far from the ideal circumstances for a ranger to do battle in. His best chance—his only chance—was to provide support for the king. Slipping around to put the giant man between himself and the enemy, Collin nocked his first arrow, then drew.

He was not his father. He was better. Collin's arrow flew with a skill and strength trained into him from before he could even recall, and it met the eye slit of a fomor just as the beast reared up. He felt himself smiling at the sight of iron burying itself in necrotic flesh, fragments of skull, ocular fluid, and brain matter frothing forth from the socket. Then the other monster was turning on him. He froze, started for another arrow, realized in an instant that the second enemy would move too quickly and unpredictably to bring it down before he was dead.

Then King Galukar stepped in.

His sword moved like nothing Collin had ever seen, or even heard about. One moment it was cocked back, held by his side, then the next it had already passed through the fomor's arm and hacked the limb off like a meat cleaver going through entrails.

The sheer weight of it actually spun his enemy, and Galukar had already readied another swing by the time it did. This one found the fomor's side, biting down to cut an angled mark as low as the monster's hips, almost opening up the groin and leaving disgusting viscera to spill out. More undead were closing in at the king's back by then, and Collin got to work quickly. His next arrow found a dullahan.

A puncture, a fountain of dark blood, then Galukar rounded on the charging undead with a roar like an entire pride of lions. The Godblade took another dark knight's head off at the base of its neck, then the king's foot sent a third crashing back into several more with such force as might have been mustered by a crumbling fortress.

Collin was given a more immediate point of comparison as the fortress continued to crumble around him.

"We need to leave!" he roared, loosing another arrow, which found that magic site between pauldron and cuirass. A fireball came for him, and he sidestepped just in time to keep himself from death.

King Galukar was quick to respond, plucking a fallen enemy from the ground with one swift motion and hurling them across the corridor. They crunched into the caster so hard that Collin swore he heard bones break even from ten yards back, both bodies flailing and spinning in separate directions as they bounced from each other. He and the king were sprinting past before the enemy could reveal itself to be either active or destroyed.

It seemed to Collin that the fortress was racing them, desperate to crumble and die before they could be free of its shadow, but if King Galukar shared his observation, he certainly didn't share his fears. The man moved as if escape from the place was merely his due and the lengthy run a scarce inconvenience in claiming it. Collin did what he could to match the pace, but it was a challenge even for him.

They were out of it, thank God, before it finished dying. Rubble fell in their wake, and stone ruptured in their shadow, each sight and sound another fist closing tight about Collin's lungs. He felt the fear taking him deep and harsh, perhaps more so than ever before. It felt sharp after his weeks of captivity, a sensation exaggerated by how alien it had become. Like feeling his gut burst from overeating after a month without food.

A more poetic man might have extended that metaphor, upon seeing the place Collin had been wishing to escape crumble just as he left. Collin had never found the time for poetry though. Kaltan lads had more practical things to concern themselves with, like watching the devastation.

It happened oddly fast, great sections of the dark spire seeming to fold inward like a punctured wineskin. Gravity and tension did much of the work, that much was clear, but one thing caught Collin's eye clearer than anything else. Despite the scale of the place, the sprawling lengths and towering peaks, despite the formidable depth of its fortifications and bedrock foundations, he still caught sight of the great pillar of flame arching high into the air.

One moment after he did, the concussion of its force reached him.

Collin yelped, humiliatingly, and took a step back, though he needn't have bothered. A normal man may have been wounded by the force and certainly would have by the chips of rock carried upon the winds, but his body was hardened beyond such considerations. King Galukar didn't even blink, just watched the display with an oddly disapproving look. Collin stared back at it and realized what the monarch had been studying a moment later.

Wings, leathery and spanning the height of five men each. Both emerged from the back of some creature so terrible as to defy description and so powerful that even Collin could feel the press of its power from all the hundreds of yards separating them.

"What is that?" he croaked, hating the sound of his own wavering voice, hating his helplessness to strengthen it even more. He'd fought the Dark Lord's armies thrice, bested them twice, slain over a dozen dullahan and two fomors. But he'd never seen anything half the equal of that abomination. It soared higher, rising as if dragged skyward on invisible strings, then its wings stretched outward, and Collin watched a new wave of fire descend upon the structure below. His heart sank.

Ten. With just ten creatures like that, he thought, the Dark Lord would be unstoppable. The entire continent could unite against him and still break against ten creatures like that.

King Galukar only sighed.

"You can stop pissing yourself now," he growled. "Relax, you're not in any danger. That's my companion."

Collin blinked, trying to make sense of the nonsensical claim just as he saw a dark streak flit out from the inferno.

CHAPTER FORTY-THREE

King Galukar's apparent companion, the creature, was swift in reacting to the attack from below. Furling its wings and dropping like a stone. Collin saw the newcomer—the lich, he realized—suddenly veer off to one side as its enemy approached. Closer as they had become, he could gauge their relative sizes and surprised himself by seeing that the surely human-sized lich was faced with a body nearly double its scale and surely many more times its mass.

Like watching an owl swoop down on a bat, he thought, just as great sword-long talons unsheathed themselves from the larger combatant and scythed for the smaller. It avoided them, barely, and replied with a flash of retina-searing light Collin knew all too well as a blast of lightning. He blinked the stars from his eyes just in time to see the larger figure take a single moment in reclaiming its equilibrium, thrown off-kilter by the strike as it had been. Then it twisted and flew after the smaller thing.

Flecks of black shot between them, each one missing the pursued monster, and the larger one changed tactics quickly. It dove, slipping beneath its enemy, then opening its wings once more. Collin realized what was happening a moment before it finished doing so.

Beneath them there blazed a fire larger and more sustained than the mostly stone construct should have permitted, and it was doubtless casting all the hot air of a forest fire skyward. This same air caught the wings of the larger beast as it came lower and closer to the source, adding extra upward thrust that let it surprise its prey.

Again the talons flashed, and this time Collin's ranger senses picked out a few flecks of blood as they grazed their target. The lich though was far more graceful and swift in the air, shortly coursing backward and beyond reach. He saw the telltale static of building lightning, readied to see the king's companion blasted.

Then the smaller figure was engulfed in a net.

Collin blinked, staring as the weighted tangle of strange fabric and tethered ceramics wrapped over the lich and started dragging it downward. The net was huge, huge to a man in the way a fishing net was to the clams and fish it smothered. Such a thing could not have come from nowhere.

He took a second to work the events through.

By the time he figured it all out—realized that the larger figure had dropped the net as it set the fires, knowing gravity would take precious seconds to let it fall a significant distance over the area it covered—it was all over. A quick flight, a final unsheathing of deadly instruments, and the lich fell back down into the burning palace as a mass of butchered flesh.

Collin had seen intestines mulched into sausage meat with less completion than the death inflicted upon this enemy. He wasn't complaining.

In only moments, the giant creature was closing on him once more, and Collin braced himself. He looked to the king, who still did not panic, and found that it didn't rest his nerves at all. Galukar was known as a decent man, but he was a monarch all the same. A tyrant by nature, a threat by necessity. More to the point, he was a man, and the giant fucking thing coming at Collin was not. Better to remain a little on edge when you were dangling over one, his father had always said.

Fortunately, the abomination changed as it neared. Shrinking, compacting, transforming so completely that as it finally slowly flapped down to land before Collin, it was a man once more.

Or something that looked like a man, he realized. There was no wisdom, and plenty of danger, in assuming a shape-shifter's original form to be the one he found most palatable.

"It is done," the man declared as he finally reached the two of them. "Where are the others?"

"The others?" Collin frowned, fearing, for a second, that there would be yet more undead to throw themselves at him. Galukar didn't seem worried, but then he never seemed worried about anything.

"Pooled out on the other side of the fortress. I was able to send them out to rally before we freed Baird, or before reinforcements arrived."

"Who are you talking about?" Baird snapped, finding his temper mounting, no longer willing to merely be disregarded like some bundled objective of value. "I will have you know—"

"Silence," the smaller man cut in wearily just as he started his march back around the castle. Galukar moved alongside him, and Collin, after a moment of frozen staring, found himself forced to do likewise. He cursed them with every step.

It soon became clear whom and what the pair had been discussing, and Collin found his heart soaring as he beheld the sight of other prisoners lined up and waiting beyond the blazing fortress. They were more numerous than he might have thought, perhaps close to a hundred, and most looked relatively healthy, all things considered.

Revoltingly, it occurred to him that their condition was likely intentional. And almost doubtlessly signified that the Dark Lord's people had intended for each and every one of the fortress's prisoners to be made undead. Healthy bodies made strong abominations, after all. Collin was glad to find the chill running his spine's length diluted by the intoxicant of freedom.

The smaller of his rescuers interrupted the moment by speaking again.

"Let it be known," the man called out, "that you are, all of you, bearing the privilege of having been rescued by Master Silenos, Esteemed Fleshcrafter of House Shaiagrazni, Keeper of the Auburn Flame, Conductor of Arts Most Ancient, and Lord of Hara'lguanta."

It was not unknown or, indeed, uncommon for magi to insist on names of a ridiculous length. Collin had rarely heard of one to match this man's pretension, however. And he just continued on, apparently far from done demonstrating it.

"Go on now and live out the remainder of your pathetic lives," the caster called. "But do so knowing that they continue only because of me. That is all. You may leave."

The man pivoted, stalking away quickly, and Collin saw the group begin to confusedly turn and leave. He almost joined them before a hand closed about his arm.

"Not you," King Galukar told him bluntly. "You're with us."

It wasn't an order, per se, but it wasn't quite a request either. Things tended not to be when made by a man capable of removing orc heads with one hand.

Silenos was back within the day, fortunately. Arion wasn't entirely surprised. They'd looked around the city before finally finding its refuse pile, and disgusting as it was, the matter there apparently served just as well in providing raw materials for his master's fleshcrafting as any living tissue. It hadn't even smelled after transforming, which was a pleasant surprise.

It had not been pleasant staying alone with the bound necromancer, but Arion had managed it. Keeping a careful eye on the woman and making sure she remained fed, even as she insisted on taunting him whenever her gag was loosed for eating. However much he'd handled the petty task, it was a relief to not have it be only his responsibility any longer.

Striding into the room, Silenos claimed the comfiest seat on the floor for himself without bothering to extend a word to anyone else, crossing his legs and peering at Arion questioningly. He'd known him long enough that the answer being asked of him was obvious, even without vocalization.

"Nothing went wrong," he explained. "And it wasn't exactly difficult to ensure. You had me watching a bound woman to stop her from causing trouble. Not exactly hard."

Silenos eyed him, then nodded fractionally. He didn't speak, sending a globule of irritation to congeal at the base of Arion's mind.

"How did things go with your mission, master?" he asked, keeping his voice from a growl. Just barely.

"It was a success," King Galukar grunted from the doorway. His own entrance was rather more difficult than Silenos's, the extra inches of height and hands of breadth making peasant doorways quite a challenge for the giant. He squeezed in after a moment anyway, and even avoided tearing any chunks out of the door-frame. "Collin Baird is safely in the city and should be on his way to reunite with the governor."

Arion felt a tug of relief. So much had gone wrong lately, seemingly everything in fact, that he'd found himself hanging his hopes onto this latest endeavor with a single fraying thread. Even hearing of its apparent success had him worrying over what they might have missed.

"Did he seem grateful?" he asked.

Silenos's face drew as close to a scowl as he'd ever seen.

"He was not," the caster replied, foul mood making itself known. Galukar cut in hastily.

"He was grateful enough," the giant added. "It's just that nobody can be grateful enough for this bastard. He expected to have the ground he walked on worshipped in thanks."

Silenos did not confirm or deny the accusation, merely huffed irritably. Arion felt a curious weariness.

No sane person could question the power at his master's command, and Arion would be at the back of the line to do so. But there was an ice to him too that was more to credit than any other aspect for the inhuman, almost otherworldly presence he always had.

That ice was thawing, or at least wetting. He was beginning to let slip more and more emotion, sometimes guarded, and sometimes without even seemingly realizing enough to try to keep from doing so. Arion would still have never even considered playing cards against the man, but he found himself growing ever more nervous.

Human volatility with Shaiagraznian power seemed a bad mix to him.

"What happened exactly?" Arion asked, deciding he could use both the information and the distraction of receiving it. Silenos didn't even glance at him, but King Galukar's manners won out, as they tended to. Arion listened while the monarch explained everything, finding himself rather glad to have missed the fighting.

"You burned the fortress down," he said once the king had finished. "Isn't that a bit . . . conspicuous?"

His question was addressed to Galukar but meant for Silenos, who seemed to realize the fact and answered it.

"It was the best way to ensure corroborating word of our claims reaches as many people as possible," he said simply. "If the Dark Lord is busy in this region, he will not be seeking us in others. Once we leave, that will make pursuit less likely."

Arion reckoned that made sense. The Dark Lord had never been one to take an insult and had historically found the destruction of his property and men to be just that. It was sound reasoning to bet on such a devastation as he'd heard described luring the conqueror's focus away.

Assuming it was he who heard about it first, of course. If the more local leaders of his forces caught wind of their flight, there'd be a pursuit all the same.

Knocking. It was abrupt, more abrupt and more forceful than Arion had heard in a long while. He'd just realized why it struck him with such nostalgia, identified it as the very same tempo of a heralded magus, when King Galukar pulled the door open and stepped back expectantly.

It was a boy who revealed himself on the other side. Tall, broad in the shoulders, and with the sort of jaw one might break their fist against. He had blue eyes bright enough to almost seem cyan and brown hair that seemed to have been militarily cropped at some point but since grown out. He wore green.

"Silenos Shaiagrazni?" the boy asked, looking to the caster without any of the surprise universal in those beholding him for the first time. A prior acquaintance then.

"I've come from seeing my father," the boy continued, not waiting for an answer. Evidently he'd spoken to Silenos too. "He sent me, knowing that I'd be recognized and hurry things along. He wishes to have an audience with you."

Silenos smiled and got to his feet. Arion realized rather quickly that the boy at the door was Collin Baird.

Which meant they'd be on their way to meet the governor.

CHAPTER FORTY-FOUR

King Galukar's mood was foul as they walked. It was a growing commonality of all the man's moods that they would be some variety of low quality, but this one was perhaps among the worst Silenos had seen. His shoulders were hunched, neck driven slightly forward, fingers twitching. It was all the same bodily shifts that tended to emerge as the king prepared himself to kill.

His history with Governor Baird had not been lost on Silenos, of course, but he'd not been yet able to wheedle any of it out of him. The man seemed far less open to answering his questions than Ensharia, and he'd not yet gotten the chance to try directing them at Arion. It was irritating in the way sulfuric acid upon sub-dermal tissue was irritating. Harsh enough that a lesser creature might have deemed it pain.

Kaltan's streets had been well explored by the time of their summons, and Silenos found no new sights awaiting his gaze on this latest trek through them. It was, however, refreshing to be moving through in the knowledge that some-thing of guaranteed worth awaited him at the end of his journey. Almost enough to distract from the scent of manure.

Ahead of him, Baird walked with a back that remained straight and a gait that remained loping despite his captivity. Silenos rather approved of that, always finding appreciation for a being able to remember itself regardless of circum-stance. Were he not a sense-dead moron incapable of even trivial magic, he might have made a Shaiagrazni. Alarming numbers of this world seemed to fit that bill.

Beneath his feet, mud turned to cobbles to smooth tiles. They came to the wealthier central parts of Kaltan.

Silenos had continued his typical habit of gleaning information about the place during his habitation of it, if only for the nonzero chance that such data would prove useful. It was for this reason that he knew already the noble quarter of the city was not actually a noble's quarter. Years ago, its revolution had seen such function obsolete, as most of those who might occupy it lost either head, property, or inclination to remain within the settlement.

These days, it was rather more militarized.

A tale as old as time, he had found. Social revolutions were not uncommon, nor even were they uncommonly successful. Almost invariably, however, the ones that actually triumphed were forwarded or directed by the military.

Soldiers. He could feel his lip curling at the very thought.

House Shaiagrazni ensured that all its citizens fulfilled their purposes. Indeed, one of Silenos's jobs when he was younger had been to scan the bodies and brains of people to ascertain which roles their genetic and environmental products made them most suited to. Soldiers were the lowliest of all these assigned positions.

To be a mathematician, one needed patience and dedication. To be an engineer, spatial reasoning and working memory. A tactician needed predictive power and logical skill, a navigator accurate memory and inductive reasoning.

Soldiers were not so demanding of their recruits. To truly excel in that field required only a trifecta of traits. Strength, courage, and a generous helping of violent savagery. They were not a stock that Silenos imagined his people would have bothered sustaining were they not beset by enemies from other nations.

Finlay Baird had been a soldier, which was why his revolution had succeeded. Might did not make right, of course, but neither did right make might. In a primitive society, it was violence and power that declared the ruler of a land.

Around them, walls rose only to moderate heights of a half dozen or so meters but frequently demonstrated ridiculous thickness. Men marched and patrolled in armor Silenos would not have expected to be common among their culture and technological peers. Quilted fabrics woven thick and tough, or even strips of steel shaped to make spines of boiled leather slabs. It was all impressive for mere foot soldiers, and it was not so uncommon to see men marching among the grunts clad in suits of full steel plate.

"Not a bad arrangement," Galukar remarked, clearly observing just what Silenos had. "Must cost a lot to keep men outfitted like this."

"We save money on training," the ranger, Collin Baird, replied. "That, and the city in general saved a lot of money. Our former earl used to hoard a lot of the product of taxation, then disperse much more among his nobility. With them gone, it's all being cycled back into the city itself. Some infrastructure but, given the state of things . . . mostly it's into the military. Nice fountains and water pipes wouldn't mean much if the Dark Lord took it all."

Galukar smiled at that, and Silenos wasn't surprised to hear his choice of focal point.

"Cheaping on training." He sighed. "You'll regret that when they see battle—"

"We don't cheap out on anything," the boy cut in harshly. "We just found a better way of doing it. We offer promotion through performance and assessed expertise and rank all the men in each squad during sessions. Those who overperform in any given week compared to their usual earn additional rations or ale, those who underperform compared to previous abilities get nothing. It incentivizes them to keep working, sometimes even in their own time. Speeds things up a lot and lets us do more with less."

His tone was insolent beyond the capacity for any Shaiagrazni to tolerate, but seeing it aimed at Galukar made the entire thing rather amusing to behold. Silenos smiled as he saw the king's face tighten. He expected to hear an argument but did not. Instead they just kept moving.

Kaltan Castle was as creatively named as so many other features of the new world, and Silenos found himself so inured to the awful monikers that he barely even winced upon hearing it. It was a thing to stand in opposition to the constructions around it. Tall, thin at parts, sprawling out in networks of spires and additional wings resting upon great stony pillars.

Impressive, he supposed, for its scope. But it would make a poor position in defense, that much was clear at a glance.

Baird spat. The gesture did not surprise Silenos, though it drew a questioning glance from Falls, which prompted an explanation.

"Built by the old lords," the ranger explained with venom in his eyes and poison on his tongue. "You can tell because it's a gaudy, impractical sack of shit."

Silenos did loathe soldiers, for reasons too numerous to easily list. But even he found that one amusing.

A portcullis lifted as they approached the castle, guarded by two men in more of the leather-clad steel and armed with coiled, steel-limbed arbalests. Once inside, they were followed at all times by no fewer than three men in plate, polearms seeming perpetually ready to bite into flesh. By the looks of their wielders, they might even have managed to break the skin of Galukar. The outermost layer, at least.

Silenos was more concerned with the surroundings than that though, and he found much of note. Namely, he found absences.

"This is a portrait hall," he observed. "With walls bleached by light, save for in rectangular patches."

Baird smiled at that, seeming proud.

"We've been selling off the old art, redistributing the funds. Actually putting them to use, you know."

"A Godless use," King Galukar piped up, clearly unamused. But not nearly as much so as Baird, who rounded on him quickly.

"Your God can eat my shit and hair," he told the king, speaking so quickly and acidically that it actually stunned the giant monarch into silence. Silenos found himself wrestling back a cackle.

Troubling how much harder that felt. But almost worth it for the joy of seeing Galukar's stunned expression.

"We're almost there," Baird told them as they came to a final corridor. "Do you all know how to address the governor?"

Galukar spat at his feet, which seemed to Silenos as eloquent a reply as the king was likely to give. Falls frowned questioningly, and he himself shook his head.

"Different to a king, I would imagine," he dared to guess.

"Couldn't be more different. Don't bow, don't refer to him by any particular title, and don't scrape at the ground. Just treat him like a man with an army at his back."

That sounded rather similar to how Silenos tended to treat kings in general, but he supposed the boy couldn't be expected to know that. Nodding, he waited for them to enter the hall.

It was true enough that the place differed from other throne rooms Silenos had been shown so far. Mainly in its total lack of a throne, but the decor in general was less extravagant and more mundane than seemed to be the preference of kings. He saw no gilded carpets or hung portraits, no marble statues or displayed weapons. Only a single plaque bearing a single item of note. A crown, dented and buckled, allowed to rust at the edges. He could imagine whose it had been.

Beneath it a desk rested, not particularly modest, nor indulgent. Sitting behind that was a man Silenos guessed was Finlay Baird. He had a strong face, though tired, with matted hair and sharp eyes. His nose was hooked and his lips thin and tight.

When the man got to his feet, Silenos saw two things. The first was a pair of long daggers hooked at his waist, and the second was his height. He seemed no larger than most of the peasants in other cities, smaller even than those of his own.

"Thank you for coming," the man grunted, and Silenos realized his accent was more similar to the peasantry of Kaltan than the more common aristocratic pattern he'd grown familiar with. Curious. "I take it you are the men responsible for freeing my son, Collin, from the Dark Lord's prisons?"

"I am," Silenos replied before Galukar could speak and thus convert their situation into a disaster. "My companion here provided aid, however, and your son in turn aided us in fighting our way out when enemy reinforcements arrived."

"I wounded a fomor," the boy added, grinning broadly as if it were an accomplishment of some kind. Finlay Baird eyed him for a second but quickly moved his gaze to other people and other matters.

"We need to talk about the attack on my people," he said after a moment. King Galukar moved to reply before Silenos could, and he did so with drawn iron.

The Godblade practically flew upward to rest an inch from the governor's nose, not even quivering as it was held aloft. Its edge halted just shy of drawing blood, and Silenos felt the magic bunching in Galukar's muscles as he aimed it, saw the lightning in his eyes.

"It seems to me that I'm standing before the one responsible," he spat. "Or do they not count as people when they're of noble birth?"

To his credit, Finlay Baird did not flinch. Even while his son aimed his own bow at Galukar and the present guards readied themselves to strike. The man might have been staring down a breadstick for all his worry.

"They count as people; they just needed to die."

His face was steady as ever, arms not even twitching toward the knives at his side. Baird either knew he would not get the chance to draw them or knew they would do nothing to Galukar even if he did. The king growled.

"There were good people among the men and women you butchered," he hissed. "And—"

"No there weren't," Baird replied. "Every single one of them was a parasitic animal. They couldn't be reasoned with because you can't reason with people who think they're simply better than you. They couldn't be negotiated with because people who already have everything stand only to lose from compromise. The only logical way to deal with them was to remove them from power and kill the ones most likely to reclaim it. I don't regret anything I did, I'm not sorry, and I'll do it to every other city on the continent if I ever have the chance."

CHAPTER FORTY-FIVE

Galukar's fury was best described through comparison to Shaiagrazni fission blasts, that rare, arcane power only a handful among them had learned to draw forth. To liken it to natural disasters was too small a testament. For one moment, Silenos thought he might actually take the governor's head off then and there; instead he only leaned forward a few centimeters, whispering his response.

"You can dress it up however you want," he spat. "You are a butcher, a savage, and a thug. People like you are the reason the world is the way it is, to protect it from the rest of you."

Baird flinched no more at this threat than he had at any others. He merely replied.

"If you think it's good to protect people from being made to provide warm housing and filling meals, then you need to be killed too."

Silenos finally cut in, realizing that the situation was only growing in danger, not shriveling.

"This is getting us nowhere," he declared. "All of us have bigger issues to attend to than the pair of you and your moronic politics. The Dark Lord will soon be responding to word of the governor's son's escape. Time is limited."

That had, of course, been the additional reason for breaking Collin Baird out so overtly. By creating such a clear disruption in the Dark Lord's territory, it applied pressure to his enemies for swift action. Silenos had hoped it would curtail the very bickering and delaying he saw now.

It seemed he had been right.

Galukar's sword came down, and it did not detach any limbs on its way. The governor remained as unflappable as ever.

"You got that out of your system?" he asked, tempting fate for seemingly no reason at all. Fortunately, fate appeared to be in a good mood because King Galukar only remained bitterly silent.

"We rescued your son, and no small number of other prisoners," Silenos prodded. "I imagine you called us here to discuss a debt owed, yes?"

Baird's eyes moved back to him, and his face shifted in some imperceptibly slight way that conveyed nothing save that the question had been heard.

"Of course," he replied.

The boy, Collin, stiffened slightly at his father's reaction, and Silenos made a note to find out why.

"You have something in mind already?" the governor asked expectantly. He was a sharp one, Silenos realized, but then those who began in a gutter and ended in a castle tended to be.

"I wish to make contact with the man known as Silhouette and have been led to believe that you are capable of arranging that," he told him. There seemed no reason to lie.

"I am," the governor told him, taking a half step back. "But it will take time. More time, given the current threat to my city. I'm afraid your breakout brought a lot of eyes onto this region, which is already rife with pockets of undead and orcish raiders, and I've heard tell that General Venka is making his way with enough orcs to choke a dozen rivers and redirect a thirteenth. That takes precedence over everything else I might turn my attention to."

Silenos hadn't lied, but he realized, somehow, that the governor was. A shift to his disposition, a sudden waver to his words. He'd stared down a sword as heavy as his leg without blinking, and it was that steel of nerves that made it so obvious how uncertain he'd become.

He thought of how best to broach the topic. Thought to the guards he'd passed, the general martial quality apparent around them, and the *delightful* abundance of organic tissue that lay ripe for the crafting. He did not think for long.

"You just lied to me," Silenos informed the man. "Stop it or I shall kill you."

The room went silent. It was all very amusing. Galukar and Falls were shocked, Baird instantly hard and wary, his son gaping with stunned, building fury. The guards were quick in closing in once more. It was the governor's answering voice that reached Silenos before bared steel.

"I am not lying. As I told you—"

"You must think I'm an idiot, so I will inform you that I am not native to your lands. People in my culture actually work for our positions. You were lying when you spoke of contacting and arranging a meeting with Silhouette. Where was your lie, and why was it told?"

It was Collin Baird who spoke next, his voice twisted with rage.

"Why don't you step outside so we can settle the matter of truth without breaking any furniture, you woolly twat—"

"*Collin*," the governor snapped, affixing his son with a glare that might have hurried soldiers into line and certainly sufficed at stilling the fury of a teenager. Collin Baird didn't meet his father's eye, pacified instantly. The governor continued in the silence.

"You're right," he confessed. There wasn't a scrap of regret, embarrassment, or uncertainty in the words. Not an apology, not an explanation, just a statement of fact. Silenos was right, he had lied, and that was the end of it.

Something strange and long absent swelled in Silenos's chest at that, and he found himself almost gasping at the sensation. This man was doing something more dangerous than lying or manipulating him, more formidable than facing or contradicting him. He was impressing him.

"What was your lie?" Silenos asked him, almost as much out of curiosity to see how he'd explain it as the necessity of learning where he'd been misled.

"I cannot contact Silhouette," Baird replied. "Because he does not exist. He is a fabrication I invented to lure possible allies into Kaltan and gain audiences and leverage with them in my fight against the Dark Lord."

Silenos felt his jaw tighten, his eye twitch, his heart almost palpitate with the molten fury now scraping past its arterial walls.

"So, to reiterate," he said slowly, carefully. Making sure to contain his incendiary emotions. "We are stuck in your city, which is halfway between revolutionary reconstruction and a retaliatory civil war, while the Dark Lord's most sadistic general amasses an army of superhuman barbarians and marches them across the country to attack it."

The governor nodded.

"Then I have no choice but to halt these issues and guarantee an exit." Silenos sighed, resisting the urge to rub his eyes like some magic-blunt ape.

"You cannot be serious," growled Galukar, eyes flitting between them. "This upstart has already betrayed you once. You think he won't do it again?"

Silenos stifled his irritation.

"Governor, I will let you know now that if you mislead me again, I will kill every tenth child in your city. Do you believe me?"

The governor studied him for a moment, then nodded.

"I do," he said. Silenos believed that he had been believed.

"Good, then I can trust you not to do something as stupid as push me a second time. Satisfied?"

His last question was addressed at Galukar, who did not look in the least bit satisfied, but neither seemed inclined to cause any issues due to the fact. That was as convenient a reaction as Silenos had learned the man would ever give him. With the issue settled, he turned back to the wider problem.

"In that case, I will ask what means you will permit me to go about purging your land of the Dark Lord's forces."

The governor hesitated a moment.

"My son saw you in the body of a great flying beast," he replied slowly. "Saw you transform back into a man before his eyes. I've asked around a bit more about Silenos Shaiagrazni too and caught a few words of necromancy along with flesh-crafting. Are these rumors true?"

There was little to gain from lying and a great deal to lose, so Silenos made his reluctant compromise with reality and answered truthfully.

"They are."

The governor studied him a moment more. It gave time for Silenos to control his boiling temper, to brace himself for what he knew was coming. The idiocy, the superstition. The sniveling, whinging, pathetic protests of an uncompre-hending animal daring to complain at losing a game when others refused to follow rules it had invented on the spot.

Magic was not to be sanctioned or condoned; it simply was. The only master a caster needed to obey was the master of possibility. And Silenos's power was more than possible, whatever the drooling imbeciles of this world said.

Baird's lips parted slowly, his eyes retaining their coherence as he spoke.

"Any means," he said at last, and Silenos took a moment to eye him. Not want-ing to let himself believe he'd heard what he had. Baird saved him the trouble by elaborating. "You have my permission to use any means at your disposal. Fleshcrafting, necromancy. Summon a demon, if you think it necessary. Just get these fucking invaders out of my nation."

Silenos smiled.

Swick had found a marked improvement in his living station, and it had come rather quickly after his offer of cooperation.

Granted, given that his previous living station had been a chained slave doing ten hours of labor each day and shitting in an open hole in the ground, it was not particularly hard to improve. Nor, indeed, did it say much about how things were *now* that they'd become better. He'd certainly had it worse though.

For one thing, he had his own chains. Linked to some large weight being carted around on a cargo haul. They were strong steel, all the same, and restricted his movements no less, but they at least meant he could walk around relatively independently. That was an immediate improvement, and not the only one.

The wine had been of particular note. Swick was not a man of especially refined taste, having burned half his tongue in a fight and lost one-quarter of what remained drunkenly kissing a woman he had no business kissing, but the taste was vaguely similar to one of those posh kinds that everyone pretended were bet-ter. In more practical terms, he'd been given access to some of the camp follow-ers. Comely sort of women, with thick lips and big eyes, and who assured him they'd spent precious little time being tossed around like dog toys by those orcs who the general had decided deserved rewarding. Swick decided to believe them, more for his own sake than anything else.

But of course, all these benefits had been nothing more than payment for services rendered. And the general Venka seemed to consider it payment enough for a great deal of services indeed. Swick was not surprised when he was called into the man's tent for the third day in a row. The general was more given to want him on any given night than not.

A clever man, Venka. And as fond of information as any clever man was. Swick answered his summons. A greedy man, Swick. And as fond of wine and women as any greedy man was.

The general's tent was as typical for the man's personality as anything could have been expected to be. Expansive but not Indulgent. Clean but not pristine. Its space was economically distributed among maps, storage, and equipment, with a portable desk used for correspondence via letter and a simple equally portable bed tucked away in one corner. That bed was the sole excess to be found in the place, raised from the ground on legs and boasting a mattress rather than the meager padding of rolls and sleep sacks. The general apparently appreciated his night's sleep more than most.

It was the desk that housed him now though. Still dressed up in a crisply kept uniform, still scratching away with quill and parchment. He didn't even look up at Swick as he entered.

CHAPTER FORTY-SIX

Naturally, Swick considered killing him while his guard was down, but he decided against it. There was every chance he'd reach him before the man realized what was happening but none of killing him. He was a warrior of some kind, with a body hardened for battle, and though his raw strength and resilience didn't seem like much, it wasn't something Swick would be getting past with his bare hands. His own powers were even less centered on bodily strength than the general's.

"Sit," Venka ordered, still not looking up. There was a chair opposite him, clearly prepared in advance, and Swick took it without replying. Eying him, thinking.

"You know I've told you everything I know," he iterated, testing the response of Venka's face as he said it. They were little and scarce.

"So you say," Venka replied. Interestingly, he did not look at Swick's face. Which meant it probably wasn't a test he'd found himself in. One did not sit a man down for testing and then look away from his expressions when prodding him with suspicion and worry.

"So what do you want me for then?" Swick asked. Venka looked up at that, his displeasure clear.

"What do you want me for then, General Venka?" Swick amended, forcing a smile. It seemed to have about as much effect on the good general as any other expression Swick might have mustered, which was to say somewhere between jack shit and fuck all. A stony man, this one.

"I have been observing you," Venka replied, finally putting the quill down. Swick was tempted to express the honor he felt at being deemed more important than a letter on latrine digging but decided better.

"And I've impressed, I should hope?" He grinned instead, still scraping the general's face for some betrayal of thought or emotion. Both were as irritatingly absent as ever.

"You have demonstrated a rare acclimation to the conditions of my camp," Venka replied. "You have, as far as I can gather, not shown any particular fear of orcs, nor distaste. You have proved steely and robust in your interactions with them and the . . . society of this war party."

It was a serious observation, and Swick sensed his humor would not be appreciated. He straightened up a bit.

"Can I level with you, general?" He didn't wait for a response. "I've been traveling this world a lot. I mean, a *lot*. You'd be amazed how big it really is, and how much it shrinks when you have a skyship. I've been north, south, east, west. I've been as high as I could go before my spit started freezing, and more. Seen things you wouldn't believe. Lands where giants herd people like cattle, mountains built by colonies of horse-sized insects that eat entire ecosystems. Other things. Dark things that we haven't invented the words to describe." He let his smile drop, feeling the mood for it gone as he revisited memories long buried and sharply recalled. "I'm not scared of a few fucking morons, no matter how big they are."

Venka studied him. Then he smirked. The smirk turned into a proper smile, which in turn bled to a grin, then finally completed its evolution into a full-blown laugh. Head thrown back, shoulders heaving, the general cackled for a quarter minute before finally mastering himself.

"Well said." He sighed at last. "Truly, well said. So many seem awed by the orcs, daunted. I've even heard some say we're doomed to fall against them before long. All hogwash."

His lip curled as he glanced over Swick's shoulder, doubtless to the pair of armored orcs who stood guard at the tent's opening.

"Orcs are never going to take this land," Venka continued. "And it baffles me that people think otherwise. Elephants are bigger than them, horses faster, lions more vicious, and many, many things stronger. Yet orcs wear clothes, and speak in their simple, grunting ways, and occasionally learn to smash rocks together until one is pointy enough to use as a knife, and so people mistakenly believe that they will one day build cities of their own. They will not, and they cannot."

Swick studied the man. As far as he could tell, Venka wasn't entirely wrong. Orcs were stupider than men, but in the same way that a few men were stupider than men too. The average simpleton was duller than the average orc, and rather less focused when they set their mind to something.

"Orcs use metal in the wild," he noted, curious how the general might react. Venka scoffed.

"Salvaged from ours clearly, or made through simple mimicry of our tactics. I have some theories on how the orcs managed to evolve what little they have . . . But that is a digression too far."

It wasn't the sort of conversation that tended to inspire a smile in Swick, but he replied with one all the same.

"So what are you digressing from?" he asked. "Something big, I'd guess. A job offer?"

Most men disliked being seen through. General Venka was the exception. He outright loathed it. The man's good humor was vaporized by Swick's response, his eyes sharpening as a slight nod shook his head.

"Your skills are considerable, and as of recently your previous career as a sky-pirate seems . . . jeopardized. You could make good money from us fighting for our side, and if you agree to do so, you will receive a skyship from the Dark Lord's own expenses as standard equipment, to be crewed by whatever undead, orcs, or other units are available." Venka leaned across the desk, eying him. "You made yourself one of the most renowned criminals in history with a crew of gutter scum and filth. What do you think you might manage commanding dullahan, lichs, belladonnan puppeteers . . . Even reanimated Heroes?"

Swick swallowed. That crew *had* been gutter scum and filth, all of them. But they'd been his. A man had to have a code, else he was nothing more than an animal, and it stung Swick's to hear his men derided so casually and say nothing against it.

But his code was a convenient and practical one too. He could speak out against indignities when doing so wouldn't dump him back in the fucking gutter himself.

"And I'd be expected to . . . scout," he guessed. "Raid particular targets, maybe disappear the occasional pesky general . . . Or Hero?"

Venka's face moved about as much as ever.

"Of course," he replied. "I trust you don't consider such work to be beneath you?"

It would have been awkward timing to decide as much after building a two-decade career off of it. Swick shook his head.

"Of course not, general." He smiled, smiled so convincingly it might have fooled a drunken idiot. Fortunately a rich, clever man was the easier mark by far, and there was never any doubt about Venka buying it.

"Excellent," the general replied, pausing, then continuing. "If so, it means I can inform you about some rather important context to our current march toward the city of Kaltan. You told me my peer, Sphera, remained with your allies, yes?"

Swick nodded, though the question was rhetorical.

"I am almost certain she is within the walls of Kaltan. There is simply no other place for her captors to have retreated, and the reports I've heard of Ebonspine Fortress's destruction all but confirm the presence of that Silenos Shaiagrazni figure. This makes a large difference for our priorities."

For the life of him, Swick couldn't think what. They had to be less vicious in their assault for the risk of killing her? That couldn't be right, surely.

Venka noted his confusion, speaking fast to rectify it.

"Good God, man, think it through!" he snapped. "Sphera is a necromancer second only to our master. With her in the city, it means that our captured enemies can be resurrected once we've taken it. Which I estimate will be tomorrow."

Swick ran cold.

"Which means the paladin . . ."

"Can be executed the hour before," General Venka replied. He did not look away from Swick as this question was asked, instead staring at his face with such focus as might be cast against a sheet of theorems by the mathematician they confounded. It was a fight for Swick not to show any of the dozen warring emotions Venka's words inspired, all while tucking away the confusion he felt at his own response. Lie now, think later. He got to the lying quickly.

"Why tell me?"

It was a fucking pointless question. Swick had already worked out the answer. But it helped to seem stupider than you were. People watched clever men more sharply than dull ones, cautious ones more warily than hasty ones. Venka seemed to buy the act as well as he'd bought everything else Swick had handed him.

"Because you will be the one to kill her," the general informed him lightly, casually, as if he were telling Swick to prove his loyalty by leading a few cows out to pasture. As if he were not suggesting the execution of the best person Swick had ever fucking met.

He'd been drinking more than his fill, could feel the laxing touch of alcohol ease the aches of his tortured mind even then, but somehow a headache manifested itself between Swick's ears. They always found him, whether he drank or not. The more he drank, the more they found him, and the more drink he needed to dull his nerves enough that they didn't register. They never weakened, once started. Not while he remained conscious. This one would be with him a day at least and grow harsher by the minute.

"And here I thought you'd suggest something hard as a test of loyalty." Swick grinned, leaning back, putting his feet up, folding his hands behind his head. Even moving that much worsened the pricks of agony. He'd seen a brain once, a human brain. Some far-western surgeon had cut it out of a dead body. There'd been folds all along the surface. Swick imagined that some invisible demon was grabbing those folds now and using them as grips to wring the whole mass of the organ out like a creased towel. It certainly fucking felt like it.

Venka smiled, oblivious to his pain as people always seemed to be.

"Good, then you may take your leave. I have preparations to see to for tomorrow's siege, and you need not have any part in them."

Which was, of course, a very polite way of telling Swick to fuck off so Venka could begin work on things too important for a yet-untested man who'd already betrayed one side to be seeing. Fair enough, he supposed, and not the sort of request he was in any position to deny even if it hadn't been. Swick got to his feet and made for the door.

Outside the tent, it was cold. Early morning. The sun was still far enough from its horizon that Swick couldn't see much of anything more than ten yards from him, let alone to any extreme of the world's edge. If they were any fraction of a day's march from Kaltan, he'd not be granted visual confirmation for quite a few hours. Preparations were already underway to pack up and resume their march.

Swick thought to that, and the notion of trudging along. It wouldn't be hard now that he'd been unchained from the other prisoners. Certainly, the paladin would have it worse. His head started to ache again.

Moving back to his tent, Swick tried to think through the bleary, painful clouds of trouble wafting about his mind. It was one of the slow days, the days where every idea he had seemed just out of reach and every problem just a hair too complicated for fixing.

What Swick needed was wine. Beautiful, brain-settling wine. Wine to blunt his tortured nerves and settle his screaming thoughts. Wine to make the world quiet and easy again. Wine to help him get some fucking sleep before the time came for killing paladins and sieging cities.

Over the years, Swick had seen a lot of men and women killed. Scum, most of them, but a few had been his scum. In all that time, he'd never once found himself turned against wine.

Some friendships were just unbreakable.

CHAPTER FORTY-SEVEN

There had been a surprising number of enemies plaguing the governor of Kaltan, Silenos found. Or perhaps not surprising. Social revolutions tended to inspire conflict.

House Shaiagrazni had been founded in the Great Alignment, some two thousand years before his birth, and even in those primitive times they had suffered inconvenience enough. Their homelands of Gwalhi had been ruled by an emperor at the time, whose armies numbered almost a million and whose military casters over a thousand. Their established order of rule by birthright and noble supremacy had been so completely at odds with the alterations proposed by his forefathers that there was no surprise violent contradiction had come.

That contradiction had been crushed, however, by the simple fact that one million drooling cows with pointy sticks, bolstered by one thousand semiliterate apes with half-remembered spell books, were no match for the supremacy of magic that had been the first elders of House Shaiagrazni. Only numbering half a dozen had made no difference for Silenos's master and her peers; they had simply unleashed magic until all who opposed them had either fled, surrendered, or been reduced to clouds of vaporized carbon wafting about molten craters pockmarking the landscape.

Silenos had rather a similar approach planned for resolving Baird's little counterrevolution.

A man screamed, that irritating way men tended to when they found their legs suddenly separated from their hips. Silenos felt his lip curl at the sight.

He had been a warrior, clad in plate and belonging to that caste these simple people called knights. Trained from his youth to hone a recognized talent for violence, instilled with discipline and skill. By all metrics, he ought to have been above such petty displays of cowardice as to *scream*. What in the world did this world teach its soldiers?

Well, evidently, they did not teach them much in the way of preventing dismemberment. Silenos took a swift step to one side, avoiding the column of splashing ichor that cut through the space he'd just been occupying, then watched as his flesh construct swung the man's torso down into the street with a single muscled tentacle. Steel and flesh both gave in more or less the same way, popping against the stone and leaving a gory painting. Its toy broken, his construct turned and lumbered off to find more pickings. There was no shortage of them.

Only ten minutes had passed since the fighting began, three hours since the announcement given. A day since Silenos's help offered. Baird had been reluctant to accept Silenos's suggestion of posting warrants of arrest for a full fifth of his known enemies, but it had worked splendidly.

Within half a day there was open rebellion, tens of thousands of men readied and marching to seize back the city, trained and armed on whatever funds were available to the aristocratic survivors and migrants.

Gathering so many in the same place had made it near effortless to destroy them all at once.

"Back, you foul monster!" a man roared, holding a sword almost as big as the Godblade in one hand and a great sphere of searing flame in the other. He cast his magic against a flesh construct, bathing it in stone-splitting heat, then thrust his sword. The keratin plates broke steel handily enough, and he was soon bowled over to be crushed.

Silenos had worked rather carefully on the monsters he'd sent out, given that he'd had the biomass for only three of them. Each was a fine piece of artistry, even by his own postgenius standards. His master might even have refrained from calling them failures.

"*Luthar!*" a woman screamed. "*You monsters! Men, fire!*" Silenos's eyes flicked over just in time to see his creation pelted by a hail of crossbow bolts, each striking with force enough to skewer a man fully through. They bounced harmlessly from its armor. Flexible stuff, woven dense and durable with deposits of iron. He'd not had time to make it as flawless as his own, but it would have turned away those primitive weapons that passed for artillery in this world. The creature opened its mouth, inhaled, then shredded the company of bowmen with a blast of its own projectiles. Slugs of calcic density propelled by a mechanism not dissimilar to his own weapon.

He had to admit, all the dirty brawling he'd been forced into had given Silenos some insight into what made for an effective armory. His grotesqueries had certainly benefited.

One particularly impressive enemy evaded the long, tendinous lengths of musculature Silenos had shaped into limbs. He sidestepped the nacre barbs tipping them, twisted aside from the volleys of cannon shot that smashed apart stone everywhere it hit, and danced around patches of burning fire that might otherwise have scorched him. His sword was an impressive, magical thing that would have carved through sheet metal, and managed to do a formidable job in scything through the centimeter of armor protecting Silenos's creations. Oxygen-bright blood frothed from the wounds, splashing across the man, who seemed to wear it with pride.

Interesting. Silenos pondered the practicality of making his creations' ichor toxic or acidic, even while sending silent necromantic commands for another grotesquerie to close in and aid its sibling.

The man who might have contested Ensharia with even odds of winning did not last long against two of Silenos's creations, and his allies lasted less time still in his absence. It was less of a battle than a massacre, the mark of a properly engineered Shaiagrazni design.

"How do they move like that?" asked the necromancer named Sphera. Silenos glanced at her as she questioned him and decided to let her impudent demand for an answer slide. There were more productive things than plucking out a disrespectful tongue, for the time being at least.

"How should they move?" he asked, drawing an irritated frown from her.

"Sluggish as a geriatric cow," she growled. "You made them from corpses slain and buried years ago."

"Decades," Silenos corrected. "Yes. It was the earliest source of human biomass that had not been cremated upon death. This war with your master has done rather a lot to shape Kaltan's burial practices."

She breezed past everything but the magic, an admirable sign.

"And undead get slower and duller the longer you wait to reanimate them. After a few hours, even I can't bring something back with all its faculties; after a day, my master can't manage it. But you did this with corpses decades old. Does your fleshcrafting make it possible?"

"No," Silenos replied honestly. "Fleshcrafting is limited in its effects over cerebral"—he sighed—"brain matter. Which is why I needed human corpses to begin with. There are simply better ways of reanimating something. Your master is rather an amateur."

She stared at him with something that could not have been mistaken for anger, humiliation, irritation, or hatred. It was not embarrassment, not fear, not awe. No, Silenos would have insulted the woman were he to misidentify her response for anything so pedestrian and worthless as those petty thoughts. What he saw in her was hunger, the very same that burned in any true Shaiagrazni.

"How?" she demanded in such a way as to deserve instant and agonizing destruction . . . were it not for her anomalous talent.

"That is a secret of my house. I have no inclination to share it with you, and many reasons not to."

Her face was blank with carefully masked thought for all of a second, then she nodded and looked away. Silenos found himself slightly disappointed, but he supposed the truly intelligent could rarely be found making decisive judgments so hastily.

Soon, he thought, this one might ask to become his student. If Silenos was confident she would not betray him, he would grant her request. More than mere cognitive or magical genius, she had a trait valued in House Shaiagrazni that even Falls lacked. A total and unbroken lack of empathy. It was marvelous.

Wetness, hotness. They splashed against his face at once, a gooey, familiar sensation that curled Silenos's lip. He raised his hand, grazing the squirt of blood with two fingers and absorbing it into his body. Curious how much less it bothered him to consume the stuff through touch and magic than feel it resting against his skin. He supposed there had been no evolutionary advantage for his prehistoric ancestors to feel inclined toward avoiding the former. Disease did not spread well through a medium that had been disassembled into protoplasmic fluid.

The sun was starting to set, sending long shadows to cut through the battlefield and making the pooling ichor dance in shades of orange and pink, complementing its natural reds.

His grotesqueries let out low, rattling moans as whatever remained of their enemies finally gave out. Silenos had structured the things to feel uncanny spikes of pleasure and fulfilment when they killed so as to better motivate them into the murderous frenzy that best suited battle, and the consequence was that they practically thrashed in agony at running out of corpses to make. He smiled. It was rather enjoyable to see, all things considered. Silenos stepped down from the roof.

Around him, the cobbled streets had been crushed, fine multistory houses obliterated into piles of crumbled mortar and splintered wood, or else scattered out dozens of meters in every direction. Fires burned where magic had struck timber, and there were mangled bodies as far as the eye could see. An army's worth.

It had taken the city's aristocracy only a half day to muster their powers and stage their coup, a testament to their rage at Baird. It had taken Silenos slightly less time to destroy them, a testament to his genius.

The grotesqueries moaned, stumbling over to kneel before their master, as was proper, and expressing their agony to him through more rumbling vocalizations. Silenos felt his lip curling. Each of the constructs had been damaged, but only one in any serious capacity. That notable soldier who'd proved a match for one of them had, apparently, not been gifted the prowess of destruction to cut truly deep. Still, Silenos would need to turn his attentions to the things if they were to continue operating at full capacity.

He did so and considered the weaknesses he'd seen exposed while he did.

Silenos's first creations had each been made with six large, crushing limbs the width and length of oak trunks. Those had been excellent for destroying anything they struck but rather poor in catching the quicker enemies. Given that his grotesqueries already towered over even an elephant, Silenos added some additional limbs.

Smaller, longer. More akin to the branches of the tree than their thicker counterparts. He structured them with more numerous flexible joints and imprinted the instinctual knowledge of how to wield them like whips to his monsters.

Their armor had been excellent, though with their score or so new weapons, Silenos could afford to reduce mobility and thicken it. He did so. He retethered nerves for faster responses at those sites that most needed them, increased the sensitivity of pain receptors, and added in a more social instinct to ensure it would not require his direct attention to have his creations cooperate. That last feature would be well needed, for Silenos had just granted himself rather a lot more biomass.

He glanced across the battlefield and did the calculations.

Each grotesquerie was some two hundred tonnes in total bodily mass, due to the density of certain supermaterials, and Silenos had access to enough rarer elements from the city's warehouses and stores that he could be certain biological tissue would be the limiting factor. Estimating the average weight of a new worlder at sixty-four kilograms, and bearing in mind the estimate of fifty thousand or so for their army, that gave him . . .

He smiled.

Fifteen new grotesqueries? Sixteen? It really depended on how well he used the materials. Silenos glanced sidelong, checking the sun's position.

Yes, fifteen new grotesqueries by noon seemed more than reasonable. A stronger force than anticipated. And Kaltan would make just the perfect stage from which to deploy it.

CHAPTER FORTY-EIGHT

They'd had mean looks, the orcs that came for Ensharia.

She'd gotten good at recognizing orcish expressions during her captivity. Garutan had spoken with her every day, and though he was far friendlier than most of his kind, Ensharia was beginning to learn that it was not at all uncommon for them to take a liking to her. Orcs seemed to like conversation, with humans above all else. They found her jokes hilarious, found her stories captivating, and she had grown to find them . . . Yes, companions. Almost friends. There was really no other way to describe it. Her old trainers would have wept.

But there'd not been a scrap of friendliness in the orcs that came for her. They weren't the chained ones, the ones driven to rebel against General Venka's cruel demands by empathy, decency, or morals. They were his elites, which meant they possessed three terrible qualities. The first was their strength, the second their fearlessness, and the third their savage brutality.

It was the size of them that struck her before anything else, however. Ensharia had grown quite accustomed to being towered over, surrounded by orcs as she was, but Venka's elites loomed a full head over their chained kin. They moved with the concentrated grace of lions, as if their dirt-compacting weights were slight enough to be balanced upon the tip of a toe. Their bodies were bound in great sheets of plate, but theirs was steel rather than the shoddier, easier iron, and she felt an uncanny power in their grips as the first of them seized her arm.

Ensharia had to resist the urge to shake the hand off and strike its wielder, knowing that to do so would be unproductive. She stifled her indignity, watching as the orcs undid the lock about her, preparing to bind her to a new chain.

And *then* she shook the hand off and struck its wielder.

Hands still bound, Ensharia could not properly punch. Instead, she simply bunched her fingers and caught the orc with a pair of horizontal hammer fists.

All her weight was behind the strike, and all her strength, but she knew at the moment of connection she'd made a mistake.

The orc was probably twice the average weight for its species and far, far more than twice the average strength. Ensharia had hit trees less sturdy than its cheek. She sent it stumbling, but not to the ground, and caught movement in the corner of her eye before she could follow up the blow. She dove, rolling from the path of danger and bouncing back up to her feet, kicking out without thinking. Her heel connected with a sternum, knocked an orc over and her hopping yards in the opposite direction.

Both the remaining elites closed, now wielding thick iron cudgels that might have been excessively heavy even for beating down a castle gate.

She flitted right, then darted left. Luring the orc guards one way so that her kick would land clean from the other, and it did well enough in sending another into the dirt. The opening was too wide for the last to miss, however, and fatigued as she was, Ensharia didn't quite manage to escape the cudgel as it found her ribs and squeezed the air out of her.

Lights, dancing, washing in her vision. Gravity, apparently taking a day off. Heels high and well over her head, head feeling like it was caught between four different times at once, not one of which contained the orcs responsible for beating her. Ensharia realized she was face down only in time to find the orcs pressing down on her again, their strength and weights all used to hold her in place now as she was shackled rather more forcibly than before.

Ensharia was limp as a rag doll as they dragged her up to her feet, head almost lolling on her shoulders. There'd not been much fight in her, all things considered, not after so many days of labor and degradation. It wouldn't have taken a hammer as big as she'd caught to beat it all out.

Pitifully, she didn't move against them a second time as they hauled her off across the camp. The orcs left bound together did more to resist with their hateful jeering, but that seemed of no consequence to her captors.

The camp rumbled past her as Ensharia was forced ever onward, her head clearing as she moved. By the time she'd reached her destination, she'd regained enough mental coherence to realize that it would be her final destination.

General Venka stood nearby, watching. Around him were yet more elites, each of them nearly half again as tall as the fencer. She was forced down to her knees and stared one way and the other, quickly confirming her fears. That she was fully encircled by gray meat and hostility.

Anger. Ensharia surprised herself with it, felt the tears brimming, and nursed the embers of her fury as a means of keeping them from spilling over. She forced her head back around to glare at the general, spitting at the ground.

"This it then?" she snarled. "This how I fucking die, hacked apart by your attack dogs? Or do you have the stones to do it yourself?"

General Venka looked at her as he might a map of some battlefield, eyes drilling through the emotion, the humanity, and perceiving only the practical facts beneath.

"It is unbecoming of a paladin to swear," he replied calmly. "You ought to take more pride in your order, unless you'd sooner spend your last minute of life killing my respect for you."

It was utterly ridiculous that Ensharia found herself concerned most with the fact that he was right. Swearing *was* unbecoming of a paladin—they'd all been taught as much, and she'd not even kept to that much of her order's tenets. Her face burned with humiliation as the circle parted, revealing a newcomer.

Swick the Swift.

He'd done well for himself since they'd last spoken, black skin mostly obscuring the flush of alcoholic indulgence, adrenaline sharpening his eyes into a focus that pierced the clouds amid them. He wasn't so much as two-thirds the height of any orc there, yet each of them parted before him as he strode on. Evidently, they were clever and controlled enough to treat a Hero the way anyone else did.

Perhaps a few weeks ago, Ensharia would have been as well.

"Traitor," she snarled, knowing full well that a glare could not *actually* impale a man but doing her best to manage it regardless. "Oh, it had to be you, didn't it? A test of your loyalty, right? A showing of how trustworthy you are?"

Swick said nothing, looking suddenly ill as he just turned away from Ensharia and held his hands out. The bonds were removed from them. Somehow it made things worse to her that he was so meek about it all. Better to be killed by a real man, better to be killed with a pair of eyes to glare the last of her hatred into before death came knocking.

"That's it?" she continued, watching as his chains fell and a great, grisly sword was handed to him. "Got nothing to say, nothing at all? Oh, I suppose you aren't being paid to talk, are you? Just to kill."

He turned. Swick could have insulted Ensharia, laughed at her. He could have proclaimed the righteousness of the Dark Lord's cause or declared the paladins an order of baby-eating demons, said or done a thousand things, and none would have punched the breath from her half so fast as his expression.

In his eyes, she saw regret. Weak, trembling, agonized regret. The sort felt so keenly as to turn itself into pain. The sort felt so keenly, indeed, as to turn itself into the very order of pain a man might be so inclined as to try drowning in wine. By the unsteady nausea upon Swick's face, he had failed.

He closed in, one foot in front of the other, each stride made swiftly, dexterously. There wasn't anything of a drunkard about him, it seemed. As if the very role of an imminent murderer had sobered him. Ensharia supposed it rather had. If anything ought to have managed that feat, it was hardly an unfitting thing.

Swick stopped only when he was within two yards of her, beyond the range of any lashing limb she might throw out but so very within the reach of that sword. She could see its edge close from their new distance, make out the numerous tiny teeth along its blade. Almost as much a saw as a weapon. Made, no doubt, to remove limbs from a target of preternatural toughness. A target like her.

"Swick, please."

It was pathetic, revolting. It degraded her, achieving nothing and costing what little pride Ensharia had left, but she begged regardless. In her position, there was simply no way not to.

"Please, you can still turn around. You can still escape . . . You don't have to do this. Please just . . . Don't kill me. Please, I don't want to die."

She didn't. There was nothing practical or selfless motivating her. Ensharia felt no great duty calling her or unfinished business preserving her. She just didn't want to die. Her tears fell openly now, with all the volume and weight of a dying storm cloud.

"I'm sorry," Swick whispered, seeming to take just as much humiliation in his own pathetic words as Ensharia had hers. He was sorry. Spectacular. She was dead.

His sword came up high, glinting in the light, and it remained there for a moment, quivering. Ensharia's heart was in her throat, beating so hard she almost felt it rattle the teeth. A weapon that size, and an arm able to hold it so steadily so high, meant there'd be little chance of her surviving the first stroke. Not with Swick's accuracy.

Somehow that only made her more scared. Better to withstand the first blow and live a few more precious moments than be obliterated into the underworld all at once.

"I'm sorry," Swick repeated, arm tensing, sword shaking, weapon remaining in place. Ensharia couldn't take it anymore.

"*Just do it!*" she screamed, looking away as she did, just barely too slow to keep from catching the blade starting its descent.

Ensharia was wincing and looking away for long, agonizing moments before she finally realized that the blow was not going to fall. It felt like a remarkably long time, thanks to her enhanced reflexes, but could not have been far from a second. She looked back around at last, still expecting to see Swick's sword hovering in place. Instead she saw only empty air, a ring of gaping orcs, and a general with a face like wrathful lightning.

"*After him!*" Venka roared, his composure truly shattered.

It was rather humbling to see. Ensharia had swung a weapon at that face hard enough to send a head flying five hundred yards from the shoulders it sat on and failed to so much as raise an eyebrow. Clearly Venka was not a man accustomed to surprises or betrayal, for his emotions were about as restrained as a kicked hornet's nest.

"He can't have gone far! His translocation is limited to a quarter mile, if even that! Now hunt! Hunt, you damned animals! Hunt him down and I shall give whoever finds him first a hundred days and nights with whichever women they choose!"

The orcs were quick to obey their barbaric orders, taking off in a storm of grunting, whooping howls. Ensharia did not see animals, as Venka did, watching them take off across the camp. Through her shock-shattered wits and fear-clenched vision, she still recalled her long conversations with their smaller brethren.

Chasing Swick now were men. Large men, gray of skin and with mouths split by tusks and fangs, but men, nonetheless.

It was something to inspire more pity for the pirate, not less. Ensharia touched her neck where the sword might have fallen and swallowed.

Good luck, captain. Good luck, and thank you.

CHAPTER FORTY-NINE

Collin liked to think himself a veteran. He probably wasn't, being fair. Even his father's rangers only ever accepted that denotation after their *fifth* battle, not their second. Still, two was two more than most men fought, and two more than a great deal of soldiers survived. If nothing else, Collin had considered himself a man inured to the shock and horror of seeing undead roam about a battlefield. He had, after all, fought them often enough.

Silenos Shaiagrazni taught him differently.

There wasn't really a way of describing Collin's contribution that made it even sound like he'd fought, because he really hadn't. Oh, he'd gotten a few bastards early on, put arrows in knights and nobles and such, but he'd been made redundant around the first time one of those giant tentacled undead slammed into the enemy formations.

Not easy to break a shield wall, certainly not one made by veterans with hours of training and a shade of Vigor in their muscles. Collin had seen trebuchet boulders break against those overlocking slabs of wood without wounding the men beneath.

Shaiagrazni's monster hadn't even looked like it noticed them as it walked through the formation. Just lumbered over, broke it apart, then waddled off to find something more to kill. Collin had almost been too shocked to start headshotting officers before they reformed.

Then things had really kicked off.

Collin had heard tales from his father about his earliest battles, before he'd spent the time needed to train his Vigor up to its natural potential and enter that wide realm between unnoticeable superhumanity and the power of a Hero. He'd told of frantic, desperate, chaotic battles where every slight movement was a threat. Collin had never known one like that. He'd gone into his first fight with the strength of twenty men and the speed of a mantis. The flesh monsters had shown him a new empathy.

He ran around, screaming, swearing. Desperately changing directions wherever he saw a tendril about to impact or a building about to fall. At one point, he gladly sprinted straight toward a ballista rather than face the rampage of a monster at his back and barely survived the business.

By the time he was done, Collin had found himself thrust into a rather profound state of ego death. A sort of zen state, his consciousness ascending past the trappings of humanity. He was unshackled by greed or loathing, ambition or rage. All that was left was the primal, simple instincts of a rat, scurrying around and mindlessly fleeing from whatever had made the loudest noise most recently.

It kept him alive, if nothing else. That was a damn sight more than could be said for most of the enemy.

All told, Collin beheld the final butchery of it all with rather a heightened perspective. Nothing would empty a man's mind—and his fucking bowels—quite as much as a fight he had no control over, and he'd never controlled one less than this. He watched as the giant reanimated mountains of flesh tore apart the remnants of noble forces, raining blood down on the cobbled ground around them and striking Collin dumb with the brutality of it all.

Undead. He was fighting alongside undead. Collin waited for the disgust, the revulsion, the loathing. None of it came. He only smiled.

About time we use the Dark Lord's tricks against him. Here's hoping I can see one of these grab a hold of that cock Venka.

For that matter, he was hoping he kept managing not to knife the things' eyes out on reflex whenever they came within range. Old habits died hard.

Collin stepped in something, looked down, and realized it was someone. He couldn't tell which bit of the man it had been; one body part looked rather the same as any other when they'd been squeezed into mulch. It made him feel plenty sick all the same. His gaze turned back to the battlefield, guts squirming with queasiness, and Collin turned altogether. He started marching through the city.

There was no particular destination in his mind; anywhere would have done. Even a street caked in sewage was better than one caked in mashed-up people.

Kaltan was growing used to revolutionary wars. It was a sorry state, but it was the state of Collin's city. Its people had all taken cover with an almost practiced organization, and its streets were empty. He studied them as he moved.

Years ago, when his father first took power, the city had had much of its wealth redistributed, but the old trappings of aristocratic greed still remained. This close to the remaining noble's homes, everything was still pristine, smooth, and fucking expensive. Dangerous too, for Collin. That much occurred to him only once he'd turned his first corner. Plenty of folks around this part of town would be all too happy to see his throat opened up.

Then again, he'd be even happier to open theirs. And if they were any good at killing, he reckoned they'd already have been popped by one of Shaiagrazni's freaks. Collin kept walking.

Unfortunately, he found battle damage present as he moved. Sometimes a roof or wall staved in by stray siege stones, sometimes impacted instead by someone doubtless thrown by one of Shaiagrazni's monsters. In other places, he saw sure signs that there had been deliberate looting and destruction, which tended to hit the wealthier areas whenever the city found itself washed by a great violence.

Criminality liked cover, after all, and there were few forms of cover more effective than a fucking war happening elsewhere. Collin only hoped none of the younger ones had been hurt; child aristocrats were about the only kind he'd ever found himself caring for.

The streets warped, degrading as Collin moved. Kaltan's class discrepancies were not so pronounced as they had been five years ago, and the differences of five years ago were shriveled compared to what they'd been the decade earlier than that, but there was still a palpable change as Collin transitioned from the area of the rich to that of the more modest income wielders. It was, he supposed, not to be helped. Probably the city would remain plagued by its economic parasites for another ten years, even fifty. Perhaps he'd still be fixing rather than maintaining it if he ever took over from his father.

Now there was a daunting thought. Give Collin a lot of bastards to poke holes in and he was at home, but he'd rather weather a few holes himself than run a bloody city.

Somewhere along the way, Collin ended up turning toward the center, toward the second of Kaltan's noble districts. This one was rather more established, though now the crux of its military rather than its upper classes—it was for this reason that the site of his battle not thirty minutes earlier had been renovated so hastily and cobbled so lazily in the years since.

There was always something in the air of the city's center that soothed him. Something that promised a hard fight to any of the Dark Lord's underlings, whatever numbers they came in. Collin wasn't sure he could quite put his finger on it.

Ah, no, he could actually. Pitch. They kept plenty of the stuff in half-buried stores all over the place, just in case they were ever attacked and needed some boiling sludge to help give a hard fight. It reeked even when not burning.

Military life. It was simple, blunt. Easy. And every now and then, it was a hot explosion of adrenaline, savagery, and glory. Collin found his fingers twitching despite the horror he'd just scampered away from. He really could have done with a proper fight, and sooner rather than later. General Venka ought to hurry.

In through the main gates of the castle, then along through its halls. Guards saluted and bowed, which Collin ignored, and his anticipation grew. The farther he grew physically from the carnage of Shaiagrazni's magic, the more he was able to let its implications settle.

For decades, the Dark Lord's armies had been unbeatable. Possible to inconvenience, even delay, but never truly stop. They grew stronger with each victory and needed only to swarm along the countryside for a few days, weeks, or months to bolster their ranks with ever more shambling undead. But now that advantage belonged to the side of good as well.

The more he pondered it, the more Collin started to question the reluctance of using undead in the first place.

It was distasteful perhaps, in the same way that fucking a man's corpse was distasteful, but if Collin could free a city by doing the latter he'd have made the choice without hesitation. What was a bit of posthumous indignity to the lives of millions?

Nothing at all.

Finally he reached his father's office, not bothering to knock before he entered, and not surprised in the slightest by what he found within. King Galukar, it seemed, was in a particularly unpleasant mood. Perhaps one day, Collin would discover such a thing as an actually *nice* one in the man.

"A murderous savage," the king snarled, looming over Collin's father by well over a foot. His eyes were like chips of flint, his jaw like a boulder. Finlay Baird did not flinch before them any more than Collin had ever seen him flinch before anything. One did not cow his father.

"I am an avenger," the governor replied. "The people I killed were all guilty of more murders than me. They simply used starvation as their weapon rather than knives and arrows."

Galukar stared at him.

"And what of me then? Am I guilty of murder by starvation?" There was a dangerous note to his voice, the sort that might have deterred most men from continuing. Most men, Collin supposed, did not know themselves to be an irreplaceable cog in a world-shaping alliance.

"That really depends." His father shrugged. "I'd need to look more closely into your legislation." It wasn't lost on him, the rhetorical slant of Galukar's questioning. Apparently it *was* lost on the king that he was talking to a man who'd act his past out all over again and think nothing of it.

"And that's where it all leads," Galukar snarled. He was victorious sounding, despite his fury, as if some great point had been proved. "A way of doing things where any leader can be accused of murder, simply for making decisions about their nation."

Collin's father stared at him with every bit of the contempt his moronic answer called for.

"Yes," he said slowly, as if fearful the king would mishear. "That's where it all leads. Leaders *should* be possible to accuse of murder. That's a good thing. It means there'll be a lot fewer murderous leaders in the world."

It was clear by the way Galukar reared up and puffed his chest out that he had no intention of letting the conversation end there. Things like total, abject moral wrongness or utter logical vacancy had never stopped a king before. Collin tuned the man out, finding his interest quickly slipping from the debate. It was embarrassing to find, as he perused the rest of the room, that he'd entirely skipped over two additional presences.

Both he'd seen before, both in Silenos Shaiagrazni's accommodations when he'd called on him. The first was a witty, potbellied young man of perhaps Collin's age or older. He had the look of one who'd seen rather a lot more of the world than he'd grown used to all at once and appeared to be doing his best to sink into a wall. Beside him was a woman of darker skin even than Shaiagrazni himself, cyan eyes glowing with loathing as she studied the governor and king.

Neither one was a person Collin felt much kinship with, but the latter had his blood boiling. He'd asked his father about her, who in turn had asked Shaiagrazni, and eventually managed to learn that she was one of the Dark Lord's most trusted lieutenants. Sphera, a necromancer. Specializing in subterfuge and sabotage, she'd probably killed as many people inadvertently as King Galukar had with a sword stroke. And not one actually deserving, he'd wager.

There were more productive things to do than walk across the room and head-butt her in the mouth, but God if it wasn't tempting. Collin noted it down on the "maybe" list for later consideration, depending on how bored he got, and how quickly.

"You're both stupid," a new voice rang out, and all eyes turned to behold the sight of Silenos Shaiagrazni himself as he stepped into the room. It felt wrong to see him so unchanged after the devastation he'd wreaked.

CHAPTER FIFTY

Collin felt Silenos ought to have been wearing a different skin because his presence had so thoroughly transformed in light of seeing what he could do. It didn't feel right that monsters as powerful as him could wear the bodies of men. Even King Galukar seemed rather intimidated.

Even his bloody father, and that was a first if anything was.

"Finished destroying my bloody city?" the governor asked, glaring at Shaiagrazni, masking the fear well enough that it would probably have taken his own son to peer through it. If the caster was bothered, or even noticed the anger, he gave no hint.

"If I wanted to destroy your city, I assure you, there are far easier ways for me to go about doing so. I have finished destroying your enemies and have made a start on preparing yet more grotesqueries—that is to say, *monsters*, to aid in further violence. I have five now, all fully repaired and patrolling around the military districts. I thought it wise to give your men some exposure to them before combat began, given the inevitable novelty of fighting alongside such things."

Collin's father considered that. If there was one thing, and one thing only, that could always be entrusted to smooth away his foul temper, it was being presented a good idea.

"That is wise," he said after a pause. "But we have other issues to concern ourselves with than morale. Venka is coming. My scouts claim he's been delayed—something about a prisoner escape. Details are scarce, but that won't last him long.

"We have a day, at best. And if we have more than that, it'll be because he's decided to take a few detours and link up with even more of the local forces. His army will already be with him by now, which means we're staring down somewhere north of one hundred thousand orcs, undead, and casters. This city's walls were never built to hold that number back."

"They can be rebuilt," Shaiagrazni noted. "It would mean cutting down on the number of grotesqueries available, but I could accomplish several things with the saved biomass. Defensive weapons, reinforcements to the walls, among other things."

"More useful than your monsters?" Collin asked. Shaiagrazni eyed him in the way a man might a child who had just urinated upon his boots.

"Situationally, yes. I would not suggest them otherwise."

Collin's face flushed, and he let the room's attention move to King Galukar as he spoke.

"If there is to be no dissuading you from using these abominations," he grunted, "then . . . we may as well do so. I imagine that even now General Venka could be delayed on the roads, given our resources. We have the advantage of Heroes, and near Heroes, and a great knowledge of the land to boot. A small group consisting of our strongest could cause a great inconvenience for his marching armies, then disappear far faster than a mass of men the size of Venka's can follow."

Guerilla warfare, he was describing. More or less. It was essentially the modus operandi of Kaltan's armed forces and had been since before Collin was old enough to even consider joining them. One did not fight the Dark Lord directly.

"Could you send undead to aid this?" the governor asked, thoughtful now. Silenos Shaiagrazni's face twitched with irritation.

"I can send my apprentice," he replied, making the younger man twitch uneasily. "And I can perhaps make a few undead more specialized in mobility and subtler attacks."

Collin's father thought it through.

"You'd be volunteering to help, Galukar?"

"Of course," the king replied, not remarking upon the lack of mention for his title.

"Then it could work, with a few rangers to make sure you can all find your feet in the terrain." The governor nodded, settled in the matter. "Alright, we'll see how much time we can buy."

"We," Silenos Shaiagrazni echoed, sounding neither amused nor derisive. A silence followed his words, which Collin hastily filled.

"I want to help," he blurted out, glancing across the wider room but mostly keeping his gaze on the governor. "Let me go with them, Father. You know I'm good for it. You—"

"No," Finlay Baird replied, speaking as if he'd just given the order to see a man court-martialed. "Out of the question."

Collin's temper frayed.

"You know full fucking well I'm the hardest bastard you have," he growled, feeling his accent slip, feeling his long lessons on hiding it fade. "And I can scout rings around any of your rangers. What reason could you possibly have not to—"

"Because you're my fucking son," his father interrupted. His father, not his commander. Glaring at him not with the icy cold of command but the molten heat of family. Collin would rather have had the former. Easier to resist by far. "You're my son," his father continued, strained. "And I've only just gotten you back."

There was no arguing with that, not in any way that wouldn't make him a complete bastard.

It was fortunate then that Shaiagrazni was present.

"That is an utterly inane excuse," the caster noted, seeming oblivious to the maelstrom of fury spasming its way across the governor's face. "If we do not succeed in defending this city, your son's lifespan will be measured in days regardless. You are being laughably irrational."

All at once, the room went quiet. Collin had only ever seen such a thing happen once. It had been a few years ago, spanning a scarce few moments between his father hearing some derisive remark about his mother and breaking a champagne bottle across the offending party's face. There were no bottles within reach now though. Only edged steel.

"And what benefit do I gain by risking those last few days of his life?" Collin's father asked. He had not headbutted the caster, which was a good sign, but there was still an air of hungry violence around them. Silenos Shaiagrazni marched through it as if it were a pleasant misting of rain.

"For one thing, a trusted leader to bolster cohesion between your men and my undead," he explained. "The battle today was not a disaster, but it might have been. Your soldiers spent more time scrambling away from my creations than aiding them."

Collin rather thought he'd barely been better but decided to hold his tongue about the fact.

"And you think this will make a difference?" his father asked, wavering. Shaiagrazni met his eye.

"Do I need to tell you how having your men make proper use of the kinds of creatures I can make would grant them an advantage? Treat my undead as an equivalent to siege towers or trebuchets, if it will put things into perspective. Such things tend to have an effect on men."

Clearly, this Shaiagrazni had never seen just how orcs differed from normal soldiers in their response to danger. The decision was still not long in being made after he spoke, however. Collin's father nodded.

"Fine," he hissed, sounding about as happy about his own decision as Collin had been about his last one. "But you keep my son alive, alright? You keep my fucking son alive, or we're done."

Collin felt a flush of shame as Shaiagrazni nodded, and the caster was leaving soon. Their meeting didn't take long to break up after that. He didn't say his goodbyes to the governor, finding himself in no mood. All Collin wanted was to prepare himself.

He headed to his quarters, packing food, donning armor. Testing the steel-threaded string of his steel-limbed bow. It was tense enough that a normal man might have taken his fingers off in the effort of drawing it, and that pierced Collin's foul mood with a smile.

Soon enough, that string would be putting bolts through skulls. He'd need to take a few hours for practice before leaving. Wouldn't want to waste the iron.

Swick really wasn't sure what had possessed him to throw the rock; he'd just sort of done it. An instinct, a reflex. A deeply ingrained, mindless urge to leave himself some means of escape. His blood would serve as a marker for a good few hours, depending on weather, and the few drops he'd sprinkled along the stone had been more than enough. His throw had even been excessive for the distance.

A quarter mile was Swick's limit on a good day. It hadn't been a good day, and he'd gotten maybe three-quarters that distance, even at the expense of dropping to his knees in a sweating heap. A thousand-foot head start was nothing to scoff at, however. Nor was a camp full of rabid orcs led by the angriest man this side of the continent. He'd gotten running.

His hands were still bound, and still bound thickly. A warrior might have broken free. King Galukar, he had no doubt, would be past holding with such restraints, but Swick would have to get clever. And first he'd have to get far from the damned orcs.

Ensharia wasn't, he knew. His first thought had been to free her, but Swick had chosen not to. Doing so would only have made her a threat, quite possibly made her a dead woman. That wasn't why he'd made his decision, however.

The sword was heavy in his hands, threatening his balance with every stride and reminding him of his failure. Swick could surely have carved her free of her bonds with it, if he'd chosen. He hadn't.

Better to leave her bound and imprisoned than himself a mere two hundred yards from danger instead of four hundred. He felt his headache reemerge.

Swick slipped on something, shifting ground. He cursed. The land here was only half transformed by the Dark Lord's touch, not held and frequented by enough undead that it had fully degraded into ashen deserts. There was enough vegetation to leave the terrain uncertain beneath him, and he found his feet an unreliable pair of allies.

He scaled a dune, reached the top, and tripped, falling, rolling, landing in a heap at the bottom. It didn't hurt. Half caster or not, very few falls could hurt a Hero, but it scraped his pride well enough.

Of course, Ensharia might well be killed anyway. Her death had been ordered, he knew, and the general Venka was certainly not a man to hesitate before ending a person. Swick wasn't sure though. His escape had made him an active enemy, and one whom the general couldn't be sure hadn't conspired with the paladin. With a bit of luck, he'd want to keep her around and alive for questioning.

With a bit of luck. Luck was in such short supply these days. Unless one happened to be Swick the Swift, of course.

He scampered along a lengthy patch of land, then pounced behind the shadow of one taller mound as he heard scraping footsteps behind him. Swick cursed his haste, climbing to a grunting stand and continuing. Orcs moved in many ways, but scraping was not among them. If he heard lumbering or crushing movement, he knew he'd be in real trouble.

In real trouble. That wouldn't be a first; precious few things were for Swick. He'd been in real trouble at Grimsquoi, in real trouble in the Snarling Forest. He'd been in real trouble when that curmudgeonly old fuck Walriq had almost snatched his ship clean out of the skies after he stole his staff. And, of course, Swick had been in real trouble when he'd flown that same ship into the side of the Flying Fortress.

Real trouble, it seemed, was something that followed Swick but killed only those around him. He supposed that was to be expected of a man who habitually threw them into its path.

Lumbering movement, sharp in his ears, ferocious in pursuit. Swick knew that if the orcs were close enough for him to hear, he was close enough for them to smell. With luck, he'd be faster.

Was it his fault his men were dead, Ensharia still bound? Perhaps. Did he regret it?

There was the real question. Did he regret it?

No, he didn't. Swick risked a glance over his shoulder and found a pair of towering orcs glaring down at him from on high. They were perched atop a dune, peering at him from some two hundred yards back. Gained, or gaining? He had no easy way of finding out.

Swick turned back and hastened his flight.

CHAPTER FIFTY-ONE

They were elites in more than just name, these orcs. Swick might have expected as much. General Venka did not like inaccurate titles within his army.

He'd managed to keep ahead of them for just a few more minutes and a few more miles, then the things had gotten him surrounded. They were four in all, big and mean, bodies covered with bolted-on steel that rattled as bulging musculature flexed. He saw pure hatred flashing behind their eye slits, and it wasn't hard to imagine why.

Slaves got that look when they saw a runaway. They hated them for a number of reasons, but none more than for having the courage to do what they themselves had not. No slave would ever fight so viciously as when they were fighting a runaway. Just his bloody luck.

There was something clotted and sludgy in the back of Swick's throat, spit and phlegm. He always felt the need to spit in a fight, particularly a tough one. He decided to use it this time, hacking out the stuff at the nearest orc even as he whirled around, sword held tight.

His guess had been right. They were quick, these elites. Quick enough that one had already pounced and come within range by the time he finished his turn, letting the heavy blade cleave down hard into the fucker's shoulder. It was a solid connection, and the half inch of steel gave way with a satisfying crunch as bright blood spurted out from the gash. Swick felt the sword bounce back and followed its momentum as he jumped away just in time to evade the third orc's hammer swing.

Then the first, the one he'd blinded with spit, smashed something into his back.

Probably it was a hammer, given how efficiently it emptied the strength out of him. Swick's feet left the ground, and he flew five, ten, twenty feet before landing hard and rolling farther. He was barely up in time to see the orcs closing in.

A change of strategy was called for.

Swick's mouth was full of blood; perhaps he'd bitten his tongue. He put it to use, subtly spitting down, then again onto his hands. He spat a third time at his feet—aware of how much utility the deed was getting in this fight—before he hurled a final spray out at the charging orcs and lunged.

Predictably, his target raised an arm and blocked the projectile rather than lose momentum by dodging. Swick translocated just as the blood settled on their bracer, waiting until the height of his sword thrust before suddenly appearing before his enemy. Charging orc met stabbing man blade first. The tip pierced steel even better than its edge. It was, after all, a sword made to cleanly fell a bound paladin of near-Heroic power.

Orcs were big, broad, and ever so slightly magical, but very few living things could survive their hearts being skewered.

Swick made sure to tug his sword a moment, shifting it around in the wound and hastening the bleeding, then he released his grip and translocated back to the dirt he'd spat blood onto just before more hammer blows could find him. He watched from those twenty feet back as the stabbed orc wavered, fell, and died. One down.

Trading a weapon for a dead enemy was not the best deal he could have made, however. The remaining orcs closed quickly, fury in their gaits.

Swick almost let himself feel a stab of hope before one of the beasts halted, sticking beside its slain ally, eyes keenly drifting to the body.

Elites. Fucking of course they'd realized the trick to his magic. Orcs weren't half as stupid as most thought. Swick backed off, cursing as he realized his plan of translocating to retrieve his sword was foiled by the one elite's proximity to it, and then cursing again as he saw the second give the marked patch of sand a wide berth. There'd be no slipping behind it, little tripping the thing with his magic at all. Swick steeled himself and closed in with his shackles readied.

The axe that came for him might have been better used decapitating elephants than men, but Swick was sure to avoid it regardless. He made to move in, a feint that succeeded in drawing the orc's next swing out prematurely. Swick went under it, raising his arms and controlling the slack of chains between them just so as to leave it in the path of the metal blade. Steel screamed against steel, and he was sent flying.

He landed, rolled, sprang to his feet, and tested his bonds. The chain remained in place, but a quick glance showed Swick a great chunk bitten out from one of the links. He squared his shoulders, yanking the shackles two ways with both arms at once, feeling a moment of resistance before the damage worsened and the chain snapped entirely.

His arms were free, more or less, and just in time. The orc was on him again.

Swick planted his feet, threw a punch with all his strength . . . and translocated at the moment before it snapped out. His fist thudded hard into the jaw of the *other* orc, knocking the giant clean from his feet and buying Swick a few precious moments to go for the sword still sticking out of its friend.

By the time the orc was up, his blade was out, and Swick started his swing. He glanced to one side, saw the other orc charging in past his previous location, waited a moment, then translocated again so that the very tip of his weapon's arc scraped along the approaching enemy's gorget. It dislodged the piece of armor, nearly cutting it in two, and drew a squirt of blood that Swick noted was too little in volume to be arterial. His enemy rounded on him, then started backing off. The orcs were together again shortly, and wary.

Wise. Swick had to fight not to grow cocky himself.

Knives were his weapon of choice, but against armor that thick, Swick was happy for the greatsword. He'd have been happier with a halberd though. The orcs came at once, both spaced just enough to watch each other's backs, both ready for an assault from any direction. Swick ran his finger over the edge of his sword, flicking his hand upward and rushing in.

His first swing was dodged, but he quickly twisted it into a second just in time to meet the axe that would otherwise have taken his arm. Both weapons rattled, shards of steel exploding outward from the clash. A common fate to mundane weapons in Heroic hands.

The other orc's hammer came down to within inches of Swick's spine before he translocated to the drop of ichor now falling, twisting in midair to turn his descent into a stab clean through the damaged shoulder of the first orc he'd struck.

Blood. Steam. Death. The air filled with all three as the dirt filled with orc flesh, then Swick hit the ground and rolled. He came up swinging, almost blinding the last orc as it tried its luck with a lunge, then started backing away. He chased it, snarling and slashing, making himself as big a terror as was possible to drive his panicking enemy farther away.

Swick's final translocation, and the subsequent sword running into his enemy's back, came just moments before the orc realized it was being shepherded to one of the previously marked locations. It convulsed, swinging in a vain attempt to kill Swick even as it hung on the end of his weapon. Then died. He let it fall, cleaning the blood-soggy steel in black dirt, panting.

There wasn't time to waste, so Swick didn't. He looked around, located the orc's tracks, and followed them back until he found a trio of horses. Big things, dark of mane and rippling with almost as much muscle as their riders. One couldn't use a normal mount to haul around a rider the weight of a horse itself, after all, and the magical beasts used by Venka's elites were well-known.

Going through the saddle bags, Swick found food enough for a day or two. Or a few months if one happened to be a twelve-stone human rather than a number of hundred-stone barbarians.

The mounts themselves were aggressive but not impossible to reason with. Swick took one and sent the other two sprinting off in different directions. With luck they'd delay the enemy finding his trail.

But once that was done, he was left with a question. Swick hated those. They were the one form of struggle he never quite grew used to. His head ached at it.

Swick could go back for Ensharia, but he wouldn't. A rescue now would be the most likely to succeed. Venka's men would be diffused, and Swick had given enough impression of his true self that he doubted the man expected him to come charging back. One Hero, with speed and surprise and plenty of stolen knives from a trio of dead orcs, might well make it to the slaves and free them fast enough to turn the hunt into a real fight.

That would be best for the paladin, but not for Swick. He urged the horse on away from the camp, head throbbing as he did.

Swick had to look out for number one, had to do what was best for himself. God knew nobody else would.

Magi were socially stunted, selfish, half-mad egotists prone to fits of volcanic tantrum followed by long periods of arctic sulks. Collin had heard as much, and heard it well. It was quite another thing, however, to see it himself.

What he'd heard of Arion Falls spoke of a man possessing singular intellect and power, destined to claim the seat of greatest magus alive, and quite possibly in history to boot. What he was met with, instead, was a whinging, petty, narcissistic twat. Even his voice was annoying. All nasally, all sneering, as if he felt slighted that each word—and the punctuation between them for that matter—were not met with a round of applause.

A day. That was all Collin had spent pinched beside him, tucked away in their dugout, kept shielded from sight more than from the elements as rain drizzled and winds bristled and the magus whinged. By the halfway point, Collin was about ready to behead him, and by the end, he was halfway to beheading himself. It was all only worsened by the damned king.

Kings were socially vacant, self-*full*, completely mad egotists prone to fits of apocalyptic tantrum followed by periods of actual war. Collin had heard as much, and heard it well. It was quite another thing, however, to see it himself.

Galukar seemed more willing to weather the elements, that much had to be handed to him. If only because nothing else could. He groaned frequently and snarled even more so. Constantly hissing out some whispered, bitchy demand for the enemy to show themselves, as a force of thousands might be hurried on their path by the anticipation of men primed to jump them.

Between the two of them, Collin sincerely wasn't sure which was more annoying. The king, perhaps, if only because his age left him no excuse at all for the childishness. It was a relief when a flash of cloud-buried sunlight bounced off a rain-wet sheet of metal ahead. The sign of naked steel. Armor.

CHAPTER FIFTY-TWO

They're coming," Collin whispered, shifting and feeling his locked muscles work themselves. They didn't numb with motionlessness the way others did, not even warriors were as limber as his kind. Easier to get muscle cramps as a cat than a ranger. By the discontented groans of his allies, they apparently were no exceptions to the general rule.

"What sort of enemies are we looking at?" Galukar asked, remaining hunched, ready to pounce like some coiled snake. Collin could appreciate the sense for an ambush, at least.

"We have a minute or three before they're on us," he whispered. "And the column looks to be about . . . Yes, one thousand," he counted swiftly. "No orcs, just undead. I'd guess this isn't one of Venka's originally. He's probably calling them in to link with his forces before the attack . . . Which means that we know whichever way they're marching now, he lies there."

Galukar nodded.

"Their strength?" he asked, absorbing the information quickly. Collin peered back.

"Twenty dullahan, three fomors. Otherwise . . . Skeletons, I think."

It wasn't good, but it could be worse. Skeletons were old reanimates, old enough for their flesh to rot away and the magic keeping them active to settle and mature. They were invariably stronger, faster, and tougher than when first created, and usually by a lot. Collin would rather take one than a dullahan, rather take four or five in fact, but even veteran soldiers would be disadvantaged against them without Vigor. He'd heard of skeletons cutting apart ten or twenty men before dying, or knights being killed by a scant few.

"Skeletons," King Galukar grunted, then smiled. His face was ghoulish in the dim light, raindrops following the curve of his grin like blood running off a scythe blade. "Good to work the knots out of my muscles, at least."

It took a few minutes before the enemy was within range, at the foot of the hill upon which Collin and his allies perched. That was quite fine by him because it took just barely less time to send the order through his side's ranks and ready them for an attack.

They numbered one hundred, their enemies one thousand. It wasn't a ratio most men would feel confident in, but Collin had more than a few reasons to let the steel lace his spine. Rangers were one thing, Shaiagrazni's undead another, and the star pupil of wind mage Walriq quite possibly another order of combatant still. King Galukar though . . . Well, he was the sort of man who defied description for his powers. Most of the contemporary words for deadliness and strength were referencing his own famous feats to begin with.

At last the enemy were in position, and Collin gave the order. King Galukar moved before anyone else by simply hurling himself from the hilltop.

He flew as if he were a stone tossed by a catapult, coming down in a great arc, hitting the ground from a hundred yards high and barely even bothering to bend his knees. He swung once, lopping an entire row of skeletons in half with the motion, then undead were falling in behind him and rangers were letting bolts fly. Collin made sure he wasn't the last to fire, having half expected the abrupt beginning anyway.

The enemy, it seemed, had not.

Undead ripped skeletons fully in half, lithe, efficient things almost like skeletons themselves. They seemed suits of bone-textured armor puppeted by economically placed weaves of musculature within and moved like sacks of vipers. Appearing wherever an enemy's strike wasn't, striking wherever an enemy's spine was. Thirteen was all they'd been given, and thirteen seemed almost excessive.

Arion Falls fought at the middle range, turning away volleys of arrows, unbalancing particularly troublesome enemies, wounding or killing others by advantageously hurling dropped weapons with subtle gestures. He seemed a conductor giving commands to an orchestra, and the song he was playing rang much the same as any other battle. Death, mayhem. Fun. Collin let himself get lost in it as he loosed one arrow after another, picking his marks as carefully as ever, grinning his bloodlust as carelessly as always.

Nine hundred or so skeletons had made up the bulk of the enemy's force, and they moved predictably. Undead always did.

A man, when suddenly peppered with arrows like ballista bolts and hacked away at by a screaming lunatic bigger than most bears, might have felt themselves influenced by such thoughts as staying alive.

Oh, that huge, horrible man is about to hit me with a block of rusty iron so hard my guts are squeezed out of my arse, they might have thought. *I reckon I ought to stop that from happening, seeing as I enjoy living and all. Running away seems like a good idea.*

Not an undead. They didn't much care for living, on account of not living to begin with, and would much rather kill an enemy than keep from being killed. It made them fucking awful to fight in some situations, but trivial enemies for a prepared ambush.

Because they always moved the same way.

The undead made two main bodies: one charging for Galukar, the nearest living thing, and the other turning to head uphill and carve into the rangers, the most numerous living things. Both were doomed, for different reasons.

At Collin's signal, Arion Falls hurried back up to the crest of the hill and splayed his arms. The ground rumbled as wind shook it, then a mountain of black dirt fell, made into heavy sludge by the rain, and rolled down to bowl them over. The arrows came shortly after, smashing open whatever skulls or limbs first emerged from the avalanche. Collin's were the most carefully aimed by far.

The other group of undead, the ones charging King Galukar, died for a rather different reason. They were fighting King Galukar. Collin had gone most of his life assuming the phrase "one-man army" was merely hyperbolic, but what the king did to stave off his own assault proved otherwise. He suddenly found the bastard's whiny arrogance just a shade more tolerable.

As his quiver ran empty, however, and his victory close, Collin realized something about their enemies. There hadn't been two groups; there had been three.

"*Regroup!*" he ordered, smelling a danger in the unexpected change. All the deadliest enemies were bunched up among that third pack: dullahan, fomors, and a few other, smaller things that were dressed in fancier armor than either. King Galukar heeded his order with a swift decisiveness, hacking one last line of skeletons to bits before rushing uphill.

Arrows, arrows, more arrows. Always more fucking arrows, and always fewer enemies after they were fired. Soon enough Collin was out, all of his quivers emptied, and as he looked down the row of rangers, he saw his was a common situation. The undead below remained where they were. They'd been the subjects of the most recent shots of course, but they'd hung back, kept their distance. Sidestepped the streaking iron and managed to avoid even a single hit.

Stronger undead did tend to be smarter too, in Collin's experience. He'd never fought something more powerful than a fomor, but he knew they were out there. Evidently these mysterious new ones were examples of that most esteemed order of might. He turned to King Galukar, keeping them in the corner of his eye as he whispered a question.

"What do you recommend we do with these ones?"

Still, they simply waited. If an undead could afford to do one thing, it was wait. Fucking immortal bastards.

The king studied them, brow furrowing as he thought.

"We should attack as one, have your best shots gather up all the remaining arrows, have everyone else switch to close combat weapons. Charge in a single group with me heading it and Falls protecting the masses with air. With luck, we'll be able to break them apart and overwhelm them. We have the numbers now, with the skeletons dead."

"We have the numbers, not necessarily the strength," Collin breathed. "One dullahan is worth five or more rangers in close combat. There's twenty there, plus fomors and those others."

Galukar growled.

"Shaiagrazni is scum, scum of the lowliest kind, but he can make potent servitors. I'd wager the undead in our forces against any of theirs individually. Mix them in among your men and you'll have units able to bear the brunt of enemy violence while the rangers strike from sidelong."

Collin thought, then nodded. It made sense. He sighed.

"Give the orders."

Their enemies waited patiently as they reorganized, apparently confident in winning the charge provided they could hold their ground. All told, Collin ended with some seventy rangers wielding blades and shields, merely twenty left with bows. He almost felt the doubt seep in, so buried it with fury.

"*Alright, lads!*" he roared, forcing himself to project a nonexistent certainty. "*Let's go and fucking do 'em!*"

Cheers erupted around him as they started downhill, King Galukar bounding ahead. Within moments, the sound of screaming bowstrings rang out, and the volley of arrows raced down just ahead.

Their enemies had no shields, and thus their options were limited. Try to slap near-sonic projectiles from the air, which was not an option. Move rapidly to avoid them, which was but would break their balance and formation immediately before the charge hit them. They instead chose the third, simply weathering the blows of thrown iron as a means of retaining cohesion. Collin's men hit them like a battering ram, and the violence started.

He was among them, of course. However good he was with a bow, Collin had no intention of sitting out of the most dangerous of the fighting. He wielded a pair of long daggers like his father, magus-wrought steel far stronger than any nonmagical metal and doing a fine job of prying open dullahan plate or scraping along fomorian tendons. King Galukar was less a man than a fate, befalling whatever tried to stand in his path, and everyone else just washed over their enemies as a tide of jagged, swearing soldiers. Collin had rarely felt so proud of the angry bastards.

One dullahan fell, another, then half were gone. Collin headbutted one, saw stars as his helmet dented against theirs, then headbutted again to knock the thing down before knifing its brain to mulch through the eye holes.

Men fell and carved around him. A fomor stumbled as one of Shaiagrazni's undead latched on to its head and started chewing through its skull. Another volley of arrows hit the back of the enemy line, which had not yet been engaged but was still close enough that any men but rangers would doubtless have hit their allies in trying the shot. Then, suddenly, the path was clear.

Undead lay in bits at their feet, some still active enough to crawl and bite at ankles, most still and destroyed. All that remained was one fomor and a quartet of the unidentified ones.

King Galukar strode forward, intercepted by the fomor as it lunged, lithe limbs lashing out. He took both off in one swing, then the legs beneath. His third strike fell before the creature even hit solid earth, turning its head into a gory mess. Then he rounded on the last four.

Collin stepped in to cover the king's back as he approached their final enemies, ten paces away, cast in shades of darkness by the cloudy sky. Eight paces, Galukar faltered. Six and he stopped. Collin stopped too, taking only another stride to glance at the man's face, suddenly fearing he'd been struck by some spell.

It wasn't magic that held the king, however. Mind-clouding spells left a man senseless or dazed, and Galukar's face could not be sharper with emotional thought. His features were twisted by agony, regret, guilt. Sorrow. The Godblade fell from his suddenly limp fingers, and a shiver took him. When he spoke, his voice was quiet enough that Collin knew only his ears were sensitive enough to catch the words.

"No," he breathed.

Collin saw he was staring at the undead and followed his gaze. They were men, clearly reanimated soon after death for the lack of rot, clearly potent for the quality of their arms and armor. He saw nothing more in them than that, however.

Not until King Galukar spoke.

"My boys . . ." The king sobbed, tears falling freely, voice as stable as a collapsing cliff. "My sons . . . What has he done to you?"

The undead came on without a word.

CHAPTER FIFTY-THREE

Two major things were needed in the defense of a city. In fact, many were. The act of holding a fortified position was fiendishly complex and composed of an uncountable multitude of contrivances. They all, however, influenced the same two fundamental aspects in one way or another. Holding the enemy attack at bay for as long as could be managed and thinning the enemy's numbers during that time.

At the end of the day, when outnumbered, the defenders of a settlement would find their best hope lay within the prospect of achieving numerical equilibrium, or as close to it as was possible. And that of course meant remaining safe behind the walls and killing them before they got in.

Silenos decided to tackle the matter of prolonging the siege first, imagining that it would prove the larger challenge. Kaltan was not a large city by Shaiagrazni standards, but a scant few days was not a long span to be worked in either. They were stony structures measuring perhaps one meter at their thickest and half that for much of their span. Not the sort of structure that would withstand even a single volley of modern cannon fire but perhaps sufficient to turn away Venka's weapons.

For a while. Venka had powerful casters within his armies, Silenos had heard, and they were the real concern. A breach wouldn't take long to find itself carved across so thin a structure of rock, when it was belladonnan puppeteers or lichs turning their powers to making it. The walls had to be strengthened somehow.

He studied them, walking along their span, considering the options.

Keratin of course was the universal first choice of House Shaiagrazni, infinitely versatile and eternally potent. It could be hardened, made springy, spongy, near elastic, and terribly, terribly tough. With molecules of ferrous compounds, Silenos might make a material like his own armor, able to turn aside any weapons this world could muster. But he hadn't the time.

The truly potent weaves of keratinous material required a great precision and care, such that even he was tested to apply them quickly. Silenos might make cubic meters of the stuff, might make dozens of cubic meters, but when dealing with a wall measuring ten or so kilometers in circumference and five meters in height, that was simply insufficient.

He could cover it all in less than a millimeter within that time frame, and even his own fleshcrafting genius could not make a material potent enough to turn aside siege engines while measuring on the microscale. Silenos considered other possibilities.

Nacre was out of the question for similar reasons, as were many of the harder forms of organic tissue. Silenos had studied sea snails with shells of dark gray and iron strength once, but the substance of their bodies had required large volumes of iron ore that the city simply could not supply. Not in the amounts needed to coat an entire outer wall with sufficient sums.

Chitin was more homogenous and simpler than the more exotic keratinous weaves, but he feared it was too weak. Silenos considered exotic mucus, arthropod teeth, protective mineral enamel. He flitted through a hundred possibilities before the obvious struck him like a catapult stone.

He would simply use bone.

Carbon, phosphorus, calcium, and oxygen. A few trace elements aside from those four, and he would have all the materials needed for animal bone mineral. Most of which were found in the very soils or air around him.

Bone was not as intricately structured as many other substances, depending on the kind. It required no careful shaping or weaving, simply the creation of its chemical substance and the molding of its volume. There was, after all, a reason it was so common in the works of less skilled fleshcrafters. Silenos allowed himself a moment of embarrassment. His master had often warned him not to overlook the basics. If she'd seen him now, she would surely have arched a smug eyebrow and whipped his pride with some steel-tipped remark.

Silenos got to work quickly, demanding he be brought the corpse piles and feeling his mild annoyance reborn at the reminder that he was expending yet more resources that might otherwise have been used to create more servitors for himself. He was soon remolding meat into osseous matter, deciding to graft it onto the wall in larger sections.

At first, he tried to attach the bone mechanically. Using fleshcrafted talons and grip strength to dig furrows into the stonework, then hooking the slabs of bone on. It was a losing proposition. Silenos found himself spending five minutes affixing the stuff for every minute he made it, and at such a rate he'd be fortunate to have finished the entire wall within the week. There was a need to improve his method, or else hope that General Venka was delayed beyond their most hopeful estimates. Silenos chose the former option.

He did it by first placing his raw materials against the stone, then beginning the process of transforming their molecules into bone from the bottom out. In doing so, he increased their density, thus reducing their volume and leaving pockets of near-empty space that he then sectioned off with further strips of bone. These pockets, vacuums, yearned to be filled, thus dragging air against them and exerting pressure from the atmosphere beyond the bone, holding it in place.

By keeping them separated in many dozens of smaller compartments, Silenos removed the risk of having a wall breach let his entire protective coating of bone fall away and guaranteed it would remain where it was.

A clever design, even by his standards. It quartered the time spent affixing bone and left Silenos's week of work reduced to barely two days. He still found himself uncertain of finishing in time, however.

It took too long to move and walk, to reach every section of the walls. So Silenos improved his system further.

He fleshcrafted a great thing of locomotive musculature and supporting vertebrae, then mounted it atop the wall. From its outstretched limbs, Silenos let himself dangle, and, his thoughts tethered to it, he commanded the construct to move sidelong or raise and lower his body, handing down organic tissue for him to work with while lesser constructs kept it supplied from the piled corpses in the city streets. Within half an hour, he had a means of removing practically all his work save for the deed of actually producing his materials in the first place.

Silenos did so hastily.

It was growing dark by the time he finally finished encasing the walls of Kaltan in osseous protection, and Silenos found his legs unsteady from the long hours spent dangling high as he finally took his place back down upon the dirt. He gazed up at his work, a wave of pride punctuating its visage.

He had not made a few dozen cubic meters of bone, as he would have keratin. He had made several thousand. Enough to encase the rock's front and back in five-centimeter shells, flexible and yielding, yet tough and sturdy. He doubted they would have fared well against a blast of cannon fire, but such protection would be more than sufficient for the kinds of wars waged in this world.

Silenos took a step back to the wall, meaning now to mount it and begin work on the second stage of his tasks. He was surprised to feel the limb give out beneath him, his knee suddenly digging into dirty ground, his palms hitting the ground a moment later for stability. Every scrap of his body was heavy, aching, and raw.

For a moment, Silenos actually thought he had been attacked, that some force of the new world had possessed both the power to enfeeble him and the subtlety to apply it without his notice. Then the true reason made itself known.

He had exhausted himself. Silenos found a dry, cracking, jagged smile splitting his face. He'd become exhausted. It could hardly be considered surprising; six million kilograms of processed meat, dirt and air, of slaughtered cattle and shoveled shit was a great sum to apply himself to. He'd grown so used to economically using what few resources he had that Silenos had almost forgotten he even had limits of magic rather than material or time.

Slowly, carefully, he got back to his feet. His enhanced musculature made little difference with a mana-deprived body. The simple mental exhaustion was what interfered with him now. Silenos sent out a command to call on one of his other undead, leaning against them until he'd felt some of his strength return.

By the time he was confident he could continue to work, the sun had fully disappeared over its horizon.

Silenos was left to rest only hours after the dark had consumed the city, his work having taken a considerable length. Shortly after, he was called back to the city's walls. This time Finlay Baird waited atop them, eyes hard as they peered out, face tight. Silenos came to stand beside the man and saw what had him concerned instantly.

The enemy had arrived.

General Venka's army moved much more like a modern one than the primitive hordes of the other new worlders. Silenos might have been impressed were he not a stupid savage pathetically laboring to serve a bumbling buffoon of a ruler. As things were, he only found himself irked by the inconvenience of a formidable enemy.

"You can see in the dark?" Baird asked, sounding surprised as he glanced at Silenos. Silenos didn't see any reason in lying, just nodded.

"My eyesight is enhanced," he replied. "What are your thoughts on the enemy?"

"Looks like we were right about what to expect. Most are absorbed from nearby forces. A lot though are orcs."

Silenos could see as much, feeling his lip curl at the sight. Repugnant creatures, they reminded him of the primitive hominids his species had evolved from. As similar to apes as modern man, by the low ridges of their brows and pronounced occipital bones.

"You said they have the strength of six or seven men?" Silenos asked Baird.

"On average," the man confirmed. "Venka's are better fed and trained than tribals though. I'd guess they're closer to nine or ten. They've been known to snap the necks of bears farther east, as I've heard it."

Silenos could believe it studying the beasts. There was a spasm of magic running through their bodies, and a great quality of musculature.

"They are not the main threat, however," he noted, peering now at a row of undead. They were of no blanket kind, all more identifiably individualistic by the different flairs and schemes of their armor. Each burned with a considerable magic, enough that any two of them might have bested even a Hero.

He recognized that magic from the things that had pursued Falls from that town, and very nearly caught him.

"How confident are you in our defenses?" Baird asked as the army began its deployment.

"Very." Silenos shrugged. "But I've been wrong before. I'll be tested in my certainty soon enough regardless of how strongly it burns."

"You could surrender," came the voice of Sphera, and Silenos glanced at the bound woman sidelong. She had been accompanying him everywhere he went, of course, as he was simply the only creature trustworthy enough to hold her prisoner. Now, she didn't look eager to flee. More concerned. "If you surrender, present the city to the Dark Lord, he will give you a high position. Higher than any of his lieutenants, I daresay."

Silenos snorted.

"Why would I wish to be second to a rat?" He looked back at the army, considering it. Yes, a formidable force indeed. Kaltan must have been a great thorn in the Dark Lord's side. Perhaps it was inspiring rebellion elsewhere; that was worth considering after the siege.

"They're waiting for something," Baird snarled, sounding rather bestial as he did. "Look." He nodded ahead, gesturing to the army. "That's not an offensive formation. They're making camp."

So the delaying tactics had worked then. Somewhat at least. Silenos found himself less surprised by that than the governor's apparent eagerness to fight.

"That is good. It gives you more time to drill the men with my new defensive equipment," Silenos replied. "And me more time to do other things."

CHAPTER FIFTY-FOUR

Silenos turned, heading back down the steps and dragging the necromancer Sphera along behind him. He'd kept her bound and collared, more for his own amusement than anything else, with a strip of keratinous material measured carefully to be the equal of her strength, then tripled for good measure. The two of them were alone soon enough, and her temper was as hot and hissing as he had hoped.

"You're going to lose, you know," she snapped venomously. Silenos had found the woman rather enjoyed taunting her enemies. He could appreciate that particular pleasure, but not as much as he appreciated her inevitable fury whenever he demonstrated that he was beyond her petty attempts at enjoying it with him.

"You can think that if you'd like," Silenos replied. He rather imagined that was the sort of vague response most likely to truly needle the woman, and as was so often the case, he proved himself right a moment later. Her fury was like hearing a bowstring released.

"I know that, you fucking imbecile. Why are you so insistent on fighting this battle when it's so clearly hopeless?"

Silenos turned to her, taking a moment to examine her before he replied. No, she wasn't angry; she wasn't blind with her emotion. She was testing him, trying to wheedle some hint of his plans, or else confirm a theory. He considered how best to reply.

All other things being equal, it was invariably best to keep others knowing less, rather than more, about oneself. He pursued that ideal in his answer.

"It is not my way to surrender," Silenos replied calmly, letting her think he was acting more out of stubbornness than he was. Her eyes narrowed.

"So that's it? You'd rather die than give in? Fucking men."

She was annoyed, infuriated. No, more than that, disappointed and even . . . Yes, worried. Intriguing.

"You have something more to say, I notice," Silenos guessed. "Might you just save us both a wealth of time and simply say it? I have far better things to do than stand here in anticipation of your drivel."

Her eyes were sharp again, considering, but her hesitation did not last long. Of this woman's numerous qualities, good and bad, quick-wittedness was certainly among the most notable.

"Your necromancy," she answered at last. "It's superior to the Dark Lord's."

The woman said it as if it were in some way significant, as if Silenos ought to have felt flattered or surprised. He only snorted.

"And it's better than a babbling infant's too. Are you going somewhere with this?"

She seemed more amused than irritated at that.

"I want to join you," the woman pressed. "To study under you. I want to learn from the greatest necromancer I can, and I think you're greater by far than my current master."

He hadn't failed to notice the signs of course, and Silenos was not such a fool as to be surprised.

"No," Silenos replied. "Was that all?"

Her face turned to surprise first, of course. Truly gifted magic casters were invariably prideful and egotistical, and any slight against them, be it insult or rejection, tended to come as a shock. They tended also to draw out the necromancer's second response, fury. Her eyes narrowed, brow creased, fists curled as the rage came on. Silenos found himself probing his mana reserves, noting that even after his rest they were still nine-tenths empty.

Enough to stave off this one, now that there was no great wealth of preparation to help her gain the advantage. Even without any power at all, he'd have surely won given the days spent skewing things in his own favor. Still, Silenos did not care for the novelty of weakness.

"You're turning down the most gifted necromancer alive?" she demanded. It was one of the funniest things Silenos had ever seen, her anger as fierce as a tyrant's, her gesticulations as impotent as a child's. This one knew exactly what the disparity of strength was in this conversation, and it was torturing her with every word. He almost couldn't bring himself to interrupt the woman's thoughts by answering.

"No," Silenos corrected. "I am turning down the second-most-gifted necromancer alive, or third. Depending on Falls's aptitude."

Her eyes could have been replaced with blobs of molten iron and not glared as hotly or brightly as they did. Silenos had not, in the end, been able to resist twisting the knife. It really was a bad habit of his.

"Might I ask why, or am I unworthy of such elaboration?" Sphera hissed, clearly struggling to rein in her temper.

Silenos almost sighed. The fun was over. He'd have to enjoy her misery another time.

"Because this situation is highly volatile," he replied, skewering her rage with the simple facts of it all. "I have no guarantee your offer is genuine, nor that it will remain so even if it is. If you are telling the truth in this conversation, then you have only proved to me that you are one who will not hesitate to switch sides when your current allies seem to be the worse ones, which means that you may well turn against me a second time should this city's defense seem to be in jeopardy. Allowing you freedom on the promise of receiving help is a large risk, and I have no reason to take it now. Ask me again later, when you do not have such a fine opportunity for betrayal, and I may answer differently."

She thought only for a moment at that before replying.

"So you have reason to be confident of winning after all then?" she noted.

He paused, studied her, considered the conversation. Then just nodded. She'd scored a fair point on getting that from him, Silenos supposed. It was his own fault for playing with his food.

"And no more reason to continue this discussion," he told her, moving away. "Now come. I didn't spend half an hour building a strong enough cell to hold you just so you could not use it."

She followed, though they got only two strides before interruption.

"Lord Shaiagrazni!" a messenger yelped, using the local, primitive title for feudal aristocracy to refer to Silenos and almost being eviscerated in a reflexive punishment for the disrespect. Silenos instead mastered himself, recognizing the messenger's uniform and terror at once.

"What is it?" he demanded sharply. The boy was hasty in answering.

"The enemy is attacking!" he gasped. "They're charging the walls already. Your power—your attention—is needed!"

Silenos froze for a single, morbid moment. Then he started away, sending out a silent command for undead to escort the necromancer to her cell and for yet more to bolster the city's walls. He stalked toward the outer perimeter, seeking a direct look at the events being so desperately described.

It did not take him long to reach the wall. Silenos was able to send himself to it by simply shaping wings and throwing himself in its general direction using a shot of blasting oil. By the time he came down, the situation had barely progressed, but it was grim enough already.

Orcs, he saw. Numbering in the thousands at least and coming on as a great carpet of gray flesh and grayer iron. They were already within two, maybe three miles of the walls, and their formation, if one were generous enough to call it that, was closing faster than any humans could on foot. He estimated perhaps ten or fifteen minutes before they reached the city.

Baird was easily found at one end of the wall, barking out orders, and Silenos heard one given in particular.

"*To stations!*" the governor shouted. "*But keep the cylinders hidden!*"

So he was eager to avoid tipping their hands and letting the enemy know of Silenos's more offense-oriented modifications. That told him that the incoming force was not such a threat, at least.

But several thousand superhumans were, in fact, several thousand super-humans. Silenos hurried in making his way to Baird so that they might coordinate their response.

Raiar struck with the very lunge Galukar had taught him as a boy, executing it with just as much dexterity as ever, and Ohm was right behind his brother to let it drive their father into his own cleaving death blow. Galukar avoided the former and let the latter catch on his shoulder, feeling skin and muscle part as the edged steel sank an inch or so into his flesh. His wound wept as he tore the weapon free and backed off farther.

More of his sons followed, however. They were well wise to Galukar's tactics, having learned to counter them in his own training halls under his own tutelage. Kanai and Kuroi came from two sides at once with two lance thrusts. Neither one missed, and Galukar could parry only the right, feeling the left bite him just over the spine.

Not one of his boys had ever been a Hero, not one had ever been close, but they were all strong, deadly men who'd have shamed ninety-nine knights out of a hundred even without the armament of princes. Now, somehow, they were stronger. Made mightier and deadlier, faster and more vicious, but the dark magics had denied them a clean death. Galukar felt his rage burn to howling intensity at the thought.

But it sputtered out as Ohm closed in from up high. How could he sustain such rage? It had been his arrogance that did this, not the Dark Lord.

An arrow came for Kuroi, striking his helm and scraping off in a grinding, tearing, spark-spitting ricochet that sent flecks of mangled metal flying out in every direction and forced the boy—the undead—one step sidelong. Galukar made to seize the chance brought by its opening but faltered. Another lance thrust caught him before he could make up his mind, and he was fighting a retreat once more.

He roared as his rage only grew, body taking a half dozen more wounds. None were deep, none were even substantial, but all of them together racked him with a dangerous pain and wetted him with a dangerous vascular spill. Galukar caught Ohm in the visored face with the Godblade's pommel, then kicked his son into two of his brothers before swiping for Kanai. The last of them ducked back, as he knew he—it—would, and Galukar took his chance to break from the fighting.

"*Retreat!*" he heard a voice ring out. Collin Baird's, the murderer's son, speaking with such command as to almost sound noble. Galukar saw plenty of men obeying plenty fast, and the battlefield was soon being emptied of rangers. He pulled ahead of them, then paused, slowing himself to ensure he was between the fleeing men and the undead.

And his sons. If anyone was to die by them today, it would be him. Galukar readied to stave off their assaults.

Fighting retreats were difficult things to manage, and it was damned good Galukar found himself among men as well trained as the rangers. Shaiagrazni's undead helped, of course, fearlessly throwing themselves at his sons the way they did, and Galukar did what he could to further draw violence away from the rangers and onto himself. All the same, it could easily have turned into a disaster.

They reached the top of the hill without incident, and then things started to go sour. They were fast, Galukar's boys, as fast as these damned rangers even living, and faster now.

It was inevitable that they'd break past the defenses, shrugging aside arrow hits and splintering apart shields. Soon enough they were threatening to leap among the half formation of men, and Galukar knew that much would be death. Every one of these rangers was deadlier than a knight and many times longer in the training; a single loss among them was felt. They stood to lose dozens.

No disaster came, however. Not to the men. Galukar whirled as he saw Kanai barge two men aside and round on the backs of those he'd slipped behind, sword ready, death held tight to be rationed out. Then he saw Collin Baird slam into his reanimated son.

A stupid thing to do, Galukar knew. Baird was no warrior, and his strength was at best the equal of a dullahan, at worst a knight. He practically bounced off his enemy, swiping both ways with those long daggers of his and ripping small notches from the edges of plate armor. Kanai barely even reacted at all, simply turned, paused, then ran his weapon clean through Baird's guts.

He landed hard on the muddy, sludgy ground, disappearing from Galukar's sight.

CHAPTER FIFTY-FIVE

It was a hollow comfort to hear about the assault on Venka's reinforcements. Ensharia's captivity was stretching more by the day, and as of her near execution, it had finally taken the last scrap of dignity from her. She'd always liked to imagine she'd be brave faced with death. Stoic, unflinching. Weeping as she had, crying and begging, was not the behavior of a paladin. It was the behavior of a damned woman.

She'd been surprised and relieved to not find herself instantly killed by Venka upon Swick's escape and rather confused at being kept near the outer perimeter of the camp from that point on. Probably the general was planning to use her as bait and lure the pirate back in; probably there were more of his undead staring at her even then.

Well, they could stare away for all she cared. It wasn't as if she was in a position to do anything about it one way or the other.

"I hear Venka's men were attacked," Garutan whispered beside her. They were working, this time at the deed of hammering in palisade posts to set up the pickets of the general's siege camp. It was difficult work, the kind where Ensharia's strength left room for an increased rate of productivity, and so she was not permitted to simply rest by exerting a fraction of her might.

The first of each hammer blow she struck a post with sent it digging close to a foot deep into the dirt, and every subsequent one managed only inches. On average she took close to a dozen hits to fully impale the ground before moving on to the next. Her current quota was five hundred posts a day. Most of the others were only being told to manage thirty.

Distracting work, tedious work, painful work. It left hands blistered rather than calloused, eyes almost blinded by sweat. Ensharia hadn't strained herself so hard since she'd been in training, wielding the heavy, lead-made practice blades to shape Vigor and build strength. It was almost impressive Venka had managed to find labor able to exhaust even her current self in such a way.

"Venka's men are attacked a lot," she whispered back between grunting swings. The trick was not to use all her strength, Ensharia knew, because that would only bear the risk of snapping the post. They were thick things, made to let barded warhorses gut themselves without breaking, but her strength had become something new since meeting the Savior. And if she destroyed one, it'd be her job to dig its remnants out of the ground. Ensharia paced her power.

"Not like this," the orc insisted hastily, driving his own post almost as deep as she did.

He might've been an elite, Garutan, a towering, strong figure who doubtless enjoyed no small measure of Vigor in his bulging musculature. He just didn't have the heart for it. The poor dear was too nice, sweeter than sugar and more likely to start crying and apologize to a wounded enemy than finish them off.

Fortunately, he did not need to apologize to the fence posts.

"You always say it's different from the last bouts," Shargon huffed, to the other side of Ensharia. He was smaller than Garutan but cleverer than most humans, let alone orcs. His gray skin was barely even moistened by sweat, muscles working shortly and economically. Stamina was his great boon, and it seemed at times he boasted more of it than any dozen other workers combined.

"This one is though," Garutan pressed. His language had much improved in the last few weeks, as had all the orcs'. "I hear they were almost wiped out before they arrived, and yesterday I saw four undead heading to the camp. The general was promised a full fousand. They'll probby arrive today or tomow, then you'll see."

Much improved, but still not great. Ensharia found her focus slipping from their conversation, considering the implications.

She'd seen the walls, of course, now surrounding Kaltan. They'd been the great point of discussion for much of the day while everyone readied the camps. Everyone had marched expecting stone because stone was simply what was used to build city walls. Those crafted by great magics might use rarer, denser, stronger kinds, but still invariably stone. And sometimes not even that.

It had taken quite some time for Venka's scouts to properly confirm exactly what Kaltan's outer defenses and battlements really were made from, but it had been clear from even the horizon that it was no kind of rock any present was aware of. The reports came back eventually, however. Ensharia had already worked it out herself before they did.

Bone. *Bone.* She almost laughed at the realization, for more than one reason. Silenos had told her of bone's remarkable strength once, how it dwarfed the strength of stone, and even exceeded steel if one measured by weight rather than volume. To find the city defended by that of all things was a very promising sign.

The second aspect to her reaction had been more personal, however. Because Ensharia knew only one man who might have the knowledge, inclination, and raw, shaking power required to clad so many miles of a structure in such a sheath.

Silenos Shaiagrazni was within Kaltan then. Her joy at the fact had only been slightly diminished by Venka's latest torturing session, which had boasted a new enthusiasm in light of her knowledge.

Apparently it was known she'd defended Elkatin alongside a fleshcrafter, and the general had put two and two together. He got nothing from her, of course. Sometimes Ensharia wondered whether he even expected to. Perhaps he simply tortured her out of habit.

Ensharia paused, letting the hammer hover for a moment. She drove it down quickly, not wanting to attract a work master's ire, but found herself thinking a shade more jaggedly.

What was happening to her? She was acting like some cow, penned in and mindless to the fact. She'd just seen confirmation not a day ago that her ally was within viewing distance, and she was simply sitting around, working on the defenses of the people who'd try to kill him?

I really am a coward. A beggar, a whiner.

She drove the thoughts aside, more for practicality than anything else, and made herself focus. Silenos Shaiagrazni was within the city of Kaltan, that much Ensharia was sure of. Even for him, it would have been a great undertaking to work such a feat as she saw now, if his claimed mana reserves were accurate at least, and she didn't see him doing that for a city he didn't plan to stay in.

The Savior was in Kaltan. Ensharia was staring at it. How many miles away? Less than ten, surely. Perhaps as few as five.

If she tried to run that far outright, she'd likely be caught before making it, even if she wasn't mistaken for a spy or enemy and shot dead by the city's guards, but it was nonetheless a tantalizing proximity. An invigorating one.

Ensharia would escape, and she'd help Silenos stave the bastard Venka off from taking that city. She swung her hammer, picturing now that it was the general her strength was aimed at rather than one of his posts.

The wood split in half, splinters and pulp blasting out in all directions, some even spraying into her mouth. The work masters were screaming within moments.

Bugger.

Finlay had been more than a little paranoid when Silenos Shaiagrazni offered to strengthen his body and quicken his limbs. It seemed the sort of archetypal flesh-crafter's deal told about in the stories, inevitably turned against him as he found himself transmuted to a toad or rat, left to roam the world as a lessened thing and serve as a reminder to all the good little girls and boys about the dangers of evil magic and trying to rise above one's proper place.

Funnily enough, the proper place of the people writing those stories seemed always to be within the ruling aristocracy. They had less appeal for the poor sods tilling fields and getting their brains cudgeled out in battle.

He'd accepted the offer shortly.

An orc closed in at him quickly. Finlay fought on the walls, with his rangers, but even with the new coating of bone, the city had proved easily scaled for its new attackers. Orcs had hurled dark iron grappling hooks over it, hauling their bodies up while men tried in vain to cleave through the carefully wrought metal links chaining their equipment up. Within moments, dozens had poured onto the walls, within minutes more, hundreds.

Finlay had not expected that, but he should have. It would have been the first thing he'd experiment with in a nonhuman unit, and yet his mind had slipped, and he'd overlooked the possibility that his enemy had done likewise. Age, getting to him, dulling his wits, proving his best years of command already in the past? Perhaps he was just having an off day. He fought no less hard either way.

The orc was a big bastard, with an even bigger bastard of an axe. It towered a yard over Finlay, bigger than the elites he'd heard Venka used, and lumbering close and snarling. It brought its weapon down in a big, predictable swing that left the haft lined up just perfectly for Finlay's longknife to eat, letting splintered shaft and severed blade fall in separate directions. The other knife was no less precise, introducing itself to the orc's brain by entering uninvited through the eye.

He twisted, blood and optic fluid streaming over his hand as a sticky, stinking mess. Bubbles of air formed and popped in the flowing leak, and the orc fell as a thrashing slab of meat at Finlay's feet. He was already turning before its death finished, picking out another target from the chaotic melee.

A ranger had fallen, slipped on blood by the posture of him, and a pair of orcs were readying to turn him into mincemeat. Finlay came flying at them without even thinking, surprising even himself with the strength of resisting wind against his face, and certainly surprising them as he took off meaty limbs. A bigger one lunged, and he caught their axe's blade with that of his knife, expecting for a moment to be shunted back. Instead he held, then overpowered the thing.

Still, strength was not his specialty. There were easier ways to kill a creature five times his weight, and Finlay picked the simplest by abruptly sidestepping and opening up its neck down to the spine.

Rangers were scarce in this fight now, having mostly retreated from the melee to focus on poking holes in the orcs still trying to climb up and meet them. That meant normal men at Finlay's shoulders. Normal, Vigorless, courageous bastards of no talent, standard training, and fifty-ton balls of steel.

They were formed into lines, shields up and spears pointed out like the bristles of a porcupine, held steady while orcs tried to barrel past and stumbled back snarling and spitting from their weeping gashes. It was an immutable law of battle that men in a formation could and would hack apart many times their strength in unformed enemies, but orcs were not human. They had a physical weight and speed that jeopardized the cohesion of Finlay's men, sending shock waves rippling through their ranks each time one slammed into a shield. They'd break soon.

He moved in to stop that.

"*Backstep!*" Finlay roared, giving his men a stride more slack in the tension of their defense, then falling upon their enemies from behind.

He was a hurricane, a pointy one. Wherever Finlay went, blood hurried after, painting limbs, faces, floors, and battlement walls. He jabbed knives into the gaps of armor and the slits of visors, even smashing an orc's eye socket in with his own forehead at one stage and taking another's head fully off. He'd heard tell of the glory of battle, and it was just as bullshit an idea now as it ever had been, but for the first time, he felt some measure of where the delusion came from.

How easy to make yourself think war was a hero's business when it felt like this. How easy to make yourself great when the choice of such carnage lay solely with you. Finlay's musings were interrupted sharply as a pain lanced down at his side, and he peered at the source.

A spear, long, steel from tip to body. A carefully made fomorian weapon, the sort that would go through both sides of a knight's armor and kill a second behind him. It was jabbed clean between Finlay's ribs.

Clean through his heart.

CHAPTER FIFTY-SIX

There had never really been much doubt of how the fight would go. Silenos had known that from the moment he saw the incoming forces. The only question was how much damage the charging idiots might manage.

Apparently, not very much.

Finlay Baird was a primitive, like all in the new world, but he had actually managed to impress Silenos. In martial terms, at least. He ran Kaltan's army in much the same way House Shaiagrazni ran its own, keeping a soldier class to be consistently trained, equipped, and fed. Each man standing atop the battlements was moving guided by hundreds of hours of training, and every squad had at least a handful of combat veterans to further galvanize them.

Swap their quilted armor with poly-alloy scale and their spears with bayoneted bolt actions, and they might well have resembled his own people's foot soldiers. They certainly fought like them, a credit to the not-so-delicate art of violence.

Of course such pinnacles of soldiering were still mere men, regardless, and Silenos could see the battle would not be an easy one, as he'd suspected. Orcs threatened human formations through simple bodily mass alone, and there were a handful of undead among them, no doubt giving aid due to flaws in their orders.

It was always a risk, having reanimates obey officers instead of the general. They'd be faster to respond to tactical changes but susceptible to getting whisked along by an overeager commander. Wasted.

Finlay Baird found out about fomorian presence the hard way, seizing up as one caught him by surprise and skewered him with a spear. Silenos noted the stab did not go as deep as it might have earlier. Judging by the length of steel disappearing into flesh it would barely have even reached his heart. Enough to kill the organ dead, in any case.

Baird hacked the offending arm off, then lunged forward. Within moments, he'd dragged his knives, now edged with nacre as a secondary aid by Silenos, along his enemy's body scores of times, leaving it to fall as tendons were cut and tissues impaled. For a moment the ranger stood, panting, then he moved on to continue killing.

Silenos's lip curled at the man's surprise. Had he really thought he wouldn't have added a redundancy for his *heart* of all things? It was bad enough that natural selection had made such a moronic design as to only have one. A senior of House Shaiagrazni wouldn't be caught dead making such an error.

Baird continued hacking and slashing; his men continued thrusting and backstepping. There were documented accounts of Shaiagrazni seniors turning the tide of such skirmishes single-handedly, crushing enemies by the thousands, even tens of thousands. Silenos's own master had, he had heard at least, once slain a million men by herself. But the new world's phenoms were not so potent as that.

Fortunately, they had a sufficient substitute. Silenos reasoned he'd waited enough and gave the command for his undead to pounce. Waiting hidden by the wall, they came on in moments, crashing into the swarm of scaling orcs just in the nick of time. All according to plan of course.

Silenos had made a few smaller creations specifically for fighting on the battlements, and he took his chance to test them. Sending only two to flank the orcs pinning down Baird's men and leaving the rest to crash into the tide itself at the grapples. His enhanced vision showed the combat progressing nicely. Limbs gave way and tore free of torsos, skulls erupted like crushed eggs, and axes and clubs bounced from keratin armor like common human-wielded cudgels against rocks. Within moments, a score of orcs were dead; within moments more, their corpses outnumbered those still fighting upon the battlements.

Grapples were soon cut, climbers soon dropped, and Silenos made his way over to the wall, landing just as he saw the enemy horde below start to convulse and surge as half fought to continue climbing while the other tried to flee. He settled the debate quickly.

Silenos's newer undead were possessing of considerable ranged abilities, using pneumatic designs within their bodies to hurl premade javelins—taken from Baird's supplies—at appreciable fractions of Mach speed. Orcs were durable, but they still died to exploding shafts and sprays of splinters as sheer velocity tore target and projectile both to pieces. Baird's rangers threw their own abilities into the mix, skewering orcs with their deadly arrows, and soon enough ordinary archers were helping too.

All of that clearly had the orcs wavering more, but it was Silenos who tipped the scales. He started with his cannon, letting the blunderbuss configuration rip bloody chunks out of the swarm of bodies, seeing little effect. Then he changed to his flamethrower.

Incendiary weapons were a growing controversy, geopolitically. Or at least they had been in Silenos's world before he'd left. Fire was an inhumane way of killing, causing undue suffering and anguish to its victims, or so the arguments went. House Shaiagrazni had no business with such trifling concerns. They would burn whatever they damned well liked, and if their enemies thought themselves above such things, they were welcome not to retaliate.

That moment, seeing the flames fall so closely upon enemy heads, he understood where the opposing sentiments derived their weight. It was a cruel, grim thing to see done to any creatures at all. The effects on his enemies were immediately felt and remarkably strong.

Orcs screamed, as immolated things tended to do, and the crowd surged back. The smell of burning oil and carbonizing matter mingled with cooking meat, almost disturbing for how similar it was to any other kind. Bodies fell crackling to the ground, skin splitting and hot fat dripping free to boil and pop upon the flames, dozens, then hundreds turned into their own funeral pyres. Silenos had plenty of material to work with, converting the slain enemies into more fuel for his weapon even as he emptied it out onto the rest, cleaning up the battlements one processed corpse at a time. Cleaning up the ground beyond the walls one score of blackened soldiers at a time.

It did not take very long, in the end, for the enemy's impromptu attack to falter, then crumble. Orcs practically scrambled over one another to flee, scurrying back along the landscape, heading toward their half-finished siege camps like a pile of dust blown away in sudden winds.

Smiling, Silenos surveyed the sight. Individual combat was rather a barbaric thing, he maintained, but there was a certain satisfaction in claiming such a crushing victory with it. He could see why so many of House Shaiagrazni's named chose to direct their magic into more direct and immediate powers than his own.

For an hour or so, all focus was on recovering from the attack. It had been unexpected, though not unforeseen by the wall's scouts, and though fighting had proved fierce, only a scant fourteen men had died, none of which were rangers. Silenos watched Baird go about his business of ordering ammunition stockpiles refilled, guard shifts rotated to account for the injured, weapons replaced and maintained.

His own undead helped somewhat, while others did their work of hauling off slain orcs and—with Baird's permission—humans to process into further weaponry and constructs. All in all, Silenos considered the incident rather an effective stroke of luck. It had bolstered their power considerably to gain so many new undead, even if the city's iron ores had long since been exhausted past the demands of Silenos's more exotic materials.

By the time Baird finally came to speak with him, demonstrating the sense to make his way over to Silenos rather than inappropriately requesting that he go to him, the sun was rather near to the horizon once again. The governor was a vision of health, even by the standards of men who had not been stabbed through the heart. His body seemed more animated than it had been when they'd first met, and his eyes were alert as ever.

Silenos's fleshcrafting had invigorated the man. Now he would see what that physical vivaciousness would do for his wits.

"A word," he asked without asking. Silenos could respect the courage there at least.

"You wish to ask about the battle?" he guessed, and Baird did not bother confirming.

"Your undead took their sweet time in joining it. Why is that?"

Silenos had decided before the conversation even began that he'd be open with Baird, simply because gaining his cooperation—which he believed was more than possible—would make the fruits of his plan far quicker in ripening.

"I decided to delay them deliberately, until such time as it became clear your defense was starting to lose ground. Not waiting for casualties to mount but sending them to arrive precisely during a momentary loss of momentum to give the illusion of saving your soldiers. My plan was that this would improve trust and cohesion in my undead among them."

Baird was not surprised, not even in the slightest. He looked like a man who'd just heard several of his own deductions confirmed, in fact, subtly satisfied and already prepared with an answer for what he was hearing.

"Good. I've been telling my men that your monsters were busy preparing other fortifications to explain their early absence. Next time, don't leave details like that for me to hammer out."

Silenos was rather surprised to find himself without even the slightest urge to behead Baird after being spoken to like that. It was, he realized, proper. This was a man more experienced in the marshaling of soldiers than he, whose knowledge of military matters came far more from hands-on practice than Silenos's largely book-born understanding. It was quite appropriate he be chided for falling short of such a man's standards.

"I apologize," he replied, amused by the sheer novelty of finding himself exceeded by a primitive of all things. Baird seemed quite mollified, and extremely surprised, but said nothing of either fact.

"That your first time fighting orcs?" he asked. Silenos nodded, surprised once more by the man's guess. Baird just grunted. "Yeah, looked as much. I guessed you were experimenting with how they reacted to fear, switching from that bloody dart gun to the fire spell you used."

Dart gun? It made sense, Silenos supposed, that a primitive would compare elongated bullets to those of all projectiles.

"I know now where their threshold for panic is," Silenos replied. "It is . . . surprisingly far from human."

"Orcs tend to go wild when they fight. It's what makes them so dangerous. They don't use formations as well, barely even possible to *teach* a proper shield wall, but most of the time you can consider their morale infinite. It's almost as much of a factor in their effectiveness as the sheer strength they have."

Almost. Silenos could imagine that, though their prowess was hard to compare with.

"The information has been noted," he replied, finding himself rather stung to have erred so completely in the first place.

"Good. Good," Baird grunted, seeming suddenly tired. Something was gnawing at him, Silenos saw, and he imagined no good could come of anything severe enough to draw such disquiet from Finlay Baird. By all he'd seen, the man was remarkably resilient.

"What is bothering you?" he prodded, then found himself surprised as the governor simply shook his head.

"Nothing," he grunted. "Just . . . men. I lost men today. Always find myself in a foul mood when I lose anyone at all, even in a winning battle with few casualties."

Silenos was almost completely sure he was being lied to, but he could think of no way in which he might draw the truth from Baird without starting an incredibly inconvenient war. Instead he just nodded, began to move elsewhere, then paused as a messenger hurtled toward Baird, face sheet pale with fear and voice tight with haste.

"Governor!" the man gasped, his words escaping as hot things, made bitter and sharp by lactic acid. "It's—Your son, governor, your son has returned. He's wounded."

Baird was instantaneous in heading off to the place gestured by the messenger, and Silenos wasn't long after him.

CHAPTER FIFTY-SEVEN

It was a nasty wound, and one given no small measure of time to worsen itself. Silenos saw Collin Baird's blood had mostly stopped flowing, perhaps only due to already being so drained, and his guts were escaping the boy's belly like a sack filled with writhing worms eating through its fabric. Without him, left alone, he'd have been dead within a day, two at most. Transhuman physicality was all that had sustained his life even this long, and such things had their limits when their wielder found themselves so thoroughly disemboweled.

But Silenos had seen worse injuries himself, much worse. It was remarkable the things a person might find done to themselves in a battle of magic.

"Back," he instructed, watching as all but one of the crowding soldiers obeyed. He took the offending man by one shoulder and hurled him aside, barely exerting himself to separate the man from the ground, not even looking as he knelt down in his place and heard him land hard out of sight.

Collin Baird did not seem to even know he was there. His face was soaked with clammy sweat, pale with exsanguination. Both of the boy's eyes were open, but they were unfocused, staring out into the empty air as his lips and tongue worked silently.

A message, perhaps? One he was desperate to see heard before he died? Silenos hoped so. It would offend him to be in the presence of something so unforgivably stupid as a prayer.

"Can you save him?" asked the governor, having the sense to remain yards back as he threw his question at Silenos like a javelin. Silenos took a moment to examine his patient further before replying.

"Yes," he said. "But ensure everyone is silent. Working with distractions is horribly tedious." He got to work extending his magic without another thought.

The difficult part about magical healing was nothing about the physicality of it. Rather, it was the magic one had to work against. All magic was intent made manifest, reality shifted and shaped by the exertions of human will, and such acts left their mark. When a suicidally stupid boy found himself disemboweled by necromantic limb and necromantic strength, the arcane forces powering such an attack dwelled in the wound and resisted their closing. It was these Silenos contested, and he found the act of doing so rather an enlightening experience.

He eased aside magical residue around the shredded tissues, studying it even as he isolated and purged it with his own power.

Such things were made easier by his arcane sight, which allowed for finer control and targeting. Without it, Silenos would have had no choice but to mindlessly exert will until he pushed the opposing magic aside rather than targeting it directly.

Even still, it was a surprisingly testing endeavor. Whatever had done this was powerful, more powerful than the Dark Lord's necromancy had yet managed to prove itself. A deadly, formidable creature in life then, further given power in excess of their own through the process of reanimation. They must have died recently for the effects to be so pronounced.

Silenos almost grew distracted from the actual work of restoring Baird, so trivial was it. But he considered the matter a moment before beginning the efforts of doing so. Instead of merely fixing flesh, he started to strengthen it just as he had his father's.

He altered muscle fibers, breaking them down and reshaping them into compact, tightly coiled bundles able to multiply or divide their length exponentially with a single twitch. He shaped the minerals of his bones, weaving in natural carbon fibers and encasing it all with yet more made for hardness and scratch resistance. Soft tissues were woven into armored fabrics able to turn aside blade thrusts, vital organs were duplicated in body cavities, circulatory channels shortened and made more efficient.

Silenos even took the time to reshape the boy's lungs entirely, converting them to a connected, looping channel that left air running a circuit through his chest cavity the way a bird's would. Far more efficient, able to sustain respiration in far more scarcely oxygenated environments.

By the time he was finished, Collin Baird's healing was the least of his changes. The entire procedure had been more difficult than was necessary, made harder by the irksome resistance of natural magic, but Silenos managed it all the same. Ensharia had been harder by far, her own durability exceeding this one's by a factor of double or more.

"It's done," Silenos informed the group, sitting back as he finished his work. Half an hour had passed, far less time than he was used to spending on such changes, far more than he would have on mundane flesh alone. Finlay Baird stared at him, expectant. "Your son will live, and he will have no long-term aftereffects. But he was close to death. You are lucky gut wounds take so long to kill."

The governor did not look like a man who considered himself lucky, but then so few lucky men did. He only nodded, relieved by a hair but still tense by a scalp.

"Good." He sighed. "Thank you, caster. Once again, it seems you have done me a service."

Silenos saw the men around him relaxing similarly to their governor, smiles growing and muttered prayers of thanks flitting around. Evidently Collin Baird was popular among his soldiers. Silenos himself stood, having little time for the sentiments. He had gotten only fifteen paces from the group when he heard more footsteps behind him and turned to see Finlay Baird closing in, moving past the necromancer as she trailed behind Silenos and eying him with unbroken focus.

"A word," he said, somehow making the phrase neither a question nor a demand.

With a nod, and a quick detour to somewhere more private, Silenos indulged him. Baird did not waste time or mince words once the two of them—save the necromancer—were alone.

"I thank you for what you've done in fortifying my city," the governor said. "I really do. You've made it a defensive position worth two or three of its previous self. Defied my expectations and understanding both, and quite possibly revolutionized warfare as a whole. The things you've done here were beyond expectation and are too great for me to fully do justice. Thank you."

No man gave so much flattery in such a concentrated stream without a "but" on its way, and Silenos remained entirely quiet as he awaited it. Sure enough, Baird continued a moment later, seeming more hesitant.

". . . But I can't continue this siege."

The words hung between them like a lynched man, kicking and jerking, fouling Silenos's mood. He took a moment in gathering his thoughts before replying, wanting to ensure he did not bisect the governor.

"You are giving up?"

"I am," Baird confirmed, still meeting his eye, still unapologetic about every word. "There's no choice about it. I've seen the quality of these orcs, I've seen the quality of these undead, and I've almost lost my son just from a skirmish. The only thing I *can* do now is give up."

"You have numerous options," Silenos replied, speaking with patience, knowing that a show of contempt only tended to make lesser men dig in their heels. "For one thing, your forces will be made stronger by the undead I reanimate from this latest attack, and you have yet to bring out my secret weapons. I also took the time to enhance your son as I did you, making him considerably more potent, and now that Venka is drawing so close to beginning an offensive, we ought to hold all of our forces behind the walls. Which means you have King Galukar to bolster your forces too."

Baird's fury grew despite Silenos's best exertions of rhetoric and rationality.

"There's easily a hundred thousand out there, and the least of them are orcs. Now we have these new undead able to draw sweat from a Hero, not to mention Venka himself, who actually *is* a Hero!"

Ah, so he had discussed the particulars of his son's failed raid. With Galukar, perhaps. That was inconvenient. It would make the act of convincing him to continue resisting only harder.

"And you have me," Silenos pressed. "I've not shown my own power yet, only my creations', and let me tell you, when I do battle in earnest, I am more than a match for even Galukar. More by far."

Baird must have believed him because he actually looked halfway uncertain. For a moment. His eyes hardened with resolve after another.

"No." He sighed. "I can't. I can't risk this. I can't put my people in this position. Have you ever seen a city taken after a siege?"

Silenos said nothing, just nodding.

"Then you know it is the most barbaric fucking thing man is capable of doing. A siege is the most awful, deadly kind of fighting there is for the attackers. I know because I came up from the ranks of conscripted scum whose job it is to die in them. You'll have siege towers if you're lucky, hot and clammy, smelling of the sweat wafting off the hundred other men you share them with, dark and rumbling. All the while you ride them, you do so knowing that most don't make it to the walls, that the enemy will need only a few catapult shots to tear enough chunks from the structure that it leaves you screaming and falling amid a hail of jagged wood and dropped weapons. If you're lucky enough to even make contact with the target, you come out finding the walls already flooded with men ready and waiting for you. Only a few of the tower's occupants can come out at once, see, five, maybe six if it's a big one.

"The enemy are equipped with long spears that let them jab you from over one another's shoulders, so you have more than a few bits of steel coming for each man charging. The only thing you can do is fight and try to widen a hole in the defense so that your men can get a foothold on the walls, and if you're very, very fortunate, you might even live in doing so."

Silenos opened his mouth to reply, but Baird was far from done.

"And that's assuming you have siege towers, of course. If you just have ladders, then you're forced to climb pelted by arrows from all sides, dying in droves until enough men get to the top at once that the fire is disrupted. If you have a breach in the walls to enter through, you can guarantee it'll be doused with burning oil and archery, then defended by the toughest bastards your enemy has. You understand what I'm saying? No matter how you attack or where, the enemy has all the chances to concentrate their forces and enough cover and space to hit you with weapons bigger than any man can carry. It's a slaughterhouse."

It seemed to Silenos that he was hearing reasons for why they had a chance, after all, but Baird's face tightened.

"And attacking soldiers blame the city for putting them through that. If you survive a thing like that, if you're fast, tough, and fucking lucky enough to come stumbling out the other side of it, you're driven half mad. Not believing you even lived, still remembering the deaths of your comrades and the near deaths of yourself, covered in the blood of men you called friends. Men like that vent their fury on the city; they take revenge. Raping, pillaging, but also burning, lynchings. I've seen men take turns trying to cut people in half with one swing, or march people up to the highest tower they found just to watch them thrown off the side and break on the ground below. They're less than animals like that, and they remain less than animals for hours."

His face turned jagged as a spear.

"And orcs will be fucking worse."

CHAPTER FIFTY-EIGHT

Arion had never really known what it was like to hate someone. He'd thought he hated Walriq sometimes, but that grumpy old bastard had never been more than a grumpy old bastard. Annoying, inconvenient, endlessly jealous of his apprentice's talent, but nothing truly worthy of being despised. The Dark Lord might have been, but magi weren't taught to really care about matters as pedestrian as human suffering or world destruction, and even if they had been, he was always such a distant figure that truly mustering any sort of emotion for him in the first place had been difficult.

But the necromancer Sphera taught Arion what the feeling of hatred was. She opened his eyes to that wide, burning spectrum of human emotion and truly made him realize how such a thing felt. And how easy it was, feeling it now, to believe those stories about crossed lovers taking their own lives, or spurned brothers waging wars of vengeance.

How difficult, even, to imagine restraining oneself from acting on such a thing when it flowed with such volcanic horror through every vein of their body.

Arion did not kill Sphera, he did not hit her, he didn't rip any of her limbs free with his magic or fall upon her with teeth and nails in some altogether bestial surrender. But he wanted to. God, how he fucking wanted to.

Evidently, she knew how much he wanted to. It seemed to amuse her.

"Something on your mind?" she asked venomously. Arion ignored her, and she spoke again. "Oh, Galukar's children, right? I heard the governor talking about them. Must have been interesting to see the old fool react to their corpses. Was he surprised? I wouldn't put it past him. He did seem slow."

"Shut up," Arion snarled, mind surging quickly to the king and his new reclusiveness. He'd not spoken to anyone since returning, not even left his quarters, and Arion's fury was sincere and solar in potence. But Sphera moved past his words as if he were some clawless kitten and not the pinnacle of wind magic.

Where are you, master? What are you doing at such an ungodly hour to leave me alone with this vicious, taunting whore?

"I do wish I'd been there. I'll bet the face he made was to *die* for. Of course you'll be reanimated too, you understand, yes? Just like your master did. You're simply too powerful not to bring back. Mind you, we might hold you captive for a few years instead. You're still young enough to grow stronger quite quickly. Twenty, right? So you'll be half again as powerful by thirty. Not a bad long-term investment."

It was pure cruelty, every word of it. He could even see it in her eyes, the same look a cat got while toying with mice. But that didn't make it any easier to ignore.

Arion couldn't hit her while she was bound; some things just weren't done. He certainly wasn't stupid enough to untie her just for a beating either, and so he decided to fight fire with fire. He smiled.

It must have been a convincing expression because a sliver of cold doubt made its way across the woman's face. Her brow furrowed fractionally.

"Something funny I'm not seeing?" she prodded, clearly hoping to turn things back against him. Arion let her curiosity stew for a moment, shaking his head slowly.

"No, not really. It's just . . . Well, a woman's still a woman, I guess. Give a monkey magic and it'll turn everything into bananas, and things aren't really much different when power finds its way into the hands of someone whose brain is mostly used for controlling the spread of legs."

The words bounced off her, as he might have guessed. One did not become a potent caster without dealing with one's fair share of magi.

"Ah, the typical insult." She sighed. "And here I was—"

"But you really haven't figured out that you'll die long before I do, have you?" Arion pressed, choosing that exact moment as the best time to unbalance her. Evidently it was well picked.

Her eyes narrowed, but with caution now rather than contempt.

"What do you mean?"

Arion smiled, the way she did, he hoped, and leaned back.

"God, even with a hint that obvious—"

"What do you fucking mean?" the necromancer growled. He decided the time to let her stew was expired.

"I mean that my master is a practical man, and he doesn't quite trust you. That, and undead he creates are a great deal stronger than others. What exactly do you think he'll do if this city starts to lose its defensive certainty? Sit around, hope he has the resources to win anyway? Oh, or were you actually hoping he'd *ask* for your help? Come on. Easier for everyone, except you I guess, if he just kills you and reanimates you. There's a certain guarantee of loyalty there."

The necromancer's skin was darker even than Master Silenos's, but Arion still saw some subtle discoloration as the blood rushed out of her face. Her lips parted, eyes widened, shock congealed to a positively stony composition. She was a long time in speaking, and more than a little hesitant as she did.

"Any reanimation can damage the memories," she tried. "I have information on the Dark Lord that would be useful."

Arion nodded.

"I'd guessed as much, based on you still being alive. How long do you think that will hold weight? It might be fun to wager on it actually. I think the moment part of the outer wall is taken and my master needs a construct for spearheading some counteroffensive, he'll just cut your throat and use you. What about you? Before then, after, around the same time?"

There was a certain joy to just being a bastard, he realized. It had been so long since Arion had been the most important person in any room, so long since the other magi had betrayed him, that he'd almost forgotten. In particular, it was bloody fun aiming such behavior at someone who actually deserved it.

"That won't help you though," she said at last, clearly trying to move back onto the offensive. "And it won't stop the same from being done to you when the city falls."

Arion forced a smile.

"Who cares?" he asked, shrugging. "I certainly won't. I'll be dead by then."

Governor Baird's quarters had been surprisingly easy to sneak into, all things considered. At least they were once his guarding rangers had fallen to the floor with temporary seizures. Silenos was careful not to cause any long-term harm or disorientation in the deed, well aware that such potent soldiers were in rare supply.

Finlay Baird himself was at his desk, smoking and drinking. He looked to be wrung out, hollowed. Beaten and eroded by circumstance, pulled in so many different directions with so much strength that he'd merely come apart rather than fly into any single one. Silenos gazed at him as he entered and noted a lack of surprise in the man's eyes. Did he know? Perhaps. He was that sort of man.

"Shaiagrazni," the governor grunted, gesturing to a bottle of drink on his desk. "You're walking in on my rare indulgence. Care to join me?"

"I am not fond of recreational brain damage," Silenos replied, making his way to the desk. "But thank you." Baird deserved manners and courtesy at least.

"Here to try and persuade me again?" Baird asked.

"In a way." Silenos shrugged.

Baird sighed.

"You can't."

Silenos studied him for a second.

"All you said about the savagery of a siege's attackers, that was a smoke screen, wasn't it? This isn't about the city. You'd sooner fight for the slightest chance of keeping it independent than hand it over to some sorcerer king."

There was no denial in Baird's eyes, only a reluctant concession.

"You're right." He groaned. "Of course, it was a thin pretense to begin with."

"This is about your son," Silenos guessed and could see he'd struck the mark a second time.

"It is." Baird nodded. "Seeing him like that, it . . . Well, made me realize that youth doesn't guarantee he'll outlive me. That things are more dangerous for him than they ever were for me at his age. He'll be better than me one day, he's close to being better already, but not if he gets gutted to death by some bastard general in the Dark Lands."

Baird had grown talkative of late, Silenos saw. The sure mark of a man who knew his own convictions were half empty. That was unfortunate. There would be no reasoning with someone who already understood reason and simply denied it.

"Kaltan doesn't have a chance though," Baird noted, eying Silenos coolly. "I maintain that much. We can fight; maybe we can even fight well. I'm sure the Dark Lord will bleed legions of soldiers and undead trying to take us. But he has legions more. How many, really, do you think we'll stave off before the city falls? Ten thousand? Doable. Twenty, even, isn't a problem. Thirty though? I'd be surprised if we managed to kill that many before we were taken, and forty is practically impossible. What you're asking is that I allow Kaltan to be crushed and made an example of, all without even halving the strength of the single army responsible. And you know that, don't you? We're not a people to you, just a means to do particularly great damage to your enemy. Am I right?"

There wasn't a scrap of accusation in his tone. Perhaps Baird was incapable of such a thought. He was entirely right of course, and Silenos found himself deciding that this man, of all, deserved his honesty. He nodded.

"You are right. I am quite sure I could escape this city before its destruction, and my main priority is ensuring that as large a fraction of the Dark Lord's forces die here as is possible."

Baird grunted.

"Fifty thousand orcs." He sighed. "Thirty thousand skeletons, ten thousand dullahan, four thousand fomors. Hundreds of belladonnan puppeteers, dozens of lichs, Venka himself, of course. And a few thousand other elites, mercenaries, or giants, other such things."

He listed it all mechanically, without fear. "I'd wager this hundred thousand or so could get the better of a conventional army numbering one million. What do you say to that?"

"I'd say my own estimate is closer to twelve or thirteen million, speaking as a necromancer."

Baird smiled.

"A sizable fraction of the Dark Lord's military power, indeed. I completely understand your desire to break them here, while you have surprise and potent defensive options to aid you. I only hope you can forgive my selfishness in denying you the chance. Kaltan is my city; its people are my people. I can't use them as ammunition to cast against the Dark Lord's empire."

Silenos nodded, stepping forward and, with only a moment of hesitation, placing his hand down upon Baird's shoulder. He did not do it out of any sense of social propriety; such things were well beyond significance now. He simply wanted to. It felt right.

"I do understand," he murmured. "And I would do much the same thing in your position. You are a great man, Finlay Baird, wasted, I think, in your station and region of birth. I would have liked to see you study Shaiagraznian magic in another life."

They locked eyes for a moment, and Baird was not surprised in the slightest when Silenos ran his blade of keratin and nacre through the governor's chest. He was very precise, passing it between ribs and clean into the hearts.

Both of them, each skewered by another of the knife's twin prongs.

Finlay Baird died as any other man might have, gasping and spasming in bodily reflex to the sudden, terrible injury. His death took only moments. Silenos had been careful about that much.

He deserved dignity, at least.

CHAPTER FIFTY-NINE

Collin woke up to a body in open rebellion, and not for the first time. He was used to the residual agonies of a fight, having spent years being subjected to them, but the pain assailing him now was different somehow. Stronger, angrier, and sustaining itself no matter how or where he moved. It was like a thing of magic, and his mind screamed at it futilely.

When he lay on his back, lances of misery ran along his spine. On his side, it was his ribs and guts that threatened to come apart with the sensation. His stomach was no choice at all; in that position, his shoulders and neck somehow twisted and writhed like nothing else. Rivers of magma, rains of acid, mists of deadly, choking toxin to leave a man thrashing as his tongue swelled and jutted dumbly from his lips. It was beyond description, his pain, and it took minutes to finally diminish itself.

Minutes didn't sound like much. Collin had tolerated minutes of agony more times than he could count. Minutes of this though made him want to die. Minutes of this were enough to leave him fearing ever experiencing a single second of it again.

"It is phantom pain," a voice rang out, cold and clinical, as if Collin's convulsive torment were merely an interesting fact to be observed, explained, and then put aside with no relevance beyond understanding the mechanics behind it. Collin glanced up, half wincing in anticipation of more pain, and saw Silenos Shaiagrazni seated at one wall.

He frowned at that, realizing this was not his bedroom, and looked around further. High ceiling, thick walls, everything smooth and clean, everything easily maintained and functional. This was a medical room, a private one originally built to hold the wounded aristocracy without tainting their sores with working-class pain.

"I was hurt," Collin mumbled, finding the memories coming back now as a steady stream. It was remarkable how much easier thought became when one's body didn't feel as if the blood was trying to escape.

"You were," Shaiagrazni confirmed. "Physically you are fine, though you may experience some whispers of phantom torment for a day or two, and I would recommend you spend a while training to adjust. I had to strengthen your body to help you survive your injuries, and that strength, that speed, will have affected the timing of your movements. Best to remaster that when not swinging your weapons in anger."

It was a lot, to be told that his own limbs were now lacking in control, but Collin found it hard to be moved. He remembered the feeling of steel through his guts now, and after suffering a wound like that, even having control of his limbs left at all was good news. He nodded.

Shaiagrazni eyed him, quiet, seemingly waiting for something.

It was the most disconcerting stare Collin had ever been on the receiving end of, not human, and somehow not even an animal's either. He imagined it was how a jar of mercury found itself studied by the alchemist planning on using it. Purely cerebral, purely cognitive, without a trace of room made for emotion or any of the other little irrationalities that made people people. He shivered, starting with a grunt as he tried to emerge from his bed.

"Would've expected my father to be waiting for me." He grinned. "But I suppose that grumpy old bastard will be bogged down and busy, right? What's the state of the city?"

Shaiagrazni was not grim exactly, but there was a definitively dark twist to his scientist's stare as Collin said that. It gave him pause, had him staring in silent question, mouth suddenly dry.

"Your father is dead," the caster said, describing the impossible as if it were some ordinary affair.

Collin blinked, made stupid by his surprise, slow by his disbelief.

"That's not funny," he growled, confusion turning to anger as hot water does mist.

"It is not a joke," the caster replied. His eyes still didn't change; his face still didn't move. He might have been explaining the loss of family to a chicken for all his apparent cares for the matter. "Your father died in his sleep, while you were unconscious. A magical complication from a wound he took defending the city," he explained. "I am sorry for your loss."

That last phrase almost sounded comical. How could a man with eyes as empty as that claim to be sorry for anything? It made Collin angry, furious. Made his hands curl into bunched fists, made his blood run hot, his lips pull back in a feral snarl. He wanted to kill something, and not cleanly. To fall on it with flailing fists and thrashing teeth, ripping out chunks and spitting them back into gaping eyes. He wanted to fucking vent his fury out with a war cry.

A tear came down his cheek, and then more followed. In the end, Collin vented his fury out with a long period of crying instead.

Most men were awkward when they saw such a display, unsure of how to respond, what to say—whether anything ought to be said at all. Not Silenos Shaiagrazni. He simply looked on with a face so consistently unmoving as to make a statue seem dynamic. He could not, Collin thought, have physically cared less about the matter of his grief. Collin broke the silence after taking a minute to master his emotions.

"How did he fight?" he croaked, not quite sure why he even asked himself.

"Well," Shaiagrazni explained. "He cut down perhaps fifty orcs himself, and a fomor. Had he not been present on the walls, they'd have fallen without question before reinforcements arrived. It was like watching some heroic myth acted out."

Collin nodded and felt nothing. His father hated fighting, hated it. He hated the dying, the killing, hated what it turned men into. Animals, he said. Less than animals even. There was a monster living in the heart of every man, and it came out to play when he found himself in battle.

"Not to be insensitive," Shaiagrazni pressed, sounding about as sensitive as a boulder. "But there is the matter of your father's duties. As governor of Kaltan, as leader of its defense. I am not aware of what succession he had—"

"My father had no succession," Collin snarled. "We were going to turn this city into one led by its people, with leaders decided on by popular vote. Like some village community, scaled up and legislated to hold it together."

Why did he speak with such fire? Perhaps Collin simply didn't want his father to be remembered for his killing rather than his building. Shaiagrazni didn't appear to care one way or the other.

"That being the case, I imagine you realize why your father remained in power himself during this particular time."

Collin hesitated, then swore. Of course he did. More voices being heard meant slower decision-making, which could be fatal when one was fighting the Dark fucking Lord of all people.

"What are you getting at?" he growled, finding himself overcome by an unspeakable weariness. He just wanted the conversation to be over. Just wanted everything to be over.

"I am speaking of you, Collin Baird. I believe you would be the rather obvious choice as successor to your father, no?"

He stared at the caster.

"What gave you that idea?" Collin asked, feeling as if he'd just been punched in the head.

"You were trained from your earliest years to exceed him in every way and have much of his talent, no?"

"No!" Collin snapped. "He's been fighting and warring for decades, ruling for almost as long. I have a few years as an officer, and I've never commanded more than a thousand men. Put me in charge of an army, let alone a city, and it'll be a bloody disaster."

Shaiagrazni shrugged.

"I disagree. I have seen stupider commanders perform passable jobs with less relevant experience. Do not underestimate yourself; it is immoral."

Collin was still blinking and reeling from that fucking bizarre response when Shaiagrazni continued.

"Years of battle experience, knowledge of units as large as a thousand men, and a youthful, malleable intellect of considerable magnitude. I have examined the history of other potential choices, and not one has struck me as being half so practical as you. Unless you know of some veteran rangers or generals who may have slipped my notice?"

The walls were getting closer together, Collin thought, and the ceiling lower down. He wanted to vomit, wanted to roll around screaming and kicking and crying about how unfair everything was. Wanted to ask his father for advice, except he couldn't do that. Could never do that again.

His father was dead. It sunk in then, finally, truly, and properly. His father was dead, and he would never again be anything but dead. The world would keep moving, its people keep living, but they'd be down one grimy, grumpy, clever old bastard with a soul made of tough boot leather and a heart made of gold.

Collin felt the tears coming back, but they were different now. Cold instead of hot, terribly, terribly cold. He felt himself sharpening, his wits growing quick and cruel like the barbed tips of arrows. His father was fucking dead, and the Dark Lord's bastards had killed him.

"I'll do it," Collin croaked, hearing his own voice as a distant, disconnected thing. "I'll take the mantle, if they'll have me."

Silenos Shaiagrazni studied him, taking a moment, then asking a calm, simple question.

"What will your first acts be, Governor Baird?"

Collin looked up at him with a start. What sort of question was that? The answer was so obvious.

"We're going to kill every single fucking one of them," he breathed, fighting a smile that threatened to spread at the very suggestion.

There was a monster living in the heart of every man, and Collin needed his to come out.

Sphera the Necromancer was happy. Not just smiling, not just smug, but happy. That was a dangerous sight, Arion knew. The last time she'd been at all happy, Ensharia had gotten captured.

His master was still yet to return. In the wake of the governor's death, he'd taken it upon himself to speak with Collin Baird. Probably he was finding out some way to get what he wanted from the boy, push him up into his father's position and use him as a tool for controlling the city's defense. Probably he'd manage it. Silenos Shaiagrazni rarely permitted failure in his endeavors.

It was all to be expected, all mundane, uneventful. And so why was it then that the necromancer sat smiling with such sincerity? What did she know that Arion didn't?

Perhaps he was being manipulated; perhaps this was simply some new elaborate torture, or a trick to gain freedom. Perhaps. Or perhaps there was more to things than he'd caught on.

Arion didn't take long to make his decision. I was rather an easy one to be made. Magi did not sit idle and roll around in their ignorance; if there was something they didn't know, they fixed the fact.

He mastered himself and spoke.

"What are you grinning at?" he growled, affixing the necromancer with what he hoped was, if not intimidating, a stare that conveyed he was not to be pushed around.

"Oh, nothing much. Just pleased to find out that I was right. And that I'm less likely to be killed and reanimated, though being honest that's not really more fearsome a thought for me than simple death."

Arion frowned.

"Right about what?"

She'd dropped that hint deliberately, to lure him into asking, to keep herself ahead of the conversation and ensure he continued following after her for crumbs of information. But that was just the way of it. Right now she knew something he didn't, and that gave her all the power. Better to focus on getting what he could rather than futilely try to turn around a hopeless imbalance.

"About your master." She beamed sweetly. "Good thinking on his part with Finlay. Damned good thinking."

Arion froze. She hadn't said Baird.

CHAPTER SIXTY

What are you implying?" Arion growled, and she looked at him in much the way he might expect a woman to look at some barking puppy.

"What exactly do you think I might be implying?" she asked dryly. "Have a think, a good hard one, and try to recall the things of note our late governor has done since we last spoke. The list isn't very long, being honest."

Arion had caught her meaning before she'd even gotten a tenth of the way into her condescension, and he didn't like it one bit.

"You think my master killed the governor," he hissed, keeping his voice low for fear of being heard. She grinned wider.

"Finally, yes, I do. Do you not?"

"He can't have," Arion replied, his defense seeming a pathetic thing even to him.

"Why? Would he have been impeded by his strong moral character or his glaring empathy? Perhaps his scrupulous, squeamish attitude toward violence and final measures?"

She was enjoying herself, he saw, and she was making one good point after another. It felt very much like being on the receiving end of a beating, sent stumbling so hard and far with each blow that he could do nothing but blink and maintain his balance before receiving the next.

It was, he knew, because she was right. Arion never had a chance at beating her out in this rhetorical game of cards because he'd been holding a losing hand to begin with. And she was not a woman to miss it.

"I've got you convinced, I can see," she noted. "You realize, yes? You're just a pawn to him, you and everyone else. Just pieces on a board to be moved, taken, and sacrificed as he sees fit. Your only value to him is what you can do."

"That's not true," Arion stabbed back. "He's fought with us; he's protected us."

"Because you're useful," she countered. "Because keeping you alive at his own risk in the short term is a worthwhile investment in the long term. That's why he was so unmoved by your paladin being captured; that's why he's not even paid the good king Galukar a visit. Really, it's impressive. I'd say he thinks like me, but I think that would be giving myself undue credit."

It was disgusting, the amount of sincere admiration there appeared to be in this one's voice. As if everything she thought good was bad, and everything she thought bad was good. How did one even reason with a person like that?

"You're working too hard on this to just be fucking with me," Arion noted, eyes narrowing. "And you're not stupid enough to give information away for free either way. What are you planning? What are . . . What are you about to suggest?"

She seemed surprised, almost amazed, but he was in no mood to derive any measure of satisfaction from the state. Arion just watched and waited for her reply.

It wasn't long in the making.

"What do you suppose your master will do to you when this city's defenses start to crumble?" she asked. "I'll spare you the effort of thinking. It's the same as he'll do to me and any other Heroes or near Heroes. Because undead are more powerful than the living."

Arion found himself once more unable to answer.

"Venka could find use for a wind mage of your power," the necromancer continued. "As could the Dark Lord himself. If nothing else, you would be spared a painful death—"

"Don't treat me like an idiot," Arion snarled. "If I try to leave instead of fighting alongside you all, I'll just be killed and reanimated like the toxicologist."

She blinked, hesitated, then shrugged.

"Fair enough. Yes, you would be. But fighting alongside us is a much safer bet than fighting under your master. I mean, he *is* powerful, don't get me wrong, but do you honestly see him overcoming the Dark Lord? He's not even doing well against Venka here. How long do you think Kaltan will hold? How many more futile attempts at disrupting my master's plans do you think yours will be permitted before he's hunted, caught, and . . . well, turned into the most powerful soldier in our army?"

It was all so sickeningly logical, and Arion hated himself as he got to his feet and stepped toward her. He concentrated on her shackles, applying sharp pressure down on the locking mechanisms and doing what he could to wrench them apart. The great steel cuffs binding her hands and fingers fell away at once, and the necromancer flexed her freed digits, grunting.

"Ah, cramping, they're cramping. God, you have no idea how good this feels."

Arion didn't let his guard down, however much she may or may not have been cramping.

"You'll introduce me to General Venka," he pressed. "Like you said, yes?"

Her eyes flickered up to him, and she smiled.

"Of course I will." The woman sighed, as if he were being horribly foolish. "Really, what sort of madwoman do you think I am? Everything I said was true, you know. I have just as much—"

Arion did not see her punch coming, and only really deduced that it was a punch at all by the particular place and way in which it connected. She was stronger than she looked, this one, perhaps augmented a shade by some Vigor along with her magic. Strong enough to send him stumbling with the surprise blow in any case. Arion growled, glared back at her, readying his power and conjuring forth more wind. Then the stone ceiling crumbled, and a block of debris caught him clean in the back of the head.

He was pinned, face mashed into the floor, vision blurring with the concussion as he gasped and groaned. Above him, Sphera looked down, grinning still.

"I had a feeling you'd be too durable to knock unconscious with brute force," she noted, as if it were a mere interesting tidbit and not a fact that had very nearly left her trapped. "So I improvized. Glad to see my guess was right. Your master enhanced your body, yes? I'd have done the same."

Shadestuff. She must have splashed the ceiling with shadestuff as she hit him, letting it weaken and fall. Arion should have seen it coming. It was such an obvious use. He'd been stupid. Stupid in more ways than one.

". . . Stop . . . You," Arion grunted, but he could scarcely even summon the focus to speak, let alone wield magic. His vision was growing less focused by the moment, but he could still hear the necromancer's smile in her voice.

"Unlikely, but don't worry. You don't need to, and you won't be dying here."

Arion remained pinned as she took her leave, gasping, spitting, feeling the salty blood fill his mouth ever more.

Crucifixion, it was called. General Venka was fond of it.

His orcs, the renegade orcs, had returned as a tattered mess from their attempted assault, and Ensharia almost felt sorry for them. Many were missing limbs, or else limb-sized chunks torn from their bodies. Most had some measure of soot or scorch marks darkening their pale-gray skin and slowing their movements. Exhaustion was present in every step they took, both the physical kind born from running miles in heavy armor and the mental kind. The kind held by beaten men, and fearful ones.

It was wise to be fearful because General Venka's fury had been indescribable.

He had ordered much of the camp gathered up to witness as he passed judgment on the survivors, just a thousand from the three or so who had attacked the walls.

Venka did not waste time in his address, always a man to value economics in his doing of anything. He simply stood high, gazed out at the watching army, and spoke.

"The orcs you see now," he began, gesturing to the rows and rows of arrested renegades, "disobeyed my orders. They thought to charge ahead without my command. To try to take Kaltan themselves, perhaps earn a reward in the seizing of glory, I really couldn't say. They disobeyed me; that is what matters. Had they succeeded, they would be punished just as they are now because what I value in all of you is your obedience."

He paused, then screamed the word again, his fury coming on in an instant.

"*Obedience!*" Venka howled. "Is that understood? You are scarcely more than animals, and I would not have my hounds of war making their own decisions. Such things lead to the disaster we experienced today, our hand tipped for the enemy, their men's morale bolstered by a petty victory. Such things lead to punishment."

Venka turned his gaze to the orcs, as did all others present, and Ensharia watched with horror as the work was done. Great wooden crosses pressed down into the dirt, high enough to leave a man—or an orc—dangling as their arms were bound to the crossbar near its top. But they were not simply bound; instead each orc was nailed to one, driven into the wood with crude iron hammered brutally through the wrists or palms. They screamed, moaned, howled their apologies and pleas.

The general heeded none of it, merely watched with a stony face until the work was done. Ensharia watched too, feeling bile threatening to rise in her throat.

"Gulgaranth," Garutan whispered beside her. Ensharia turned to see him staring ahead at the display, his face tight, his eyes wet and wavering. "That . . . Gulgaranth."

His friend. Ensharia's heart broke as she saw the grief on his face, and she found herself placing a gentle hand down on Garutan's shoulder.

"Come on," she breathed. "We don't need to see this. We—"

A tear rolled down his cheek as he interrupted her, voice a mess of confusion and misery.

"Why . . . Why does he do this?" Garutan turned, staring at her, lips trembling. "Humans . . . You build so much, so many wond full thing . . . Why do things like this? Why . . . Why are you cruel? What did we do to make you so cruel?"

Ensharia thought about it and couldn't tell him. Years of education seemed somehow useless, seeing the orcs for herself. They weren't snarling animals, and yet her order still treated them as if they were. How could she fall back on the old justifications of raids and barbarity after seeing what she'd seen and learning what she'd learned?

"Because we are cruel," she said at last, finding herself speaking from the heart.

Ensharia's mind drifted back to earlier days spent coughing in a gutter, starving on the streets. To a little sister who failed to wake one morning, to a little brother who failed to smile.

"Even to our own, we're cruel," she continued. "And we always have been. But . . . We can learn." Ensharia felt the tears building, the guilt growing. "I think, at least, we can learn. And a lot of us try to do better."

Garutan eyed her, silent. Ensharia could bear the sight of his sadness no more and spoke again, more fiercely.

"Garutan, I'm going to get you out of here. I'm going to get you all out of here, if it's the last thing I do, I promise."

It was a ridiculous thing to say, an impossible promise to make, but somehow Garutan's face lit up with hope all the same. Ensharia felt a curious feeling in her gut, an impossible strength in her spine, and found herself repeating the words.

She was a coward, a weakling, an idiot. But by God, she was a paladin. Her vows might not have meant much, seeing now the things they deemed monsters, but the promise she'd made to herself . . . That still did.

Ensharia got to her feet, tightening her hands to fists. She was a paladin, and whether the order agreed or not, there were people around her in need of protection.

CHAPTER SIXTY-ONE

Orcs were not something Silenos had ever taken the time to study, and he found the practice quite a refreshing one. It had once been the spine of his work, dissection. That and all the other intellectual tools he now employed in the work. It was crucial, after all, for a fleshcrafter to possess a keen understanding of what exactly he could work with. Nature provided material in bottomless variety, with some of the most formidable weaves of organic tissue coming from the strangest places.

Had he not taken trips to the deep ocean, he'd never have found the blends of keratin and iron that made for the sturdiest armor. Had he not thought to examine the semicrystalline stones within the body of a clam, he'd never have discovered nacre, or how it might be tweaked into a diamond-hard substance of limitless sharpness.

Knowledge was to a caster as arrows were to an archer, and Silenos's quiver was deep indeed. He had carefully filled it for half a century of independent research, and nearly a full century of apprenticing before that. To repeat the measures he'd used in doing so was . . . refreshing.

A return to his roots, and rather enjoyable for it. Silenos had almost forgotten the joy of carving apart flesh, of shaving bone, of scrutinizing tissue for its magic and carefully unraveling it to gaze at the merits of its physical biology alone.

He felt a flash of irritation as he indulged himself. Were it not for the idiot calling himself a Dark Lord, he'd have spent the past months doing precious little else and be doing it now with a brain still optimized for such work. An unacceptable delay that he would simply have to punish.

But later, for now he needed knowledge.

Orcs seemed to be of simian descent, much like humans, for Silenos found several telltale signs. Their brains were the most notable, neuronal size and structure a near-identical match to other great apes. He noted that they had a mere nine or so billion within their cerebral cortex, though did not appear to have any neurological structures that might be expected to emphasize aggression or violence. Could he have been misled in stories of their savagery by a cultural bias on behalf of the new world's humans? Or perhaps orc culture itself was what encouraged such behavior rather than any natural inclination. He made a note to study further.

Their musculature was considerable, making up some two-thirds of their body mass, which itself was already several times greater than the norm among humans. The individual fibers were nothing particularly special, though Silenos noted far more fast-twitch strands, which explained their explosive physical potency. Bone tissue was denser than in humans or apes, but mostly it seemed to derive strength simply from its thickness.

It was the orc's organs that truly interested Silenos, for he had rarely seen anything like that. They seemed far too small to truly sustain the creatures, far too feeble to power such hulking masses of meat and bone. He soon discovered how they functioned regardless.

Magic, of course, considerable volumes. Less than even a journeyman caster, but enough that it made a marked difference upon their biology. It seemed that arcane forces worked to compensate for the lack of truly developed sustaining organ tissues just as they worked to increase the potency of muscular strength. Silenos pondered that, examining further.

Yes, as he'd suspected. The orcs' very cellular structures were augmented on such a scale, kept safe and sustained as magic destroyed whatever pathogens threatened their equilibrium and subtly aided the biological processes they carried out. An entire structure of mismade, patchwork tissue sustained only by the supernatural.

No natural cause was behind this; something had made them. He would find out what.

Silenos worked, and worked, and worked some more. Feeling himself slip into the fugue of intellectual dedication, his awareness seeming to leave the body in which it resided to more tightly wrap itself around the task at hand. It was a familiar feeling, a good feeling, and in the absence of all his preventative measures and self-preservative magics, a dangerous one.

It left Silenos quite unaware of the footsteps behind him until they'd already come to within half a stride of his back. Left him quite slow to act against the sound of scraping steel until its edge had already come down to kiss his neck.

Arms closed around him; hot breath hit the base of his skull. The voice followed but a moment later.

"Your apprentice was quite easy to fool, all things considered. Underestimated a woman, I think. Typical magus stupidity."

It was the necromancer, Sphera, but there was no magic to her danger now. Just a simple physical force, concentrated along a few millimeters of steel.

"Then I had to sneak through the keep, but that was barely hard either. Shadows, you know. Useful for us necromancers, aren't they? Good for hiding. It was smart of you to keep me from knowing what time it was, but I got lucky and picked the evening. After that I just followed the scent of your magic, which wasn't hard. Like searching for a bonfire in an eclipse."

She sounded proud of it all, and Silenos supposed she had done an adequate job.

"Now, if I wanted to, I could kill you. I'm not a warrior, or even a ranger, but I'm powerful, holding a knife and a damn sight stronger than any normal person you'll ever meet. I could drag this pretty little edge across so hard and fast that it'd scrape through a gambeson and still open up a normal man's guts. How do you think it'll do against you?"

Silenos wasn't certain. He tried to calculate the most likely eventuality, using what he knew of textile mechanical properties. His skin was resilient, his body too, but in his standard form, and with the blade held so carefully between his armored plates, there was every chance he'd still be killed. He could feel the strength in her arm as she grabbed him, and it was just as impressive as she'd claimed. Slicing him would ruin the knife, but that meant nothing to Silenos if he died in the ordeal.

The knife's pressure vanished before he could complete his calculation, weapon drawn back away from him, grip released as the necromancer stepped away. Silenos turned to her, eying the woman, reassessing her.

"You want to negotiate," he guessed, and she nodded.

"I needed you to know that I was serious, and in my experience, the only way to truly see a person's intentions is to be left completely under their power. I do hope you'll forgive the impoliteness, but it was really the only practical choice I had."

Silenos could appreciate that, and so he decided not to melt her. Breezing past onto more important issues.

"Very well then," he replied. "I accept you as my apprentice. Bow."

The woman seemed surprised for a moment, blinking. Silenos wondered whether she'd expected more, whether she'd truly been stupid enough to think she might get anything else from him, that he might forget the dynamic of power that existed between them both simply because his life had been endangered for a few measly moments. Then she lowered herself to both knees, a smile flicking across her features as she did.

"Thank you, Master Silenos," she breathed, and Silenos eyed her as she knelt, taking a moment before he replied.

"Call me Master Silenos, Esteemed Fleshcrafter of House Shaiagrazni, Keeper of the Auburn Flame, Conductor of Arts Most Ancient, and Lord of Hara'lguanta," he instructed.

Unlike Falls, she did not hesitate before repeating him.

"You'll want to learn more about necromancy before anything else," Silenos guessed. She looked up at him sharply, considering.

"You imply I could . . . learn more?"

Silenos allowed himself a smile.

"I imagine you can. It will take a while, perhaps a century, before your magic has matured enough, but you will one day be capable of learning a second discipline just as I myself did."

He might have told the woman she would live forever and not received a grin so wide or hungry as that.

"I will begin with whatever kind of magic you think to be best, master," the woman answered, her natural deference making rather a pleasant change.

"You will begin by obeying me." Deciding to first strike at that expectation of receiving anything at all from him without earning it. "And my first order is for you to bring my other apprentice here. I would have words with him."

She seemed downright eager at the idea, nodding and grinning.

"Of course, Master Silenos, Esteemed Fleshcrafter of House Shaiagrazni, Keeper of the Auburn Flame, Conductor of Arts Most Ancient, and Lord of Hara'lguanta."

Silenos smiled.

As far as sieges went, Collin was not the most experienced boy. But he was fairly sure this one was going about as well as a plague.

They had enough food stores for maybe two months, three if he got nice and mean with the rationing. Their walls wouldn't be an issue, in all likelihood, but the incident with the orcs had proved that even intact, they wouldn't be too difficult to scale. And to top it all off, he saw siege towers ahead.

Orcs were dull things, he'd always been told, but here in Kaltan a bit more was known about them. They'd been dealing with orcs before he was even born, before the Dark Lord's bastards started showing up, and one of the most dangerous and overlooked abilities they had was their knack for metallurgy.

Perhaps it was just strength, sheer muscular power letting them work the stuff harder and easier than humans. Perhaps it was instinctual. Perhaps it was something to do with their habitats because orcs tended to enjoy dark, low places rich in iron veins. Whatever the cause, orcs were better at actually working metal than even humans were. He saw the proof of that poking out of the siege camps now.

Siege towers, big ones. And not just wood. The great structures were all clad in wide sheets of bolted iron almost like armor themselves, glinting dull and gray, nasty and cold in the evening light. Such a weight of metal would be untenable for human-driven structures, that much he knew, but orcs were different. Any of them could do more work to move a thing than most draft horses, Collin reckoned, and they had far more than just a few for each tower.

Footsteps caught his ear to the left, and he turned just in time to see Gyvain hurrying over. He was a tall man, like most rangers, and as light on his feet as a cat, moving with the same innate grace that all with their training managed. His scarred face was not a pretty sight, more categorically resembling a well-used shield than a normal visage, but Collin only felt a stab of relief at it.

He was among the most veteran from among the rangers, and the most powerful to boot. Within them, only Collin and his father were deadlier in a fight.

Just Collin now, of course. His mood darkened.

"What have you seen?" he asked the ranger.

"It's thick," Gyvain replied, speaking in that grunting, clipped tone he always did. Hard to make this one string more than five words together. A life of getting stabbed and shot at tended to have that effect. "Half inch thick, at least. Not sure where they got all the iron, but orcs have always been better at finding and refining it than us."

Collin racked his brains. A half inch of iron wasn't as strong as the same thickness of steel, but it was doubtless still plenty tougher than plate armor. Maybe even four layers of it at once. That, and the wooden frame beneath, would make the towers difficult to destroy.

"Shall we sabotage them, governor?"

He thought about it, then shook his head.

"No, there's enough men in this city that we won't be losing to the first wave no matter what. This siege is going to end only when they've exhausted our fighting bodies. We'll test the new weapons on the towers' approach. If they stop them, then it'll make sabotage pointless and save us the risk. If they don't, then we'll weather the first attack and be able to send rangers out to dismantle the towers in the night, after making sure we have to."

Gyvain nodded, heading off to give the word. It felt strange to hand such a man orders. Collin looked back out at the siege engines. They, at least, he could understand. They were familiar. An enemy at his front, allies at his back.

Collin couldn't wait to get his hands on them.

CHAPTER SIXTY-TWO

Arion had woken up to a lot of things, and for the most part they tended to be rather pleasant. Nice furniture, nicer women within squeezing range. The smell of cooked breakfast, sunny weather, or even the rare day off from his studies. All in all, waking up was a typically enjoyable experience when one was the most gifted magus alive.

In recent weeks, the experiences had soured somewhat. Hard ground instead of soft beds, dry rations rather than fresh meals, and no women at all save for a steel-clad scowling paladin who seemed to regard him rather like something she'd just scraped off her heel.

Nothing though had yet compared to the sight of his master's fury. Silenos Shaiagrazni demonstrated his displeasure subtly for the most part. A stiffened jaw, a curled lip, the very occasional arching of an eyebrow. His glare was like burning magnesium now though, and his anger crushed in around Arion like the great weight of stone.

He still felt that on his back, and it was a testament to his master's sheer presence that he had taken so long to even notice it hadn't been removed.

"You allowed her to escape," Shaiagrazni noted, speaking as if to some drooling child who might be inclined to misunderstand if he did not temper his rage with a careful clarity.

Arion did not need to ask whom; that much he was sure of. He didn't really need to ask anything at all, in fact, his head suddenly clear, body suddenly refreshed. Obviously his master's work, which would only enrage him further.

"I'm sorry," he hurried. "She—"

Silenos Shaiagrazni kicked Arion hard, his heel slamming into his nose and flattening it. The cartilage caved so quickly it barely even felt solid, as if it were a snail's shell being stomped on rather than the body part of a grown man. Blood filled his nostrils, tears filled his eyes, and Arion felt suddenly strangled by the weight crushing down on his back.

"Apologies are for simpletons," his master snarled, punctuating the words with another stomp, further mangling the crushed meat of Arion's face. "An apology comes after a failure, and only simpletons fail. Are you a simpleton, Falls? Have I accepted a simpleton as my apprentice?"

The stomping finally stopped, leaving Arion to gasp in air and huff the thick blood out from his crushed nose. Everything hurt suddenly, face, jaw, neck, and the rest of his body somehow to boot. His head was clear as anything though. As coherent as the flight of a ranger's arrow. That clarity gave way slowly to anger.

"You don't give a shit about me, do you?" he snapped back, forcing himself to meet his master's eye. "You don't care about any of us. I know you haven't visited Galukar even once since what happened with his sons, and . . ." He hesitated. Arion saw a fury in Silenos Shaiagrazni still burning, a dangerous one. If what he was about to say turned out to be wrong, he might well pay for it. But he had to say it. Some things just needed confirming. Some truths just needed speaking.

"You killed Finlay," he accused, finding his mouth and throat suddenly terribly dry. The words hung between them like a deadweight, dangling there in silent anticipation of a nudge to send it tumbling one way or the other.

His master provided it first.

"You accuse me?" he asked slowly, calmly. "Me, the greatest fleshcrafter—the greatest caster—this world has ever seen? You demand truths of *me*? You complain to *me*?!" His fury remained quiet, as always, but the molten heat of it was enough to blister even Arion's wits regardless. He saw his master raise a hand, flinching, expecting a blow, but it never came. Instead magic wrapped around the man's fingers, and a new sensation swept over him.

Arion knew pain, somewhat at least. He'd felt blows strike him, felt cold iron chafe against his skin, felt the toxicologist's venom eat him alive from the inside out. Nothing could have prepared him for the agony unleashed by Silenos Shaiagrazni.

It was like fire, running through his veins along with the blood. Like ice pricking every nerve he had. He'd read about flayings, a form of torture so horrendous that men had been known to die from simple shock upon experiencing it, but even that hardly seemed a comparable thing to what he felt now. How could the mere mundane mangling of flesh measure up against this? How could any physical sensation at all?

His mouth opened silently, and his lungs tried desperately to form something, anything to project their torment outward. A moan, a groan, even a whisper to tell of his torture. But nothing escaped him; it was all held tight and compressed by the bottomless torment. Arion was crying, he realized, and by the wetness around his groin he knew he must have pissed himself. Humiliation was no more significant than the physical agonies of his past might have been. He didn't care for how he looked or how he'd been embarrassed; he just wanted the pain to stop.

Finally, finally, it did. Pulling away all at once, like a rug dragged out from under him. The shock of it was so abrupt and jarring that Arion almost started laughing, sure he must be imagining his lull.

A gasp escaped him then, followed by a groan. Long, low, and scraping his raw throat even more. He looked at Silenos Shaiagrazni through eyes flooded with tears.

"I did kill Finlay Baird," his master told him with a voice so casual he might have been admitting to eating the last slice of beef. "And I did it intentionally. I skewered him through both his hearts, then healed the damage away after he died and twisted his innards to resemble a death by necromantic poison or magical influence. I did it intentionally, and I do not regret its doing. It was for the greater good, serving a higher purpose, necessary."

Arion was torn between barely focusing enough to hear and desperately clinging to every word for fear of being plunged back into the depths of his agony if they stopped. If his master noticed, he didn't communicate the fact.

"You, however, served nobody and nothing in your betrayal. The necromancer you released might have killed me, or else left me seriously wounded, in her ambush. And had we been forced to leave, we would have done so without making half so large a dent in the Dark Lord's forces. Every possible eventuality to come of what you did was a poor one, save for your own self-preservation. You are a petty, stupid, selfish rat of a man unworthy of the name Shaiagrazni, and perhaps unworthy of even my tutelage."

The bile was rising, sickness made solid. Arion could scarcely believe what he was hearing, could scarcely believe it was all real. Surely he was in some nightmare; surely the world was not this cruel. His master though showed no hint of stopping.

"I had an apprentice like you once," Silenos Shaiagrazni murmured, seeming distracted suddenly.

His eyes were incoherent, unfocused, his words soft and distant. It was as if his thoughts were on another place, another time, as if Arion were some specter ephemerally drifting before him.

"He rebelled constantly. Complained about everything, a great, gushing heart of sentiment and idiocy. He complained about how I treated our servitors, about how I conducted my research, about how House Shaiagrazni itself operated. And that was a transgression too far. I twisted his spine, leaving it just an inch from breaking, then left it to naturally fix into that shape. The look of a cripple, I thought, suited him rather more given his crippled intellect. What do you think, Falls?" His hand raised; his magic built. "How might it suit you?"

Arion felt the tears running down his cheeks, tried to speak, but found his words leaving him as a blubbering, clumsy wave of inexplicable sobs and half-formed syllables.

"Please," he croaked. "Master, please, I'm sorry. I'm sorry. I'll never do it again. I'll never act against you again. I'm a fool, an idiot, but I'll do better. Please let me do better."

His master hesitated, hand remaining aloft, eyes remaining sharp and grim. He stared at Arion for a few more moments, some subtle shift running under the skin of his face. Then he nodded shortly.

"You are more useful to everyone alive, for now," he replied, then with a gesture, the stone at Arion's back was pulled off. Some undead, he saw, hefting the boulder aside without any visible exertion at all. His master was leaving by the time he looked back to him.

Shaiagrazni was almost at the door when Arion next spoke, and he found himself unable to meet the caster's eye.

"I'll do better," he breathed, repeating the promise, not even certain why. A silence followed, and Arion looked up only when it had persisted a few seconds more to see his master's staring, cold face.

"It would have been better if you had died instead of Ensharia," he replied.

There was a lot of work to be done in holding an army together, particularly an army who had just recently lost the man responsible for leading them across a decade. Particularly when that recently decapitated army was staring down a force ten times its size and a hundred times its strength from behind fortress walls they'd long since been trapped in.

One surprisingly notable issue, he found, was in keeping them behind the walls. Collin would have thought that men might go placid over something like a giant, snarling army threatening them. Apparently not.

Some men, it seemed, went fucking insane under such conditions. Fear displaced from them as surely as air was by smoke, replaced with a bizarre sort of maddened, vicious aggression that drove them toward the enemy like loosed pit dogs against a juicy steak. It was half his challenge just to keep the men struck by their random bouts of lunacy from making impromptu charges. The other half was resisting his own.

Out there, somewhere, in the dirty gray plains, there were the fuckers responsible for killing Collin's father. Could he really stay put and mess around with logistics and planning while they went about their business without so much as an ounce of steel in them?

Yes, he told himself. More to the point, he had no choice in the matter.

Some idiot had mixed up an order for defensive stones, intended to be dropped over the walls on attackers, and piled three loads in the same area. Collin had to

rectify that himself. He'd had heavy axes prepared to hack apart the grapples apparently used last time, but those were delayed in arriving, which had forced him to
investigate the matter personally. It turned out the load was being smuggled and
sold in the city for profit, thus necessitating new action to resolve the entirely separate issue *that* posed. Collin hated that part. He'd never liked hangings.

He recalled what his father told him about thievery within a siege, the way
hoarded food suddenly became the most valuable thing within its walls, and so
he had the known criminals rounded up and disposed of all at once. That one
stung in particular, but it was necessary.

Forty years ago, his own dad might have been among that class, but today
anyone in it was a threat to the people. He couldn't tolerate those at this of all
times.

Collin worked for hours, distributing ladders, checking over firing slits, supplying ammunition, working men, working forces, working bloody officers.
Everything was his problem, everything his duty, everything his fault. He was so
smothered by the scale of it that it took him rather by surprise when word finally
reached him that other matters besides drunken arseholes knocking out teeth in
a pub brawl demanded his attention.

"General," Gyvain said, looking about as happy as ever to be bringing the
news. "Venka is here for a parley."

Collin was so suddenly cold at the knowledge, he barely even noticed being
called general.

CHAPTER SIXTY-THREE

Watching Silenos Shaiagrazni work was an exercise in insignificance. Sphera had considered herself a clever, educated, knowledgeable woman. She'd worked hard to become so. Like most who excelled, she had been born with a natural gift for magic and natural studies. Like all who excelled without peers, she had hammered that fluke of nature until it was tempered well beyond the limits of mere talent. Within her head lay a thousand secrets and a hundred thousand facts, each one contributing to an ever-growing web of genius and enlightenment.

At least, she had considered it genius and enlightenment. That was before the towering, lithe man she'd made her new master had shown her otherwise. Had revealed to her that what she'd called genius was mindless idiocy, that what she'd called enlightenment was the half-known truths of a simple child stumbling onto an apprentice's book.

He had an orc, or rather an orc's corpse, laid down across the table before him. He eyed it as if it were a book to be read, scrutinizing it with inhuman eyes and probing it with fingers made into long, needle-thin instruments by his own magic. Sphera watched, thoughtful, silent, and just a hair irritated to be so far behind his cognition as to not even muster any meaningful deductions.

"You will learn much faster if you ask me about my work," her master noted, speaking without looking up. Sphera felt the blood pool in her face. Somehow it had felt inappropriate to do such a thing, as if she might defile the sanctity of this testament to intelligence simply by adding her voice to the room.

"What are you examining in that body?" she asked immediately. The question had been bubbling for a while and was practically launched from her lips the moment her master gave it permission.

"Microorganisms," he explained.

The man could not have gauged Sphera's confusion from her face because he did not look at her. Nonetheless he must have sensed the need for elaboration after a moment.

"You are familiar with insects, I take it."

"I'm not a fool," Sphera replied, carefully keeping her frustration from showing.

"Good. Then picture things smaller, so small, in fact, that they are to insects as insects are to you. Now imagine smaller things still, that are dwarfed by these new beings as much as these beings are by an elephant."

She tried her best, but it was no small thing to be asked. Sphera wasn't sure scales even functioned at such minute levels. How could life exist as small as that? How could anything?

"Are you picturing it?" he prodded, and she nodded, though she was still not sure whether it was the truth.

"I think I am," Sphera whispered. "What you just described, they're microorganisms?"

"They are. 'Micro' meaning one millionth, in this case one millionth of a meter. A meter, before you ask, is approximately thirty-nine inches."

She tried to envision that and promptly failed. The human brain, it seemed, was not designed with millions in mind.

"And 'organism'? What does that mean?"

"It simply means an individual life-form, which makes a microorganism . . . ?"

He was testing her, she realized, and Sphera was eager not to fail so early in her education. She would have been eager enough not to fail so simple a test as that in any case.

"An . . . An organism that measures smaller than one millionth of a meter?"

"Yes." He nodded, sounding slightly satisfied, if not pleased. "One millionth of a meter is called a micrometer, for future reference. You must learn proper units of measurement if you are to study under me."

Sphera hadn't wheedled her way into his apprenticeship to learn proper units of measurement, but she knew enough to keep her displeasure hidden as he continued his work.

"So what is it about microorganisms that you find cause to study?" She frowned. "It seems hard to believe such small things could matter much for such large creatures."

He did not look pleased at this question, rather annoyed. As if the very asking of it were failing some subtle standard he'd laid out. Silenos Shaiagrazni nonetheless kept his voice level.

"Your body is made of structures as small, and smaller, than microorganisms, at its most fundamental level. The way these are arranged and built is what determines the difference between bone, muscle, or blood. There is much to be changed by affecting matter on the microscale. In more direct, immediate terms, I am looking into which microorganisms live within orcish anatomy."

"To try and remake them?" she asked hesitantly.

"No, such a thing would be an uneconomic use of my time and power against an army of tens of thousands. I mean to see if any of the microorganisms living within their flesh are vital for life, responsible for sustaining it, or managing some bodily function they cannot do without."

Sphera thought about that, frowning.

"Why?"

"Because any weakness, or fault in their design, is a possible avenue of attack," Shaiagrazni replied.

It was a lot to swallow at once, but Sphera did her best. She supposed if she really could learn this most powerful of magics, however far into the future, it would not hurt to gain some intellectual grasp of its mechanics first.

"Can you not create your own species of servitors?" she asked finally. "Something that reproduces itself, rather than requiring your magic? Surely that would become a mighty army within years even without you altering anything, especially if it bred like rats or rabbits."

He actually looked up at that, eying her, looking rather pleased.

"That is an intelligent question," the caster replied. "And no, I cannot. Complex creatures, ones capable of reproduction, are made in accordance with . . . The best way to describe it would be design details, I suppose. We call it DNA, standing for deoxyribonucleic acid, a pattern of sub-microscale matter contained within the tiniest components of your body and ordering how they replicate and function. For sexual reproduction, you require it to be further adaptable through things called gametes that are designed to combine patterns with those of external sources, thus creating an offspring based on the material of both parents. Such matters are . . . beyond me. For now. My master and one other are capable of it in all of House Shaiagrazni, and I have not yet developed the raw skill and power required to mimic her."

Sphera reckoned she didn't understand even a single word of that, up until being told that her new master couldn't do it. A pity, she decided. There was something rather appealing about creating life, doing as God did . . . Doing better, even. She'd seen the sort of creatures Shaiagrazni could make. There was no comparing them with the petty efforts of nature.

"Do microorganisms attack one another?" she asked suddenly. Another smile.

"They do, in a way," Shaiagrazni replied. "Diseases are caused by them, or rather, they are them. A cold, a cough, a deadly plague. All of them are one kind of microbe or another. They enter the body and multiply within it, their simplicity letting them do so without the need for complex reproductive patterns, and are quickly numerous enough to negatively affect the activity of the body's smallest components—its cells. Some, called viruses, are even more efficient, small enough to actually sink inside the cells and affect them from within."

Sphera glanced down at her hands, feeling suddenly, terribly sick. It was a pointless effort, trying to see any microorganisms that might be clinging to the skin, but she found herself doing it, nonetheless. Shaiagrazni evidently took note.

"You needn't bother. We are all of us covered with microorganisms at all times, more or less whatever we do. Most are harmless, however."

That didn't make her feel better about the damned infestation, not in the slightest. It was simply too big a thing to be told all at once, like having it revealed that the world was actually hollow under her feet and falling through a crack may leave her falling forever.

"How . . . How did you learn such things?" Sphera whispered, staring at the man with new eyes now. She had taken him for a genius, for a being with knowledge beyond her world. She had underestimated things to a grotesque extreme.

A rush of something ran down Sphera, starting in her chest and blooming as it shot straight to that spot between her legs. She'd not felt such a feeling since the Dark Lord first demonstrated his might to her, and it hadn't been mingled with such a delightful, dangerous touch of fear then. She found her lips dry, voice uncertain, as she spoke to her master.

What she was going to say, however, was swallowed by the sound of an opening door, and Collin Baird stormed in. Sphera's first thought was to punch the stupid bastard for ruining the atmosphere so thoroughly; her second was to study him.

Kaltans were a hard people, harder than most. Generations spent choking in mills and workhouses, then decades more being sharpened by one of the finest military minds alive, had left them about as difficult to shake as boulders. Which meant that it was more than a shade concerning to see their new governor, and general, soaked so thoroughly with his own sweat.

"Venka," the boy gasped, clearly having sprinted the entire way to the workplace. "Venka is here, to parlay. What—"

"Take care of it yourself," Master Silenos snapped without looking up. "I am busy."

Baird stood there, blinking and dazed as if the retort had been a blow between the eyes. Sphera let her amusement show with a grin, and he recovered quickly.

"But this might determine the fate of the city," the governor pressed. "We need—"

"It is your city," Shaiagrazni interrupted irritably. "And I would entrust it to no other. Now go and take care of the matter yourself. My incredible mind is required for the task it is currently applied to."

If Collin Baird considered it comforting to hear that such an incredible mind was being worked, he did not show the fact. Merely scowled.

"That's it then?" he snapped. "You spend all this time working on defenses, and now the time's come to actually negotiate with the fucker they're made for, you—"

"I am making defenses at this very moment," Shaiagrazni interrupted. "Now leave. I have given you more leeway than I would most other men, out of respect for your father and talents, but my patience is finite and rather lacking compared to what you are doubtless accustomed to. I will snap soon, and painfully. Begone."

Baird paused, stared. He worked his mouth in silent, considering discontent. Then nodded sharply, glared jaggedly, and made his way out through the door he'd come in through. Shaiagrazni spoke again only when he was almost past it.

"Two days," he called. "That is my current estimate. Give me two days and I shall give you a victory."

Baird hesitated, and Sphera half expected to see the boy crumple under the demand. Instead he hardened, like molten brass setting into a cast.

"Two fucking days," he replied, voice like a starving dog's. "If I can resist taking that bastard's eyes out for that long." He was gone a moment later.

Sphera found herself turning back to her master, and only one question had any true weight in her mind.

"Do you really think you can turn the tables in two days?" she asked.

He did not look certain.

"I can, but there is no guarantee. It is, however, the only hope any of us have."

Sphera nodded at that, thoughtful. One city, one outer wall, and a few thousand normal humans against the greatest army assembled on the continent in over a century. Any other time, she'd have fled from such odds like they were death itself.

But she'd seen too much, glimpsed too much more, to live satisfied with not wringing out all the secrets her master had. She realized then why he'd been so encouraging of her questions.

What better than promised knowledge to ensure a caster's loyalty?

CHAPTER SIXTY-FOUR

General Venka marched with quite an impressive staff, Collin had to admit. He'd gathered his own best men, of course, a dozen of the finest rangers in Kaltan. Two of which were even at his side, rather than perched in buildings primed and ready to start taking heads off with near-sonic arrows. Even still, he'd half expected to be outdone, and he found he was not surprised.

Venka moved with a procession of orcs and undead, which very much mirrored the general makeup of his own army. These ones, however, were all something past elite. A pair of lichs came first, hovering slightly above the ground, their desiccated flesh neatly wrapped in linens and empty sockets somehow filled by intelligence rather than ocular tissue. The magic from them was felt at fifty paces, and overwhelming at ten. Collin found himself wondering whether he and his pair of bodyguards would have matched even a single one.

They would not, he decided.

After the lichs came Venka himself, his march framed on either side by a giant armored reanimate that Collin recalled was one of Galukar's sons. There were only two of them present, but two was two more than he'd have liked. Even weighed down by all that plate, they moved like cats, lighter than air on their feet, and seemingly primed to lunge one way or the other in an instant. Venka himself was more graceful by far. A Hero.

Collin always hated that term, "Hero." There was nothing Heroic about power and strength, his father used to say. The great Finlay Baird claimed to have seen at least one real hero die in every battle. The magic-filled cunts who always lived? They were just human siege engines.

Venka had his back covered too. Probably he'd heard that Kaltans were dirty, cheating cutthroats who'd sooner stick a knife in it than meet for peace talks. Bastard. It was a lucky guess, at best. Collin wouldn't have *had* to do such things if he weren't so bloody outnumbered. Breaking parleys was a great way to ensure you were never parlayed with again.

"Governor Baird," Venka said, speaking calmly as his little group came to stop just a few paces from Collin's. Oh, that was strange. Rage. Pure, molten rage unlike any Collin had ever felt, coursing through his veins, animating his muscles, urging him to come flying at the Hero and start biting chunks out. He'd thought he had a handle on his fury, thought he'd calmed himself with the bigger picture, but here it was, waiting for him. Springing its ambush and bowling his wits over with a storm of animal hate and soldier's savagery.

"General Venka," Collin replied, surprising himself with how coherent and calm his voice was. Was he calm? Would he be a calm man today? He didn't know.

Could be he'd lose his wits and start sticking steel in things any moment. It felt like he was watching the conversation from the outside, looking in on some scene he had no part in and no ability to influence. He was actually curious to see how it ended.

"I will be brief," the general replied. "You are grossly outnumbered, and more grossly outmatched. Surrender and we shall spare your city."

"I'll be brief too," Collin replied. "Fuck yourself with a pike, you shit-eating twat."

Apparently he would not be very diplomatic today, interesting. Gyvain snorted with laughter. General Venka did not seem particularly surprised by his response, but he was certainly annoyed. Brow creasing, face suddenly lined in all the ways his uniform wasn't.

"I had expected you to conduct yourself with a bit more dignity," he noted.

"I had expected you to not throw a few thousand idiots at my wall and watch them burst like grapes," Collin shot back. "Seems neither of us is living up to our reputation."

Venka's eye twitched a moment, his lip curling, cheeks thinning. The man's fury was well hidden but rather too great in volume to be fully missed.

"You know, I had nothing but admiration for your father," he answered, speaking with the forced calm of a man resisting the urge to draw steel and start hacking away. "Nothing but admiration. He was a man after my own heart, I should think. A man of iron, of intelligence, of drive. One who understood the need for a strong leader in hard times, who . . ."

Collin didn't stop listening, but by God did he want to.

He'd read Venka's books, of course, and his half-thought philosophies had always been good for a laugh, but hearing them in person was an exercise in tedium. Every good thing that had ever happened, the man seemed to think, was because of some individual, great man seizing power and initiative, while every single bad thing was the fault of some vague weak men growing soft in times of peace.

It was laughable to hear him try to reconcile that with the existence of King Galukar, pathetic to hear him try to explain Elrai the Cruel's coming up from his almost-as-incompetent father, and downright infuriating to hear his own dad used as further evidence of the fact.

But Collin listened because that was what a lad in his place had to do. He wasn't a noble really, and though he had wealth, most would call it stolen. When the whole world considered you a rowdy, violent thug sitting on a throne you didn't own, you learned to take what advantages you could get.

The younger, brasher, and stupider Venka thought he was, the less he'd try to keep himself from giving away whatever subtle hints Collin could catch and the less he'd notice them being caught.

You had to take whatever advantages you could, particularly when you were dealing with a general twice your age and a hundred times your experience.

"Am I boring you?" Venka asked irritably.

"Hmm?" Collin blinked, making a show of having let his focus slip. "Oh, no, not at all. Please go on."

It seemed Venka bought the performance, for his lip curled with disgust.

"Nothing like your father at all." He scowled. "Very well then. If you have any counteroffers to make then I will hear them now. If not . . . This is your last chance to surrender."

"Or what?" Collin asked.

Venka seemed stunned, almost disbelieving.

"I . . . I beg your pardon?"

"Or what? What will you do if we don't surrender?" Collin pressed.

"We'll attack your city, breach the walls . . . Seize it by force, and punish its populace for resisting."

"If you manage to get past the walls," Collin replied, making a show of confidence. Pure, unbroken confidence, of the kind that only an absolute fucking moron could possibly humor. For a moment, he feared he'd overdone it, but Venka seemed to swallow the performance well enough.

"We will get past your walls," Venka explained. "Our forces are a power not sent to field on this continent for centuries, even more. Whatever modifications you've seen made to Kaltan's outer defenses, they will not withstand us. Not our siege towers and, at worst, not our sheer numbers. Your father, no doubt, knew as much, and it surprises me that he apparently did not think to inform you." His lip curled, disgusted. "Such a waste for this to be his legacy. In any case, you have heard my warning. If you wish to ignore it then that is your mistake to make."

"Oh, I'm not ignoring anything," Collin snarled, letting his rage seep through—a shade—and letting Venka mistake it for mere pricked ego. "If you want to test your men against mine so badly, you can be welcome to it. We'll be waiting for you, us rangers, by the front gate. Send your best and we'll see how they fare. I should warn you though, my boys plan on getting a thousand of you fuckers each before they drop, and I reckon that's without counting the other help they'll get."

Venka's face was unreadable, but even that told Collin that his words had hit home. The general had not hidden his expressions before. That he did now . . . It implied he considered them something worth hiding. Something that might tip his hand.

He'd believed him. Had he? He couldn't be sure.

Venka was staring, scrutinizing, studying Collin. That was bad. His mask wouldn't hold up long under as practiced an eye as his. He had to do something, and do it fast. His sole advantages would be surprise and secrecy; he'd hold on to them even if it killed him.

"You might want to think twice before your bombardments, by the way," Collin added. "We have your necromancer, Sphera, in our city. Tied up, bound, powerless. Very much at risk of being killed by a stray catapult shot."

The general didn't wince, or flinch, or even hesitate. He only smiled.

"I see," he answered, voice slick like oil on water. "Excellent. Then with luck, she will perish in the siege and allow me the chance to further rise in status unimpeded by her emotional idiocy." The man turned, moving away without so much as pausing, and relieving Collin by leaving his eyes off from his face.

"Good day, Collin Baird," Venka replied frostily. "And good luck in your pointless last stand."

Collin watched Venka leave and tried to work out whether he'd won the exchange or not. He'd find out, he supposed, by either dying or living the next day.

Venka was long gone when Gyvain next spoke, his voice a tight growl.

"Good work on not skewering the smarmy bastard," he grunted. "Barely avoided it myself."

Collin just nodded, finding his mouth suddenly dry. He'd expected more rage, or to feel it more harshly, but he hadn't gone hot and blind when Venka arrived. Just cold and jagged. Like his father always talked about.

"Think he bought it?" Collin asked, his voice made a strangled whisper by sheer nerves. Gyvain laughed and slapped him on the shoulder.

"I nearly fucking bought it myself for a second there, you magnificent little bastard!" He chuckled. "Now come on, sir, we have more preparation to do."

Collin was escorted back to the inner fort and felt the sour taste return to his mouth. The governor's quarter, the military quarter, the center of the city. Their last stand. He'd neglected it for a good few days, kept himself focused on everything except it, and then he'd finally run out of other things to do. Finally run out of excuses not to start fortifying the place they would die.

It was a sickening task to work on. Hard to feel it had any relevance, not out of skepticism but simply because to seriously consider it meant humoring a scenario in which the city was lost, its citizens rendered the playthings of their enemies. It was a scenario where Venka would have all Kaltan's supplies to salvage and sustain his army, where he would control the territory around it, using the outer walls as his own refuge. Where he could camp indefinitely until starvation displaced the remaining defenders from their remaining defense.

But Collin put himself to work quickly, all the same. For no other reason than the simple, immutable fact that he was governor. Governor, general, leader. And if that meant the most he could manage was buying his people a few months more, then that was what he'd do.

He started setting up the ranged defenses, calling on wood and twine to assemble catapults, ballistae, and trebuchets.

If the most he could do was buy a few more months, then he would. But Collin rather wanted to make that fucker Venka bleed a few more troops in any case.

CHAPTER SIXTY-FIVE

Venka had fallen for Collin's feigned stupidity, and he'd sent a great mass of his forces to attack the center of the walls. Doubtless, he had believed his enemy to be a fool, believed that there would be a hundred rangers awaiting the assault with longknives and shortswords. He had been wrong, of course, because awaiting them there had been only one thing. Silenos Shaiagrazni's new weapon.

Collin would have been a liar if he'd claimed to understand what it was or how it worked, but he understood the results. He understood the results very, very fucking well, and he was rather fond of them.

Weird things, they were big, bony. Like they'd been carved from the skeleton of some great creature long dead and rotten. The main structure was cylindrical, maybe a half foot wide and stretching as long from arse to face as a tall man lying down. The back end of it curved down into a thickly built platform welded into the bone surface of the walls, built onto a platform designed to shift forward when pushed. That was the part that made it possible to keep them hidden from the outside, just a few feet, just a few degrees, but it ensured the enemy's scouts wouldn't be getting a clear line of sight to them.

Not that they'd have been likely to recognize the weapons, no more than Collin had. Far as he knew, they were something new, something unheard of. Something more sudden and unprecedented in the ugly art of killing than anything else since one man had first taken a rock to the skull of another.

The enemy found that much out the hard way.

Orcs, mostly. Made sense. Venka had been sending them against rangers in his own mind, against death itself. He'd want savagery, and he'd expect death. Orcs were always the most replaceable and expendable for that bastard.

It was orcs he sent, and it was orcs the weapons—Shaiagrazni had called them cannons—spat their burning death out into.

Collin didn't understand what they were, or how they worked. But he understood the results, and the results were a wave of falling bodies running deep along the horde of charging enemies, a flight and rain of shredded meat and severed limbs, then a twist of blasted dirt and bloody mist. Too many died at once to be counted, entire chunks simply disappearing from the thousands-strong mass of bodies that came surging for Collin's wall. Their ladders disappeared as panicking orcs dropped them, then crushed them to splinters in retreat. It took only three volleys of the weapons to send the enemy scurrying away.

Another minute had passed before the air was clear enough to let the ground look back up at them once more, and Collin almost puked when it did. He couldn't see the dirt, not really. It was covered in that many bodies. Pooled with that much blood, carpeted with that many smashed and discarded weapons.

Collin didn't understand what they were or how they worked. But he understood the cannons' results. He understood them enough to hope with every fiber of his being that House Shaiagrazni remained absent from his world.

Crossbows weren't complicated; most men could learn to use them. Henri had learned enough, over the years, to use them fast. But it was the fear more than the knowledge that had his fingers dancing along the weapon; it was his desperation more than the experience that kept his muscles dragging the winch back tight.

An orc came on with a ladder, a big bastard of an orc with a big bastard of a ladder. No human could have carried such a tall thing, no five humans, but it barely seemed to slow this bugger. The quarrel did a better job of that.

Orcs were tough, and this one was well armored, but the bolt was well aimed. It found that magic spot between heavy iron plates, cutting through the ringmail that protected its joint and digging a few inches into the meat below. Henri was already cocking another one by the time the blood was visible, and his next quarrel hit within a finger of the first. This time the mail was already weakened, and he saw half a hand less of the projectile as it embedded itself. The orc stumbled, gasped, fell. Its ladder took some of its bulk, left propped against the ground where one end bit into mud, and the thick wooden frame snapped. Henri turned his focus to the next enemy.

Bolts, that was his work. There were men around him with spears, axes, swords. Rangers, the odd hedge knight, some mercenaries with Vigor and vinegar in their balls, but they were the dessert. He was the main course. Every siege started with bolts, and he'd fought in more than a few sieges in his days. Twelve years of soldiering, all under a Baird, and he'd be fucked if he outlived the old one by less than a decade.

He drew, fired. Drew, fired. Drew and fucking fired. Snarled as he saw bolts bounce from thick iron, grinned as he watched them bite into the mail-wrapped gaps, laughed and whooped and bit back the urge to dance in satisfaction as one of them sank right through a helmet's eye slit and mashed up the soft brains beneath.

A veteran was a reaper of souls in any fight, and none so much as a siege. Henri felt the snap of string in his weapon, the jitter of wood as it threw another murderous splinter out, and he reloaded again just as the first orc reached the walls. He nailed it in the spot where pauldron and gorget parted ways, and the angle was such that he nicked an artery deep enough to leave half its body painted red in seconds. The orc wasn't dead for even a moment before yet more came onto the wall, and a ladder with them. It was up in seconds, enemies scaling it in seconds more, angry iron flashing about in the dawn light.

Dessert had arrived.

Patrick had a simple job. Jobs tended to be simple for him. As complex as the actual study of magic was, as taxing and demanding as attaining true mastery had always been, there was an invariable lack of contrivance to the things one was generally asked to do with it.

Focus, destroy things. That was about the gist of it, ninety-nine times out of a hundred, and this was certainly not the hundredth. Today, his target was incoming catapult stones. Patrick focused well.

His power was one over flame, as potent a war magic as could be hoped for. He threw it out in great jets, concentrating the power such as to leave it forceful and kinetic as it struck the incoming projectiles, smashing rock into shrapnel, leaving chips of smoldering stone to rain down on attackers en masse. Each success was a dozen men saved behind the walls if he'd stopped a lucky shot. Each failure was a dozen deaths allowed. Patrick didn't feel any particular weight to either fact.

They were people he held in his hands, but there was no time for that sort of consideration. He could ponder the philosophy of what he did when he had the wits to spare; for now they were all needed. Focus and destruction.

Something scraped just a few feet to Patrick's left, and he looked down in time to see an axe. A great big axe with a great big orc on the other side of it, closing fast, swinging faster. He gasped, screamed, just about pissed himself, and took a full step back all before thinking to do the one thing a man of his talents ought always to think of doing first. Use his magic. The flames wrapped around the orc like burning oil about a figure of wax, and he just barely caught its silhouette through the eye-stinging light. One step, two. By the third it was losing shape, iron armor running off its body in molten streams, pooling to form a hissing, spitting puddle on the battlements at its feet. The orc fell in that puddle before taking a fourth step.

Patrick never got to laugh. Globules of metal splashed out from the impact, and a few caught his face. He fell just as the orc had, screaming louder than ever, and more clambered over their burning comrade's corpse to crush his underfoot.

Gyvain hadn't run out of arrows, but he'd run out of time. The orcs were on the wall, and that meant that in a few more moments, the humans wouldn't be. Unless he was quick.

He was always quick though. That was what it meant to be a ranger. Not shiny and proud, not grinning and smug, not strong and tough. All of that was knight's business—fool's business. Rangers were quick, careful, nasty. Baird had been teaching that lesson for decades, and Gyvain reckoned he'd learned it before anyone else.

His knives were quick too. And they were most certainly nasty. Each one found a different eyehole as the orcs stormed on, plucked back out of helmeted skulls with a twist and a jerk to leave the newly made corpses thrashing on the ground. Some idiot splashed himself with molten metal a few yards to the right, and Gyvain saw more orcs glance over at the heat and light. By the time they'd focused again, he'd cut another dozen arteries and cleared the section of wall up nicely.

That was when the easy part stopped because it was an elite that came up next. One of Venka's favorites. It towered a full stride over Gyvain's height and probably a warhorse's weight over his mass, coming at him like some giant statue had gained the power of movement. He feinted low, then darted left, knives flashing, scraping uselessly along iron plate and iron mail. Armor that thick, he might have pissed on it and done more. At least piss-soaked metal might rust.

A hammer was this orc's weapon of choice, its shaft as long as Gyvain was tall, its head as big as a brick and seemingly solid iron all the way through. It whipped for him fast, almost catching him, sending a few hand-long cracks along the bony shell of the wall as it impacted it. Gyvain swung his own weapons, felt steel scrape off mail, swore, and backed up. He'd spun his way around the orc's body, kept his back to the side the rest were coming in from. If another one cleared the ladder while he fought, he was fucked. But that was combat: risks. Sometimes the best you could do was work out which one measured the smallest, then take that instead of the others.

The hammer came again, again. Gyvain kept on backing up. He was two yards from the wall's edge, then one, then barely a foot. The orc closed just as he found his arse kissing the fringe, its hammer forgotten in favor of a single grasping hand.

Gyvain's knives bounced off its visor, blinding the orc for a precious moment and letting him move with his newly freed hands. He grabbed the outstretched wrist with both, hopped back to plant his heels on the wall, then kicked out. He and the orc both fell back, bodies tumbling over the edge inexorably, and Gyvain moved fast.

Rangers were quicker than men, and quicker than warriors. They couldn't cut through armor, not even with Gyvain's talent and experience, but train enough, fight enough, grow enough, and even gravity felt slow to a person. Slow enough for him to climb the orc's body even as it sluggishly accelerated downward and leave himself rolling back onto the wall just as it fully fell off.

A ton of meat and metal landed hard just moments later, audible even over the snarling fight occurring at every place around. Gyvain stood, grunting, and readied his spare blades. Another orc was up just as he was, this one barely smaller than the last.

CHAPTER SIXTY-SIX

It wasn't going well, not at all. Collin recognized a testing blow when he saw one, mere fodder thrown at the walls in great volumes, sent to die in droves and expose useful weaknesses in the process. Well, they were certainly dying. And the fact that Venka could order so much death for knowledge alone said more about the general's resources than his skill.

Galukar, where the fuck are you?

Easy to call the king useless, easy to spit at his feet, when the bastard was standing idle and passing judgment on workers. So much harder to prop himself up by his morals when the matter of killing turned up. Collin watched his right flank threaten to crumble, orcish elites mixed in with the grunts, easily one for every score, and found himself wondering how quickly that tide would be reversed if he had the Godblade's master to throw into it.

Then he pushed his thoughts elsewhere. Wondering about what he didn't have was a surefire way to waste that little time remaining in his grasp.

He didn't need to look around to find the suitable bunch of reinforcements, not physically. Collin had reserved a dozen battalions for just such occasions and memorized each one. There still came a few moments of mental flailing as he searched his own mind for the information, thoughts somehow slowed by the daunting scale of his novel new assignment.

"The Third," he commanded, knowing without looking that his orders were being sent down the line. "I want the Third up there on that section. Order them to form a wall before they ascend. It's going to be bloody vicious fighting, and I don't want to lose any more than is necessary in this shit of an assault."

It was already vicious fighting, as far as the eye could see. Collin saw nothing but dying men and killing men and three or four enemies for each one, their defense sustained only by the sole grace of being affixed to a wall that kept the foe from really bringing their numbers to bear. But there were siege towers coming now, tall and plated in iron, ready to meet whatever counterfire would strike them and come on anyway.

"I want the cannons on them," he barked, a cold fear rushing through him. Four or five orcs at once spilling onto a wall from a shielded passage would be the end of it; that much Collin knew. There'd be no displacing them by simply cutting a chain, as with the scaling force from the other day. If a siege tower touched down, it might well spell the defeat of their entire defense.

He watched the cannons move out and found himself able to do nothing but pray.

Gyvain hadn't expected the wind mage's help, and he hadn't needed it. But he'd have died without it. He was a big enough man to admit that much, and a desperate enough man to not feel the slightest twitch of bitterness at seeing the killing power thrown out by a man so much more youthful and greener than himself.

Cutting currents scraped the air, picking orcs and undead up to send them spinning from the walls, or driving chunks of mortar into them with bone-smashing velocity. It was a destruction possible only to one with magic, and no small measure of it. But Gyvain had seen far more skilled casters of far less talent. Falls was distracted, he realized. There could not have been a worse time than that moment for such things, but it was the nature of a magus to be inconvenient in their disposition. He got back to killing anyway.

The attack had lasted a day, and the focus had intensified into a crescendo, when Ensharia finally made her move. It felt almost surreal to do after her time of inactivity and imprisonment. Minds had inertia just as bodies did, and to suddenly spur oneself into action was a jarring thing. There was no choice now though.

General Venka, fortunately, seemed busy conducting his siege still. Ensharia had counted on that, counted on the old narcissist being obsessive over his enemy's unexpected resistance, counted on him monomaniacally focusing on breaking through their defenses regardless. Counted on the nice, big lull that would leave in his observations around his own camp.

Of course he had not been so careless as to leave them entirely unobserved, perish the thought. Ensharia had to keep herself cautious, and keep her allies well hidden, as they made preparations. But the moment came eventually. A particularly dramatic flourish of the siege, a row of distracted guards, a carefully worn-down chain then snapped in one explosive lunge. She had cleared the way in moments.

It was thanks to the Savior that, even worn down and exhausted by the passing days, Ensharia had enough strength to wring the necks of two orcs before either could make a sound. A stab of guilt hit her at the deed, but she buried it. These weren't her friends; they weren't even innocents. They were enemies, serving perhaps the worst man she'd ever seen.

She turned to find Garutan eying the display, a look of hurt disgust painted across his features. Ensharia felt it inspire very much the same sensation within her.

"They are . . ." he breathed, looking away suddenly. Ensharia forced her heart to harden. There were times for kindness and compassion, times for steel and resolve. To be a paladin was to be capable of both, and she knew that now called for the latter.

"Dead," she replied. "Now let's hurry. We don't have long."

Shargon was the first to move, as Ensharia might have expected. He was no colder or crueler than the others, but far more mentally nimble, and endlessly practical. He knelt beside one guard to claim their arms, then handed the other's weapon over to Garutan. The larger orc hesitated a moment before accepting it, swallowing with nerves.

It hadn't been hard to free them, numbering only three as they had, and boasting such an excess of physical strength. What came next would be harder still. There were thousands of chained orcs in dozens of rows, and all were watched by their own squads of guards. Ensharia would need swiftness and brutality worked as one to manage her task.

Not for the first time, she felt the loss of her companions. Not a group of friends—never that—but they had been beyond effective. Falls or King Galukar might have made a considerable distraction, and the Savior would surely have defeated any chains Venka had mustered with no issue at all. She buried the sense of worry their absence sprouted, moving on.

First, Ensharia found the hardest band of slaves she could. One composed, she had carefully learned beforehand, of former warriors from the many tribes crushed and absorbed by Venka's war machine. They would serve as a vital aid in keeping their momentum going.

Guarding them were orcish warriors but not elites. Their bodies clattered with boiled leather bound around slabs of iron, but none so solid as plate, and their wearers not half the equals of Venka's greatest warriors. Ensharia fell upon them like a plague. Her only weapon was the half-severed length of thick chain once used to bind her, but its sheer weight proved enough to split open skulls and ruin limbs wherever it touched. Within the span of a half minute, she'd slain each of the ten or so guards around her prize, then she got to freeing the slaves.

"What is happening?" asked one of them instantly. He was a large orc, as the most confident and assertive of their kind tended to be, but did not seem as aggressive as he was cautious. Ensharia spoke with as soothing a tone as could be made, in spite of the adrenal convulsions of her vocal cords.

"We're freeing ourselves," she replied quickly. "And you may help if you'd like."

The orc blanched.

"Venka will kill us," he replied, staring at her as if she were the one to pass the sentence. In a way, Ensharia supposed, she was.

"Only if he captures us all again. If you don't want that to happen then you'd best get to work on helping us gain more slaves on our side and bolster the breakout."

If it had been a human she was speaking to, or a particularly clever orc like Shargon, Ensharia might have feared he'd think to simply attack her with his hundred or so companions and try to apprehend her. She wasn't certain a hundred slaves would even fail to best her, unarmed as they were, with such warrior backgrounds and natural strength. But the idea did not seem to occur.

Precious minutes slipped by as Ensharia helped free the rest of the line, and the orcs soon armed themselves in a fashion that was as crude as it was practical. They tore tent pegs from the great pavilions set up around or smashed great clubs out of the palisades at the edge of the camp. Some even thrust their hands into dirt and ground to pry free boulders as bludgeoning weapons. It seemed the world was malleable for creatures with so many times a man's strength, and soon enough she had behind her hundreds of shoddily armed, but armed nonetheless, warriors tested in combat and growing more eager for it by the moment.

It was just in time for them to be unleashed as the first wave of guards came to investigate the noise of their disturbances.

Ensharia had seen undead eating men alive, and more besides. The years of war against the Dark Lord had washed the continent with some of the worst carnage in its entire history, and her earliest years had been spent in the beginnings of that conquest. But she had yet to see slaves turn upon their jailers, or men swarm against traitors. To witness both at once was a sight so savage in its violence as to almost transcend savagery.

Guards were simply taken from their feet, like leaves caught by a gale. Those few who were far stronger than their brethren lasted moments before being seized from enough sides and bludgeoned in enough ways to surrender likewise, and in seconds the battle was done. What followed grew only more twisted.

Clubs came down upon armor, then limbs and skulls as the iron quickly broke away. Punches and kicks fell like rain, interfering with one another in their volume, their victims kept alive only by the inefficiencies of so many at once attempting to strike them. Bodies broke, then broke more as they were hoisted up, grabbed and torn in every direction. Skin parted, blood spilled, limbs detached from torsos while skulls gave in to leave gray brain tissue spilling out in a visceral shower.

There was no concern of quietude or stealth, only hurting the men who had spent so long watching the slaves hurt. Ensharia didn't even consider trying to stop it. Whatever control she'd had as the one to free these orcs, she had lost it the moment they fell into their frenzy. Within the span of this barbarity, anywhere touched by blood, there was no master but murder itself. And it was obeyed with relish.

By the time everything had finally finished, their position was known. Ensharia stood high atop a flagpole to watch as guards hurried over by the dozen—too many to simply be swarmed as the first few had, with their weapons and training.

"We need to galvanize," Shargon growled from below. He always had a grasp of the most important things. "You go and get the other slaves. Leave this to me and Garutan. We'll be trusted more than you."

Ensharia didn't need to ask why. Fellow prisoner or not, she was still a human, and these orcs hadn't exactly had the best experience of her species. She hurried to do as he said, letting only one glance fall over her shoulder as she saw Shargon growling something to the half-maddened slaves, gesturing repeatedly to Garutan as he did. Their own group at least had not joined in the carnage.

But that wouldn't help anyone if they didn't gain some measure of coherence, and even that would mean nothing without yet more numbers. Ensharia hurried.

It was long work, hard work, dangerous work. But it was work Ensharia did well.

One chain of freed slaves became two, then five, then twenty. By the thirtieth minute since her escape, the alarm was ringing out among the camp, and thousands of orcs stood waiting and twitching with nerves. Bereft of their chains and bequeathed with an urge to unleash no less than the monstrous violence she'd seen before.

Ensharia forced herself not to look at Garutan or those few others who seemed more sickened than excited by the idea, speaking quickly.

"We can run now!" she called out. "But Venka will probably take Kaltan, and once done he'll only hunt us all down to recapture. Our options to flee are non-existent. But he's distracted now, busied with the siege. And if we were to crush his forces from behind . . ."

She watched the distant horizon, where a siege tower was torn nearly in half by some impact so quick and forceful she couldn't even make out the projectile as a blur.

". . . Then these defenders might well exhaust his armies enough that they can't pursue us. Might well let us into their walls to further defend them. The choice is yours."

The choice was theirs because there was simply no other way to draw in recently freed men for another fight but to make it their decision. Ensharia was not surprised to find many choosing not to follow.

But she was not surprised to see so many more choosing to do so either. Perhaps they were practical, perhaps they simply wanted blood, or perhaps the thought of fleeing scared them. She really couldn't guess why they began plucking stolen weapons from the dead guards.

And it truly didn't matter. She had her force and was not slow in leading them on.

CHAPTER SIXTY-SEVEN

It had been long odds from the start, Ensharia knew. Numbers aside, her newly recruited orcs were far from the finest soldiers, and nothing near the equals of those under Venka's command. She fought at the front as they slammed into the edge of the war camp and took a horde of soldiers just around a siege tower. Shock and the confusion of seeing fellow orcs falling upon them bought precious minutes and yet more precious lives as they cut into Venka's forces, Ensharia herself wielding a stolen mace to take off heads and ruin torsos with every swing.

But there had always been long odds.

A spear came at her, a big, nasty spear with great big points on one end and a great big orc on the other. Ensharia didn't have time to parry, so she blocked with her arm—felt the metal sink a half inch through her reinforced flesh, then brushed it aside and brought the mace down on its wielder. Her blow squeezed brain matter out through the helmeted orc's eyeholes, and she stepped over the thrashing corpse to find her next enemy.

Behind her, Garutan had finally started fighting in earnest. The man was not blind with rage, like some of his allies, but he didn't hesitate either.

There had been no missing Garutan's size from the start; between his height and breadth, he surely weighed double or more what most of the other orcs did, even starved and worked in slavery. But Ensharia couldn't have known the Vigor dwelling in his body beneath the bulk.

A grunt escaped him, not a roar. Nothing more than the product of exertive muscles and tensing lungs, powering his arms along in a great arc as the axe they held split an armored orc almost fully in half. Entrails spurted out, sloshing across the faces of an entire row among the enemy, blinding them for the vital moments Garutan needed to take his weapon to them once more. He slew in every direction, felling enemies like they were trees, standing, it seemed, in a fathom-wide circle carpeted by blood and pulped flesh and rimmed by wavering, hesitant enemies too intimidated by the orc's bottomless might to come nearer.

Another spear. Ensharia swatted it aside only to find a great hammer slipping in under her guard. She had no armor of fleshcrafted resilience—that had been taken from her when she was captured—and so only bare ribs were left to resist the impact. It was enough to throw her from her feet and back into the ranks of her orcs, knocking the wind from her. Ensharia was jostled, shoved, and fell into the mud, wheezing for breath while feet and weapons slammed down all around her.

Her head was clipped by a heel, then caught outright by another. Vision blurring for a moment as preternatural resilience contested impossible weight, then her thoughts regained clarity.

Ensharia barely even realized she was screaming as she rose, swinging, then swinging again. She'd soon smashed a space out of the enemy's mass of bodies no smaller than Garutan's own, but it was too little.

She was one woman, her enemies a thousand orcs, and among them were elites. She could tell even then her hastily assembled horde of starving slaves was thinning quickly in numbers, and more quickly by far in morale.

There hadn't been enough orcs on her side, or else too many on Venka's. They had chosen the wrong moment, waited too long or too little. They'd missed their chance, and she'd led thousands to death.

Ensharia swung one last time, saw an orc step into her guard even as she downed another, and braced herself for its sword to fall. But the blade did not oblige her, and when she fought back her wince and opened her eyes anew, blood was wet and warm on her face where it gushed from the enemy's opened-up throat.

She saw a flash of spinal bone poking out through the jagged wound, then the orc dropped back and Swick the Swift stepped out from aside its jittering corpse. He had knives, two of them. Ugly things, crude and thick, but more than sharp enough to do the work that needed doing. More than sharp enough in the hands of a Hero, in any case.

He moved like quicksilver, and the orcs like slow lead. Swick merely appeared in one place, with dead men falling away from him, then disappeared to reemerge elsewhere amid another spout of ichor. Ensharia couldn't tell what was his translocative magic and what was sheer, simple speed, but she knew where he was always by the living men who weren't there with him. And their own side saw it too.

It was palpable, the realization among her orcs. Then tangible, and then it was a mighty current of will and rage resurging at their backs. They charged on ever more fiercely as their enemy's cohesion broke around Swick's attacks from within, and Ensharia charged faster and harder than any other.

Collin's father had been balding before his death; he'd been balding for years. He'd always wondered why, always laughed when he'd been told stress might have something to do with it. His first command, as a general at least, had educated him on exactly what the causal relationship there might have been.

If he felt any greater weight of emotion against mind, his wits would surely be squeezed out the ears like butter from a churn. He could hardly have retained less control of the fucking conflict in that eventuality because it had long since progressed from disadvantaged fight to bloody chaotic mess even in spite of his orders.

"Sir, the retreat is finished," said one soldier, whom Collin didn't recognize. He was his messenger, he thought, one of them at least. It was rather hard to track them. Half the originals had been killed, two-thirds of those who remained were in comas, and most of the ones now serving were hastily conscripted noncombatants made to keep the chain of command from snapping like—

One of the walls imploded, crumbling as Venka's new weapons finished chewing through and letting dozens of tonnes of stone and mortar fall inward like the perfect metaphor for Collin's situation. Bastards. They'd made him poetic.

Venka's new weapons. Oh, those had been a surprise. And about as pleasant of one as a spear up the arse. A few weeks ago, Collin would've been stumped as to what they were. Now he was just suspicious.

After all, Silenos Shaiagrazni had taught him to recognize cannons when he laid eyes upon them.

"I want the rangers, all of them," Collin replied after a moment, watching the wall further crumble and drawing the very obvious conclusion. Their defense in the martial district would not live long past its infancy. Another withdrawal would be needed. Into the very keep itself.

Into the very laboratory of Silenos Shaiagrazni.

"General, you must—"

Another cannon shot. Collin was rather amused by the regularity with which they seemed to be interrupting conversation of late. This one struck the stone far above his head, the projectile gouging a great, jagged rent from one corner of a towering building and leaving mortar to rain down. He moved quickly, shoving the messenger down, shielding him with his own body and wincing as fist-sized rocks peppered and bounced from his back.

It was a petty pain, less than the punches of orcs—and Collin had long inured himself to those.

"Leave, now," he ordered the messenger, watching him scurry away, then sweeping his eyes back to the final wall of the district. The men were fleeing from it already, unable to continue their defense now that enemies were swarming through breaches to attack them from behind.

Less than half, Collin thought, would manage their escape back to the rear lines. His error had been calling the retreat too late, and it had killed men. He buried the thought like so many others of its kind and turned himself to hurry back as well.

Collin found his own path easier, guarded by soldiers and wardens, as the ways of generals seemed always to be. Within minutes, he was surveying the entire battle from a new vantage point, one of many balconies in the keep. He did so with an eyeglass, finding a rare limit to his ranger's sight in the extreme distances involved.

It had been hard to deny from the start, but after seeing the bizarre chaos at the back of Venka's forces diffuse into subsequent, smaller explosions of violence over the following days, Collin had come to conclude that his initial instinctive guess had been right. There was friction in the general's camp—a lot of it.

He'd spread word at once, of course, having not coined even a lie that would have positively imprinted on morale as well and extensively as the simple truth of such a thing. Over the hours though, that fact had started to wear thin as far as comforts went. No doubt it was the main reason their defenses still held strong, but even it couldn't distract from the ever-tightening noose of orcs and—increasingly now—undead closing in around them.

The keep was all they had left, and they barely even had the men required to fill it. Collin wondered idly how many he'd sent to their deaths by insisting upon fighting Venka. Most who had defended, he was certain of that much, and it was no small thing to admit.

Of all the battles he'd read up on throughout history, and all the great victories or crushing defeats, a scarce few had featured losses so severe as even half of either side's starting men. And here he was, standing bereft of surely more than two-thirds of his own soldiers. What sort of general was that?

A bad one, Collin decided. It was, perhaps, the first correct decision he'd made over the course of this entire smegging siege.

"General!" came a messenger's voice, speaking that wretched, sickening word apparently heedless of the chill it sent crawling down Collin's spine. Call him scum, animal, but not general. Anything but that.

"What is it now?" Collin asked, forcing his voice to the appropriate heights of arrogance and certainty. It was, surprisingly, not hard. "Is the sky falling, or has the devil come up from beneath? Both at once maybe?"

If the messenger found his joke funny, he was in too much of a rush to even reply with the ceremonially appropriate nod.

"No, general, I . . . I'm sorry. It's Gyvain."

Collin's blood ran cold.

"Where?" he asked.

"At the first breach," the man replied, misunderstanding the question entirely.

Collin had wanted to know where the old bastard was resting with his wounds. Evidently, he hadn't been taken back.

"One of the enemy's new weapons. A piece of debris from the impact clipped him, then the orcs overran his position. I . . . I am sorry. I was told he died well."

That, Collin knew, was a lie. There was no dying well, just dying sooner or later. Gyvain's sooner had been staved off longer than might have been expected, at least. He sighed.

"How long until we have all the remaining rangers assembled, and what are their numbers?"

"Minutes at most, general," the messenger replied. "I'm told there are fifty-two remaining."

Fifty fucking two, less than half their previous numbers. Kaltan was a ruin already, and ruined more with every passing moment. Collin let a snarl of anger escape him, throwing an aimless punch that clipped a fancy bit of stonework and sent it cracking free of the railing.

"Have them diffuse across the highest places in the keep. I want their range put to good use picking off enemy officers. Waste none of them in melee any longer. They're to snipe only."

Was that another order he ought to have given sooner, or would they already have been defeated had he not left his quickest, greatest killers fighting in the various breaches? Always decisions, never answers.

The messenger looked to be on the verge of agreeing, then paused and stared out. Collin followed his gaze, wincing as he anticipated the sight of some lich flying at him ready to tear him apart.

He saw none. Instead his eyes were met by the sight of King Galukar.

CHAPTER SIXTY-EIGHT

Galukar was so old. He had been old fifty years ago, even. Venerable thirty years after that—and then the disease had come to chew at his vitality. His body had wasted and rotted until all the strength that was available to him was derived from the Godblade.

He was not a Hero anymore, just a human vessel to channel the power of that relic, and even its magic could only prolong a man's life for so long. Galukar knew his days were limited, and he could feel the weariness of all those he'd yet lived weighing down upon his shoulders. One day, one day soon, he would die. The thought was a candle in the dark.

But for now he lived, and while he lived he had to fight. It had been selfish enough already to keep himself chambered in isolation for so long. Selfish enough for even his long lifetime. Galukar surged on to put an end to his petty failure.

They were potent, these enemies, and numerous too. Swarming in for the keep from every direction there was. Evidently something had gone very wrong in the siege, something he hadn't the time or means to check, and the results were an attack that could be bottlenecked only in the very corridors of their fortifications.

And so that was where Galukar met it. With the Godblade held tight and a roar erupting from him, he announced himself in a storm of screaming iron and rippling air. The enemy seemed as pleased to meet him as ever.

One orc came in, one of the huge, ironclad ones he'd been told were called elites. There wasn't much difference between it and the others, so far as Galukar could tell. Perhaps its elite training had been to keep the head hanging on by a thread rather than removed entirely, for that was all that separated it from its kin. Then he was crashing past the corpse and swinging again. A row of orcs was split apart, another dismembered likewise. One of the undead—a fomor—shot for Galukar like an arrow, and he barely sidestepped in time to take its legs off as it stumbled by him.

The thing was not permitted to rise before his Godblade found a new sheath in its torso, cutting deep through until it found the point where the skull met spine, then separating them from each other with a sharp twist. Rotting blood filled the air and tortured his nostrils as Galukar turned back to the hall of his enemy's entrance, surveying the flood.

If he estimated their numbers to a thousand, he might have killed five. As things were, he knew he had slain a great deal more than that, and yet the tide of bodies seemed to be swelling, not receding. It was the dangerous sight of a siege close to unwinnable. An enemy already past city walls in such numbers could scarcely be further reduced by whatever remained inside.

Well, that was fine. Galukar was certain he'd fought himself from deadlier spots, once or twice. Though none quite came to mind. He got on with the killing, doing what he could to thin the tides ever more.

An orc fell from him in two pieces; a fomor spasmed as its neck bones were crushed to paste. A dullahan, insanely, attempted a mere frontal assault that ended in predictable carnage, and through it all the Godblade came up and down like the scythe of a farmer. It had grown muddy with blood, that's how much blood there was, necrotic fluids and viscera now forming a repugnant crust around the metal where it fissured one body after another. Galukar was struck by the reek of it all at every moment, almost overwhelmed. He knew a lesser man would perish to the innate toxicity of such close undead exposure near instantly. For him, it was just an annoyance adding further fuel to the flames of his rage.

"Galukar!" He heard a voice, almost felt it pull him from the killing frenzy that befell all effective warriors. Galukar did not turn, realizing it came from his back and was made by human lungs. "It's King Galukar! He's returned!"

There was hope in that voice, and with hope came a bolstering of morale and rigidity that could, and had, turned the tide of many battles. He'd seen it himself, relished it himself. But he was old now. So very old.

Don't cheer my coming, fools. I could have been with you all this time if I'd not been such a coward.

They cheered in spite of his thoughts. As if the sun were shining from Galukar's body, as if he had brought with him a body of ten thousand knights and five hundred magi to bolster them. As if he were a man made of stories and myths rather than weakness and fear.

A fomor almost caught him in the side of the head with one of its razory tendrils, and Galukar felt a surge of rage displace the guilt. He killed it slow and savagely, then kicked its carcass into the front row of enemies to keep them tied by its weight while he fell upon them from the side.

Galukar swung, swung, swung. Then he gasped as his blows finished peeling back the ranks of putrid undead to reveal a new quartet emerging from them. His eyes stung with tears at the sight of his reanimated sons, and his muscles froze with indecision. They came nearer, readying their blows, and still he remained. How could he fight them? How could he even move aside, if they wished for his life?

How could he deny his boys the justice of seeing their killer's life end?

Something coursed through the air, and it became solid in an instant. Smashing sidelong into a falling sword to send it off course, and before the next was coming, Galukar felt a wind cast him backward along the corridor. He landed behind Arion Falls.

The boy was different, and perhaps not for the better. He seemed leaner, haunted, but the look in his eyes was that of a killer. Desperate and emptied, with nothing left but the fight. It was a useful one to see at his side, and it spurred him into motion. Galukar got to his feet, staring, searching for the right words.

"What are you doing?" King Galukar asked, and Arion had to resist the urge to sneer at the moron. Perhaps his master was influencing him more than he thought.

"Saving you," he replied. "Now get up and start fighting or we're both dead."

There was no exaggeration in his words. The armor-clad undead—Galukar's sons—were coming on fast as anything Arion had seen before. They moved like knights, long hours of training and care evident in every motion, but had that feral magical potency noticeable in all undead. Writ large. It was easy to recall the fear of being chased by them now, but Arion found himself without any scrap of it.

Was it just what had happened with his master? A simple fact of realizing his own worthlessness that made the thought of fearing death laughable? Certainly, his new powers could not have hurt.

Arion drew on his magic quickly and shaped it into shadestuff. His lessons all clicked together like some Rartychan mechanism, gears grinding, cogs sliding, and he found the substance answering his call as will seeped in through the abyss to give it form and mass. It was off-center, he knew, far from that perfect median point of the spectrum that made Master Shaiagrazni's able to eat through so much steel, but there was an instinctual fear of it imbued within him, nonetheless. Superstition, or his gut sensing that that his higher thoughts lacked the knowledge to predict? There was only one way to find out.

Walriq had made issues for Master Shaiagrazni by deflecting his shadestuff with potent currents of wind, exploiting its mass to send it flying back at the creator. Arion used much the same technique now, but with his own. He cast the shadestuff out in rapid globules moving arrow fast and pelting the approaching enemies faster than they could react, watching as it burst apart to coat armor and mail.

Black steam hissed from wherever the shadestuff touched, and Arion watched the metal recede like ice doused in boiling water. But the erosion was too slow, and too little. His enemies were on him the instant later, primed and ready to end his life.

Then King Galukar barged him aside, catching three swords at once along the edge of the Godblade. For a single instant, he remained locked in place against the trio of undead, even while the fourth moved to slip around his side. Arion sent that one stumbling back with a jet of wind, and a moment later, the king let out a roar and forced his strength against the enemies' with a mighty heave.

A tree might have stood before him and not offered as much resistance, or even a castle gate. Nonetheless, the undead were sent sprawling as their balances gave and their bodies shot back before Galukar's prowess.

For one wonderful moment, Arion thought the old king would actually snap from his stupor and start helping. Then he froze again and stumbled back as his sons rose to their feet. Arion snarled, more shadestuff leaping to his hands, winds carrying it out as another volley. The undead's armor was looking worn now, but not nearly as much as it needed to.

The closest was on him within the moment, sword barely missing as Arion helped it to one side with a blast of wind. More shadestuff, this time carefully angled into its face, globules breaking off to slip through eyeholes and eat at the flesh below. It started twitching, froze up just long enough for Arion to throw it back at the others, and he continued backing away as one was knocked down and two more continued to close.

"I need your help!" he cried to King Galukar, not having the time to so much as glance his way before the undead closed further. Arion put up a wall, which shattered instantly as they crashed into it but bought him time enough for another blast of shadestuff. It might have hit an already-eaten part of the closest one's armor, might even have put it down, had the sword not come up to block the magic substance. That single move kept an extra enemy in the fight, and so when Arion sent the other stumbling, there was one left to attack him.

The sword came low and bit him right under the ribs, cutting through meat and gristle, then exiting around his belly. The strength left him instantly.

Arion was falling, and it felt like a long time. But the ground was all that caught him. His body hit it without sensation, mind bouncing around, drifting suddenly. It was hard to focus, hard to notice where the sensations of his flesh were starting or stopping. From one corner of his eye, he caught movement, tilting his face slightly to see King Galukar closing in. There was a look of horror upon the man's face, a novel sight that Arion might almost have smiled at. Had he still possessed the strength and responsive flesh needed to produce a smile.

Galukar's sword was out, shoulders squared, voice hollow. It all felt so surreal.

"I'm sorry," he croaked. "I'm . . . Forgive me."

The undead came on, and so did the king.

CHAPTER SIXTY-NINE

A man was dying, and it was Galukar's fault. Many men had died already, many more were dying as he moved even now, but this one had happened in front of him. This one he'd known. He was no Hero, just a worm writhing in the dirt.

One sword came, and Galukar slapped it aside. Another slipped around, missing as he ducked it, then the Godblade found that crease where pauldron and breastplate parted.

The offending undead lost its arm in a single stroke, falling back from the momentum as two more swings came after Galukar. Neither caught him, parried just as the first, space newly reopened between him and his adversaries.

He was fighting again, and he hadn't even noticed it start to happen. Galukar waited for the freezing cowardice to strike him once more, but it didn't. He felt nothing at all except the bodily instincts of movement and combat. Nothing until his heart ached anew at one son's approach.

It was worse than cowardly to keep from clashing with them. It was cruel. Galukar would not stand by and watch his boys left in their torment, not when it was within his power to end it. He surged on, roaring out every one of the molten emotions burning at his lungs and swinging in a great overhead arc that cleaved a streak of stone from the ceiling above. At the end of its path, the sword proved deadlier still. Undead strength, even bolstering his own son's might, was no match for the Godblade, and steel gave in with a scream of agony as the old iron edge bit deep. Rotting juice spurted free as the reanimate fell back. Galukar turned just as the others were charging.

They had learned from their previous bout, and perhaps even from all the decades he'd spent sparring with them as living men. They swarmed Galukar carefully, bringing numbers to bear in a diffused weight, ensuring that their blows fell from many angles at once. Speed was of limited aid in such conditions, but

Galukar found himself striking first and used the edge to keep them from over-whelming him completely.

A sword bit his shoulder, and a morning star bounced from his cheek. The latter actually left him stumbling, blood filling his mouth as teeth loosened, but he was within their reaches a moment later and swinging hard enough to take two of the three from their feet entirely.

It was nothing like the fights they'd once had, and growing more dissimilar by the moment. Galukar had always held back then, fearing even with his own sons that his strength would break them if wielded unfettered. That was no con-cern now, and strengthened though they were, he still saw the truth in his past fears with how they failed to withstand him.

Galukar's side erupted with a sharp, cannibalistic pain that reminded him of the other disparity between his situation and those long hours in the training grounds; he had no armor on him now. His body had always been steel enough against most blows, but these were no ordinary strikes now facing him, and he'd taken three already. He focused his wits, retaliating against the cut to his side with a long stroke that tore a pauldron free of his enemy.

The morning star was back, then its head fell from the body as chain was cut before ancient iron. Galukar followed his swing with a kick, twisting to sidestep another sword slash and wincing as a second caught him across the shoulders. He ignored the foe behind, swinging for the one in front.

His son's head came free in an instant, and his suffering was ended in that single stroke. Three remained.

Weight, speed, force. Galukar's world became no more than the sum of those spheres acting in opposition and unison, working in one way, then the other, reduc-ing all of creation to nothing more complex than the ebb and flow of a single bout. It neared its end quickly, and more quickly still with each undead he slew.

Soon enough, only one remained. The eldest, the strongest, relatively unmarked and at the fullness of its Vigor compared to Galukar's own weakened, wounded body. Ten gashes and bruises welled along his flesh, where edges had opened and blunt heads crushed the bare meat of him. None were grievous, but together they proved an issue. Galukar could feel even his own stamina running out.

"It's you, isn't it?" he asked, feeling his fear grow as he spoke. "I can recognize you, armor or no, undead or alive. My oldest, my first. My boy."

The undead said nothing, but Galukar didn't dare hope it was beyond under-standing him. He had to fight back the tears clouding his sight, knowing that even so much as distorted vision would be neither missed nor overlooked by so sharp an enemy.

He moved toward Galukar, the eldest. The first, his. The one whose name he dared not speak, even now, for fear of the torrential emotion doing so would bring forth. Galukar forced other words out of himself, wincing as they came.

"I'm sorry," he repeated. "Know that. And know that the Dark Lord will be leaving this world too. But I mean to send him to a different place than I will you."

Galukar had been right, and his son did still understand him. He chose that moment to charge his father, swinging in the precise way Galukar had expected he might, opening himself up for the blow that removed one arm, then his head. It was all over in an instant, dismemberment taking no longer than the blink of a man's eye.

It was his first instinct to take a moment staring at the ruined corpse, but Galukar resisted that. He turned instead to Falls, hurrying to the magus and kneeling down beside him.

"Boy, do you live?"

He did, that much was clear, but the wound was a nasty one. A normal man might have been cut fully in half by such a blow, but whatever magic or fortune had spared Falls, it had not done so fully. He seemed to have been slashed right down to the spine and was bleeding in a volume that might have threatened men twice his size. He was pale, shaky, gasping. Galukar had seen injuries like it, and they were rarely survived.

Arion's guts felt as if they were falling out, and a quick glance down to his waist confirmed the reason as to why. They were. He felt his agony intensify just from the sight alone, desperately looked away as the queasy feeling washed over him and threatened to strip his consciousness all over again.

His thoughts were solidified once more as a new spark of pain rang out, this time born from movement. King Galukar's arms slipped around him, hoisting his body up as if it weighed no more than a sheet of paper and starting the process of hauling it back through the corridor. Arion was seized by wheezing torment for only a moment before managing to sputter out a protest.

"What . . . are . . . What are you . . ."

"I'm saving you," the king growled, words barely audible over the sharp wind rushing around them. It was strange; he seemed to be moving barely faster than a jog, and yet the space was vanishing underfoot as if he were a sprinting horse. Vigor was a force in and of itself, Arion supposed, particularly the kind fueled by such weapons as the Godblade.

"You can't," Arion croaked. "There's no point. I'm . . ."

A petty, stupid, selfish rat of a man . . .

"I'm useless," he breathed, finding tears, pathetically, rising up to accompany the words. "There's nothing to gain by saving me. You have other things to do—other men to save. Every moment you spend carrying me is one you're not fighting for."

Galukar didn't even hesitate, not missing a step, not pausing a moment, and not revealing a single breath strained by the efforts of speaking as he moved.

"You are my companion, under my protection, and I will not leave you to die. There'll be fighting enough once I've left you with your master for healing, and you might still be able to join it once repaired."

Arion surprised himself by feeling a stab of . . . something. Contempt, perhaps, or something categorically akin to it. He felt that same niggling wrongness, heard that same echo of his master's words, and decided to change tactics.

"And what if I distract him?" he snapped. "What if healing me costs him precious moments that could be spent on whatever plans he's working, or else delays him even more? What if you kill everyone in this city and doom them to be reanimated as undead servitors of the Dark Lord?"

That finally gave the king pause, and Arion jumped on the chance.

"Please," he gasped. "Do what's right. Leave me."

Spare me.

"Keep from disturbing my master."

From dropping another of my failures at his feet.

"Focus on what truly matters."

On anything other than me.

Arion was no fool, and he was not stubborn. His magic was no special thing in the grand scheme of things, his power no worthy virtue. After meeting Silenos and learning of House Shaiagrazni, he couldn't possibly have continued to live with such a delusional view of his importance as he'd once enjoyed. After failing them, he could barely bear to live at all.

"Boy . . . You will die," the king breathed, turning a corner now, jostling Arion in his speed and jostling himself in his consideration. He was close to convinced, Arion could see. His every word would count to weigh against the man's decision from now on.

"Better me than us all," he forced himself to whisper, then felt King Galukar tense, hesitate, and slowly lower him to the floor.

"If you're sure," the monarch breathed, eyeing him, still wavering. Arion realized then, with the jolting weight inherent to any such realization, that he was looking at his own last chance for life pass him by. Oddly, he felt no sudden urge to seize it. Only a bizarre peace.

"Tell . . ." He coughed, and his guts squirmed at the motion. Arion's pain lasted well more than a second, but it was within that time frame that he managed to make himself speak anew. "Tell my master . . . Tell him I'm sorry." Tears wet his eyes, though for what, Arion wasn't sure. "Tell him I'm sorry I couldn't be better."

King Galukar stared back at him, long and hard. Then nodded. He was gone an instant later, back to the fighting, leaving Arion where he leaned against the wall.

He didn't take long to die, at least. And he was busy in the dying. Arion thought to old lessons of magic and new lessons of necromancy, recalled the half-remembered hints of prolonged life and onliving spirits let out by his master during their travels together. What could the consequences of an amateur's failure in such arts truly be?

No worse than death, he thought. And so he began to work on them promptly. Arion seized his spirit with grasping fingers of magic, feeling none of the trembles in his metaphysical hands as might have racked those bound physically to his failing muscles and dying flesh. He worked to weave a net around his spirit and keep it tight and strong, a trail of arcane webwork tethering that vital core of his mind to the body it inhabited, carved through abyssal paths and necromantic avenues.

Whether it worked, Arion had no idea, and no way of so much as guessing. By the time he was finished, it was all he could do to even recall that he had done such a magic at all. His life slipped from him within the minute, magic soon following. Then Arion Falls was nothing but cooling meat pressed against a cracked stone surface.

Like so many other men slain in the fighting.

CHAPTER SEVENTY

In hindsight, Ensharia realized, it had been too good a target. Too obvious, too exposed, too open. Not the sort of thing the famed General Venka would permit to exist within any of his war camps, even ones so great and expansive as these. Except as a trap.

She was a paladin, and proud to count herself as one. But paladins were warriors, not commanders, and though she had studied the tactics of history and learned what she could from memoirs and accounts written by the very greatest geniuses ever to conduct men in war, she was no general herself. Perhaps the Savior could have foreseen her error, or King Galukar. Perhaps they could have prevented the ruin that followed it.

After his sudden appearance the day before, Swick the Swift had remained by Ensharia's side. They had not spoken much to each other, and she would have had things no other way. The man had left her, had *betrayed* her, and returning hero or not, that was a hard stain to remove. She'd forgiven him, but her heart did not seem to realize it. Even if it had, there had been more productive things to discuss than their camaraderie in any case.

It had been a crushing blow to Venka, and a rallying victory to her, that they had managed to kill so many of the general's orcs in their attack. Almost half perished before the rest fled, and some remained. They were quickly taken as prisoners, bloodlust not so strong in victory as it had been in freedom, while the corpses were picked over for arms and armor. The siege tower, of course, was destroyed. They carried the salvaged wood with them as they disappeared across the plains.

Parties followed, large ones, fast ones, but none were able to chase them down. Swick's translocation proved an invaluable scouting tool and was almost as useful in misleading the enemy as to their location as it was keeping his own side accurate and informed about their foe's. Only one of Venka's numerous chasing hordes actually made contact, a force of some half dozen elites and two hundred warriors.

There was no contest as to the victor of that conflict, and soon enough yet more equipment was being shared out among their men. Bolstered by this, they had grown hungry for yet more victory—and hastened in their hunger by the sight of Kaltan's outer wall falling. Once the siege was done, Venka would turn his focus on them. All remembered that well, and none so well as Ensharia, so they had turned to the attack.

It might have been clear to her, had she not been blinded by the novelty of freedom and the thrill of revenge, that a man of Venka's experience would have known their advantages better even than they did. The first easy target they stumbled onto, they attacked, and it was then that the forces came to encircle them.

Among the ambushers were ten thousand warrior orcs, close to double the numbers Ensharia herself laid claim to, a hundred elites . . . and Venka himself. Any hope they might have enjoyed before that point died with the sight of him striding across the battlefield, saber drawn and eyes cold as icicles. Ensharia readied herself.

Orcs crashed into orcs, and instantly the difference was there. Ensharia's might well have been the higher-quality soldiers, less formally tried and tested but consisting largely of former chiefs and warrior castes from the tribes, greater in size and strength, and fighting with a ferocity impossible to any but a freed slave. Venka though had the numbers, and he used them well. His formations were nonexistent, forgotten in favor of simply made columns that struck her forces like bludgeons. The carnage was great, the effectiveness greater. Ensharia grabbed Swick, gave him the signal, and they translocated past it all in one go to come charging at the general.

If any chance was to be found in the battle, it was by taking Venka's head. Clearly he had known it himself, because he was well guarded by elites as Ensharia and the pirate drew near. They split apart into twinned attacks, closing from different sides and each contesting two of the lumbering orcs. Ensharia baited a swing from one, then opened its jugular up just as the other grabbed her. Venka was moving behind it, almost skewering her before Swick translocated between them to parry the thrust, then, while the general was stunned in shock, headbutt him hard and savage across the nose.

General Venka stumbled back, and Swick and Ensharia both made short work of the remaining elite beside her. Of the other two, the ones fought by Swick, only one was able to continue fighting. They came on for Venka like a thunderstorm, and this time the general seemed cautious.

When last they had fought, Ensharia had done it without her armor and with barely even a weapon, Swick half drunk. Now they were armed, armored, and sober as a winter chill. The elite fought well, defending his master, but died quickly. Then it was just Ensharia, Swick, and the general.

Ensharia's war pick was unbalanced, but it served her amply enough as it chased after the general. Swick, for his part, seemed perfectly comfortable with the daggers he wielded, slashing out in great circles whenever Venka sought to slip within Ensharia's own strikes. A nick appeared along the general's wrist, then his cheek. Her pick's blunt end clipped his shoulder in a stumbling blow, and his wince of pain was doubled as the tip snagged his leg and gashed it just over the knee.

He was dying a slow death, that of a cliff eaten away by tides, but he was dying, nonetheless. If one such scrape could cause a man pain, then fifty might well kill him. Ensharia had only another forty-five to land.

Of course, it had always been Venka's trap, and the man was a Hero in more than just name. He did not make his killing easy, sword emerging to parry nine would-be wounds for every ten that came at him. Ensharia was faster and stronger than she'd ever believed possible, thanks to the Savior's touch, but she was no great threat to an enemy like this. Not when he needed only play for time.

A sling bullet caught Ensharia in the back of her head, and the one after it struck Swick in much the same place. Both projectiles were stone, not iron or steel, and thus fractured on impact with the Vigor-infused skulls they struck. Neither failed to stun their target regardless.

Venka's sword caught her weapon, not her body, and easily cleaved through the shaft. Before Ensharia's pick had even lost its head to the dirt, the saber was back around and thudding its blunt side against Swick's face. The man dropped like a stone, and orcs fell down upon her before she could surge on to try to best the general with a tackle. Strong arms, numerous arms. Three, eight, a score.

All crushing grips and compressive holds, strength compounding strength until even Ensharia was no match for the sheer weight of musculature and Vigor brought to bear against her. She fell, knees hitting the ground so hard that stones broke beneath them, the rest of her following a moment later.

It was all she could do to raise her head and affix Venka with a glare, and all she could do after that to keep from snarling in her rage as the man refused to so much as glance back at her. Ensharia bucked her body, twisted to give herself more space, then lashed out with both feet and lifted an orc from her. Before the ranks of bodies closed again, she was sliding through them and breaking out at a sprint, bowling over a quartet of others trying to pin Swick and hauling him along beside her. Both of them moved quickly.

Ahead, they saw their forces. Or what was left of them. The orcs were encircled by their own kind, ranks thinning as enemies broke through and hacked apart the defenders. There was no saving them, not all. Ensharia took all of a second to make her decision, then turned to Swick for verification.

"We need to take the left flank," he gasped. "They're the only ones with a chance to cut and run."

A chance, perhaps. But not a big one. Ensharia braced herself, cursed herself, then charged on, only pausing to snatch a fallen weapon from the ground.

It really had been too good of a target, in hindsight. And there was no time to do anything about that now.

The siege was over; Collin could see that much. The people had long since finished their retreat into the keep, and the orcs had long since begun their final assault at it in earnest. For hours, the building had been surrounded, and those hours were starting to run out. He watched it all, waiting for the fear, the dread. Instead he felt only a quiet discontent.

I won't be avenging my father then.

It was laughably pathetic that a thought like that stuck itself out so far above the others, but Collin couldn't control his thoughts. He couldn't control his city anymore, for that matter, either.

From his telescope, he saw Galukar was still fighting. It wasn't a normal telescope, of course, to be perceiving such a thing through solid stone walls. Some magus had been commissioned to craft it decades ago as a means of looking through the correspondingly enchanted structure of the keep. Fitting, because it wasn't a normal fight Collin used it to observe.

Regardless of the verbal trouncing he rather fancied his father had given the man . . . Galukar still impressed. Collin hadn't thought of him much, merely sectioning all recollection of the king off to a distant, resentful corner of his thoughts, but he was grateful to see him back again. No doubt, the corridor he held would have long fallen otherwise.

For hours, he'd carved his way through undead and orcs alike, until their mangled forms made a bloody carpet at his feet. The walls, the ceiling were all coated with congealing ichor spurted out by the wreckage left where ancient iron came down on fragile meat.

Collin had heard the stories, everyone had, and he'd seen some measure of them acted out in their joint ambush against Venka's forces beyond the walls. It was another thing entirely, however, to be exposed to such a distilled, prolonged demonstration of King Galukar's prowess. How easy to imagine there was some truth to the theocratic propaganda of his sword, seeing it used with such impossible strength. How tempting to actually feel some whisper of hope, witnessing such a potent creature fighting on his own side of the conflict.

But no man could kill forever, and the army feeding itself into Galukar's corridor would have crushed five or more times its number of conventional attackers. He was a creature, in the end. Not a god.

With each new blow, the king's fatigue was apparent. Movements made slower, weaker, clumsier all in degrees that would have been fractional and near imperceptible in another man but proved stark reductions of the near-perfect might he'd been so recently doing battle with. Where before he had slain undead by the dozen with each passing moment, he now killed precious few, ceding ground as their numbers swelled before him, rotting masses climbing over the piled-up corpses to force him ever deeper into the tunnel of stone. Others made to dig through the walls, testing their strength against the ancient architecture and creating their own passages with its yielding. The siege was over, and the slaughter was drawing near.

CHAPTER SEVENTY-ONE

Sphera was exhausted, in every way she believed a woman could be. Her magic was drained from hours of emptying her mana out into one newly retrieved carcass after another and directing them all back to the front lines. Her body was drained from the mild physical element that came with the rituals needed to make her necromancy reach the heights of its power. More than anything else, her *mind* was drained. She'd not slept in almost forty-eight hours and had only even been kept conscious by her new master taking an incredibly irritated moment to touch her forehead and work some unknowable fleshcrafting upon her brain to purge it of its fatigue.

Some of its fatigue, not all. Apparently leaving her entirely without the need for sleep was an alteration more than he had time for. Most things, other than his damned research, were more than he had time for.

Her work, in the siege, had been a purely support role. That was not a surprise. It was by far the best way for any necromancer to serve in any capacity. She had conjured undead, imbued them with all the power she could, and sent them on to fight the enemy. Rested when necessary, paused when forced, and did precious little else.

Of course, Sphera knew there must have been at least one ranger using that preternatural perception of theirs to watch her servitors. Had even a single one turned against her new allies, she doubted it would have perished fighting in the front lines before she herself had been put down behind them. Amusingly, that fact would have made a rather promising strategy for Venka in having one of his own undead disguised as hers, if only for the slim chance of actually fooling a ranger, but she supposed even the greatest generals could only work with the information they had.

And Venka was a damned imbecile too.

For the first day, that had been all Sphera had worried about, nothing more than the most unpleasant twenty-four-hour stretch she had ever found herself subjected to. By the second, it was worse by far. By the second, she'd understood what the ranger was there for.

Her undead died, and Sphera felt each one. They'd always been dying, of course, but suddenly their expirations came rapidly and easily. On no less than a dozen occasions, she felt her creations destroyed within moments of reaching combat, and the carefully built-up surplus she'd been flooding the keep with for the past day rapidly withered as enemies found, seized, or made new paths into the building to bring the full force of their numbers to bear. It was scarcely even a massacre, more akin to the sight of her creations being crushed beneath some natural disaster. A flood of bodies, a hurricane of blades, a storm of ruin.

Sphera's fears worsened as the siege did, enemy approach keenly felt with the growing proximity of her slain undead. Soon enough, Sphera realized, she was sending her creations out to be destroyed without even leaving the corridor adjoined to her master's laboratory where she raised them.

After that, Sphera stopped sending them out entirely. She simply focused on the pile of bodies still left beside her—which had long since halted its replenishment as defenders were killed in the fighting—and began concentrating undead directly by her side. It did nothing to smooth over the turbulent waves of her strengthening horror, and the enemy were scraping at their doors shortly.

It was the second thing Master Silenos had taken the time to focus on, if only briefly, that door. Its wooden frame had been removed, its bands of reinforcing iron replaced with the same inexplicable materials he worked into his other creations. Sphera had no reference for how strong they might be; she'd not seen much of the grotesqueries in battle. She had only hope, and that was a fool's comfort.

A thud shook the door, sending dust to drift from the stone into which it was built. She jumped, stepped back, swallowed, and turned to her master.

"They're coming, master."

Silenos Shaiagrazni did not even look up. Sphera might have whispered the words to him, or giggled them, and elicited no less perturbment or shock. He simply continued his work on the latest of numerous orcs, replying without so much as a glance her way.

"Hold them," he instructed. "Falls ought to be returning soon. Once he does, we will galvanize and prepare to flee from this city. Assuming my work is not done beforehand."

It was comical. What work could possibly turn the tides now, of all times? He might have obliterated the entire city in a single, great blast akin to the one he'd used to destroy so many of her own undead, and Sphera doubted Venka would even have been left with an army too small to besiege another. No, they had failed;

they had lost. And her master, it seemed, was falling toward outright delusion in his refusal to accept as much.

More impacts struck the door, then yet more. The noise was almost beyond belief, like hearing trebuchet stones break against the surface mere feet from her. Each time, Sphera expected to see the curious construct break and fall away, but instead it held. She almost found a scrap of hope welling up, then saw the cracks appearing.

They were in the stone, not the material of House Shaiagrazni. A wall made carefully thick and defensible—and chosen as the necromancers' base of operations for just such a feature—was being broken apart long before the door it held. Sphera had gauged the thickness at two, even three or four feet. A sturdy structure, but far from invincible. It would not have withstood a Heio, and she had no doubts its span would be short as the assault continued.

Of course she had no doubts. She could see it shortening with her own two eyes each time another blow came upon it.

"Master!" Sphera cried in a tone that might have left her feeling embarrassed to portray such weakness were it not for the significant fact of her standing mere yards away from a visceral end.

"Silence," Silenos snapped as if she were some petulant, whinging infant at his feet. "My work is nearly done, and Falls is not yet here. I need but minutes, less than an hour, then we will be ready to meet them."

It was laughable, insane, and—worst of all—something Sphera was utterly without the means to contradict. Venka would know that she had sent her own undead against him now—such traces would be provable in their bodies—and there would be no mercy for her in the Dark Lord's army.

She had gotten herself killed in a momentary impulse of ambition, and there was nothing more to be done about the fact.

The wall screamed in agony as cracks lengthened, thickened, widened. Chunks of stone the size of a man's fist fell from the space between them, then those architectural discards grew until they were almost head wide and landed with an audible crash. A minute passed, five, ten. Then Sphera saw images through slits in the wall, shadows and forms shifting behind, barely perceptible through the wafting cloud of dust-clotted air. Her body felt suddenly disconnected from the rest of her, as if the terror unfolding was happening to someone else. Someone distant, someone whose death would have no bearing on her.

And then the largest piece yet was smashed from place, and Sphera's frightful dissociation was halted by the sight of an undead scrambling through the newly made gap.

Her first instinct was barely resisted, and very nearly killed her. Sphera had prepared a globule of shadestuff, somewhere, and had she loosed it then, it might well have spattered the walls and widened the gap already made. Instead she curtailed herself, sent undead on with a thought, and watched as a reanimated orcish elite split the invader's skull like firewood beneath an axe. Its corpse remained in the hole for all of a second before being violently shoved free, exposing another reanimate, which perished in much the same way. This time, Sphera had another orc shove back at the carcass, aiming to keep it lodged in the gap.

It was a functional tactic for the next four or so holes that emerged. Soon enough though, the wall was being eroded from so many points at once as to begin collapsing. She felt her heart lurch at the sight of so many rotting faces coming on, even as her own surged forth to meet them. Within the close confines, the violence felt somehow enhanced. As if it were forcibly compressed, intensified, by being denied the room to expand. She felt putrid flesh and the reek of sweat and combat stench, pressed herself back against a far wall and watched as her forces were slowly taken apart.

The quality of her undead was greater; there could be no doubt. But they were finite, and the enemy, functionally, was not. One by one they fell, even as Sphera started hurling shadestuff into the enemy masses and melting off limbs and heads. Soon she was virtually alone, and then the horde was upon her.

It was a streak of fire that stopped them, and a tendril of meat. The latter came down first, forming a new wall, impeding them long enough for the broiling chemicals to wash over them and ignite with an intensity she recalled perfectly well. Recalled, and recognized the improvements to. Steel had not melted from flesh when last she'd seen Silenos Shaiagrazni unleash his fire magic, but it did now.

"I have finished," her master proclaimed, striding forth with nothing more than those words alone. He looked around at the room, curled lip illuminated by the flickering blaze he'd set among the enemy ranks. "So many corpses, and most untouched by magic. Your mana capacity is not so impressive as Falls's."

Sphera didn't have the chance to reply, nor was she even certain she would have, before her Master raised a hand and gestured. The world moved around him.

It was a large chamber they were in. Large enough that a full company of one hundred soldiers might have occupied its center and still found room enough to maneuver and march with space to spare. Despite this expansivity, it had been filled almost to its totality with corpses. Orc corpses, human corpses, even the occasional other species who had somehow found themselves conscripted into Venka's army or trapped in the slaughter of Kaltan. Some were undead themselves, beyond reanimation for a second time, but those were pooled near the entrance, and elsewhere the place was practically choked with dead meat.

Thousands, at a glance. Too many for Sphera to have possibly animated in her weakened state, perhaps too many for her to bring back at all. Her master did not even change his expression as he shattered her sense of scale, possibility, and pride all in a single flourish of magic.

Everywhere Sphera saw, corpses rose. Not the lumbering behemoths made by hours of Shaiagraznian genius, nor the half-possessed vessels stuffed with some ancient Hero or abyssal force, but reanimates nonetheless. Imbued with all the power their bodies could hold without bursting apart, each lurching forth with the physicality of a knight and the savagery of a rabid dog. All crashing into the incursive enemy like a tidal wave.

It took less time to force the undead out of the room than it had for them to force themselves in, and Sphera stood on trembling legs as she watched. Turning to her master.

". . . So that was your weapon," she croaked. He slapped her, hard. Hard enough that she hit her knees again, head rocked by the blow, eyes staring up confusedly at him.

"Idiot," he replied, good mood apparently dissipating. "As if such a pathetic reanimation as that would take me even a minute of work. No, that was the contents of roughly one quarter of my mana capacity. Ugly work, crude, but it had to be done. It wouldn't do to be savaged just as I finished sealing our victory."

At a gesture, his arm was that strange, cylindrical weapon he called a cannon. The wall burst apart, revealing the cityscape out beyond. Sphera's heart lurched as she saw just how thickly the orcs crawled across it, light spilling in, hope spilling out. But only for a moment.

Because then she realized that the orcs swarming outside the keep—swarming in their tens of thousands—were not standing, nor climbing, nor holding formation. They were lying around, rolling in the dirt, convulsing. Their noises were not hungry war cries, but agonized squeals. Their bodies were not moving with victory, but with death.

All of them, without exception. As if the general Venka himself had ordered his men to die. Sphera turned to her master, stared, and saw him smile.

"I will admit their biology was strange enough to delay even me," he mused, good mood apparently restored as some great beast lurched around beneath them. It was no more or less terrible than any of his other abominations, disparate only for the fog diffused out from its body. Sphera saw now that it was this mist that set the orcs to dying. For those who lay in the most thickly congealed clouds were already still and stiff.

"Now tell me, apprentice," her master continued. "Where is the fighting exactly?"

CHAPTER SEVENTY-TWO

Silenos's newest grotesquerie was more finely made than the others, so far as he'd been able to manage. There had been no true function to such a feature, but he had expended the effort to work it in such a way as a kind of artistic flourish. It was not often, after all, that one introduced a new kind of warfare to the world. Such occasions called for some drama.

It was an impressive thing, and he took pride in it. Standing affixed to the top of his creation's scalp as it slithered up around the keep's largest tower, almost buckling the stone structure beneath it with its fifty-tonne weight and convulsive motions. From such height, Silenos could see the entire battlefield, and see it well.

There was no doubt how things were going, and he was not surprised by the fact. Orcs overwhelmed defenses, innumerable and potent. Undead too intermixed with their numbers, but mostly orcs. It seemed those reanimates among Venka's forces were near entirely serving in an elite fashion; the bulk of his army were the creatures. Just as Silenos had thought.

"People of Kaltan!" Silenos called out, feeling the musculature of his throat and tissues of his lungs tense with force enough to rend apart normal flesh. His voice came out so powerfully that he had no doubt a man might have been deafened for life hearing it from too close. It was an intriguing prospect for future weaponry but for now served only to announce his glorious presence. Sure enough, the words cut out over the chaotic sounds of killing and dying, soon drawing eyes up to stare vacantly at him. *"Behold me."*

He considered saying more but decided against it. Why bother? What could words possibly do to convey any more than was seen by simply gazing upon him. Silenos felt a smile curl his lips.

He had been attacked in this world. Savaged by mindless cavemen, beaten and wounded by grunting apes fighting him on a level he'd never before had to learn or master. Now, at last, he had turned the tables on them. Now, his vengeance was nigh.

"Exhale," he ordered his creation and felt the movement of its body beneath him as lungs worked to project the mists his carefully crafted organoids were so efficiently synthesizing.

"Breeding," perhaps, would have been a better word. "Cultivating" certainly would have found use, for the substance was little more than a sustaining home made to keep Silenos's true creation from death. The virus he had worked so tirelessly to engineer, designed carefully around the alien orcish biology he'd been studying for days, moved like a breath from the grim reaper itself. It was heavier than air, its medium, and so came to settle down below in broiling clouds that further unfolded one way and the other where gusts of wind pulled at them. Washing out to engulf yet more orcs and infect their bodies just as it had the first few rows.

They fell, convulsing, coughing, clutching and clawing at their primitive flesh just as the rest of their kind did. Bodies eaten from within by a work of destruction deadlier and more invasive than anything natural selection was likely to produce. Silenos watched the blood oozing from orifices, heard the strained gasps for breath that wouldn't come, and smiled again.

It was all good. All appropriate. All a serviceable step in his plans for the world.

Motion underfoot, and Silenos glanced down to see his grotesquerie quivering. It was eager, he realized, hungry to kill. That had not been in its design, but he'd anticipated the effects. It had, after all, been fleshcrafted from the arcanically infused tissues of orcs, and he had expected some measure of their nature to move over. Their will, culture, dying thoughts. He would have to further experiment in removing them later. For now . . .

Well, for now he saw no reason not to indulge his creation. Silenos ordered the grotesquerie on.

The grotesquerie descended, body moving with a feline grace and lithe delicacy that left it seeming almost to glide above whatever surface it drew near. Silenos was quick in fleshcrafting as he rode it to the battlefield, configuring his cannon promptly, then awaiting the chance to use it.

A fomor gave him one soon enough, then fell as its head was almost torn from the neck where his shot hit. More were coming, dullahan and other undead around them. Silenos decided to let his grotesquerie play.

Barbed and thick with muscle, its tail came around like some aerial bombardment and cleaved an entire row of them in half with the same stroke. Before it had even halted its momentum, the grotesquerie was opening its maw and exhaling an acrid streak of new gas. A single click rang out at the back of its throat, and the fluid ignited.

So help him, Silenos actually had to cover his eyes from the nitrous as it detonated. The overpressure would have killed him where he stood, even shielded by the shaped crest of his monster, had his body been of lesser composition. There was no barrier to protect the enemies.

Bodies ripped, burst, tore to shreds as the shock wave bellowed out to crack stone and clear square meters by the thousand from before Silenos where buildings were blown back and carcasses sent sprawling. Silenos examined the blast and studied the damage to his grotesquerie's crest. It was less than he'd anticipated, no doubt due to the Vigor now reinforcing it, but apparently he'd been optimistic in constructing the stuff. A note for later.

A scream, a rush of air, and an imminent impact that Silenos just barely turned in time to intercept. His cannon ripped the orc's arm off at the shoulder and converted its flight into a twisted, off-kilter fall that left it bouncing off the hard plates of his grotesquerie. The creature tried to take hold but perished beneath another shot, skull coming apart much as a normal creature's might under musket fire.

So some of the orcs still lived, even this close to the grotesquerie, inhaling such a potent concentration of Silenos's virus. He felt the irritation gnaw deep. His work had been careful, and ingenious as ever, but time had not been an ally. Silenos had cut vital steps of his process to avoid the inconvenience of death. Now, it seemed, he was seeing the limits left by his decision.

Another glance around showed him other orcs still active and moving, now that he knew to look for them. Some seemed half-affected by the virus, others entirely immune. In total, however, they were but a small fraction of the full number of their kind. Silenos would have to satisfy himself with killing only eight- or nine-tenths of their masses.

With the virus, at least. Silenos's grotesquerie shifted again, preparing to destroy the remainder of Venka's forces through clumsier and more traditional means.

It was not easy to notice the mist, at first. A subtle thing, insubstantial, barely even something Ensharia was aware of. That all changed when the deaths started.

They came on suddenly, almost instantly. As if coordinated, as if planned. As if God himself had reached a hand down from the heavens and started plucking out lives. Ensharia found herself smiling first, as she saw Venka's men fall and bleed. Then the mists washed over her own, and she realized no distinction was being made in which orcs dropped.

"W-what . . . ?"

Ensharia might have been embarrassed to respond so stupidly and simply in any other circumstance. Instead, she felt her focus snatched by the moment, by the ruin spreading outward. In minutes, the clouds had covered everything, even her. She hadn't tried to run, hadn't even thought to. How could one escape from an act of nature? How could one flee from *mist*?

She awaited her own death, and when it didn't come, her next thought was as natural as the breaths she felt so relieved to still experience. Ensharia began searching her men.

Her heart broke with each new carcass she moved past, orcs rolling around, coughing and gasping, hands clawing at nothing in particular as agony spun their bodies into sickening spasms. She had to keep from being grabbed in a blind frenzy by the men dying around her, had to bite back the shedding of her tears at the sight of it all.

Garutan. It was the only thought in Ensharia's head, and a desperate one. She had to find Garutan. Sweet, kind, innocent Garutan. Garutan, whom she'd forced into a fight, who might well be dying in the middle of a battlefield because of her. Ensharia's panic, her terror, grew with each moment that passed without her finding him. He couldn't be dead, not now, not like this. His last moments couldn't be this.

"Enshar!"

She froze, then spun. Ensharia was not so used to speaking with orcs, but weeks and daily hours of familiarity had been enough for her to recognize the voices and words of her friends without the slightest chance of failure. It had been Garutan who spoke, and it was Garutan her eyes now fell upon.

Thank God, he was alive. Garutan was kneeling, though almost as tall as Ensharia even in spite of it. His body was stooped, miraculously unharmed— though that may have been more thanks to the elite armor now encasing it—and folded with concern as he stared down at something. No, someone. Ensharia's guts lurched as she realized his gaze was focused upon an orc.

Upon Shargon.

"Ensha . . ." Garutan croaked, looking up at her, face unhelmeted and eyes wet with tears. His lip trembled, throat tightened, body quivered with all the panicked, weeping fear of a little boy grasping for understanding.

Ensharia was down beside him within the instant, almost reluctant to turn her focus onto Shargon, even as her friend spasmed like the other orcs.

"Shargon, Shargon, do you hear me?" Ensharia reached out, touching the orc with only a moment's hesitation—deciding quickly that if she hadn't yet been plagued by whatever pestilence was taking him, it was unlikely she'd suffer it through contact—and gently shaking him to try to capture his focus. It worked quickly, keen intellect peering back at her from behind a thick fog of agony.

"I . . . hear . . . You. Ensharia." he grunted, speaking in flawlessly polysyllabic Common even in spite of the agony clearly blossoming with every word. "What . . . is . . ."

"I don't know," Ensharia cut in, answering hastily to spare him the exertions of speech. "Hold still. I'm going to see what I can do."

Her hands warmed up as the divine magics flowed through them, seeping down into his skin, then past it. Sinking into muscular tissue, the wafer-thin fat deposits so rarely found in orcish flesh, even the bones and organs. Infusing every scrap of his biology until Ensharia felt as though she were holding his entire living body all within the span of two hands.

It was a sensation she'd grown well used to, the feeling of flooding a body with God's light. Of healing it. Usually, Ensharia felt a change near instantly, but this time she could tell within moments that something was wrong. Very wrong. Where there ought to have been a reversal of death's inexorable touch, she instead felt only a slowing, a delay. As if she were merely digging her heels in and offering resistance to a cart as it slid downhill. Shargon's groans lessened fractionally, but his pain was still clear as day, and the slow decay of his body was something she could feel all the more keenly for her efforts.

Ensharia pushed herself, desperately willing the light into Shargon's body with ever more intensity. She'd felt this before, or something similar. When the toxicologist had left Arion Falls dying from his vicious blends, and her power had been stripped apart in the effort of repairing him. But there were differences. It felt alive, this new killer, somehow. Like an animated, breathing thing, or a swarm of maggots infesting the blood and tissues of her patient rather than merely some inert substance.

Like disease. It was impossible, ludicrous, but it was undeniable. Ensharia was feeling the miasma of adaptive, pestilent evil infesting the wounds and eating them from the inside out. The divine healing of a paladin was not so great as to purge natural rots, and this decay was something beyond any she'd ever encountered. Almost malignant in its consumption of Shargon, it was to ordinary disease as an edge of sharpened steel was to a jagged strip of iron. Evolved, perfected. Terrible.

Tears were welling up again as exhaustion started to rear its head, and Ensharia tried to blink them back. It was a futile effort. She saw the recognition bloom in Shargon's face almost as soon as her despair started. Always quicker than the other orcs he was. Quicker even than most humans.

"Is . . . okay," he croaked, grunting, gasping. Blood built in the corner of his lips, then ran down his cheek in a thin streak as the movement of mouth and tongue left it slipping free. "Ensharia, it is okay."

It wasn't okay, and it was laughable to even say otherwise. Ensharia didn't even answer him until Shargon's voice rang out again.

"Ensharia, look at me, please."

So help her, she almost failed to even do that much too.

Shargon looked worse than when Ensharia had started, and not by a small degree. His face was paler than its usual gray, skin clammy with sweat, eyes tight with agony. There was a resolve to them that hadn't been there a minute earlier, and it shattered Ensharia's last dwindling sheet of hope.

That resolve was not found in living men, she knew. It was something she'd seen born before. Always in the last few moments of a brave man who'd finally realized he was dying. She'd yet to find it anywhere but in a person soon left a corpse.

"Listen, please," he continued. "Keep healing me if you must but listen. Garutan is alive, fine even. And I am dying slower than . . . others." He made to glance, at that, but seemed unable to quite manage it. Ensharia didn't need to follow his attempted gaze. She could hear the other orcs around them, and more specifically she could hear where the dying groans just yards away had fallen silent long before. Shargon continued. "Vigor keeps us alive, I think. Other things too perhaps. Some of us may . . . may live."

Some of them. Ensharia realized the meaning instantly and almost cursed herself as she looked up to Garutan.

"Leave," she hissed. "You need to——"

"Go with him," Shargon gasped. "Please, Ensharia, leave me and go with him. Take care of him. He . . . He needs you."

"I need *you*," Garutan groaned, tears now falling openly. It seemed he'd realized what was happening, and like so many others, the knowledge brought him nothing but heartbreak and misery.

"I cannot come, my friend," Shargon replied, forcing a smile, then coughing as even that motion seemed to send a new wave of twitching pain down his body. "I am sorry, but I cannot. Now go, both of you . . . Please."

Ensharia's vision almost failed her, so clotted by tears had it become. She got to her feet, seized Garutan by the wrist, turned, and then froze.

A monster was bearing down on the armies, tearing apart hordes of orcs that, as she could tell, still futilely obeyed Venka's orders. It was a new thing, not one she'd seen before, but the philosophy behind its body was something she recognized well. Careful, scrutinous, perfectionist, and aligned in ways far too flawless and delicate to be the product of nature or God. One of the Savior's grotesqueries.

She cleared her eyes and looked back to see that Silenos Shaiagrazni himself rode the top. Orcs dangled in agony at the end of great spearing limbs as the thing fought, and from its mouth came a blasting cloud of mist.

The mist that was killing Shargon.

"*Stop!*" Ensharia roared, putting every ounce of her body's might behind the cry and watching with relief as the Savior heard it. Her relief turned to horror as he failed to so much as pause.

The carnage continued, blood running in rivers and pools, all while Ensharia stood to watch in impotence.

CHAPTER SEVENTY-THREE

There came a time when a man had to accept his fate, and Venka was not such a fool as to deny that of all things. Not when it was his own being stared down.

He had assembled his armies, trained them well, and wielded them like razored scalpels against Collin Baird's idiot defenses. Aside from a single trick, which he had repaid tenfold, his stratagem could not have been more perfect; his successes could not have been more definitive. By all measures, he was a credit to battle and a great man among mere sheep.

But he could not have won a battle against the sun. He could not have held ground against a falling sky or splitting earth. Could not have outplanned a shower of meteors or a flood. Some things were just nature, or God.

And some other things were neither natural nor divine, but something altogether more terrible and potent. It was one of those rare, wicked few that he gazed upon now. It made him shiver.

Whatever foul magic had made it, Venka saw nothing right in the workings. It was elegant, ingenious, but twisted and abhorrent. Like a sculpture made of human viscera. The lumbering thing moved, and as it did, great plates of either chitin or bone shifted and rattled along it, all interlocking with a perfection in their overlap that left precious little area exposed, all thick and dense enough that he had no doubt they'd have staved off blows able to skewer an armored knight.

Below there was a dark flesh, bundled and tight like ropes about a sailing ship. They moved its great weight as if it were no mass at all, leaving the towering creature to slither, almost to glide, like some serpent. It was before him shortly, coiling, drawing back. The head came down just enough for Venka to meet the eyes of its rider.

It was not a man he had ever seen before, and he suspected he would never see him again. Never see much again. There was no pity to be found in that gaze, only molten hatred and fury.

Like gazing into the face of the Dark Lord, he realized with a start that left his guts writhing.

"You are General Venka?" the man asked with a tone of one who did not do much asking. For a moment, Venka actually considered lying, but he steeled himself. How would he even be believed? He was the only human in his army, and his face and appearance had been well seen during the parley. There would be no fleeing from this. Better to face his fate like a man than scramble back like a rat.

"I am," he replied, forcing his tone to remain hard and edged. "And you are?"

Venka saw the motion, but it was a near thing. The creature upon which his enemy sat sprang into movement so quickly and instantly that it had almost reached him by the time Venka noticed. His blade was flashing out, saber coming down hard between the skin-thick gaps separating armor plates, biting deep through the softer tissues below. It was a stroke that would have bisected an orc.

It did not take off the tentacle though, and he was grabbed before he could step back to try again.

There was a strength to large creatures that Venka had learned well. Oftentimes it was fragile, as if their bodies' size forced whatever power lay within to be spread thin, and only sheer mass kept them forceful at all. None of that was felt now. Somehow, despite measuring thicker than his own shoulders, the great limb boasted more proportional power than a panther, hauling Venka through the air as if he weighed nothing and ignoring his struggling even in spite of the Vigor infusing his muscles. He was like a rat caught by a viper, and he'd seen that dance play out enough to know how it ended.

Within moments, Venka had been drawn close to the man atop the creature, his kicking legs and thrashing arms failing to move its grip an inch. The caster continued speaking, as if he were watching nothing more eventful than the assembly of a shelf.

"I am not surprised that you do not know me." He sighed, sounding almost irritated suddenly rather than wrathful. "I did not arrive in this world with the circumstances needed for my genius to find its use. But now I have the means to demonstrate my power. I only wish you could see what will be done with it."

Venka spat, glaring his defiance. Every man had to accept his fate, and he had long made peace with his.

"Do what you will," he growled. "I don't fear death. I have established my legacy and fought my battles. Thirty victories will be remembered with my name, thirty for each of my deaths."

He hadn't expected his words to make much of a crack in the caster's smile; heroes rarely had much effect upon their villains, after all. What unnerved Venka was how he seemed only to widen the twisted grin already splitting his enemy's features.

"Kill you?" the caster murmured. "How unimaginative. No, I will not kill you. You see, general, you have crossed me, and crossed me dearly. Delayed me, attacked me, killed—" He paused, inhaling, exhaling. Mastering himself for a moment before continuing. "Killed precious opportunity for my progress through this world. And I am well aware of your proclivities . . . No, I will not kill you. I am not so simple as that."

More tendrils wrapped around Venka, pinning his limbs entirely as he was drawn nearer, and then he saw the blade raise up. It was a sharp thing, rounded and edged, bound into some curious limb that pulsated with musculature. A bizarre noise rang out from it, and it took Venka a moment to realize that it was some circular, serrated edge spinning so quickly he could scarcely even see. The caster spoke over the sound, calm as ever.

"This is a circular saw. It is not something your idiotic people will likely develop for some time now. My own people use it for cutting, precisely and against hard and durable targets. Like a skull."

Venka's fear was an engulfment of frigid water, squeezing the breath from him, leaving him panting and kicking as his eyes widened and throat choked with horror. There was no use though; he might have been King Galukar and still failed to break such a hold as the abomination now enveloped him with. His desperate spasms seemed only to amuse the enemy.

"Ah, comprehension. It took you some time," the caster breathed, and then with a gesture the mechanism—the saw—was closing in. Venka felt a stab of pain as it cut the skin of his forehead, then yet more. Wider, as the slice ran the length of his head. There was a deep agony as he felt his scalp lifted, sickeningly and wetly, from the surrounding tissue to be peeled back. His skull was exposed. Venka knew it, and he felt the fact burn around within his mind like an arrow coated with searing oil.

"What . . . What are you—"

"Be silent," the caster interrupted, crushing his panicked speech with speech no louder or more hurried than before. "Be silent and relish this. It will be the last sensation you are ever equipped to consider."

Before Venka could even wonder what that meant, he felt the saw touch his skull and screamed as the bone yielded. It was quick work the caster made, opening his cranium and exposing the interior near instantly. He was panting and sweating, all the time, by its conclusion. Never had such a torment touched him, and never with such a confusion alongside it.

"What are you going to do to me?!" Venka cried, panic flooding his words with volume. He didn't care about composure, not now; the uncertainty was stronger than anything else.

But his uncertainty was left to fester because no answer came but the sensation of parting skull and the feeling of sudden, cold air on some place of him that oughtn't to have ever been touched by a wind.

"Hush," the caster replied, looking at—no, looking through—Venka. As if he were glass. "As I said, I will not kill you."

The sensation of touch caught Venka's head again, and he gasped. His body kicked, jerking without thought, as new limbs wielding other, smaller instruments disappeared over the top of his sight and began jostling atop his exposed head. His mouth flooded with a bizarre sensation, taste. Minty somehow, and the air filled with a grotesque, pungent reek of bloody iron.

"The cerebral cortex," the caster began, as if he were giving a mere lecture. As if he were speaking to some hall of students, and not a man gasping and gurgling under his power.

"You have not, I assume, heard of it. It is a region of your brain—of most brains, for that matter. So named due to being the seat of what might be called higher cognition. In short, those measures of thought that humans overwhelmingly do, and most other creatures overwhelmingly do not."

Venka was enraptured, in the way that was perhaps only possible for a man receiving a speech while feeling his brain probed and sliced.

"This is a simplification, of course. There are very few cognitive functions that a human categorically can do that most other animals categorically cannot, but there are, of course, enormous differences. What is less enormous, of course, is the difference between a human's cerebral cortex and an orc's."

A gasp left Venka, and he blinked as the caster continued talking.

"Theirs is not so far from ours, rather less dense in neuron composition but otherwise similar. What I am doing here will leave you roughly as far from them as they are from a normal human. A normal human, mind. You will . . . Well, you will no longer be that."

Venka tried to think of something he might say, but nothing seemed to occur. Somehow he was having trouble focusing, blinking at his confusion as the . . . The things. The things on the big arms, they kept coming, kept poking. Cutting.

"I imagine you've noticed already," said the caster. "But don't worry. I'm not done. For what it's worth, you're now roughly as intelligent as an average ten-year-old. I will be further reducing this, and doing so uniformly. Historically speaking, lobotomies tend to be rather unpredictable. My people have learned from that history and have turned them into something of a science."

It was all so exhausting, so difficult to pick through, but Venka managed. He was a clever man, always had been, the smartest, even. This was an enemy, and he fought against it as well as he could. If he just wrestled the limbs harder, surely they would break apart. Big things were easier to hurt than small ones, he thought, and he was a Hero.

"Around now, you should be finding your grasp of language somewhat reduced," the mean man said. "Vocablibrary dimished, compensation reduced.

You may grow confused at curtain words, miff them up or mishandstand them." He smiled. "Ah, I see by your face that it is happening already."

What was he talking about? And why did Venka's head feel so . . . so . . . hard to see through.

"You are now as intel gent as a chimp," the mean man said. "All be hit, with the able tea to speak and handstand speech. How do you feel? I took care of a few member trees as well, those apple pie-ing to me at least."

Venka stared, trying to know what was being said, frowning. His head hurt, and he was tired. He wanted something to eat, and he wanted somewhere to lie down too. He didn't like this man; he looked all mean and spoke corn fussedly.

Opening his mouth, he tried to reply, frowning deep her as his lips did not do as it were told.

"Want go home," Venka mum bled. The mean man smiled, maybe not so mean.

"Of course you can go home." He nodded. "In fact, I will take you there. How a boat we get you some paper and ink too? I know you love to write."

General Venka did not look much changed once Silenos was done with him, his scalp repaired, hair regrown. He stepped back from the lobotomite, smiling at his own handiwork.

"Perfect." Silenos nodded. "Now nobody will see anything wrong. They won't worry about you. They won't judge you. They'll know that everything you say comes from you, and they can enjoy your new books while you write away to your heart's content. What would you like to write about next, Venka?"

The moron thought for some time, about as slowly as might be expected of a man missing roughly two-thirds of his cerebral neurons.

"War," he said confidently. Silenos nodded, smiling.

"Of course, war. You're good at war, aren't you, Venka?"

"The best," the imbecile replied, speaking with the kind of certainty that nature reserved for the truly, stultifyingly stupid. Silenos thought for a moment whether he'd gone too far in stripping away his cognition.

Then he smiled again. No, this was just as he liked him. This was perfect.

From the corner of his eye, Silenos caught movement. Not the sluggish, twitching kind of a dying creature melted from within by his virus, nor the rapid, explosive kind of an imminent attack. It was slow, purposeful, deliberate. A woman walking, and as he turned to the source, he felt a sensation too strong and unfamiliar for him to even identify washing through the reconstructed centers of his brain's emotional processors.

Ensharia, the paladin. The first face he'd seen in the new world, and the body that seemed ever between him and danger.

"You live," Silenos breathed, taking a step toward her before he'd even realized he was moving. She surprised him then by stepping back just as he did, flinching and gazing up at him as if he were something dangerous. Something unpredictable.

"You did this," Ensharia whispered, speaking with a tone left hoarse by emotion and . . . something else.

Silenos only frowned, his confusion blooming instantly.

"Did what?" he asked.

"*This!*" She snapped, gesturing at the sights around her. The dead and dying, the ruin Silenos had made of the battlefield.

"Ah." He understood instantly then. "Yes, I did. I used a virus—imagine a grotesquerie too small to see and able to feast on flesh to multiply its number by the moment—to infect the orcs and kill them. It was the easiest way of destroying the army."

Her stare was the sort he might have received from Venka had he not known better than to try polysyllabic communication with the man. Pure incomprehension, followed by rage, and then . . . Then it was disgust.

"These were people," she snarled. "You . . . Silenos, you didn't kill animals, whatever they say; you killed people. They were capable of kindness, compassion. They could learn—"

"I am well aware," he cut in. "Yes, I examined their brains. Less intelligent than humans, but not by so much, I know."

"Then why did you do it?" she snarled. "*How* could you do it?"

Silenos frowned at that.

"I did it because they were a threat to my plans, and as for the how . . . Well, my fleshcrafting provides many—"

"*How can you bring yourself to do it?!*" Ensharia screamed, her fury, apparently, reaching a critical mass and boiling over entirely. "Every one of these people had friends, hopes. They . . . They had lives!"

It was then that he realized the miscommunication between them and sighed. It was such a simple thing.

"I see," Silenos replied calmly. "You still cling to your simple ideological quirks. I really had been hoping to avoid truly conversing on this. It was my wish that you might simply learn a better way yourself by watching me, but if we must discuss it openly, then I will start by telling you that there truly is nothing about any of what you just described that holds moral weight to House Shaiagrazni. I needed them dead, and so I killed them."

She stared, as if the ground were falling out beneath her. Speaking slowly, quietly.

". . . Could you have spared them?" Ensharia asked. Silenos thought about it.

"Hmm. Yes, I suppose I could have, if I'd been so inclined. A less deadly virus would still have incapacitated them. There would doubtless be deaths in the fighting, but they would not all have perished. I achieved plenty already, in any case, and have more biomass to be used now that more of them have perished. It would not have saved time to make a weaker pathogen."

Ensharia took another step back and just stared at him. Stared like he was a man she'd never seen before, like he had just told her his name was not Silenos, and his house not Shaiagrazni.

Silenos felt a stab of irritation at that and was not certain where from.

"I have a lot to explain," he continued. "You have missed much during your . . ." He considered the facts. Ensharia had seemed rather attached to the orcs. "Imprisonment." Silenos decided. "We will soon be moving on from Kaltan, whenever I have finished mustering our new army. Come with me and—"

"No."

That single word halted him, like a jutting strip of iron choking the gears of his speech.

"No . . . ? No what?" Silenos frowned. "What do you mean no?"

Ensharia stared, and for a moment he wondered whether she'd even heard him.

"No," she said at last. "I will not be coming with you."

Now it was Silenos's time to pause, mind halting somehow, delayed and clicking precious moments late as some new flash of emotion ran through it and slowed the cerebral brilliance like thick tar in a mechanism.

"Be serious," he replied at last. "You summoned me to this world. You knew you would have to—"

"I have made up my mind," Ensharia spat, and Silenos saw tears now glistening in her eyes. "I . . . took too long to do it, spent far too long denying what was right before my eyes. But now I see. Kill me if you want, but I'm leaving. And I'm not fighting alongside you again for as long as I live."

She turned at that. Storming away from Silenos and leaving him alone. He watched her go, trying to think of something to say, to do. Something to give him direction toward anything but the internal storm leaving him near witless.

Nothing came to mind, and the paladin was out of sight before he next moved.

Ian B. Urns is the coauthor of the Author's Nightmare series, originally released on Royal Road. He writes dark fantasy stories with all the action, humor, and horror he can cram in. Having penned six novels thus far and developing his skills with each new book, he hopes to continue expanding into other genres. Urns lives in the United Kingdom, where he avoids natural light and eye contact with other living things.

A. C. Erinle is the coauthor of the Author's Nightmare series, originally released on Royal Road. A Nigerian novelist who favors character-driven fantasy and worldbuilding, he has penned several books now, sharpening his writing skills with each one. He spends his free time frolicking in nature and otherwise enjoying life, before marching back into his Writing Hole. His stories are dark, but they never fail to be optimistic. Erinle currently resides in Lagos.

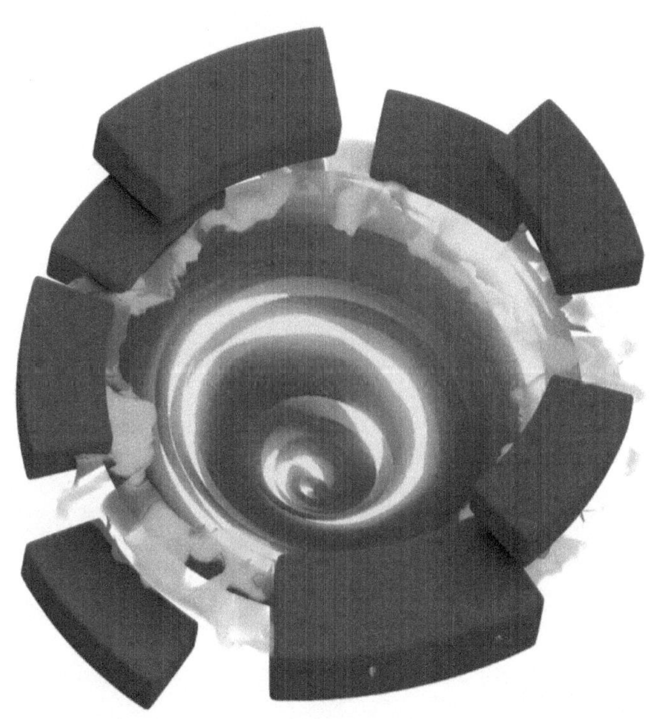

RESPAWN YOUR CURIOSITY

ollow us on our socials

podiumentertainment.com

@podiumentertainment

/podiumentertainment

@podium_ent

@podiumentertainment